Of Enchantment, Enigma, and the Infinite

an anthology
edited by

Jendia Gammon & Gareth L. Powell

ISBN: 979-8-9907055-3-1 (trade paper)
ISBN: 979-8-9907055-4-8 (hardcover)
ISBN: 979-8-9907055-5-5 (ebook/ePub)
Library of Congress Catalog Number: 2025941574

First printing edition: August 5, 2025
Published by Stars and Sabers Publishing in the United States of America.
Cover Artwork: Niall C. Grant | Cover Design and Layout: Dash Creative
Edited by Jendia Gammon and Gareth L. Powell
Proofreading and Interior Layout by Scarlett R. Algee

Stars and Sabers Publishing is an imprint of Roaring Spring Productions, LLC.
Los Angeles, California

https://www.starsandsabers.com/

For everyone who needs a little magic in their lives.

Table of Contents

Of Enchantment,
Enigma,
and the Infinite

Introduction

Magic might be one of the most evocative words in the English language, yet it leaps into all cultures and across languages in story and myth. The easy way of trying to understand the concept of magic is to say it is a manner of handwaving away logic, that it embraces the unexplained. But there's also the argument that even the ordinary can be, on a personal level, quite magical. The twinkling in-between just out of the corner of our eyes, whether in a cup of tea, in an unfurling vine, in mists, or in the nebulous concept of time.

As with our first anthology, the cross-genre *Of Shadows, Stars, and Sabers*, we collect here several tales from writers hailing from across the globe. You will recognize some from that prior anthology, and you will meet new ones as well. Each has offered to pull back the curtain just a bit, so that you can see the glimmer of enchantment, enigma, and the infinite beyond. And while each story deals in various forms of fabulism, the real trick for real stories is not something any true writer could ever reveal. Telling stories is the truest form of magic there is. We hope you are as enchanted by these stories as we are.

Ad astra per fabulas,
Jendia Gammon and Gareth L. Powell

The Princess and the Golem

David Quantick

The princess sat alone in her room. She was reading a book. It had very few illustrations and was bound in leather with an annoying golden clasp that snagged her beautiful dress every time she opened it. But she had nothing else to do with her time: she had learned all the accomplishments open to a princess. She could understand and speak the languages of flowers, birds, and reptiles. She could play the spinet, the lyre, and the crumhorn. She could row a boat and ride a horse. She could weave a tapestry, sew a kirtle, and knit a suit of armour.

But the princess didn't want to do any of these things. She didn't even want to read the book with the annoying golden clasp. She wanted to go out into the world and see what was what. Only then, she felt, could she be truly happy.

"You can't go out," said her father the king.

"Why not?" she asked.

"Because you need to be presentable for your suitors," answered her mother the queen. "And how can you be presentable if you're out all day, riding in the forest, falling into bushes, and coming home covered in briars and brambles?"

"I'm a very good horsewoman," the princess protested. "I never fall off."

"That's not the point," said the king, even though it was.

~

So the princess sat alone in her room, waiting for suitors. And the suitors did come, from near and far, because she was a beautiful princess, and her father was wealthy, and owned many lands and many castles, and had no son. The princess was a fine catch for any man.

And the suitors were not all awful. Some of them did not wipe the snot from their noses on the backs of their hands. Many of them did not belch or fart in her presence. One or two of them kept their hands to themselves. There were even a few suitors who were charming, or witty, or intelligent: but the ones who were charming were not intelligent, and the ones who were witty were not charming, and so on. So the princess rejected them all, every man jack, and she continued to sit in her room, alone, reading the book with the golden clasp, and her parents despaired of her, and wondered what would become of the kingdom.

One day, the princess sat down and was about to open her book when the gold clasp snagged on her brand-new silken kirtle and unravelled the thread. Annoyed, she threw the book across the room, where it fell flat on its face, sprawling like a drunk. The princess watched in horror as several pages fell out. Feeling slightly remorseful, she went to pick the book up.

A sudden gust of wind caught one of the loose pages and blew it into her face. She took hold of it and was about to reunite it with its companions when she looked at the page and realised that it was the beginning of a story. What's more, it was the beginning of a story she had never read before.

"That's impossible," said the princess. "I've read every story in this book a hundred times. There isn't a page I haven't seen before."

And yet, there *was* a page she had never seen before, and she was holding it in her hand.

The princess put the book on the table and sat down with the mysterious page in her hand. "How To Make a Golem," it said. She wondered what a golem was and yawned. It had been a long, boring day, and more suitors were coming in the morning.

"Time for bed," she announced to nobody in particular.

That night, the princess dreamed that she was walking in the forest. It was the early morning, and beams of sunlight thrust through the canopy of trees like shining golden swords. Birds sang in the treetops, and from not too far away came the sound of a babbling stream. Perfume filled the air, the scent of flowers whose bright colours attracted bees and butterflies.

"This is nice," said the princess.

She wandered about for a while. She sheltered in the shade of a large chestnut tree, but felt the need of rest, so she sat down on a small heap of earth about the size of a sleeping man.

"Please get off me," said a voice.

"Who's that?"

"You're sitting on me."

The princess leapt to her feet in fright. She looked down at the heap of earth that she'd been sitting on. Was it her imagination or did it now resemble a man lying down?

The heap spoke again, and the princess gasped as a mouth seemed to appear in the earth.

"Thank you," said the heap. "You have done me a kindness."

"It was nothing," the princess said, "I merely stood up."

"Nevertheless," the heap replied. "I shall now perform a kindness for you."

"You?" she laughed. "A heap of earth? Help a princess? Sorry, I didn't mean to be condescending, but—"

"I gather that you are troubled by unsuitable suitors," said the heap.

"Yes," the princess replied. "How did you—"

"This is a dream," said the heap of earth. "And there are no secrets in dreams. I can help you create a suitable suitor."

"How?"

The heap told her.

The princess awoke.

"What a strange dream," she told herself.

But when she stood up, leaves fell from her kirtle. There was earth on her feet, and she could still smell the sweet perfume of the forest flowers.

"It wasn't a dream!" she said.

She knew then what she had to do.

Riding out to the forest before her mother and father awoke, she found the chestnut tree from the dream. Beneath it was a heap of earth.

The princess took the leaves of the chestnut and scattered them on the heap. Then she crushed some flowers, and let their scent fall through the air. She took the sunlight from the sky, the babbling of the silver stream, and the sudden sight of a fawn in a clearing.

And then she took a piece of paper, on which was written the name that meant the most to her (it was her own name, for which of us can do without his or her own name?), and she placed it in the earth where the heap's mouth had been.

Then she stood back and waited.

Time passed slowly. Time passed quickly. Time stopped.

The heap of earth shrank, grew, became formless, took on form. It filled itself with light, and flowers, and scent, and sound. It grew arms, hands, fingers, fingernails. Earth turned to clay, clay to flesh.

The earth became the golem, and the golem was a man.

The man stood up. He was entirely naked.

"I should have brought a kirtle," said the princess, but she didn't turn away.

The golem opened his mouth. Some ants fell out. He spat onto the forest floor and said:

"What is my name?"

She told him.

"Thank you," he said.

"May I offer you a ride back to the castle?" asked the princess.

"No need," said the golem. "I can run."

The princess mounted her horse, and she galloped back to the castle, the golem running alongside her.

"You're very fit," she told him.

"How would I not be?" he said. "I am made of the entire world."

Back at the castle, the princess introduced the golem to her parents.

"At last," said the king.

"He seems very suitable," said the queen.

"What?" said the princess.

"Do you have any land?" the king asked the golem.

"I am land," the golem replied.

"Do you have any gold? Or precious stones?" asked the queen.

In answer, the golem stuck his hand into his own chest and pulled out a ruby the size of a goose egg.

"Do you have an army?" the king asked.

"As numberless as the trees in the forest, and as strong," the golem replied.

"Well," said the queen. "I think our little girl has found her prince."

"But—" said the princess.

"We accept your proposal," the king said to the golem. "You may kiss the bride."

And so, the golem was married to the princess, and in due time, they became king and queen of that land, and they both ruled over it wisely and well. If she ever felt any regrets about the marriage or any misgivings about her husband, she never expressed them.

But some claim to have seen her, each and every night, flicking through the pages of an old book with a golden clasp, looking for a page that wasn't there.

Hems and Hexes

Eliane Boey

Every Lighted tailor knows that brocade curtains can only be unpicked with deconstruction spells. Whispered *along* the length of the seam, and not chanted any which way over the mass of drapery. You might get away on jacquard with a quick unravelling curse, but only brocade would do for His Brilliance's Ceremonial Tent(-in-progress). Now, if I hadn't had two privates and a mess cook loitering behind me while I was trying to unpick curtains, I wouldn't have attempted a quick unravelling curse in impatience. I wouldn't then have gone at it with the seam ripper and a swifting chant when it failed, as it would have.

Pulling down the runner on the Altar of Incandescence in the process.

Then none of all that followed next would ever have happened, leading to me having to *share* a worktable. All of this because His Brilliance's touring army was not on the move as it should have been, but instead was lost in the province of Wuliao. No thanks to His Brilliance's Geomancer, the Learned Zaowei.

Three days ago, His Brilliance was not ensconced in his well-upholstered tent at the heart and hub of the camp, but was, to my social horror, blocking the light from the doorway to the Ceremonial Tent(in-progress), which I've come to think of as *my* tent. Seeing as, being the camp's only trailing tailor, and the tent requiring still more spell work and manual stitching to complete, I'd rationally set myself up in it. Alone.

The Learned Zaowei was speaking. "Until the altar is repositioned to face the west, and the trigrams on the hangings and runners corrected to reflect the number of monarchs of the Incandescence, it would be inauspicious for Your Brilliance to enter Heng-Po."

His Brilliance pressed the skin between his eyes. "Of course the altar is built into the central beam of the tent. And the hangings will take days to re-sew."

To *alter*, I said to myself.

His Brilliance continued to moan. "My army has been stuck in the wetlands for two seven-days, and now, we are told not only to expect longer, but that it all hinges upon mystic altar linen. Every day that passes with no news of progress, the Court expects deeper disgrace of the tour."

Indeed, behind His Brilliance stood an elderly man with pointy ears and unblinking eyes. The Fourth Addressor of the Seal. By the looks of it, and most of all the way that he looked on the prince with chin tucked, simmering in disapproval into the many folds of his neck, this court official had been a personal informant to Her Incandescence ever since he'd caught His Brilliance with hands sticky with malt crackers and sesame cakes before dinner.

There were two errors in His Brilliance's speech. Technically, it was the Queen, Her Incandescence's Army, and everyone on the peninsula knows that she'd put the prince to this tour of might to keep him busy with something that wasn't endless games of Courtyards and Cockatrices. And second,

"It's not linen, your Brilliance. It's Shanponese silk and cotton lawn. And I followed the pattern from Her Incandescence's last tour."

"Which directly clashes with the killing stars of this tour," the Geomancer interjected. She pulled her ridiculous cloak of trigrams around herself. "Thanks to your unfortunate tangle, which I heard from outside the tent, it has been spotted."

It wasn't quite as dramatic as sparks of hate at first sight, but it was close.

"Can't you simply recite an unravel curse and go in with a seam ripper, and then affix-chant it together? I don't see why this should take any longer than a half-day."

Unless you want it to, her eyes narrowed.

"Because." I lifted my nose at the Geomancer. "Tailoring, working fabric with Light, doesn't belong to unfixing and affixing. It's *construction*. And the garment or furnishing that's made with Light isn't just a garment or furnishing, but a carrier of protections, charms—curses too, if one wishes." I hoped she knew that in a world of 'no question is a stupid question,' hers were the exceptions. "And with construction, only spells will do."

"Spell away, then."

"I will. If you would stop moving about like that. It's bad enough you have all your wheels, charts, and compasses on my worktable." And your questions. "That thing you do with your hands. And must you shake that foot?"

"Ah, she means my very existence. Forgive the intrusion. But it was His Brilliance who placed me here. To oversee your work."

"To work together," I hissed. And instantly regretted acknowledging it.

I tried to ignore her, and bent my head over one of the hangings once more. I whispered a deconstruction spell. It's a long spell and I began with acknowledging that its current structure was artificial. Its fusion a violence. And that I will now separate it gently into its parts. But that its parts alone did not define it. And that these parts and non-parts, for certain, will once again encounter one another. And that, as a matter of fact, what I believed to be it in-itself was only what it could represent itself as, and not the entirety of what it was. So, in truth, I will never know all-that-it-is.

And so on. You understand, now, why deconstruction spells are a nightmare of spell gymnastics. And why I couldn't very well carry on with any amount of distraction. But I could feel her disdainful eye on me.

I said, "Tailoring is proper magic. Geomancy is humbug and interior design."

"Geomancy is as old as the reign of the First Empress, and is one of the five Alleviated Light Reflectors of the Empire. Tailoring is at best practical Light-spinning."

"I'm not listening. I couldn't possibly hear with the sound of your *breathing.*"

I tried to return to the spell, but I'd forgotten where I left at on the spell.

"Why were you skulking about outside my tent anyway?"

"It's not your tent," she said. And she dropped the fold of her cloak like boiling water.

"I can't work with her in the same tent. At the same table, no less."

The Under-Functionary of Logistics looked at me over the tops of his eyeglasses.

I have been on His Brilliance's Approved Tailors for two annums now, and a camp-follower for three moons. I don't always care for the packing up all of your things with no notice, humping it a few *li*, unpacking and setting up something like home again, only to pack it all up that night because His Brilliance's Geomancer got the star reading wrong and mistook the Dancing Fish for the Flying Bloodworm. But at least the army and its followers humping along means everyone having occupations of their own and not milling about looking for somewhere comfortable to idle away from Higher Up. That includes the now three soldiers who'd taken to dozing in the Ceremonial Tent(-in-progress). And Zaowei.

"Qiuyi. You are a Master-Probationer Tailor. The Learned Geomancer is a Master."

"Only for the lack of Geomancers, and for traditionalists who believe trickery for magic."

"Might I remind you that His Brilliance himself believes in Geomancy?"

"I said, Zaowei is a distraction."

The Under-Functionary smiled with benevolence. "I thought so. Men and women both have found it impossible to concentrate on their work in the company of His Brilliance's Geomancer."

"That is *not* what I meant!"

It was pointless to continue in the face of the Under-Functionary's indulgent nods. True, Zaowei was tall, with cheekbones that most people find attractive, and arched dark eyebrows that those same people would not disapprove of. But that was not the point, really.

There was a card on my worktable, when I sat down the next morning.

<Shake the cup and take a stick.>

I looked around the table. Two types of fabric, spools of thread, my heavily dogeared spell notes from Imperials—what was I supposed to have done, keep it all in my head?—and a bamboo cup with what looked like fortune sticks in it. I looked across the table at Zaowei. She pushed up her sleeves and made an encouraging gesture with her chin. Geomancy stuff and nonsense. But I shook the cup, and drew a stick, and read it aloud.

<If you could only watch one play for the rest of your life, what would it be?>

"Phoenix and the Cowherd," we both said.

I laughed. "Please. You can't be old enough to have watched it. *I'm* <<Phoenix and Cowherd>> generation."

"When you grow up near Last Stand Marsh, all the plays are new for five years, or until the mayor's son makes a contribution to the local theatre."

"*You're* from Guaji? I had you for Fugui with your airs."

The Geomancer snorted.

"Flatter me again, and I'll claim more than half the table. Take another stick."

I whispered the deconstruction spell over the altar runner.

You are a whole of symbiotic parts that have never stopped becoming.

You are always becoming.

Now, interrogate your separateness…

The runner glowed. The threads stood out at the joints. Slowly, they lifted away from each other.

"One more stick."

"Not now."

Separate-ness is not other-ness.

The thread had stopped moving.

Zaowei shook the cup once more. "You want to. Separate your lack of fun from your personality. Dullness does not become you."

The runner was no longer glowing. I threw my hands in the air.

Might as well pick a stick.

But I was still tetchy.

"You ought to stop pulling at the lapel of your cloak, or it'll stretch and then you'll look even more ridiculous. On top of being the worst bench mate ever."

Zaowei smirked.

"If you'd opened with that from day one, you'd be rid of me sooner."

I tried to pick up the strands of the spell in my head, but it was useless.

"Wait. You started this game just to talk to me?"

"It wasn't just any bush," Zaowei sulked.

Without her cloak, she looked less ridiculous. More like any other camp follower. Only taller, with silkier black hair cascading down the sides of a tight top knot, with a narrower chin, firmer lips… you get the picture. Disgusting.

I ran a hand over the cloak.

Interrogate yourself.

The cloak shifted, with some reluctance. It shimmered a little as it did, which was more due to the velveteen—*not* real velvet—make of it, than its Light. (Very tacky, not very demure.) It revealed a tear where a set of trigrams was, effectively ripping them in half.

"And you couldn't have just taken a queue stick and waited your turn for a mending."

"I couldn't risk His Brilliance knowing that the cloak was that important. To me."

We all have our crutches. I stroked my lucky scissors.

"Well. I'm sure it was the baddest bush." Was that reassuring?

"A hawthorn."

"Love the berries. Hate the claws."

"Right? I was thinking hawthorn juice, hawthorn fruit leather, hawthorn candy."

"Didn't notice the rip until after."

"And nothing's been the same since."

I flexed my fingers and ran them over the tear, eyes at the level of the fabric. It smelled of rosewood under warm hands, and red date tea. Damnit, it smelled of her.

"It only looks awful, but it's a clean rip. A simple patch and stitch would do it."

Zaowei's eyes narrowed.

"Nevertheless, I'll cast an inseparability-in-flux to make the patch extra tight." I lifted my chin. "Because I have standards. But on one condition."

"Name it."

"You tell His Lighted Brilliance that the Flying Cowherd and the Dancing Spiders are in alignment, and we *move on* into Heng-Po, or anywhere the Incandescent Army may wander, because I have had it with sitting in camp on my arse in Wuliao."

Was it two, or three seconds after, that I wondered if that would move her from my tent as well? And if I cared for that at all.

"Fix the cloak, and I'll have His Brilliance tying on his armor for the road in seconds."

Thus, in no time and with much haste to make up for all the idling—that is to say, in two and a half days—Her Incandescence's Army was on the move again.

The Army was pleased for the exercise for all of a half day before they began complaining again, over the dinner campfires, that soldiering was a rough job and they wouldn't have gotten into it if their first brothers hadn't inherited the family business.

His Brilliance was pleased because he could finally dispatch his mother's spy back to her with news of the triumphant continuation of the tour into Heng-Po.

Zaowei was pleased that her cloak was mended with the spell work and Light restoration befitting His Brilliance's Learned Geomancer. I didn't tell her that I'd whispered a humility charm over the bottom hem, to finish.

And as for myself, I found half a table to be more than sufficient for stitches and spell work. And the Leaned Geomancer's continued company in the tent and at the bench, whenever the army stopped to set up camp, better than intolerable. Mollified somewhat by a steady supply of hawthorn berry leather, and new games. Although I must confess that I much prefer a good old Courtyards and Cockatrices campaign to her quizzes. I'm just waiting for the right time to tell her. Perhaps when the Cantering Calthrop and the Reluctant Beetle are in alignment.

A House of Faded Glamour

Eddie Robson

Edith needs a new truffle hound. This has been the case for several years now, but she is finally going to have to do something about it, because she's down to her last few scraps of catalyst. What she has left will fit in a small jam jar: a cotton reel, a seashell, a lolly stick, and a badge bearing the crest of Hull Kingston Rovers. Maurice hasn't brought her anything new in weeks, keeps saying there's nothing out there to find. Last time she saw him, he gave her a roof tile which he tried to pass off as catalyst when it was literally just a roof tile. Like he didn't think she'd be able to tell. That upset her more than if he'd brought her nothing, because it was like he'd stopped caring—about her, about what she thought of him.

Late on the afternoon of Good Friday, Maurice called her from a phone box, telling her he'd found "a motherlode" of catalyst in some big house. He was obviously tripping at the time. He claims it makes his sense stronger, helps him find stuff. This is untrue.

"It's not someone else's store, is it?" Edith asked.

"No, no, it's not marked at all," he replied. "They obviously don't know what they've got." Then he said he was going in to take it.

Edith has called his flat several times since then, but received no answer.

It's now Easter Sunday and Edith has a client sitting in her front room—Gerald. He's got to take a business trip to America on Tuesday, he's an anxious flyer and wants Edith to cast a simple luck spell. Edith can't stop the plane falling from the sky, but a luck spell will mean if it does, by some happenstance he won't be on it. The likelihood of the plane crashing is tiny, so Edith could probably get away with not casting the spell and telling Gerald she had. After all, if it does crash and he dies, he's not going to come back and complain. And then she could save some catalyst in case she really needs it.

With some clients she'd just con them and not give it a second thought, but Gerald is one of her regulars. He may be an upwardly-mobile sort with a semi-detached house and golf club membership, but he grew up in a Norfolk village that was kept safe by the craft many times over the centuries, and respect for it is drilled into him. When he moved to London, his aunt put him in touch with Edith so he had someone nearby he could bring such matters to. It seems cruel to trick to such an earnest believer, especially when others are so glib.

Edith takes the lolly stick from the jar and places it in her palm. She pushes down on the stick with the fingers of her other hand and it melts into her skin, prompting a ripple of gooseflesh. Then she returns to Gerald in the front room, apologises for keeping him waiting, then performs the spell. It will be mild, but enough to give him confidence and her the satisfaction she's done right by him. As the luck is now active and will last long enough to see him safely to the other side of the Atlantic, she suggests he fits in a round of golf before he sets off. He agrees with a smile, then he leaves Edith's house, gets back into his car and drives home to his wife, to whom he will not mention any of this.

Edith has held back a little of the energy, and she has plans for it. She lifts her telephone's receiver and thinks back to the call she received from Maurice. With a slight effort she can see him standing in the phone box, talking to her with reddened eyes. The image spreads out like a watercolour dripping onto blank paper: the phone box stands on a grass verge, on a wide, quiet suburban street. A hedge runs behind the box. It's a street corner, so there should be a sign bearing its name—and there is. The image is already dimming but Edith concentrates and reads the sign: GIDEON ROAD.

Edith opens the drawer below the telephone and brings out her London A-Z.

Gideon Road is a short bus ride away—Maurice never wanders far from home. When Edith finds him, she will tell him she's looking for a new truffle hound. That's why she needs to find him, so she can make that clear to him before looking for someone new. She's not doing this because she's *worried* about him or anything like that.

Edith steps off the bus and opens her umbrella. It's a drizzly, quiet afternoon in one of those former villages that's been absorbed into the London suburbs, with a row of old workers' cottages and a small church standing opposite attractive 1920s bungalows. Gratifyingly, Edith sees the phone box exactly as she envisaged it. She managed to get that from a few leftover splinters of lolly stick. Imagine what she could do if she ever got her hands on a *proper* supply of catalyst, rather than the scraps she must make do with.

Amid the buildings in the immediate area is an obvious candidate for the "big house" Maurice spoke of: set back from the road, with a driveway that slopes up and curves around, a three-storey manor with maybe six or eight bedrooms and a large, well-tended garden. Edith crosses the road, walks up the driveway and knocks at the door.

The door is answered by a diminutive, plump South Asian woman with soft features and shaggy, shoulder-length black hair. She is young, no more than half Edith's age. She wears a loose green dress that has been hand-modified, with yellow and purple flowers made of felt stitched onto it: the effect is amateurish, but charmingly so. Her dark eyes are bloodshot.

"Hello?" she says in a Birmingham accent.

"I'm looking for a friend," says Edith. This is untrue—Maurice isn't a friend—but it is simpler than explaining what he actually is.

"I could be your friend," says the young woman, smiling. "My name's Uma."

"Hello, Uma—yes, you could be my friend, but I'm also looking for a particular person called Maurice. Has he been here?"

Uma's eyebrows rise. "Oh, Maurice, yeah, he's… you say you're his friend?"

"Yes."

"Not… his wife?"

"Do I look like his wife?"

Uma considers Edith: her loose canvas trousers, her pinstriped blouse, her dark purple cardigan, her greying red hair gathered in a high ponytail. "You look like my old art teacher."

"I'm not his wife, or anything in that area."

"Oh good, because, like, he said he wasn't married, and I thought maybe you'd get all *uptight* when…" Uma tails off uncertainly.

"When what?"

"Oh, just him and Muriel were…"

"Muriel?"

"This is her house. Would you like to come in?"

The interior of the house is a little untidy, and the décor is a little tatty and dated—but it's not squalid. It smells of freshly cut flowers and hashish. Edith glances through a door into the front room, where a black-and-white movie is playing on a new colour television set. A young man in a kaftan lies asleep on the sofa in front of the screen. Another young man sits in the corner, softly playing a xylophone at a slow, unsteady tempo. Books and magazines are scattered across the floor; unwashed mugs languish on tables.

Uma has asked Edith to wait in the spacious hallway while she goes looking for Maurice. The door opposite the living room opens and music spills out—something contemporary Edith doesn't know, reminds her of the curly-haired boy with the guitar she saw on *Late Night Line-Up* the other week. Another young woman emerges, this one blonde and gamine and willowy. "Hello," she says sleepily in cut-glass tones, offering Edith the reefer she is smoking.

Edith politely declines.

"Are you a friend of Muriel's?"

"No, I'm looking for Maurice."

The blonde woman's face lights up. "Oh, Maurice! He's such a darling. We all love him." Then she hesitates. "He's not your –"

"He's a friend."

"Well, if you've never fucked him, I recommend it."

Edith is forming a strong impression of how Maurice got waylaid here.

The blonde woman peers at Edith and her eyes narrow. "Ooh, what have you got?" She intrudes into Edith's personal space and reaches into the pocket of her cardigan. Edith brushes her hand away and steps back, but the woman suddenly doesn't seem so sleepy: she pins Edith against the frame of the living room door with one hand, and her other hand dips into Edith's pocket again. The hand comes out holding the cotton reel Edith brought with her, just in case she needed it. Edith tries to snatch it back, but the blonde woman turns and skips up the first few stairs, examining the cotton reel.

"Hmm," she says. "Not much, but it'll do. Thank you." And she continues up the stairs, calling for Muriel.

Edith is still considering how to react to this turn of events when Uma comes down the stairs, leading Maurice by the hand. Maurice is dazed, dishevelled, and unshaven: he can usually get away with pretending to be younger than he is, but not today. He's wearing the trousers from his brown corduroy suit with a lemon-yellow T-shirt. Edith has never seen him wear a T-shirt before.

"Maurice," says Edith. "Been enjoying yourself?"

Maurice peers back at Edith. "Who are you?"

Edith met Maurice one night in the summer of 1953, after he broke into her house. She'd come downstairs to find him blundering around her kitchen, knocking things over, because she'd cast a protection spell that meant anyone who tried to steal her catalyst would have their perceptions reversed, so what they saw was a mirror image of reality. It was a low-powered spell which Edith could keep running with only a sliver of her resources: some witches used imprisoning spells, but those were much heavier to maintain. Also, perception reversal was funnier.

The spell rendered Maurice harmless, and after his anger burned out, he was just embarrassed. He was drunk and Edith realised he didn't even understand why he'd tried to rob her, or why he'd made a beeline for the locked cupboard in the corner of her kitchen rather than grabbing anything more obviously valuable. He said he was just doing it "for a lark." He was a student, he said. It was a student prank. She made him a cup of tea, lifted the perception spell so he could drink it without spilling it down himself, and then she explained to him that he'd been looking for magic.

He laughed his high-handed, public-school-educated laugh because he didn't believe in magic.

"How do you think I made you see right as left and left as right?" she asked.

He wasn't convinced and demanded further proof. "Turn that sugar bowl into a frog, or something."

"That would be a dreadful waste."

"Of sugar?"

"No, of magic. That's actually what I'm trying to explain—even people who know magic is real tend to think it's a power, when really, it's a resource. Some of us have the skills to use that resource."

"So, you can't do magic for me right now… because you don't have any."

"No, I have some. As I say, that's why you broke in. You sensed it was here."

"No, I didn't."

"At home, do you have a collection of odds and ends you've kept for no real reason? Pebbles from the beach, an old toy car, bits of string, clothes pegs…"

Maurice shifted in his seat. "Everyone does that."

"It's not your fault no-one's ever explained it to you. You can *find* magic."

"What?"

"We call it 'catalyst' in its raw state. It leaks through from another world and takes on a mundane physical form, something that fits in with our world. It could be literally anything. Only people like *you* can recognise it for what it is."

"Why me?"

"Genetics. You were born able to do it. But those who never learn why they're attracted to seemingly random objects never make proper use of the gift."

"So how do I use all this *magic* I've found?"

"You don't. Those who can find it have no affinity for using it."

"The irony." Maurice considered this a while. "How many people can do this?"

"Very few."

"Do people get paid for doing it?"

Now Maurice's expression is blank, he's not joking with Edith: she's a stranger to him. And Uma is looking at Edith oddly too.

"We've known each other nearly fifteen years, Maurice. Your family paid for your flat in Belsize Park, but you never speak to them, except your brother who you sometimes tap for money. You tell them you earn a little from your poetry, but really you work for me. You telephoned me from that call box across the street on Friday."

Maurice looks confused, aware there's a contradiction in his memories but unable—or unwilling—to resolve it.

"Someone's done this to you," Edith stresses. "They made you forget me. Who?"

Just then the front door opens, and a young man enters (everyone Edith has seen in this house, except Maurice, looks to be in their early twenties). He's not tall, and his frizzy hair hangs around his shoulders, and he looks very pleased with himself. He pays no attention to Edith as he greets Uma, takes off his army surplus rucksack and reaches into it. "*Look* what I found," he says.

"Ooh, let's see," says Uma, crouching down.

The young man produces a garden gnome from the rucksack. It's a tall one, about 18 inches, with a pointed hat and a moronic expression.

"Wow!" says Uma. "That's *amazing*."

Edith doesn't hesitate. She reaches down and presses her palm onto the gnome's hat and breathes deeply—and in a matter of moments the entire gnome disappears into her hand.

Uma and the young man look up at Edith stupidly.

"Bloody hell!" Maurice says.

Edith wasn't *certain* the gnome was made of catalyst, but if she was wrong, the worst that would have happened was a bruised hand. She has never absorbed so much so quickly. If she had a chunk as large as this—and she very rarely gets a chunk as large as this—she would use a little of it at a time. But Edith feels she is not safe in this house, and needs to protect herself and Maurice, and her decision to absorb the gnome was made on the spur of the moment: she needed to convert it into a form they couldn't take from her. Now her body feels like it's exploding, filling every corner of this spacious house and lighting it up. She yelps with exhilaration and astonishment. Melodies pour from discarded acoustic guitars in the library. The balls on the snooker table in the drawing room perform an extraordinary trick shot. A monochrome Bing Crosby steps from the television in the living room and awakens the slumbering boy on the sofa with a rendition of "Easter Parade".

It feels utterly glorious, but Edith calms herself: she's wasting it. She reins herself in and the hallway of the house comes back into focus. Maurice and Uma have both shrunk back against the walls. The young man who brought the gnome isn't there: his rucksack lies on the floor.

Edith points to the rucksack. "I didn't destroy him, did I?"

The stunned Uma shakes her head and points to the stairs. The young man's voice is up there, calling for Muriel.

"That's a relief." Edith turns to Maurice, and he flinches. She already had a vague sense of what had been done to him, but she can see it very clearly now. Undoing it is like untying a knot—an awkward, clumsily tied knot, pulled much too tight. It takes more energy than Edith expects, but she frees it. Maurice moans in pain as the binding leaves him, and he looks up at her accusingly.

"Couldn't you have done it a bit more gently than that?" he asks.

"Good to have you back," says Edith. "Where's the catalyst?"

"Room in the attic. There's absolutely *scads* of it."

Edith nods and marches up the stairs. As she approaches the first-floor landing, a woman steps out and occupies the top step, blocking her way: a tall woman with a sleek dark bob and sly, refined features. She wears visibly expensive pyjamas, and her face is fully made up: she looks like she belongs to a slightly earlier age. Edith is in no doubt that this is Muriel.

"Do you usually come into other people's houses and cause this kind of disturbance?" she says.

"I do when they kidnap my friend and wipe me from his memory."

Muriel snorts. "I didn't *kidnap* him; he's been having a *lovely* time with us. And I've seen his memories of you, you're not friends."

"Why do it? Because you didn't want him to tell me what you've got here? Or because you wanted to keep him for yourself? Or both?"

"I think it's time you left."

"The young people you've collected, are they all truffle hounds?"

Muriel's forehead creases. "Truffle hounds?"

"You know. Magic sensitives."

"You call them *truffle hounds*?"

"It's what everyone called them where I grew up. What did you call them?"

Muriel says nothing.

"Ah," says Edith. "You *didn't* grow up with this. Yes, it shows."

Muriel is irked by this and is about to ask her to elaborate, which might provide the small distraction Edith needs. She has plenty of energy still to draw on from the gnome, but usually takes her time over spells, and if it's complicated, she writes it out. If she casts something quickly, it will have to be simple. Her focus is already firmly on Muriel, which gives her an idea. She blinks hard –

And when Edith opens her eyes, she and Muriel have exchanged places. Edith is even wearing the posh pyjamas. She didn't intend that. Muriel is now a couple of steps below, wearing Edith's blouse, trousers and cardigan: she looks down at herself, plainly disliking what she sees. Edith takes advantage by kicking Muriel in the chest, sending her stumbling back down the stairs.

Edith turns, runs up the next flight of stairs (how *luxurious* Muriel's pyjamas feel against her skin as she moves), and emerges onto a hallway that runs down the centre of the attic. Most of the rooms up here would have been servants' quarters once, but there's one at the near end that formerly served as a nursery, which has wallpaper with whimsical illustrations on it. The rain outside has stopped and the late afternoon light shines through the dust and cobwebs. The room is crammed with boxes and tea chests and loose objects: toys, books, clothes, tools, decorations, kitchenware. To the casual observer it might look like the owner had put all their things into storage up here while someone else was using the house. A closer inspection reveals no unity of taste—a crystal decanter next to a cheap toaster, a Virginia Woolf novel on top of a Mickey Spillane—so have they been gathered by someone with an eclectic mindset? No, Edith knows they all have something else in common. It's no surprise Maurice has been struggling to find any catalyst lately. Everything in the local area has been brought here.

This is not how things are done. No-one hoards this much. It must have attracted all those magic-sensitive hippies like it attracted Maurice. He said it wasn't marked—because Muriel doesn't know how to mark it. And anyway, she *wanted* the truffle hounds to come.

Edith reaches out and picks up a corkscrew that lies atop the contents of a tea chest –

And she feels a sudden, unpleasant shift. Her vision sinks lower, her feet move further apart—because she herself is shrinking. The corkscrew seems to be growing in her hands, and she drops it, realising with alarm she is now shorter than the tea chest and still getting smaller. Of course, idiotic of her to touch these things—Muriel will have protected them from theft, just as Edith does her own supply –

And Edith turns and sees Muriel towering over her, still wearing Edith's clothes.

"Bloody thief," says Muriel.

"I didn't come to steal it," says Edith, now just a few inches tall and unsure if she can even be heard. "You *can't* have this much. What do you *need* it all for?"

Muriel smiles and shakes her head.

Edith looks down at herself. Has the shrinking stopped? Or will it go on and on until she falls through the gaps between atoms? But then she realises the pyjamas have shrunk with her. It's possible a shrinking spell could shrink a person's clothes along with their body, but Edith has never seen it done. She thinks of the spells she uses to protect her own stash against thieves. Spells affecting perception are much lower-energy and easier to maintain than those affecting reality. Muriel doesn't have to worry about running out of catalyst, but…

Edith still has a little of the gnome's energy left. There must be something else alive in this room. She probes outward with her senses… and yes, sitting on a web in the window is a spider. Pushing her consciousness into smaller creatures is something she does regularly; sometimes as an indulgence she does it for pure pleasure, projecting herself into birds to feel the joy of flight. She quickly forges a pathway and enters the spider's mind. Spiders are difficult to manoeuvre, what with all the legs and eyes, but she manages to get a view of the floor. Exactly as she suspected, her human body is still its normal size, and lies immobile on the wooden boards. The spell only made her *believe* she was small.

Muriel stands over the body, wondering aloud why Edith has stopped moving or speaking.

There will be no lasting effects once the spell wears off—but right now, Edith's body is still affected by it. She must somehow find a way of fighting back. As a spider.

Muriel is looking around the attic room. "Where are you, Edith?" she asks. She knows enough of the craft to recognise consciousness projection, and it's possible she knows how to trace someone's consciousness. It's much easier if you've got their real body in front of you.

Muriel picks up a candlestick holder and lets it melt into her palm as she continues to scan the room for signs of movement. With all the catalyst in here, Muriel could do a lot of damage to her, and to others. Edith is surprised Muriel hasn't already done so, in fact. She would love to take the catalyst and distribute it around to people who could make good use of it, and keep a little for herself, but that doesn't seem a viable option at this moment. There is a way she can quickly remove the catalyst from the equation, one of the first things any witch is taught—the method was once used a lot more, back when people in power took magic more seriously, when you could be dragged from your home for possessing even a scrap of catalyst. Edith can open the way back to where the catalyst came from. No-one knows what forces it through to our world, but when the way is open it slips back easily, just like gravity pulls things to the ground when there's nothing holding them up. Edith should still be able to cast this while inhabiting the spider, but her unfamiliar body may make it hard to find a point of focus…

And then she recalls she is sitting on the spider's web. The fact she is in the body of the creature that created it generates an affinity with the strands of web, and her focus falls on it easily. She crawls off the web, up the windowpane –

Suddenly Muriel's gaze is on her. The light is shining past her spider body, making the movement glaringly obvious. Muriel grins and reaches out –

Edith must act now, so she creates an opening at the centre of the web and lets it spread out. The effect is immediate: all the catalyst in the room starts moving towards the window, the boxes and tea chests sliding across the floorboards. Muriel hears the movement and turns to see some of the smaller, loose items rising up and spinning lazily through the air: she snatches them, grabbing pocketknives and rusty keys, but there are too many for her to get them all, and her eyes flare with panic as the first few slip through the gate in the web. She starts absorbing them into her hands and Edith realises this could backfire: if she forces Muriel to convert all the catalyst here and now, the woman will become more powerful than ever, probably hosting more magic than she can control –

But the catalyst is being drawn out of the room faster than Muriel can absorb it. One of the biggest pieces, a rusted tractor wheel with no tyre on it, slides across the floor towards the web, and Muriel grabs onto it desperately. The gate is growing wider, larger than the web, to accommodate the larger chunks of catalyst, and Edith scuttles further up the window to ensure she is clear of it.

Muriel pokes her fingers into the holes around the rim of the tractor wheel and starts to absorb it into her palms. She digs her heels into the floor and leans back, trying to counteract the force. But the gate is only growing stronger as it accumulates catalyst, and Muriel cannot now grab onto anything for support: both her hands are stuck to the wheel.

"You *can't* have it!" she half-whines, half-screams. "This is *mine!*"

This is not what Edith intended. No-one who has crossed that barrier has ever come back. She tries to close the gate before it draws Muriel in, but it has its own momentum now: it won't stop until it has consumed every bit of catalyst in the room. Muriel loses her footing; the wheel is dragged through the gate and a wailing Muriel is dragged after it.

When Edith returns to her body, the spell that made her believe she was tiny has either worn off or been cancelled because the caster is no longer in this world. All the bric-a-brac that was in the attic room has gone. The spider has returned to its web, which is just a web again. Not a strand of it has broken.

"What happened?" asks Uma, who is standing over her.

With help from Uma, Edith clambers to her feet and asks if they might be able to discuss it over tea.

Downstairs, the young people inhabiting the house are milling around, confused, comparing notes. A spell has literally been broken. Some of them seem aware Edith has something to do with it, but no-one dares approach her except Uma. Maurice has gone.

In the kitchen, Uma boils the kettle while Edith sits at the table and explains what transpired upstairs. Uma doesn't appear at all defensive of Muriel, and doesn't question Edith's version of events.

"How long have you been at this house?" asks Edith.

Uma places a mug of tea in front of Edith, and sits down opposite her. "Eight months, I think? I wonder if my family have been looking for me." She looks out of the window. "I haven't called them. I just… stopped thinking about them altogether. Was Muriel making me do that?"

Edith nods. "And she was sending you out to collect catalyst?"

"All of us." Uma has explained there are seven truffle hounds living at the house. Maurice would have made eight. "The feeling you get from being close to such a huge collection of it –"

"I know. Or rather, people have told me. I've never seen that much in one place. What did she want it all for?"

Uma shrugs.

"She must have been collecting it for a reason."

"She never said."

"Did you ever see her use it for anything else? Apart from to influence you and the others here?"

"I think she used it to make people give her money, or cancel debts. Get rid of anyone who asked awkward questions."

"Did you ever see her do anything that affected the world in a physical way?"

"How d'you mean?"

"Changing things into other things. Altering the weather…"

"No, never."

Edith thinks back to Muriel's last moments before being sucked into the web. There were things she could have done. Set up a counterforce to draw things in the other direction, or block the gateway altogether. Maybe she didn't have the presence of mind to cast those spells. Or maybe she didn't have the skill.

"I wonder," says Edith, "if she just wanted to have it. She knew it was valuable, and it drew people like you to her, and she just liked having so much of it."

Uma nods. "Yeah. From knowing her, I can believe that." Then she asks, quietly: "Where is she now?"

"I don't know. We don't know where it comes from."

Uma nods and reaches into the pocket on the front of her dress. "Maurice left this for you," she says, bringing out a folded note and handing it to her.

Edith unfolds and reads the note. It isn't long.

"A pity all that stuff got wasted," says Uma. "We put so much work into finding it."

Edith folds the note back up, looks the young woman in the eye and smiles. "Would you like to find it for me instead?"

The Exchange

Dana Gricken

"Magical items for sale!" the wizard, Ozaris, shouts from outside his village shop. His grey hair is messy, matching his long beard, and his purple robe sparkles under the sunlight. "But let the buyer beware, these items come with a price. Are you willing to make the exchange?"

Some townspeople seem curious, entering his shop. The wizard smiles and follows them in as the door chimes. The sign above the shop reads "Caveat Emptor's Emporium," the phrase some kind of old elvish saying, and Astrid Hain wants nothing to do with it.

She'll buy things the old-fashioned way, thank you very much. With what little gold she has these days.

After browsing the village shops, spending her last gold coins on food and other necessities, she heads home through the dusty streets. Her legs are tired when she reaches her small hut on the outskirts of town. She has to do everything now, from cooking to cleaning and shopping, as her mother has slowed down in her old age. After unlocking the door, she finds the home quiet.

"Mama?" she calls out, setting down the bags of food. "Are you here?"

A quiet groan comes from her mother's bedroom. Rushing down the hall, she enters the bedroom and finds her mother lying on the floor, clutching her head. Astrid steps closer and realizes her mother is bleeding.

"By the Gods, Mama!" She bends down to her level. "What happened? Are you all right?"

Mama, so weak and fragile these days, glances around the room. "I was just getting up to fetch a book before heading back to bed…and I think I fell. Dear, can you help me up?"

"Of course, Mama."

Pulling her frail mother to her feet with a groan, Astrid brings her to bed and tucks her in. Just like her mother did for her so many times as a young child. Those warm memories keep Astrid going when life gets tough. After fetching the book Mama wanted, she gets her a glass of water from the kitchen.

"Here you go. Drink up," she says, handing it over. Her mother takes a long sip. "You know, Mama…I'm a bit worried about you these days. You're falling down a lot, forgetting things. I think the town doctor should take a look at you."

But Mama shakes her head, setting her glass down. "Oh, no, I'm fine. Just tired. Could you fetch me a blanket, dear?"

Astrid tries to give her the benefit of the doubt, but when she falls again the next morning, she takes the stubborn woman to the doctor. Mama is examined by a man with large glasses and a stethoscope in the office. After many exams and blood tests, the doctor finally has an answer. And it isn't the one Astrid wants to hear.

"…we call it Wither's Disease," the doctor tells them. "It causes confusion and loss of coordination in the early stages. Later on, it causes bleeding from the mouth. It's a rare but fatal disease. Most people only live about a week once they've caught it. Don't worry, though, it's not contagious."

"A week?" Astrid stares at her mother in horror, knowing it will only get worse from here. "No. No, this can't be happening. There has to be a cure, right?"

The doctor shakes his head. "I'm afraid not. Not with traditional medicine, anyway."

Astrid thinks back to the Caveat Emptor's Emporium. Would the wizard Ozaris have something that could help?

"How about magic?" she asks the doctor. "Is there a magical potion that could save my mother's life?"

"Possibly. But the closest magical college is days away." The doctor pulls out a map of the continent from his nearby cabinet. He points at the college's location—a far journey from their tiny little village. "And then you'd have to petition the college to help you, and we both know how long paperwork can take. I'm afraid that by the time you made it there and got their help, it would be too late."

Too late. The worst words ever uttered.

"But there's that wizard in town," Astrid says as the doctor puts the map away. "Ozaris. I see him every day as I do my errands. He runs the curio shop of magical items and elixirs. I could ask him for help."

"That wizard? All his items come with a price, you know. And a very high one." The doctor shakes his head. "My nephew wanted to become a king's guard. So he goes to Ozaris, asks for a magical sword that can make him a better fighter. And it does. But do you know what the catch was?"

"No. What did the wizard do to him?"

"The sword made him fight better, but weakened his immune system. Permanently, thanks to some spell the wizard cast on him. More like a curse. And no one can break it." The doctor shakes his head. "My nephew's in here every week, suffering from something. Broken arm. Near fatal allergic reaction. Worms in his ears. A weakened immune system, no doubt. That's the price he paid for getting such a powerful blade. I'm afraid if you went there, looking for a cure for your mother, Ozaris may ask for something awful in return. I really don't recommend it."

That's it, then. They're out of options. The room turns silent as Astrid holds Mama's hand, trying not to cry.

"Anyway, I'm very sorry," the doctor says. "I'm sure this is difficult for you both. I'll give you a moment."

After leaving the exam room, everything turns quiet. Astrid can't believe she's going to lose her mother—and so soon. And then she'll be all alone. With her father's sudden death last year, her mother is all she has left.

"Don't fret, my dear," Mama says, patting her hand. "Everyone has to die eventually, right? This is my time. You'll be just fine without me, I'm sure of it."

But Astrid isn't. The doctor gives Astrid instructions to keep her mother comfortable, and they head home, where Astrid tosses and turns all night. And the wizard Ozaris is the only thing on her mind.

The next morning, after taking care of her mother, she heads out to the village shops as usual. But this time, she walks into the Caveat Emptor's Emporium. The bell chimes above her head before she browses the shop. Magical items of all kinds—swords, amulets, rings, ointments, and more—line the shelves, all of them emanating a multi-colored supernatural glow.

Astrid touches nothing, making her way toward the back of the shop. The wizard Ozaris speaks to a middle-aged woman from behind his desk. With a smile on his face, he hands her a brown seed.

"…and I believe this will cure your farm," he tells her. "Plant it in the ground. When you check on it in the morning, your garden will be lush and ripe again."

"Oh, thank you, thank you!" The woman takes the seed, on the verge of tears. "Our fields have been infertile for too long, and my family has suffered enough. How much do I owe you? I don't have much, but I've saved up some gold that you can have."

He smiles wider. "Not gold, my dear. But an exchange. You may have that seed, but I'd like something in return. Your eyesight."

The woman pauses. "My…eyesight? What do you mean?"

"I'll pluck out both your eyes in exchange for that seed. You won't be able to see, but your garden will burst with life. You'll never have to worry about growing anything ever again. Don't worry—if you agree, my magic will make it painless and quick. And remember, all sales are final."

The woman stares at the seed in her hand. "But…but that's ridiculous. I need my eyesight. I can't agree to this—"

"Then no deal," the wizard says, snatching the seed out of her hand. "You must not want the seed bad enough if you won't give up your eyesight. Next customer, please!"

With a horrified scoff, the woman turns and leaves. Clearing her throat nervously, Astrid steps toward the counter, Ozaris' gaze settling on her.

"Hello there, young lady," he says. "Welcome to Caveat Emptor's Emporium—where all my magical items come with a price. What are you looking for today?"

"Well, uh, my mother is very sick. Sick with something called Wither's Disease," Astrid stammers. "She's been given a week to live and the doctors can't cure her. Do you have anything that could help?"

Ozaris reaches under the counter, pulling out an elixir in a blue bottle. "I sure do. This magical potion can cure anyone of anything. One sip and poof! All disease is gone."

"And my mother will live?"

"Indeed. I swear it."

Astrid takes a deep breath. "Then I'd like to purchase that elixir, please. Go ahead—take my eyes. No price is too high to make sure my mother survives."

Closing her eyes, Astrid just wants it to be over with. But Ozaris laughs. "Oh, no, my dear. Blindness was the price for my last customer. For you...I have something else in mind."

Astrid opens her eyes gulps, wondering what it will be. And how much it'll cost.

Before Astrid can ask, she sees something moving quickly out of the corner of her eye. She turns, noticing a young boy has grabbed a magical flying carpet off the shelf. He tucks it under his arm and rushes toward the door.

But the wizard doesn't seem upset at all. He sighs, shaking his head. "Another thief. When will they learn?"

When the boy reaches the door, pulling it open, a magical mist of different colors falls on him. He groans and drops the carpet. To Astrid's astonishment, the boy's hands vanish, leaving him with two stumps. Then he starts screaming.

"My hands, my hands!" he cries. "What did you do to me?"

"You tried to steal from my shop, young man, so I punished you. The door is rigged with magic to prevent thieves," the wizard says. "Now, you'll never be able to steal anything ever again."

As the boy continues screaming, Astrid walks over, helping him to his feet. "You poor child. Why did you try to steal the carpet?"

"To go see my father. He lives so far away, and I wanted to visit him. But I don't have any money." The boy stares at his arms, missing his hands. "I didn't mean to cause any trouble, I swear!"

Astrid turns to the wizard. "The boy's harmless. Give him back his hands, please."

But Ozaris shakes his head. "No can do, I'm afraid. Perhaps that'll teach him to not steal in the future. If you would've asked me for the magic carpet, boy, we could've worked something out."

"I've seen the way you work things out," Astrid sneers. "What you ask of people is cruel. Why do this?"

Ozaris sighs, walking out from behind the counter. His purple robe sashays on the ground behind him. "You must think I'm evil, don't you? Unreasonable?"

Astrid and the boy nod.

"Well, I'm far from it. You see, magic is a powerful thing. Too many people try to use it without realizing the consequences. They take it for granted and misuse it. I saw that up close when I worked at the college of magic." He shakes his head. "So this is my way of getting them to understand what they're dealing with. My customers will never forget how strong magic is, and how much it should be revered, thanks to my shop."

"I still don't think it's justified," Astrid sneers. "I'll be leaving now. And telling everyone I know to stay away from this shop."

The boy runs away in tears, the magic carpet flying back to its position on the shelf as Ozaris nods. "Very well. But we both know that without my elixir, your mother will die. I hope for her sake, it will be quick and painless, but from what I've heard about Withers Disease, it won't be."

As Astrid flees the shop, those words replay in her head for a while. And over the next few days, her mother's condition worsens, causing her to fall more often and bleed from her mouth. When she can't bear to listen to her mother's cries anymore, Astrid returns to the wizard's shop.

"I knew you would be back," Ozaris says when he sees her walk in, his smugness obvious. "Let me guess. Your mother is still sick?"

"Yes. And not getting any better." Astrid approaches the counter. "Name your price, wizard. What do I have to do to cure her?"

Ozaris smiles, reaching under his counter for the elixir. Astrid briefly thinks of stealing it before remembering the boy's awful fate. "Hmm, let me see. As you know, magic is powerful and must be respected. If I give you this elixir for your mother, that means someone out there won't get it. That person will die while your mother lives. So there must be an exchange to make up for it."

Astrid holds her breath. What will it be?

"I'll give you this elixir of perfect health," he says, pushing it toward her, "in exchange for your memory."

Astrid frowns. "My memory? What do you mean, wizard?"

"The cost is your memory—specifically of your mother—if you take this. She'll be completely cured, but you won't remember her at all. Her existence will be the only memory affected."

Astrid takes a moment to think about it. The exchange seems callous, barbaric even. She'll forget every laugh she shared with her mother, every precious, fond memory she made growing up. The very thing that keeps her going when she feels down. What's the point of a life if you don't have your memories?

But without it, her mother will die. She has no choice.

"Very well," Astrid says. "I agree to your terms. Give me one hour to prepare."

The wizard nods, setting the elixir aside. Astrid buys some ink and parchment from a seller in town. She then writes down everything she can think of about her mother—all the happy memories they shared over the years. Her tears stain the parchment before she dries them and places it in her pocket.

When she returns to the shop, the wizard's waiting for her with a smile. The elixir sits on the counter like a forbidden fruit. "Ah, there you are. Ready for the exchange?"

Astrid takes a deep breath. "I am. Do it—quickly. Before I change my mind."

Ozaris pulls out his wand in the blink of an eye, muttering some incantation under his breath. Astrid's vision goes black before it returns to normal. When she opens her eyes, she remembers entering the shop, but not the reason why.

"A pleasure doing business with you," Ozaris says with a smile, tucking his wand away. He then pushes the elixir toward her. "Remember to leave a good review for my shop and tell others about me. Oh, and you'll want to get this home to your mother as soon as possible."

"My mother?" Astrid frowns. "I don't have a mother."

Ozaris scribbles something down on a piece of paper. "I see the spell worked, then. Run along now—back home with you. Take this note and pass it to the woman you see in your hut."

In confusion, Astrid takes the elixir and the note and heads home. When she unlocks the door, she finds an old woman sitting on the couch, just as the wizard said. The woman coughs before their eyes lock. And right away, just by the blank stare on Astrid's face, the old woman's wrinkled face twists in concern.

"Dear?" she asks. "Is everything all right?"

Astrid hands the note over. "I'm sorry, I don't know who you are. But I was asked to give you this note and elixir."

The old woman takes the note, reading it over. And then again to make sure she fully understands. When the truth sinks in, she begins sobbing.

"Oh, Astrid!" she cries. "How could you do this?"

Astrid has no idea what the woman is crying about. All she knows is that she has to take the elixir. "Here, drink this. I'm told it can help."

The woman studies the elixir, clearly wondering if she should take it. After a while, she finally gives in, drinking the elixir in one gulp. She starts to immediately look better. The next morning, the woman who claims to be Astrid's mother is up on her feet, completely cured of Withers Disease. The elixir bottle lies empty on the counter.

"Remind me again," Astrid says, plating breakfast for them both. "Who are you?"

"Your mother," Mrs. Hain replies with a sad sigh. "You sacrificed your memory of me so the wizard would cure my disease. While I understand why you did it—and it was selfless of you—I wish you wouldn't have."

Astrid blinks. "I did? Huh. I must've really loved you, then. To make that sacrifice."

"Indeed." Tears prickle at her mother's eyes. "You don't remember me at all? How I would sing you to sleep as a child when you had nightmares? How I held you when your father died? How we adopted a sheep and buried him in the backyard when he passed, crying our eyes out for days? We loved that little guy. You named him Pickles, remember?"

Astrid shakes her head. "I'm sorry, I don't remember that at all. Or you."

Those words haunt her mother for days. She finds the note Astrid left for herself in her pocket, forcing the young woman to read it over and over again, but she still doesn't remember her mother. Her mother cries herself to sleep every night, missing the close bond they shared, one that was forged over the years. And one that was stolen in the blink of an eye.

By the end of the week, after awkward silences, her mother knows what she must do. A deal has to be made to save her daughter's memory—for both of their sakes. She dresses in a long cloak and heads to Caveat Emptor's Emporium without Astrid's knowledge.

Ozaris stands behind the counter as always, looking up when he hears the chime of the bell. "Welcome to my shop. How can I help you?"

Mrs. Hain places the empty elixir bottle on the counter. "Ozaris. You sold my daughter a cure for my sickness, but wiped her memory of me. Is that right?"

Ozaris stares down at the bottle. "It is. A fair exchange for such powerful magic, I think. And I should remind you there are no refunds. All sales are final."

"But—"

"Sorry, can't help you." Ozaris looks up when the door chimes again. "And now I must attend to another customer. Excuse me."

As Ozaris scurries away, Mrs. Hain leaves the shop, disappointed. She thinks of her daughter every night before she falls asleep, cherishing the memories they made and the relationship they once had that kept them both going. To be forgotten by her own daughter feels like a dagger through her heart.

When another week passes, and then another, she can't take it anymore. Mrs. Hain returns to the shop, prepared to offer anything—and truly anything—to get her daughter's memory back, even if it means dying. There must be something the wizard can be persuaded with.

But as she approaches the front door, a city guard stops her. "The shop is permanently closed, ma'am," he says. "This is a murder scene now."

Mrs. Hain gasps. "A murder? Whose murder?"

When the door opens, a coroner drags out the wizard's body on a stretcher. His chest has been stabbed a dozen times. An unfamiliar middle-aged man is then led out of the store in chains, his hands bloody.

"Oh my."

The guard nods. "Indeed. Apparently the wizard cursed some little boy. Turned his hands to stumps for stealing from his shop and wouldn't change them back. When his father found out, he came to town and murdered Ozaris."

Mrs. Hain's face lights up. "Does that mean that all the deals Ozaris made are null and void? Will things go back to normal?"

"Sadly, I don't think so. I just saw the little boy and his hands were still stumps. Whatever magic the wizard used was powerful. Even in death."

Disappointment tugs at Mrs. Hain's chest. With the wizard's death, there seems to be no hope anymore. Her daughter will never remember her—a cruel fate. She heads home to find Astrid pulling weeds in the garden.

"Oh, hello, Mrs. Hain," Astrid says, wiping dirt from her brow. "Are you all right?"

Her mother blinks away her tears. "Yes, yes, I'm fine. Do you need any help?"

"No, I don't think… Oh." Astrid pauses, pulling an object from the soil. "There's something in here."

When her mother bends down, she realizes Astrid has pulled up a collar. The same one their pet sheep wore for so many years. Astrid runs her hands along the frayed collar, and a smile rises to her face.

"We buried the sheep in the garden," she whispers. "He was such a good boy. Everyone thought I was silly to mourn for a sheep, but my mother didn't. She helped me bury him and we said a little prayer. His name was…Pickles."

Her mother's eyes widen. "You remember all that?"

Astrid looks up at her mother, her face going blank. "Remember what?"

And just like that, the memory is gone. But it was there—if only for a moment. And from that day on, her mother hatches a plan.

She spends every day doing something that'll help Astrid remember her childhood, and by extension, her mother. She cooks Astrid meals she enjoyed when she was a child, finds her old toys, and sprays the perfume she once wore all over the house.

One day, Mrs. Hain finds the old overalls her daughter used to wear. She holds them up to Astrid in the kitchen. "Do you remember these, my dear? You used to wear these all the time when you were young. You always got them so filthy from playing in the mud."

Astrid pauses, studying the overalls. Then her face lights up as she reaches for them. A dirt stain on the knee catches her eye. "We washed them every night in a basin by the river, but some stains just wouldn't fade."

"Yes, that's right!" Her mother sets down the overalls. "Dear, please. Think really hard. Don't you remember me? Don't you remember your mother, how you saved my life? The times I held back your hair when you were sick, and all the times you took care of me in return?" Mrs. Hain falls to her knees, nearly begging. "I love you, Astrid. I love you and I want you to remember everything. I want you to remember *me*."

It's fleeting, but for a brief moment, their eyes lock. Then Astrid utters the word Mrs. Hain has been dying to hear. "…Mama."

"Yes—I'm your mama," she says through tears. "And I always will be, no matter how old you get or if you've completely forgotten me."

When she pulls her daughter in for a hug, she can feel it. Somehow, by some miracle, Astrid is beginning to remember. With each small piece of her childhood, the memories come flooding back, despite the powerful spell Ozaris put her under. And Mrs. Hain thinks she knows why.

"There's one thing the wizard forgot when he uttered that spell," her mother whispers into her hair. "The one thing he didn't count on."

"What, Mama?"

"That love can and will overcome anything. Even the strongest of magic." Her mother smiles. "I just know it."

Seedlings

Kali Wallace

It was only a bit after eight o'clock, but the morning was already warm. Dee worried that she might have waited too long. After Mother's Day, everybody said, to be certain the last frost has passed. Spring weather on the Front Range was unpredictable.

So she had waited. Today was Mother's Day. Her daughter might not call, but the sun was bright, the sky was blue, and she would plant her garden.

The lawn was crackling and brown after a dry, dry winter. There was almost no snow left on Pikes Peak, just a few wisps in the mountain's deepest folds. The gentle *sh-sh-sh* of a sprinkler carried from a neighbor's yard. She didn't know which yard or which neighbor; she and Carla hadn't met many of them yet, for all that they were pressed up against each other. The subdivision was only a few years old and the houses were small, the gaps between them non-existent, the backyards no more than patches of optimistic grass enclosed by fences already weathered gray by the Colorado sun. It wasn't much, but it was what they could afford, two sisters settling in to grow old together.

Carla wanted to tear out the grass completely, give up the foolish idea of lawn in this climate, and replace it with hardy plants, paving stones, maybe a firepit. She read a lot of design blogs and had a box of magazines she'd picked up at a garage sale. Dee was going to let her do what she wanted. The outdoor living—as the magazines called it—was Carla's domain, but the garden was Dee's.

It wasn't much of a garden. Along one fence, the previous owners had built a row of raised beds out of landscape timbers. With her back to the morning sun, Dee sat on the timbers and reached into the dirt with her bare hand. She had her gloves and her spade, but she liked the cool, crumbly feel of the soil. She couldn't decide if she needed to add more. She was new to gardening, and she wanted to do it right.

She reached into the dirt once, and twice, thinking about her tomato starts and all the packets of seeds she had waiting inside. On the third reach, her fingers brushed against something small and hard. A stone? She pinched it between her thumb and forefinger. No, it was metal. She brought it to the surface and broke away a clump of fine root hairs and clinging soil. It was a ring.

Dee rubbed her thumb, brushing over the flat surface on one side. She felt a pang in her chest, like a plucked spring, when she saw the Greek letters pressed into the metal: alpha, tau, omega.

"Oh, bother," she muttered.

She did not want to deal with this today. She scowled at the ring, as though that might make it dissolve back into wherever it had come from. She didn't know where they came from, the lost objects that came back for her to find, only to vanish again after they had startled and annoyed her.

That was what she had always called it: *came back*. She had no control over it. It had been happening since she was a child.

This was Richard's fraternity ring. He had given it to her when they were young, during Christmas break of her second year of college, his third. She had been trying to find the courage to break up with him when he rolled up to her parents' house with a bouquet of roses and a smug smile. Dee had not been expecting him, but her parents had; Richard had shaken her father's hand and kissed her mother's cheek. Later, after dinner at an Italian restaurant with candles on the table, Richard had given Dee his fraternity ring and said, with a laugh, "Now all those hippies will know you're mine."

It had not been a proposal, but everybody acted like it was. The waiter congratulated them; the other diners murmured and smiled. Mom was excited, Dad was proud, and Dee's friends squealed and hugged her when she told them. She had tried to imagine it, the church, the white dress, the ribbons on the car as they drove away, and found that it hadn't been so hard. Everybody had treated it as a proposal except Carla, who had come into Dee's room one night and asked to see the ring, rolled her eyes, said it was bulky and ugly. Dee had secretly agreed, but she lied and accused Carla of being jealous that her younger sister was engaged before she could even find a proper boyfriend. Carla had never liked Richard, but she had also never thrown it back in Dee's face when she turned out to be right about him. She had agreed to be Dee's maid of honor anyway.

Dee didn't know why this ring would come back now. She hadn't been thinking of Richard. He lived in South Carolina with his second wife. They rarely spoke; when they did, it was only about Alice and the grandkids. The ring had been lost ever since Dee and Richard had moved from their first apartment near Richard's law school to their first house, before Alice was born. Dee had done all the organizing, the sorting, the packing and unpacking, and the ring had been misplaced in the chaos. That was the first time Richard hit her.

She hadn't told anybody about it, not until last year. A cold January night, sitting in the passenger seat of Carla's Honda, heat blasting to chase away shivers that would not fade. Driving up I-25 so late at night it was early in the morning. Classic rock station low on the radio and both of them talking, telling stories they had never told before, secrets they had never shared, talking until their throats were dry, until the eastern sky pinked. They had fallen silent abruptly when a state patrol car flew past them, lights flashing. Dee had held her breath until she felt dizzy.

Carla's sharp laugh had broken the tension. "Jesus. I thought... Just for a second. You too, right?"

It had been almost a year and a half since that night, those secrets. Dee didn't flinch when she saw police cars anymore. She hadn't noticed when she stopped. If she felt anything at the sound of a siren these days, it was a frisson of nerves, swiftly dismissed. She understood now how people could learn to live with themselves, no matter what they had done.

Dee set the ring on the landscape timber and picked up her trowel. Today was Mother's Day. She did not know if Alice would call. She began to mix the soil, old and new, turning it in determined scoops until her hand stopped trembling. She had a proper shovel in the garage, but this inefficient approach was nice, sitting in the sun with the scent of dirt around her, thinking about how she would lay out her vegetables. Tomatoes and their cages, beans and their stalks. Carrots, even though the neighborhood was replete was wild rabbits. Zucchini, even though everybody warned her she would be overwhelmed. She rather liked the sound of that: a vegetable bounty so great she would have to bake bread and learn new recipes and give it away. She had never been the kind of person who filled the house with warm, sweet smells and put together gifts for acquaintances. She had never been the kind of person who had so much of a good thing it made her generous.

The trowel clanked faintly against something solid in the dirt.

Something like dismay squeezed in her chest. She could hope it was a rock or a piece of wood, but it wouldn't be. It was going to be that kind of day, the kind where she found herself caught in a bothersome maze of memories. She twisted the trowel a bit to pry the object free. What she lifted from the soil was dark and smooth, almost like skin.

Dee startled and withdrew the trowel, her heart thumping.

As she leaned forward for a closer look, she heard the back door open. Carla came outside, a coffee mug in each hand. She left the door open, even though she was the one afraid of bugs and spiders getting inside.

The momentary annoyance was enough to jar Dee out of her shock. She nudged the object with the trowel again and felt like an idiot. It was plastic, not skin. She had given herself a start over nothing.

"Coffee," Carla said, extending one mug to Dee. Her gaze fell on the garden bed. "Oh. Are you finding some of your objects?"

"I guess so," Dee said.

Carla was the only one who knew about Dee's objects. Dee had told her when they were young, the second or third time it had happened, but Carla hadn't believed her for years. She had only begun to understand after Dee had opened a grocery store mailer to find an embarrassing old love note of Carla's, one Carla knew for certain she had burned in a bonfire when she was in high school. They had been in their thirties when the note came back. A few more objects presented as proof and Carla had surrendered her skepticism entirely.

There wasn't always a pattern. Things just came back, and Dee didn't know the reason for it. A pencil case she had lost in third grade appeared in her college dorm room. One of the baby blue pumps she had worn to Carla's wedding, the left one with the heel that had broken when she and Richard had been drunk and laughing on the dance floor at the reception, had shown up in the glove box of her car one day after Dee dropped Alice off at school. The objects never stayed. They would vanish again, days or weeks later, as though they had never returned at all.

Dee nudged the new object out of the soil. It was a plastic horse. She set it on the landscape timber next to the fraternity ring. It stood upright on three legs; its fourth leg was raised but broken off. Dee's heart was beating quickly again.

"Isn't that one of yours?" Carla asked. "It looks like those ones you used to collect. One of those… What are they called? Breyer horses."

Dee nodded. "It's the American quarter horse."

Carla sipped her own coffee, then stifled a yawn. "I tried to get Laney into them when she was a kid, but she only ever wanted the kind where she could brush the hair. I thought you still had them."

"Not this one," Dee said.

"I don't remember that you ever broke it. Was it—" Carla tilted her head at the sound of a phone ringing inside the house. "Yours or mine?"

"Yours," said Dee. In truth, she had no idea. She couldn't hear the ringtone well enough, but she wasn't about to admit that to Carla. They were locked in an endless feud over whose hearing was failing faster. And she didn't know if Alice would call today. Carla's daughter Laney called every weekend, even when it wasn't Mother's Day.

"Probably." Carla sighed and turned to head back into the house. "How did I ever raise such a morning person?"

Carla didn't remember when Dee's quarter horse was broken because it hadn't happened when they were kids. It had been later, after they were both married and in their own homes. There had been a few years when they hadn't spoken much, occupied as they were with their daughters and husbands and separate lives. Alice had been four or five. The age where she got into everything, a whirlwind of unrestrained emotion so inexhaustible Dee had sometimes felt like her little girl was sapping the life right out of her. And as soon as that thought entered her mind, the crushing guilt would follow. Alice was just a kid. She wanted to play with her mother. Dee had to do better.

That night, she and Alice had been prancing the toy horses across the kitchen floor, because Dee hadn't seen the harm in it. Anything to keep Alice happy, to have an hour of laughter rather than a tantrum. The plastic hooves made satisfying taps on the linoleum. Then Richard came home, and he had a headache, and Dee hadn't started dinner. He jerked the quarter horse from Alice's hands and hurled it across the kitchen. Its front leg, the bent leg, snapped off when it struck the edge of the counter.

Later that night, Dee tried to put the leg back on with superglue. It didn't work. She had loved this horse since she was a little girl and Alice loved it too, but she didn't know how to fix it. She carried the horse out to the trash can in the garage and stood there for a long time, sick with indecision. The master bedroom was right above her. Richard would hear if she bundled Alice into the car, opened the garage door, and drove away.

Dee scraped at the broken end of the horse's leg with her thumbnail. There was still a bit of dried glue clinging to the plastic. She lowered the trowel and took a swallow of her coffee. It was lukewarm and too bitter. Carla didn't use sugar and never got the amount right. Dee drank it anyway, half the cup, before jamming the trowel into the soil again.

It clinked on something right away. Dee let out a huff of breath, too feeble to be a protest. Sometimes the objects came back in batches, but three in a matter of minutes was absurd. It was more normal for there to be one or two over a few days, then nothing for months or years.

As resigned as she was curious, she set the trowel down to dig with her hand. Her fingers brushed against something thin and rigid, not a shape she recognized, not until she pinched it and brought it up.

A belt buckle, the big kind that men wore when they wanted to be cowboys. Dee rubbed the dirt away and laughed softly. The image imprinted in the metal showed a bucking horse in front of a dramatic mountain backdrop, with the word FREEDOM written across the sky.

She had remembered FREEDOM, but she had forgotten that it was a horse. She didn't remember the man's name at all. Tim or Tom or Tony, perhaps. Something ordinary. Maybe Todd. It had been a Friday night. Alice, twelve or thirteen years old, had been at a sleepover; Richard had been on a business trip. Dee had gone to a bar in a part of town where she didn't know anybody. She gave a fake name to the men who approached her and noticed the ones who made a move even after they clocked the tan line left by her wedding band. If they didn't care, she didn't care. She had wanted to feel young and daring. She wanted to feel wanted.

Inside the house, a phone rang again. Dee recognized it that time as her phone, but Carla would get it for her. She placed the belt buckle next to the toy horse and the ring. She finished her coffee and put the mug down on the grass, apart from the little trove of objects. Through the open windows she heard Carla talking, but she couldn't make out any words.

Recklessly, almost angrily, Dee plunged her hand into the garden bed again. If that box of dirt had more to vomit up for her, she might as well find it.

Something sharp sliced into her finger. She hissed at the sting, but she didn't withdraw her hand. She felt around cautiously. She found a thin and delicate edge, then a curved and smooth surface. Carefully, wary of another cut, she tugged it out of the soil. It was a broken wine glass.

The back door opened. Carla emerged again, carrying both phones. With one raised to her ear she was saying, "She just called. That's all I know. Just a second." She lowered that phone and raised the other. "I'm bringing you out to your mom now, okay? Here she is."

Dee's left hand was bleeding where the glass had sliced it; she pinched her fingers together to staunch it. She reached out to accept the phone with her right hand.

"It's Alice. It's important." Carla was already turning away and speaking into her own phone again. "Okay, I'm back. What were you saying?"

Dee said, "Alice? What is it?"

"It's Phil," Alice said.

A gentle roar filled Dee's ears. Quiet, like the rumble of tires on asphalt, or wind though the tops of tall pines. She felt it in her chest and in her veins. Her mind supplied the words Alice would say next. *He's back.* Impossible. *He told me what you did.* Impossible.

The cops found him. They know what you did.

Much more likely.

Dee cleared her throat. "Have you heard from him?"

"They found his truck," Alice said. She exhaled shortly. She wasn't crying, but Dee had a hard time discerning how calm she was. "I mean, they found him. His body. In his truck. He's been dead for months."

Sixteen months. Longer than Dee and Carla had expected.

"Oh. Oh, honey." Dee took a breath and let the fear knot in her gut, let the anxiety spark across her skin. "Where was he?"

"He was in the fucking—in the mountains. One of the places he used to go hunting." The words erupted from Alice, jittery and fast. "It's a fire road, I guess? He's been there since last winter. They said he was drinking and he slid off the road and the hill was steep so nobody saw it, the rangers didn't—I guess they didn't notice? Because nobody uses that road and looks down there? He was just there, all this time."

Phil liked to be alone in the mountains with his guns and his camo, a case of beer and a bottle of Jack Daniels on the seat beside him. Afterward, when they had climbed down the steep hill to make sure he died, Carla had said, "He sure made it easy."

Dee prompted, "Since last winter? All that time?"

"Yeah. The sheriff—a county sheriff came by—he thinks... God, I don't know." Alice let out a faint groan. "He asked if Phil liked to do illegal hunting in the off-season. Of course he does. Did. *Did*. He was always doing stupid things like that. I should have thought of that, when he first disappeared. But I thought—I don't know. Maybe I did mention it. I can't remember."

The tiny cut on Dee's finger had stopped bleeding. She used that finger to nudge the broken wine glass she'd pulled from the garden. It was one of a set. A friend of Alice's had hand-painted them as an engagement gift. Flowering cacti, desert mesas, Alice and Phil's names in flowing script. All of that was still visible, even with a chunk missing.

For a few years, the wineglasses had sat on a shelf in Alice and Phil's little stucco house in Santa Fe. But two Christmases ago, when Dee arrived for her visit, one of the pair had been missing, and Phil wasn't home. Alice was wearing more makeup than usual and hissed in pain when she used a bruised wrist. Sierra and Noah were jittery and clingy. And Dee knew. She knew what she had been trying to deny since before Alice's wedding, knew what lay beneath every white lie Alice had told her over the past few years. She looked at her daughter and saw herself. She had failed to guide Alice away from making the same mistakes she had made. She had failed to keep her daughter and grandchildren safe. She felt like all her skin had been scraped raw when she saw how little fight her bright, bold daughter had left.

Dee ran her fingertip over the rim of the wine glass. "That's awful. It must be such a shock."

There was that sharp huff of breath again. "You don't have to pretend to be sad about it, Mom. I know you never liked him."

Dee couldn't deny it. "That doesn't matter now. I'm sorry for you and the babies. Are you okay?"

"I don't know. I just keep thinking, he was drinking, even though he knew better. At least he didn't hit somebody else. The coroner said he hit his head in the accident. He wasn't wearing a seatbelt and that shitty old truck didn't have airbags. So he hit his head and he was unconscious and he just... died. It was the impact and the cold and... That's what they said."

It had been Dee, with the flat side of a shovel, catching him by surprise when he'd laughed at her ultimatum to leave Alice and the kids. Afterward, Carla came up with the idea to stage the car accident, and it turned out to be less messy than their original plan of finding some way to dismember him and disperse the body parts. Dee still woke with a start some nights, hearing the noise the shovel made as it broke his nose. It had been enough to stun him, to wrangle him slurring and confused into the car. It was enough. He had never fully regained consciousness. They had stood in the snow, Dee and Carla, shivering and waiting until his pained wheezing stopped. It had taken a long time.

"It's awful that you had to hear all those details," Dee said. "You shouldn't have had to hear all that."

"I asked. I wanted to know. I just don't know... God, what am I going to tell the kids?" A rustle as Alice moved the phone; and for a moment the faint sound of the television carried over the line. "What am I supposed to say? Sorry, kids, we have to turn off the cartoons for a minute so I can tell you Dad isn't ever coming back, because he got drunk and drove off a road?"

"Oh, honey," Dee began, gently. "Maybe they'll want to know that when they get older, but right now all you have to tell them is that Dad has died in a car accident. They know what that means. You talked to them when Phil's father died."

"I know. It just seems like it should be different." Alice still didn't sound like she was crying. It was more like she was puzzled, trying to work out how she ought to feel. "They've asked where he went, I mean, obviously they did, but not as much as I thought they would. They don't mention him much anymore."

Dee had gone back down to Santa Fe about a month after Phil went missing. One night, after Dee had read three extra picture books before bed, Sierra had asked in her sweet little voice if she and Noah could come live with Grandma when Daddy came home.

"I can come down and help you," Dee said. "For the service, or whatever you decide to do."

"Yeah. I guess I need to do that. I don't even know where to start."

She wouldn't ask for help. She never did. Dee used to be proud of that. She would boast about how strong and independent her daughter was and puff up when people commented that it was hard to imagine anybody pushing Alice around. All because Alice never asked for help.

"I'll come down tomorrow," Dee said, more firmly. "There's no need for you to have to deal with all of this by yourself."

"Yeah," Alice said again. As close as she would get to agreement.

They talked for a couple more minutes before Alice said she had to call Phil's stepmother. Dee told her that she loved her, told her to pass the same along to the kids. She hung up just as Carla was coming back outside. Her call was finished too.

Carla sat beside Dee with a sigh. She looked at Dee, then looked pointedly at the objects gathered on the railroad tie. "Are you going to be able to plant anything at all?" She picked up the toy horse and turned it over thoughtfully. "Or are you going to be digging old shoes out of there too?"

"Which shoes do you want back?" Dee wondered.

Carla had an answer. "Those leather boots you borrowed and ruined in high school."

"I didn't ruin them."

"You wore holes in the soles."

"They already had holes."

"They did not." Carla put the horse down. "The cops aren't going to look into it?"

Something tight in Dee's chest unknotted. It wasn't relief, not really, but it was close. It was the same feeling she had felt on that January night when Phil's breath finally stopped and all they could hear was the sound of icy sleet rattling on the pine trees.

Dee said, "No. It was an accident. He was drunk and the road was icy."

"He shouldn't have been drinking and driving."

"And his old truck didn't have airbags."

Nobody was eavesdropping on them, but this was how they always spoke about it. They weren't pretending. They knew what they had done. They didn't need to say it out loud.

After a minute or two Carla stood. She picked up the belt buckle and smirked a little. "You want me to toss this stuff?"

"Go ahead," Dee said. "Don't cut yourself."

There was no reason to keep the objects. They would disappear soon enough anyway, as quietly and inexplicably as they had appeared. She used to try to keep them safe, to fear the feeling of loss and panic when she realized it was inevitable.

She didn't do that anymore. It was easier to let them go the second time.

So she thought instead about her seeds and starts. About how the middle portion of the long garden bed got more daytime sunlight than the ends. About keeping the rabbits away and watering only after dusk. Tomatoes, cucumbers, beans. She would get them all in the ground and give Carla instructions for watering while she was out of town. She would encourage Alice to bring the kids up later in the summer, maybe for the Fourth of July.

Dee picked up her trowel and started turning the soil again, listening for the sound of the metal hitting something else. But there was only dirt, old and new, and tangles of dried-up roots. She would probably need the extra bags of soil after all.

Ivy Wood

Lili Hayward

The crows tell a story, and while they are generally not to be believed, they insist they had it from the bees, who had it from the flowers, who had it from the web-veins in the soil. And so, I am inclined to think it's true.

They tell a story of a hidden place on the banks of a slow green river, deep and full as the heart of a woman who has seen thirty summers. A wood, and within that wood a thicket, and within that thicket a ruin where the stones wear thick hides of moss and lichen spells its secrets upon fallen walls. Where beams surrender their strength of centuries, becoming one with furtive moulds and fungi that have never been named by a human tongue.

You won't find this place on any map. Open your trusty paper guide, creased and rain-spotted, trace a dirty fingernail down the sinews of the river and the most you will find is a tiny square, the code for *ruins*. Go back, to before a time of theodolites and metres and you might have better luck. When maps were made by memory and paces, string and sun. Unroll a map drawn on crumbling parchment and you might see— scrawled in a script so faint you can barely read it—a single word. *Ivywood*.

Not that it will help you much. Even in language, the place is hiding, using two English words to mask its face. Ivy. Wood. You might make the mistake of thinking you understand it. Trees thick with ivy. Timber from an unusual source. All true, without being truth. Like calling the moon a circle and thinking that explains it.

Go back even further. To maps that are lost to fire and time. To maps made from breath and memory and knowing, and there you might find its old name. Treidhyowen. And even if you know the midjans and jouds of the language you'll struggle. Because "tre" is *home* and *hearth* and *village* and *return*, and "idhyowen" is *bind* and *tie* and *walk* and *fall*, all at once.

Now do you understand?

No, I can see you don't. To understand you have to be there in the leaf-blotted half-light and let it creep around you, a tendril at a time. You must wade ankle-deep in green and let grit and sap smear your skin, work its way into your system. It will not be easy. She does not like to give up her secrets. She will trip you and pluck the hairs from your head, scratch you, punish you with welts and hives. She will set small lives upon you, woodlice and mites to lay siege to your skin. If you want her story, you must let them. You must give up your sad habit of thinking of yourself as separate, as if you were a knife to cut the meat of the world, or a spoon to stir the pot. You are the meat. You are in the pot. Lie down in the leaves. You're made of the same stuff as everything around you, after all. Ash and dirt. Juice and germs. Water and stardust.

Only then, when green fills your vision and you let your edges dissolve, blurring into matter and time, might she speak to you.

She sings in the old words. She speaks in leaves and shoots, in the murmur of late autumn bees and the groan of branches locked with cold. Where she walks, vines grow, tendrils unfurling from her fingertips.

She guards these woods, so the stories say. She *is* them. And some say that her skin is pale brown as bark and that her hair is thick as shadows, so twined with ivy it could never be untangled. That her eyes are gold as sunlight on stone, yellow as dying leaves, ochre as lichen.

Sometimes, she will guide a traveller. Old tales tell of children who strayed from the river path and found themselves lost in the wood in the dead of winter, when not a soul is to be seen and even the birds are mute with cold. One child spoke of an owl that ghosted through the trees with a freshly killed rabbit in its talons, the spots of falling blood marking the way out of the wood. Others whispered of snakes that moved like vines, roots wriggling from their skins, swarming into the figure of a woman who raised a seething arm to point the way. Others remembered nothing, only woke at the edge of the trees with nectar dripping from their lips and their lungs full of sweet, stinging pollen.

Some, she leads back to the path, out of her world. Fewer still she takes to the heart of her, to the place of *home* and *falling*, beginnings and endings…

Some say she was once an ivy tree, as old as the first thing to grow, who felt the tread of humans on the soil and heard the cut of iron in the earth and wanted to know the new creatures that walked her land. And so she built herself a carcass using climbing vines. She clothed that frame in a skin of waxy new leaves, and let sap fill her woody veins and swell the blue-dark berries of her eyes. She called the ladybirds to her and bid them huddle into hard, shining lips. She opened those new lips and asked the wasps nestle inside her throat to be her voice. She gave herself teeth from the bones of the beasts that had died inside her. She grew sharp nails out of flint. And then, when she was ready, she crowned herself in sunbursts of ivy blossom and walked out of the wood.

And where she appeared, people fled in fright or fell in worship before her.

Duwes gwedhek, they called her. *Bocka glas. Idhyowen-el.*

All save one woman, who was too weak to run, dying from a sickness that stole the strength from her body. Where others fled, she stood and looked into the midnight eyes of the woman made of ivy, and in them, she saw life.

And when the woman of the wood extended a hand, her fingers long and tough as twining branches, the woman of the village took it. They walked together, back into the darkness of the trees.

It was many a summer and many a winter more before anyone was brave enough to go to look for her. When they did, one Midsummer's Eve, they found a small cott, made from a pile of stones held together with ivy. And inside the cott, they found what remained of the woman: her bones so intertwined with creepers that it was impossible to move them. And nestled among the bones they found a baby girl, with eyes as blue as berries and skin as waxy as new leaves and a laugh that sounded like bees in blossom, her lips sticky with the nectar that had sustained her.

And though some whispered that they should leave her to the teeth of foxes, one man gathered her up, snapped away the tendrils that swaddled her, and took her home.

Gwenenen, he called her, for the swarm of bees that followed them out of the wood. Gwen, she became as she grew.

And though she loved her father, she missed her mothers, who she insisted still lived in the thicket. She became known as a cunning woman:

a pellar, a white witch who saw things others couldn't, who knew how to heal and hurt with what grew from the land.

In summer, adders would creep to her as she lay dozing in the grass and twine their dark, supple bodies around her neck and kiss her ears with their tongues. Hares would rest their soft heads beneath her palm. Beetles lived always in the hems of her skirts, woodlice in the seams of her sleeves. And in winter, when the village coughed and shivered, she alone brimmed with life, walking from house to house with bare brown feet that never seemed to feel the cold, bidding people drink bitter wine boiled with ivy leaves, from a cup carved from ivy wood: her own mothers' bones.

Then men arrived from across the narrow sea, bringing with them beautiful books of sparkling gold and mottled inks that gave new names to the gods and spirits the people had always known, and made them fear an old man who saw into the dark places of their hearts. And Gwen, they say she began to fade, little by little. People did not want her cup and her cure, trusting in words and breath and shame to save them instead.

So Gwen left them and retreated to the place of her birth, the cottage in the wood, where—it is said—she would greet those who came seeking help with love and honey, and those who came seeking harm with poison and death.

No one knows when she died, or at least, when she stopped being flesh and went back to being bark and root. Sometimes—driven by pain—people still made their way through the overgrown paths to the cottage. Some said they found hives of wild honey that cured their ailments or soothed their souls. Some would not say what they found, only that *she* had aided them. Over the years, ivy swallowed the stones. Its vines grew thicker than a ploughman's arm, hard wood twined into fantastical shapes, like smoke frozen solid.

That was when the bards came, from the north, from the south, seeking wood to make pipes. The stories say the songs they played on such instruments were strange and haunting. That so long as they played, the breath never ran short in their lungs, and when they finally lowered the pipe from their lips, all they could taste was blood and sweetness. Those who played on pipes made from the wood of Treidhyowen said they dreamt of a woman with golden hair who gathered them up in her arms and prized apart their bones with a love as tender as spring's first bud. And when they woke, they would attempt to play the songs she had hummed to them in her wasp's voice. Songs of branch-snap and sapseep, wingbeat and slow roots: they would try until their lips cracked and bled and they fell to weeping, because the songs were not of human making and could not be summoned in this world.

But after a time, they too stopped coming. No matter. The land is ever changing, ever becoming. A seed becomes a shoot, becomes a sapling, becomes a tree, becomes a lightning-stricken trunk, dead, but not gone. Ivy climbs. Beetles burrow. Butterflies feast on nectar. Life becomes death, becomes life.

And there were those who did not forget. Who still fought their way through the undergrowth to Treidhyowen, to place their offerings there. Centuries on, they would come walking on Midsummer's Eve, led by the best singer in the village, the one with a voice as clear as a bird's, echoing in the heavy summer branches:

'Ivy, chief of trees it is. *Veni coronaberis...*'

'The most worthy she is.' Other voices, deep and hushed, joining in song.

By candlelight, by lantern-light, they would come, flames dancing through the woodland darkness.

'Ivy soft and meek of speech, against all woe she bringeth bliss. Well is he that may her reach...'

A shape watches them, always; a shadow on the leaves, a smirr of pale dust, a hand like peeled twigs. They know better than to look at her directly. Instead, they reach the ruined cottage with its green tresses of ivy, and leave their gifts: blood and milk, locks of hair, pelts and shells, rings and beads and spilled wine. And in return, when the wind stirs the leaves and brings a scent of bittergreen and pollen, they take what they came for: ivy sprigs for buttonholes, boughs for the cattle stalls and fishing boats and milking pens, for the mantel and the doorway, for the inn and the stable, to bring her blessing on the night of the year when the door stands open to the other world...

But as candles flickered out and gas banished the darkness and oil and electric lit the world, so eventually even they forgot how to fear and respect what waited beyond the edges of their vision. They forgot that their bodies, filling new squeaking shoes, were made of the same stuff as the wood. They forgot the way to the thicket, forgot she was ever there and on the maps *Treidhyowen* became *Ivywood*, became *Ivywood (ruins)*, became □, became nothing at all.

Until you came, following the broken treads of the old tales and their half-forgotten meanings. You followed the path, you obeyed her laws, and now, you are rewarded.

Darkness has fallen while you've lain there in the leaves, listening. Did you sleep? A snail moves slow across your cold hand, tracing secret silver on your skin. A beetle nestles beneath your earlobe. A ladybird creeps across your upper lip. Move them gently. Stir yourself. The night is thickening, deep enough to fall into and keep falling. Above, the trees are beginning to roar in the wind, like men in battle. It is time you were going.

You will walk out of the wood changed, with a fierce, living sweetness on your lips, and a tingling across your scalp, like the seep of sun on the crown of your head. A green bitterness of boiled wine on your tongue. Ivy dust and pollen in your lungs.

Only later will you find the sprig of ivy caught in your collar. Only later still will you realise you lost something of yourself, there in the wood, and gained something in return. You will press the sprig between the pages of a book of stories and feel a thrum under your palm: the knowledge that you, the cover, the pages, the table it sits upon are all one and the same. And on midsummer nights—miles away from Treidhyowen—when hearts and eyes are open and the busy currents of the world still, you might hear the hum of a wasp, or the stir of leaves or a note of pipe music and feel as if you are being watched.

You are. You carry her with you, now, in your skin, in the fibres of your being.

Just as she carries you.

A Mortal, an Archer, a Hare, a Bridge

Ai Jiang

Rather than love, adrenaline and fear drove me to tear into the bedroom shared between my husband and me in our small hay hut while he was out on a hunt and pry open the small wooden case within which we had hidden the thin vial.

In between delicate, porcelain fingertips, I held the precious liquid that would extend life forever, suspend the age of the body, of the mind, of the soul—a simple sip would allow me to attain immorality, strip away wretched mortality, perhaps even humanity. But staring at the vial and its content that seemed like it would evaporate if left too long, I took not a simple sip, but rather a generous gulp screamed my betrayal down my throat. The translucent liquid ran years through my veins, lifted my hair in the air. I felt weightless, as though the age that death had added to my body since the day I was born no longer existed.

But it wasn't enough.

I drained every last drop, tapped the bottom of the vial for good measure as to not miss any of the liquid, and ran my tongue around the thin glass opening. But the vial fell from my hand, shattering into a thousand shards on the wooden planks beneath me when the sprinting footsteps approached the hut. My love.

My husband, the glorious archer returned home, standing by the entrance with the corpse of a doe, my favourite meat, on his shoulders and a wolfish smile—one that shattered my heart with guilt and left it among the broken glass by my foot. In his free hand, he clutched his famous bow and arrow. The playful grin upon his lips dropped as soon as he noticed the residue of immorality dripping from my lips. His eyes roamed my face and I knew it looked ageless, devoid of the crevices that dug deeper his own weathered skin from sunbaked days and sleepless nights.

We both knew it was only enough liquid for one, and we both promised that because there was only enough for one, neither of us would drink it and kept it as a symbol of our loyalty to each other.

And though my love held himself back, his fearlessness far greater than my cowardice, I could not do the same.

With a thump, the doe met the wooden flooring of our shared mortal cabin. The one we built together, saying that we fell in love as mortals so we would also die, perish, as mortals.

A rumble worked through my body and lifted me from the floor. The nicks made by the broken glass on my feet disappeared, healing in mere seconds. In horror, I watched as my love dropped the doe, lifted his bow, nocked his arrow, and aimed at me—out of impulsive anger, out of tainted passion—as though I were prey. So I fled, floating towards the opened window, but turned my head to look at my beloved.

Veins bulged in his arms as he drew back, quiver held against the cheek, one eye shut. Heavy panting shook his entire frame. He could have shot. We both knew his arrow would be faster than light. But he didn't. The arrow clattered onto the ground, bouncing off the doe's hide, allowing for my escape.

Not a moment later, from below, my husband rushed from our hut, light as air itself. I almost thought he might fly after me. Bare feet pounded against the grass. Eyes never strayed from me now floating backwards toward the moon. I shifted my gaze from my racing love towards the large glowing entity looming ever nearer.

Tears fell and rolled down my cheeks and cut through the air, dropping down towards my love like rain. And as I entered the moon's welcoming embrace, I nestled at the bottom curve of the moon's connected, mirroring, wicked grins, and the thoughts of my foolishness cruelly attacked my mind. Even immortals, it seemed, could not escape pain, nor love. I rested my head against the single swaying tree within the celestial body, as though it had grown itself just to comfort my sorrows.

My love watched from below, with anger, with longing. And I wondered what my expression held—regret? A hand extended upwards as though carried by the wind, muscled and sun-kissed. I felt his caress from afar, shuddered, then withdrew from the faraway touch as though seared by my own betrayal and his adoration—it was a love that I did not deserve, or at least did no longer.

A guardian, a white hare, stood guard at the bottom of the full moon. It told me that I was now an immortal goddess, and that the moon was my new moon. With a cautioning gaze, the hare challenged my husband to enter. It denied his anger. But in turn, also denied his love. I wept for the loss of my love, and I wept even for the loss of my mortality, as my home, earth, looked so much more beautiful, so much more colourful, from up here. Surrounded by pale moonlight, I had never felt so alone.

With a gentle hand, I pushed away the hare, pressed my quivering lips against the smile of the moon, and whispered, "I'm sorry."

As though drenched by cold rain, the remnants of my tears, betrayal washed from my love's body almost as quickly as it had entered, seeping into the dry soil beneath his feet—a feeling long lost.

"A mortal life was too short to hold grudges, after all," my love cried.

And in silence, I asked myself: What would I do after my love's mortal body and mind perished?

The hare stretched its body, while I immersed in the thoughts of my action's consequences and created a bridge between mortal and immortal—a meeting between the dying and the forever alive. A second chance to reunite, once a year. Time I would never again take for granted—time I did not realize would wane within a single breath's notice.

Blaze Of Glory

Sarah L. Miles

It started, as so many unusual things do, with a healthy dose of the mundane. An average Thursday night in a lowkey bar. Too far out of town for the tourist crowd, too expensive for the students, and with a weird enough clientele to remove the last of any appeal for the alcoholics and locals. We had spent years working on that, developing just the right kind of bad staff attitude to put off the people that we wanted to put off. Even the name was a bad joke, designed to misdirect the better class of clientele while admitting we were exactly the dingy little underground bar that we appeared from the outside: Glory Hole.

Benny was in his usual position, leaning against the doorway. Or rather, in the doorway. He's big enough to fill the space when he needs to, and the combination of his heavy tattoos and oversized muscles is only appealing to two very specific crowds; the female students quickly learnt that a short skirt or flash of cleavage wasn't going to improve his mood, and the twinks gave up batting their eyes at him after they realised that his whole 'strong and silent' thing wasn't flirting. It works, though, the regulars know him and he knows the regulars. The local police don't mess with him because they know he can stop any trouble before it starts, and the rest of us know that he's a big squishy teddy bear under the rock-solid exterior, and that he'd rip our limbs off if we told anyone that. From his viewpoint he can see up the short flight of steps to the pavement above, keeping an eye on the passing footfall as usual, and giving him the chance to size up customers before they even make it to eye level. Or rather, eye-to-chest level for most.

Being a Thursday night, Cassandra was up on stage. She had her backing track—dodgy karaoke music illegally downloaded from a pirate site—and was working her way from the upbeat jams that work well early evening through to the 80s power ballads that she'll use to close us out once I've called time. Until you've seen Cassie reduce grown men to jelly with her rendition of "All I Want To Do Is Make Love To You," have you really lived? This particular evening she was going a little more upbeat, some GNR, a bit of Alice Cooper, enjoying herself more than anything. Some of our specific type of regulars liked to have a bit of a singalong, but nothing overly raucous—we're not that kind of place.

I was behind the bar as always, trying to keep myself busy and out of the way, whilst also making sure no one had to wait on a drink. I was pouring a pint out for Jean-Claude, a Canadian import to our fair city with a talent for thievery and a habit of spending his ill-gotten gains in our fine establishment, and making some sort of generic small talk, when there was a minor ruckus near the door. Assuming Benny would deal with it, I didn't pay much mind to the slightly raised voices, or the distinct sound of a bladed weapon being shifted in a scabbard. The thud of a body hitting the floor is what caught my attention. Benny was usually more subtle than to knock anyone out for their first offence.

Cassie was still belting out a tune—"Let's Get Rocked"—when I looked up and swore loudly. Which wasn't unusual for me, in general, but the speed with which I followed up the cussing to get my staff out was. I generally keep it tucked under the bar for "emergencies," which in the years we've been here have almost all been related to someone needing an impromptu crutch or walking stick. Not this time, though. This time I had looked up to see that the body slumped in the open doorway was Benny. Standing slightly to one side was a smug-looking woman dressed head to toe in black, with silver jewelry dripping from every piece of visible skin. She looked like a horny teenage boy's vision of an 80s pirate warrior queen, all corsetry and lace. Except that she has somehow bested Benny, and that was extremely bad news for everyone else in the bar right now. Cassie immediately switched up her singing, adding an inflection to the vocals that hadn't been there previously.

The woman in black flicked her wrist almost imperceptibly, and was joined in the doorway by a pair of near identical youths, each the negative of the other: one dressed in white, with black hair and dark skin; the other pale as a ghost, hair as white as a winter blowout, wearing identically styled clothing but in black. Just as Cassie got to the chorus of her song one of the youths ghost-stepped to her stage and wrapped a black gloved hand around her neck, strangling the charmed notes out of her. She gasped as the youth effortlessly lifted her off the stained wooden floor, and dropped her microphone with a small squeal of feedback.

I held my hand up, having thankfully remembered to put the full glass down first, and started to open my mouth to ask for calm, but in the blink of an eye the other youth was by my side, something sharp and pointed sticking in the gap between my bottommost ribs in a decidedly unfriendly way. I closed my mouth as fast as I could and simply raised my eyebrows instead.

The woman in black casually dragged Benny out of the way of the door—not an easy feat given his size and muscle mass—and smiled smugly before sauntering over to lean on the bar next to Jean-Claude, who had the forethought to keep his eyes down and his hands on the bar. She licked her lips as she eyed him, which was a reasonable response; his being easy on the eye was just one reason I enjoyed having him as a regular and let him nurse his drinks at the bar. Everyone else cleared out of the bar at a flick of her chin, deserting drinks and carefully avoiding looking at the rest of us. They knew the rule of old—don't ask, don't tell—and it was easier to walk away from a drink and danger with your regular number of limbs attached.

My new companion eased off with the poking slightly, and I allowed myself to draw a breath. Before I could speak, though, they placed one finger gently on my lips, a weirdly intimate move as they stood close to me, almost a caress. I waited to hear the woman in black speak:

"Well, well, well. You're not an easy person to find. We must have visited every town on the south coast before we finally got a lead on you. Not many places that can keep someone Ebenezer's size hidden, but plain sight clearly did the trick here."

She smiled as I blanched at her use of Benny's name, pausing to let it sink in.

"Cassandra too, such a sweet songbird."

My eyes flicked to her on the stage. Thankfully Cassie's feet were back on the ground, but the albino youth still had hold of her, and I felt a flash of guilt that I hadn't checked on her sooner. My friends here were the closest thing I had to family now, and I should take better care of them, we both knew that. She glared at me in a way that told me I would pay for that oversight later, but I had bigger—or at least sharper—things to worry about.

"Did you think that it would be so easy to simply vanish, after stealing what was so rightfully ours?"

Even JC flinched at that one, a barely perceptible twitch of one eye, but we'd known each other long enough for me to see his tells. Hard to stay in our line of work without knowing each other inside and out. Sometimes literally…

"So, sweetie, where is it? You couldn't possibly expect this silly retirement idea would last as long as it has, so now is the time to cough up. Maybe we'll even let you live afterwards. Although your brute was rude to me on the way in, so maybe not."

I racked my brains for what the hell she was talking about, trying to remember what we might have stolen, or where we had encountered her before. Annoyingly, I drew a total blank and, given that I was supposedly the brains of the operation, I wasn't even going to bother checking in with the others at this point, even if they could have helped. For some reason the youth hadn't taken my staff away, so I grounded it as best I could whilst standing on the rubber matting behind the bar and attempted to channel something out of them, the fact that they still had a finger lightly on my lips being my best hope of information. Big mistake. My brain flooded with images, the vast majority of them utterly unpleasant, the stuff of horror movies or nightmares. I had a fleeting thought of how a person could have contained so much intestine before the youth broke contact with me and lazily punched me in the kidney. The woman laughed at me, bent over double and gasping behind my own bar, as she continued to casually lean on the other side.

"The greatest team in the country! The scourge of the continent! Undefeated and uncaught! Yet here we are, your fighter knocked out, your bard bound and gagged, and your thief trying desperately to pretend he is anywhere but here, and hoping I haven't recognised him. But you keep trying, don't you, poppet? You really think that your little parlour tricks are going to save you here?"

It was the 'poppet' that did it. No one spoke like that in real life. No one except for the bane of my youthful existence. My tormentor. My bully. The only person I had ever truly hated, and the reason I fled my childhood home and biological family to travel with this band of reprobates. She'd really grown up since then, was barely recognisable with the new hairstyle and piratical garb. But I knew. Only one person had ever called me poppet, and I had stolen the thing most precious to her in the world—her power.

I might use a staff to help me channel, but the woman in black used a demonic grimoire. Classic, she called it—I said basic. No one needed to chant ancient languages or turn pages in time to their made-up words. She loved it, though, she was all about style over substance, which is just one of the reasons we hated each other. I had worked damn hard to get where I was, with the people I was with, and she just wanted to look good and have the world handed to her on a plate. Probably a black one with some stupid twirly silver details. At least it explained the pair of youths she was sporting about with: they were painfully fashionable, from their pseudo-punk hairstyles to pointy-toed boots. Gods only knew where she had found them, but they were effective. Cassandra was struggling against what appeared to be well tied knots, Benny was still unconscious, and Jean-Claude was desperately trying to make himself inconspicuous.

Sighing in defeat, I licked my lips and went to speak, parting my lips before thinking better of it and raising my hand to speak, like a child at school. She smiled a Cheshire Cat grin and simply nodded at me slowly, reveling in the defeat she could read in my face.

"There's a chest. We kept all of our spoils in it. No, not spoils. Memories. All the things that we couldn't fence, or barter, or work out what the hell to do with. It's hidden here in the bar. Just let the others go and…"

She cut me off with a swiftly drawn rapier that was under my chin before I saw it move. Style, always.

"No, I don't think so. I think that you are going to tell us exactly where the chest is, and you are going to open it for me, and all your little friends are going to watch while you realise that I've won and you've lost, because I am simply better than you are."

Her smug grin hadn't changed over the years, and I wondered how it had taken me so long to recognise her. I kept my eyes on her while my hands moved through a series of complicated movements, trying my best not to notice Cassie desperately trying to get my attention in the corner of my eye. We had poured almost everything we had into the bar, and the contents of the chest were our backstop, the tiny remainder that we'd need if this first attempt at retirement fell through. That's why we kept the chest so close, the large table in the middle of the room slowly losing its glamoured appearance as the magic fell away.

The woman in the black was by the chest and opening it even before I had finished moving my hands, deftly working the mechanism to reveal the contents. No magical inner light blazing out of it, though—probably to her dismay—just a wooden box half-filled with the remnants of a life lived… if not well, at least *lived*. We'd been through scrapes worse than this, faced off with brigands and pirates and evil sorcerers, and somehow always come out of it on top, thanks to the way we worked so well as a team. We kept each other in check, buoyed each other up, brought in new recruits when we needed them. Looked after each other.

Finally, the realisation dawned. No one is coming to help us. To help them. The entire crew was relying on me, and I have always been the weakest link in our chain. Physically I'm one step above useless, but barely. No matter how many times Benny or JC tried to teach me how to throw a punch or grapple someone to the ground, it just never took. So I only really had one option left. The one thing that I promised I wouldn't do here. But I caved, whether out of desperation or something else, something baser…

The scent is intoxicating. No matter how long I've been away from it, it always brings the memories flooding back. It's almost visible, dancing up into the air in front of my face, soft red tendrils insinuating their way into my imagination. The woman and her companions were too distracted to notice me now anyway. I breathed in deeply, allowing the smell to fill my nostrils, closing my eyes briefly as the pleasure of it filled my head, the bubbles of memory popping against my tongue. Only the good ones, though, the victories, the praise. That's how it gets you. Reminding you of the good times alone, ignoring the lonely mornings, the defeat, the embarrassment.

Maybe this time, I thought. Just once more won't hurt, and maybe this time it'll be the final time I need to lean in, to allow the power to fill my body and burst out of my chest.

The air began to warm around me, the scent thickening as I pulled on the threads of magic in the air, time slowing as I focused on the urge I've kept buried deep for so long. I could see Jean-Claude start to turn his head towards me, realisation slowly dawning on his face as he pushed himself off the stool and away from the bar. Away from me. It feels so good to let it out, to uncage the beast. I caught myself just before I started laughing, one step ahead of what feels a little too much like madness. I couldn't stop it, though; you can always bolt a door after the horse has started running, but it won't help you. It won't help anyone.

I realised too late that this time isn't different. I'm not better than I was before. I haven't learnt any lessons from the past, no matter what I've told myself or my friends. They're the ones who are going to pay the price. Again.

The power swelled within me as my staff dropped from my hand, overwhelming all my senses, building to an unstoppable crescendo. I succumbed to it, feeling the heat flow into my body from the ground, the air, the bar itself: directing it, manipulating it, channelling it into my palms and finally, finally the sweet release. I moved my hands into position and thrust them forward, towards the knot of thieves who chose the wrong night to steal back what we stole, the glow of the fireball forming between my palms before I could think better of it, reflecting in Cassie's panicked eyes, casting a soft glow over the bar that belied the chaos I was about to cause.

Their backs to me as they gazed into the chest, the pair of youths didn't realise what was about to hit them, but the woman in black was facing my way, looking up at the sound of my staff falling. Her one mistake was assuming that I was as weak as I looked, thinking that retirement meant I'd given up my skills. She was about to rapidly learn from her mistake, though. Cassie and JC both ducked away from the bar, Benny was still prone on the floor, and I gave in to my basest of desires and blasted the fireball into the trio ahead of me, not even noticing when the scent of magic was covered up by the smell of burning flesh, or the way that the flames didn't stay where I sent them but gleefully flickered over the tables, dancing towards Cassie's beloved wooden stage as she fumbled her way off it. I calmly watched as my sister, black-clad and hated, was consumed in the flames I had thrown at her. I was too intoxicated with the power I had released to even pay attention to the others pushing me towards the door, rolling Benny ahead of them as the flames starting to lick up the wood panelling that we'd installed in the first week, and the smoke started to fill the room, covering the photos of us on the walls, showing all the years we'd spent here together.

Spells for the Afterlife

P.A. Cornell

Before an embalming can begin, we verify that we have the correct person lying on the table, and that they are in fact deceased. My colleague, Andrei, has already completed this step. In spite of this, and even as I look down on my twin sister's face and know it's her, I can't help glancing toward the toe tag to read her name: Frances Young.

"You don't have to do this, Elyse," Andrei says. "The fact that she's your sister's bad enough. I can't even imagine what it must be like..."

He leaves the rest unsaid, but I know he's imagining the horror of standing next to a corpse that looks exactly like you. I suspect it's worse for him than it is for me. Frances and I may be identical twins, but we could always spot the subtle differences, even when others couldn't. Our uncanny resemblance has meant that all our lives we've been able to pass for each other when we wanted to.

A fact that ultimately cost Frances her life.

"Let me do the embalming," Andrei says.

"That's not necessary," I tell him. "I can do this."

I must do this. I owe it to Fran.

"Fine," he says. "But if you change your mind and need me to take over or assist, you know where to find me."

I watch him leave and wait for the sound of his footsteps to fade down the hall before locking the embalming room door. Then I head back to where my sister lies supine, naked, head slightly elevated. She looks so vulnerable.

"I'm sorry, Fran," I say. "It's my fault you're here, but I promise, I'll make it up to you."

There are many reasons why we do what we do to prepare a body for burial. Some are for the safety of the living. Some for the preservation of the body. And there are of course the rituals surrounding death, which vary by location, faith, and culture. The way we treat our dead and manage their passing has fascinated me my whole life. People think it's morbid when I tell them what I do for a living, but it's not. It's an expression of love and respect for life, and the way we mark its end, that says something profound about who we are. But it can be more than that too.

The first time I heard about the embalming process, I was just a kid, flipping through an old copy of *National Geographic* magazine I'd found while exploring my grandparents' attic. Of course, this referred to the embalming practices of ancient Egypt, which involved far more than the simple preservation of the body. For the ancient Egyptians embalming was a ritual imbued with magic that would serve them in the afterlife. It was that magic that first caught my attention, sparking a life-long interest in the burial practices of ancient Egypt and calling me to this vocation, even if I ultimately learned that the way we preserve our dead is far more mundane.

It's that same magic I'm counting on now as I retrieve the bag I brought from where I'd hung it earlier, reaching in to remove the two statuettes I purchased yesterday at the museum gift shop. The first, a jackal-headed deity. Anubis, Egyptian god of embalming. The other resembles a pharaoh holding a crook and flail. Osiris, god of the underworld. Both often referred to simply as gods of death—far too broad of a description for their actual roles. I'll need them both for this to work.

I only hope they find the offering I've brought acceptable.

Setting the statuettes on the table just above Fran's head, I then take out a pair of incense sticks, placing them on stands next to each god. I light the one for Anubis, leaving the other unlit for now. Next to this, I place the envelope with my sister's name on it that contains the letter I wrote, setting the bag aside until I need the other things it contains.

Aside from these out-of-the-ordinary elements, I begin the embalming in the usual way by washing my sister's skin, taking care to clean her as best I can. I then massage her, attempting to relieve the stiffness of her muscles, checking for damage caused by the accident or the subsequent handling of her body as I go. Next, I wipe down her mouth, nose, and finally her eyes. I prepare the eye caps, lubricating them with petroleum jelly to facilitate their insertion beneath the eyelids in order to maintain the natural shape of the eye and create the illusion of peaceful sleep for the sake of the living. At this point I'd normally suture the mouth closed, but this time I don't. For the ancient Egyptians it was important to leave the mouth open to allow the deceased to speak and breathe in the afterlife. Reaching once more into my bag, I take the copper ceremonial blade, or adze, also obtained from the museum, and touch it to my sister's mouth, as per the ancient ritual. The blade is only a replica, but a good one. I hope it will suffice.

Laying the adze down, I next take a scalpel—the blade I usually work with—and make an incision at Fran's neck to expose her carotid artery and jugular vein. I've done this countless times, on countless bodies, but as I insert the needle for the centrifugal pump into the carotid and make a small incision in the jugular, it feels wrong, somehow. Still, though my hands shake and my heart quickens, I manage. Then I start the pump to introduce the embalming fluid, displacing the blood in the process and allowing it to drain through the jugular. I help it along by massaging Fran's body for even distribution.

I think about how squeamish Fran always was around needles and blood. She would've hated this.

"It'll be okay," I soothe, as though she can hear me. "I'll take good care of you."

It's not the first time I've spoken to a corpse. I started doing it in college, mostly for my own sake, I guess. It just felt like less of a violation to treat them as though they were still among the living. My colleagues find it amusing, mostly, but I've caught one or two of them doing it now and then.

"Remember when we were kids, Fran, and I'd make you play Mummy with me? I know you hated it—having to lie still while I wrapped you in toilet paper. You were always so patient with me, though. You never complained. You'd just lie there while I read my made-up spells for the afterlife. I never said it enough, but you were the best sister I could've ever asked for. My best friend, too."

I proceed to the cavity embalming, taking my time, treating her body as though she can feel it. All the while I continue to speak to her, explaining what I'm doing and why it's important. As I work, I can't avoid thinking of that night, though. The night that brought us both to this moment. How many times have I thought about all the things I could've done differently? I should've gone to bed earlier the previous night so I wouldn't have been so tired. I should've just picked the damn parcel up the next day rather than let Fran go. I should've remembered that she wasn't as good a driver as me in the rain. That as much as we might look the same, there were differences that put her at risk.

"Tea," I say aloud. "You died over a stupid tin of assorted teabags. Because the damn courier insisted a tea sampler required a signature and I.D. Because I lied and said I was starting to get a migraine so I wouldn't have to go out again. Because you offered to pick it up for me and I let you." Just like all the times I'd let her make my life easier. All those tests she'd taken for me in school when we were kids. All the boys she'd dumped on my behalf so I wouldn't have to see their sadness or face their anger. All the times she'd taken calls for me, or dropped off forms, or stood in line. Fran had always been there for me, and my repayment was long overdue.

As I continue to work the embalming fluid through my sister's body, the skin discoloration is beginning to lessen, but there's still much left to do. When that's finally complete, I close the incisions and begin the process of moisturizing her skin. Again, I vary from the norm, and rather than use the regular moisturizer, I reach into my bag for a jar that contains a blend of wine and oils once used in the ancient burial rites. I work this into Fran's skin with my hands, gently coating the surface of her skin until her entire body is covered.

Now begins the cosmetic step, starting with the face, matching the color of her skin to my own, then adding more makeup to give her a healthy glow. I've always excelled at this step. Families routinely thank me after the services for making their loved ones look as they were in life. My sister is no exception. She really does look as though she is merely asleep. But I know Osiris and Anubis require more.

I take a small container from my bag and open it to reveal a loose powder that shines golden in the light. I brush this on over the cosmetics I've already applied to her face, then continue down her body to give it a golden sheen. Gold was an important element in ancient Egyptian practices. Often, bodies were coated in a gold resin, in part for protection and preservation, but also because it was believed that divine beings had golden flesh in the afterlife. My hope is this will appeal to the gods and make them take notice.

I then brush out Fran's hair, and part it in the center like she used to. Like I do my own hair. After this, I comb through oils and extract from aromatic plants like juniper and cypress. The scent is not unpleasant. I hope it will please the gods.

Now I take the remaining items from my bag. First, a picture of Fran and me together on our last birthday. The most recent photograph I could find of the two of us. I place it between the statuettes of the gods and take a moment to light the incense next to Osiris. Next comes a stone scarab. This I place over Fran's heart. It's meant to protect the organ until the moment it is weighed against the feather of Ma'at. A crucial step during which the heart is judged, and the gods will either accept or reject my sacrifice. The last item is a scroll I've personally prepared. I set this aside for the time being.

I now take a white linen sheet and cover my sister's body with it, leaving only her head exposed. She looks even more like she could wake at any moment, which seems fitting. Taking the scroll, I begin to read the words I've written. A made-up prayer that speaks from my heart—just like the ones I'd write as a kid. This one talks about what we've always meant to each other. It tells my truth. How I failed her. How my own shortcomings and selfishness cost Fran her life. How I can't live with the guilt. And, most importantly, what I want to do to atone for what I did to her. I beg that the gods will accept my terms. I offer them all I have to give that could possibly come close to being worth my sister's life.

Contrary to popular belief, the Egyptian Book of the Dead was not a single canonical text. It was often personalized to the deceased and imbued with prayers and magic to suit their specific needs. I stayed up all night creating spells to achieve my goal today, researching the sorts of things I might say to appeal to the gods, and which gods to address in particular.

"Just like when we were kids," I tell my sister. "Only this time, the gods will answer…I hope."

It's now that I call to Osiris and Anubis. Osiris was not just the god of the underworld, but also one of resurrection. According to the mythology, Osiris died, but had his life restored by Anubis. I ask them to work together to return my sister to the realm of the living.

For their trouble, I offer them a trade.

As a child, I believed there was magic in who my sister and I were, due to the circumstances of our birth, having come into this life together. My hope is that this mirrors the Egyptian belief of Ba and Ka. The ancient Egyptians believed in two special abilities the dead had that allowed them to walk between the afterlife and the living world. Ba allowed for an invisible twin to leave the body to return to the living and help their family, while Ka insured this twin's return to the body.

As I read the final words of my prayers, I think about how some of the oldest burial rites included a practice that would later fall into disuse. Human sacrifice. The ultimate sacrifice, and one I hope the gods have longed for.

The ritual complete, I set down the scroll and look at the photograph of Fran and me. Twin spirits, Ba and Ka. The magic that allows family to care for family, even beyond death. I hope I've done enough.

"Please," I say aloud, closing my eyes as I speak. Please, I think in my mind, calling to the gods for their mercy. Calling to my sister to return.

When I open my eyes again, they don't actually feel open but, somehow, I still see. I'm no longer standing. I now lie on the table, looking up at my sister who clasps her hands to her mouth and breathlessly says my name.

"Elyse."

I know this must be shocking for her, but the letter explains everything, and with that thought, I see her eyes dart up to it. She tears open the envelope and reads the letter that tells her about the ritual I've performed, and how I've taken her place. How if she's reading this, it means the gods have accepted my offering—my sacrifice.

She's still reading. The letter goes on to tell her what to do next. How to tidy up. What to tell my colleagues when she leaves. How to replace me in life as I replaced her in death.

As she reads, I see faint shadows approaching behind her. The shadows materialize into Osiris on her left and Anubis on her right. Slowly, the embalming room fades away and is replaced with a vast hall—the Hall of Truth. Without a word, the jackal-headed god reaches inside me and pulls my heart from my chest. A set of scales appears before him and he places my heart on one side, weighing it against a blindingly white feather. The two balance perfectly.

Fran wipes away tears, seeing none of this, as Osiris gestures with his crook for me to rise and follow him through a golden field of reeds.

Spells Don't Happen with a Bang

Eugen Bacon

all things are a price.
she met a myth and a story—
now time is a panel
*   for the first edition of a brand new night sky*
*   like the antiquity of cosmic love*
*   an ultraviolet replay of mindless songs*
there are no drifting memories,
just death spiraling hot
to beat the sunrise.

— Take me with you.
— No.
— Why?

Karesta doesn't answer. She has no wish to speak the obvious. Her world is ending. She feels her body eat itself. Her life is a code she can't read. It's a menace. It runs like a dog, the direction unclear. If only she could catch glimpse of a sign listing destination right here: bright-eyed planet. But there's nothing bright-eyed about Earth. Karesta feels herself spinning in lava that's a calamity of failed loves. If only she could die in peace. But she worries if she's damned to eternity in a museum of apocalypses, dioramas of flood, earthquakes, heatwaves, pandemics, hate, intolerance, poverty, misjudgments and bushfires. Here's a selfie with the angels of death.

Medina pleads, asks questions. She's not a failed love, but perhaps she's the planet. A failing hand does not rub coconut and lavender essence that way on Karesta's spreading lesions on her ears, her face, her scalp.

— I'm the alpha in this relationship, Medina says with a laugh. Tosses her head back and in a way that catches the light in her hair just so.

— I don't know what… to say.

— That you'll take me.

Karesta thinks all this in a grip of insomnia. Sleep, when it comes, is full of shadows but they're out of focus. Walls, doors, and windows that come and go. The walls drift further into a blackwater world, and she sleepwalks after them with outstretched hands. She pats here, there, feeling for place. Now her touch is in a flood, then her body flows into the cold. She needs granular sunlight, clear photon rings to spell out her infinite dislocation. If she could bound for a quantum supposition, it would be pure joy like none she's seen in eons. Her body falls apart somewhere new. The wind plays music inside the grotesque.

— No.

— Seriously, why?

— It's a matter of… context.

Karesta is short of breath. It hurts to speak. She has no appetite for food or drink, but—under Medina's watchful gaze—clasps her tea with both hands to the porcelain, gazes at the maps of her dying in its dregs. Mortality is a finger poking into her eyeballs. It's the cutting call of a solitary magpie caroling her memories and regrets toward light and shadow, everything she's been unable to accomplish culminating in a loud and terrible squawk.

His name was Eos, the man who splintered her heart. He cheated on her with his own wife. Funny that. She blamed herself for not asking the right questions. Like why he never invited her to his place, why he mostly called her when he was en route, why he sometimes spoke on phone in muffled tones as if he was talking from under a box in the attic. But he always had the right answers for her wrong questions, was so earnest in his statements of affection, she said sorry for mistrusting him. Turned out allegories were slippery, and separated wasn't that separated after all.

Heartbroken, she summoned her only solace. She was born with this magic, or is it witchcraft? A gift she never sought. But she has glowed and drifted in it, recited herself to places she once only saw in books. Twinkle. Twinkle.

Ake-tay e-may o-tay e-thay ilderness-way! Take me to the wilderness!

She shapeshifted into a white eagle and soared over a mountain pass, where her stomach nearly fell out of her buttocks, such was her sadness, her disorientation. She was a seasoned spell traveler, accustomed to heights and plains. But she had to flap hard her great white wings with black tips to stay airborne past wind-lashed dunes and across the striated grassland. Fly, fly… She dipped, feet first in a gust of wind, stabbed the river and snatched with outstretched claws a baby tilapia. Caused quite a stir. Oh, there—the stampede of a pod of hippos parting seas in a river.

— That's fucken pointless, she whistled at them. Escapism. The hell do you think you'll go?

She was asking herself the same question.

Take a fucken guess, her mind said, as Karesta circled the mangled carcass of a calf.

Are there simple memories? Each is a haiku, always with a punchline. How can she adjust recall, calibrate detail such as how cold or warm the touch, whether the lips were a 'hard agree' or something in the direction of soft? Eos had minimized the nature of his true relationship and, in so doing, had ripped his connection with hers. What's his alter ego, she wonders now?

Even though he doesn't have enchantment, as in magic or witchery.

Storks, eagles, cheetahs and dingoes are her alter ego when she traverses the African savannah and the Australian wilderness. She doesn't know what animal, bird, or form she shapeshifts into when she soars the galaxies. She hasn't mastered the water world. She'd love to be a great white shark swimming rivers and estuaries and gliding into the sea. She'd siphon tilapia, crabs, lobsters, squid, octopuses, seals, and Eos. She'd regurgitate him and chomp him head down in two halves with her serrated jaws.

She chooses a form with a spell:

Ing-bray orth-fay a-ay iconia! Bring forth a stork!

Ing-bray orth-fay an-ay aquila-ay! Bring forth an eagle!

Ing-bray orth-fay an-ay acinonyx-ay ubatus-jay -ay! Bring forth a cheetah!

A form chooses itself if she doesn't specify it in her spell.

Ing-bray orth-fay a-ay anis-cay upus-lay ingo-day -ay! Bring forth a dingo!

Karesta's favorite form is the dingo. She feels the most alive, standing lean and alert. It's the body that gives her the most respite from the dry eyes and migraines on her deathbed. In this form, like a vulture or a hyena, she's a hunter and a scavenger.

Her body is loose as she lopes high up a tree, higher, highest. She looks, listens, smells. Spots a fire-tailed skink, its bright-red tail masking it well against red rock. But it's a little far, too many crevices for it to slip into. There's no koala for her to stalk on her tree, none plummeting dead weight on a cool night. Maybe, yes, on a hot day. Ah, there's a bush stone-curlew pestering the dusk for worms, leatherjacks, and snails. The dingo leaps silently and without effort from the tree. She accelerates her lean body and tight chest, turns at speed, and paws the bird flat, lunges for the throat. A sea of feathers, gobble.

Sometimes she haunts river estuaries, wades through fern fronds, mangroves on waterlogged silt. Plucks out shellfish and sea turtles whole.

Such adventure! She sees why Medina would want to come along.

— When did you last pass urine? Medina asks now.

she's breathed a life—
now she's the epitome of hollow,
a ghoul with a non-body.
her end is, of course, not fabulous
but when she remembers how it was
>*before she was this gone—*
>*her skin the color of forgotten—*
she feathers her dawn so she can stork the skies,
and pads her paws so she can gallop in cheetah
after kudu she might catch
>*and she commits to memory the sun on her back*
>*the rush of platelets down her throat*
>*the wind's snivel on her face.*
her eyes are the same,

ancient and full of lifetimes.

Eos—what stupid name was that? His own mother couldn't call him Eros.

After Eos, taking to the night sky, hurtling over the waters below, became Karesta's pastime. Canyons, mountain ranges that were grass—then snow-covered... Still, she was hurting. So she magicked herself light years away.

Ake-tay e-may o-tay e-thay alaxies-gay. Take me to the galaxies.

Whirl! Oh, what a nebula. She floated on freefall in the Milky Way. Swept into a black hole into a galaxy called Quasar, where she first met the little doctor, whose eyes gleamed with zodiacal light. His skin was keratin. He pored over a middlemist red camelia meadow, plucking vibrant pinkish reds for his apothecary.

— Tell this man he be legend, because find. He spoke of himself in third person.

— What did you find?

Stars effervesced in his eyes as he stroked his long, white goatee.

— This respectable vegetal.

— Were you hard out trying to find it?

— It beget so erratic, sprout only night when the moons finish one dimension orbit. Can you just cogitate that? Tell the man he be legend.

— I think he already knows.

— I'm like be love, love, love this respectable vegetal.

— You're a legend, she said.

He turned to her the most solemn eyes.

— This is really suck.

— What sucks?

— You be Earthling. We have many problem. *You* have many problem.

— Don't tiptoe around me with words, I'm not a rabbit. What problems do I have?

— Black hole no decent. It chaos your body.

— Maybe I have dodo DNA.

— Let we see.

— Sure. Yeah.

She murmured her spell.

Ake-tay e-may ome-hay! Take me home!
And instantly overrode it.
Ake-tay e-may o-tay a-ay oved-lay one-ay. Take me to a loved one!

She fell into a whirlpool of gas, dust, and particles. Tumbled across spiral arms of the universe in spectral radiance. A color-coded topography interspersed with voids recreated her every sense and overwhelmed her with the unimaginable beauty of it all. She flew herself light years back to planet Earth, plummeted from the iridescence of silvery-blue noctilucent clouds to exactly three minutes after midnight. She found herself precisely in a bar named Virgo that reverberated with *doof-doof* beats, as a DJ named Scorpius permeated gyrating bodies on the dance floor with his supermassive mix that gave gravity a new name.

Karesta reached the bar, tossed a blue and red hybrid that smoked down her throat and said:

— How about another?

— Really? the bartender said.

She looked at his name badge.

— Ben, what did you expect?

The second didn't burn as much, the third not at all.

She took a spot under a mirror ball sizzling a complex radiance of light into her brain, and it told her feet to stomp out their own rhythm, and she thought the bones on her face would explode right off her skin.

Then a rapper named Soul Fa'You came on, ate the mike and blasted the stupidest song with dumbass lyrics:

The women—gotta be the women—
Daylight, bright torches, tutting in stilettos—
The women—gotta be the women—

Hips ticking to a timeless hum unfix the men to their windowsills the hot breaths of a barking dog!

The women—total-assed women—
Dismantle, glass ceiling, with a snap of heels—
The women—total-assed women—

Disassemble suppositions and set milestones in the tomorrow take silence to the Wowsa Book of Records!

At a pause in the beat, someone leaned close, yelled into Karesta's ear.

— What? Karesta shouted back.

— Said how ya doing. Name's Medina. Drink?

— I've had six shots, feel only a little drunk, said Karesta.

— The fuck are you made of?

— What?

— Can lose your hearing on this junk, said Medina.

— Shit, yeah.

— Songs are dumb shit.

— Damn, right.

— Let's get out of here. You got a decent pad?

— Yeah. Kind you press a button and water spurts on the whole fucking lawn.

— Say less.

They raced giggling and holding hands past the bouncers guarding Virgo's doors.

— What, already? said one with serious tatts around his neck that said: Cut Here.

— One day, someone will, said Karesta, still laughing. She'd never felt so giddy in her life.

Medina's boots stamped like a whole fucken army on the asphalt pavement. Karesta hopped onto Medina's all-souped-up 2200cc motorcycle—she made a living jacking up bikes—and, damn, the thing flew.

— Is it even legal? laughed Karesta.

— I fuck with it, said Medina.

Her black leather jacket had the pungent odor of a hyena, but Karesta clutched Medina all the way to an apocalypse ready to happen in a night of unprovoked deadliness. They made love like lightning, baptized every room of Karesta's pad to open a live-in relationship that was a cyclic kaleidoscope of predator and predated.

Medina touches Karesta's forehead with the back of her hand.

— You've got a fever coming.

—Ease up, Moses. Enough with the commandments.

— You have the mood of lightning.

— Funny you say that.

And the mood in the room changes.

Medina is no longer fierce in her taking. She handles Karesta gently, as if she would break.

— The fuck are *you* made of? I weigh some kilos, Karesta says. Keep touching me like an invalid, I'll flick you so quickly.

— Jesus.

— Now you gone do something serious about us, or will you keep sniffing me so intensely as if my pheromones are bringing on an orgasm?

— Sweet Jesus.

Karesta's goading does it, and they fuck like equals. Karesta feels her body tense, then she cries out. Their climax is a nebula. They lie holding hands, Karesta's body pulsing, naked legs astride Medina.

Their sex is still good, thinks Karesta. But it's changing.

Her head hurts. It's like a massive 4WD rolled over it, reversed and trolled over it again.

Nobody, until the little doc, warned her of magicked travel. All those odysseys with dark matter she unprotected herself from. Now her body is gobbling itself.

Ending her.

What started with a rash, then a niggle, took a whole lot more.

Without her magic, her joints are useless asteroids.

Lethargy overcomes her.

who she is now or then is a question mark,
    not a semi-colon.
if she could live forever in the dying suns—
    she can't.
hers is the lifecycle of a star
she yarns her twilight with magic
so she can scale the universe—
    to first loves that are real, until they're not
    blueprints for the debris of who she is,
    the infinity of how she fights or fucks.
her lover here is a comet
who makes her feel—
she feels.

— Take me with you, says Medina. Those places you go.

— No.

— Why?

— It's a matter of context.

— It's a matter of the right moment. Take me.

— No.

Karesta knows she cannot, even if she wanted, especially now. And that's all there is, in the brief dialogue of a heartbreak, the erosion of big and little things. She wants to float in super bubbles to black holes and neutron stars, but this taking has no return.

She needs a granular sun, clear photon rings to ease her dislocation to infinity. She wants to drift to a quantum supposition of pure joy like she's not seen in eons, to reach a place where wind plays music inside the grotesque, as her body falls apart to its nucleus.

Maybe she'll see the little doctor one more time, find middlemist red camelia in a meadow that's the miracle she needs to recharge her new.

The room stays quiet, but the moment is a violent volcano. It's a silence Karesta must break—she can't bear the tectonic rumble and rupture of everything she and Medina have left unsaid.

Ake-tay e-may o-tay e-thay aurora-ay orealis-bay.

Her spell slips from cold lips in the jade, crimson, and amethyst light of an aurora borealis. She levitates, her body gaunt in faded overalls, gently spinning from her bed and her lover's arms. She feels faint headed.

Medina is out of focus, her expression unclear, and it's a blessing. Because Karesta cannot bear to linger in her mind the face of her lover raining with tears. She slips through the walls into the cloudy night, spreads her arms, rests her head backwards to the hush of the wind.

She closes her eyes beneath the sky, face up to luminescence in bright-eyed planets, and gives herself to the stretch and warp of space and time.

The Point of Art

J.L. Worrad

ONE

"Is it true, father?" Sanzo asked. "There is a devil in our house?"

Lucandro Il'Lunadella, Duke of Ribot, chuckled. "My son, who feeds you such nonsense?"

"The stable boys, no doubt," his wife Bianca said, walking alongside with her austere grace. "He spends too much time there."

"He must become a mighty rider," Lucandro replied. "A great knight like his grandfather."

The young family were walking the grounds of the inner estate, as was custom after church. The summer morning was warm and blackbirds sang in the cypresses beside the path. Lucandro felt good, like he had not felt for some time. The kidnap had succeeded and the ruse could begin. It would work, it *would*, and his family name and his wide estates would survive and prosper. Better still, no blood would have to be spilled to ensure such survival. He was a man of peace, Lucandro, unlike his father, and peace would win him victory over the man who would destroy him and all he cherished. The sun's rays fell tenderly upon Duke Lucandro. The gravel crushed delightfully beneath his boots.

"Is she from the lake, father?" Sanzo asked. "Is she an *anguana*? Doesn't she want to drown us?" When his parents ceased walking and looked at him, he said: "The kitchen boy told me."

Bianca frowned at her husband. "So our son frequents the kitchens now. This too will make him a great knight?"

Lucandro sighed. He looked at Sanzo. "Son, you are heir to the Il'Lunadella name. We refuse to countenance idle superstition. There are no nymphs in our estate's lakes, nor anywhere in this world. We are a practical family; we deal in the calculus of power." Sanzo frowned to hear that; he hated his arithmetic lessons. His father pressed on. "We *do* have a guest."

"*Lucandro*," Bianca muttered. She was a woman. They feared bold endeavors. They clung to what they knew.

"She is from a far-away island," Lucandro told his son. "A strange place few men of the mainland have ever seen. You will not meet her, Sanzo. That I promise."

"And she will not stay long," Bianca added.

"Now that we have made our prayers and sloughed off our sins," Lucandro told his family, "it is time I greeted my guest."

"I shall accompany you," Bianca said.

"That is not necessary, my love."

"I am the lady of this house. She is *our* guest."

There was no arguing with that logic.

"Sanzo," Lucandro said. He smiled and cupped his son's chin. "Go play with those stable boys."

TWO

The guest was being kept in the south-west wing, where Lucandro's father had kept his more furtive projects. It seemed fitting somehow. The wing had gone to dust, for no one had visited it this last decade and the servants had fallen into slovenliness there. Two phenomena that would soon change.

Two guards waited outside the double doors of the chamber, one armed with spear, the other with a crossbow. Beside them stood a footman with an arm-long item wrapped in cloth.

"We'll need more protection," Bianca said.

"There is another guard inside," Lucandro replied.

"I meant a priest."

"Really now, woman."

"They say these people are the progeny of demons and sinful women."

Lucandro chuckled. "Then you have nothing to fear, eh?"

"My husband…" Her brow knit in that way he adored. "Is this not a gambit too far? We treaty with creatures infernal…"

"These 'creatures,' the commrach, they are mortal and foolish as any." He looked to his head guard holding the crossbow. "Dulenci, how was she found again?"

"Duke," Dulenci replied hoarsely, "with deference, is that something a lady should hear?"

"Come, man. My wife is a strong woman."

"Unconscious from drink…" Dulenci answered.

"See?" Lucandro told his wife.

"…and abed with two whores," Dulenci continued.

Bianca drew breath. She tottered.

"Oh," Lucandro said. "I had not heard that part. Apologies my dear."

Bianca adjusted the pendent around her neck, a little golden hook, symbol of the Holy Pilgrim.

"Let us face this dissolute goblin," she declaimed.

Dulenci opened the doors and Lucandro stepped through and into the parlour.

The commrach lounged upon the cushioned longbench, one booted foot atop the bench's arm. She looked human on first glance, and boyish, for she wore male finery: shirt, doublet and—most scandalously— trousers. Her black hair she wore in a tail and below the fringe stared two inhuman eyes of fiery amethyst. The tips of her ears peaked out from her raven locks, sharp as falchions.

"Here he is," the commrach announced, her voice a razor in honey, sweet yet sharp, "the smug prick with his big smug plan. So, what is it?"

"I wanted to see if you had awoken from your stupor," Lucandro said.

"I like that." She waved a finger at him. Her grin revealed two rows of pointed teeth. "Most of my kidnappers start with, 'Ah, but you are my guest, madam,' or some self-satisfied nonsense. So, you're ahead there. However, the sack your thugs threw over me was orange in color. Orange. It clashed with my outfit. Quite unforgivable."

"You have been kidnapped before?" Bianca asked the commrach.

"Don't be jealous," the creature replied. "None were pretty as you." She winked.

Bianca stepped closer to her husband.

"That my sword?" the commrach said, nodding toward the footman holding the object wrapped in cloth. "Ah, you'll return it soon enough."

She had a constant smirk to her, this one, like she knew something no one else did. "You require my skills with it, naturally. You'd have killed me otherwise."

Lucandro laughed. "I require your skills… Kyra. Kyra the hellcat they call you, no? Made that name for yourself in the city of Hoxham, selling sword for coin like everyone seems to do there." Lucandro stepped over to the footman and, carefully, unrobed the blade. "And why not, eh?" He lifted the sword. Long, thin, like a needle. The whole—from tip to swept hilt to pommel—was all one piece of metal, some strange black alloy that glittered beneath the candlelight. For a moment, Lucandro was lost in the beauty, the art. "What a work."

He drove it into the bench's back, just before the commrach's knee. It slid through cushion and oak like they were thick mud. He withdrew and stepped back.

The commrach had not flinched, not blinked. Yet her smile had vanished.

"No fiercer point," Lucandro said, "no sharper edge. It is not the metal that makes it so. Why, Kyra, you could make any sword in my armory similarly as sharp, for your people's touch is magic. You simply caress the metal…" he pretended to do so, careful not to slice a finger off "…concentrate on the caressing… and the thing is sharp enough to make mockery of shield or mail. The imbuing. That's what you call this sorcery, yes? The imbuing?"

"I don't like being awake this early," the commrach said. "Fetch me some wine." When Lucandro said nothing, she added: "You want me to kill the Duke of Balanetti, yes?"

"Why do you say that?"

"Because you must be the Duke Il'Lunadella." She gestured at the drab grandeur of the room. "This is certainly not the knocking-house you stole me from. I've only travelled a night, so I can only be on Il'Lunadella land. Everyone knows dukes Il'Lunadella and Balanetti are poised to have a good old border skirmish between your estates. Again. I wasn't on the mainland ten years back, but simply *everyone* says Il'Lunadella and Balanetti fought a most lucrative land war. All the veterans rhapsodize about it. A golden summer of coin, hot weather and, er…" She looked at her empty hand and then to the footman "…wine."

"You pennyblades have journeyed for nothing," Lucandro told her. "There shall be no second war. I shall see to that."

"With assassination," the commrach agreed.

"With art."

For the first time the commrach looked non-plussed.

"We men of Mancua delight in beauty," Lucandro explained, "and when a man pays a great deal to put more beauty into the world, others respect him for it. And if he should pay for something truly glorious? He gets whatever he desires. Without a war."

"You jest."

"You have loitered in my home country for some weeks now. You will have noticed all the fountains and statues and public buildings. Great men paid for them to get some leverage from life. Otherwise they would have used the sword. I am one of their kind." He smiled. "I have to be. I am a man given to peace. And besides, I can hardly lift a sword against my brother-in-law."

The commrach's gaze shifted between Lucandro and Bianca. "How awkward."

"How practical," Bianca corrected her. "Our marriage put an end to the last... indiscretion."

"Oh, I quite understand." The commrach, with her animal eyes, gave Bianca a tender look. "A marriage of practicality was half the reason I fled my isle."

"I love my husband," Bianca said blankly. "I adore my son. My brother is a villain. He was greedy for land then and ravenous now. If not stopped, he shall take and take until House Il'Lunadella is but memory and dust."

You say too much, woman, Lucandro thought. But she was right enough. These were trying days indeed.

The commrach looked to Lucandro. "You have fallen for a misconception irritatingly common among you humans: you think every commrach can make some wondrous statue or painting. Not so. My only art is that blade you hold. Hire me for that. Your war is inevitable."

Lucandro passed the sword back to the footman and sat down on the bench beside the creature. She was fascinating in aspect, with her eyes and teeth, yet comely too. So were all her people, tale had it. It was why they were monsters.

"Kyra, I know you are no Attawan. Yes, I know the names of your people's great artists. I also know that any commrach's touch can make poor art good and great art beyond words." He nodded toward a figurine on a nearby table. "That is a simple enough piece, a brass statuette of the miracle at the well. Use your fingers. Your 'imbuing.' Make it astonishing."

"How dare you?" the commrach said. "You'd have me fondling tat and bringing out its luster? That's what the servants in my family's tower do! You'd have me a scullion like them?"

"Who would know?" Lucandro said.

"I would. So fuck you."

Bianca sighed. "We have a lake on this estate," she told the commrach. "Our dear son thinks there is a she-devil at the bottom of it. Don't make my husband prove him right."

THREE

The thing was a triumph. Oh, she had been miserable, the commrach, sulking as she went about it, stroking her fingertips over the brass figure of the Holy Pilgrim and the lamb he held, and when she had finished, she had crossed her arms and stared at the floor, embarrassed at what she had been compelled to do. Yet what splendor her reluctance had wrought.

Lucandro thought of the statuette now as he lay waiting in his wife's bed, his wife beside him in her nightgown. The statuette depicted a rather small miracle when all was said and done—the Holy Pilgrim had brought a lamb back to life that had fallen down a well—but it was an event said to have occurred in the village of Triere on the border between his own lands and his brother-in-law's. A disputed place. The commrach's power of imbuing had lent the statuette a serenity beyond words. The faces of man and animal seemed alive, or near-as-damn, and the brass seemed some other metal now, some shining alloy of heaven.

"The cardinal will be entranced," he told the ceiling above. "He will speak for us, Bianca. The moment he sees it. He will stand for our cause."

"Is it so wise, husband?" she asked. "Dazzling our peers is one thing, but a man of God? He will see through such devilry."

"He will drop to his aged knees and pray. Have faith." He rolled on his side toward her, and she stiffened. "Relax."

She was always like this before her wifely duties. No woman truly enjoyed the act, after all. But Bianca knew her obligation to husband, family and God. Lucandro respected that. He always gave her a little time to prepare.

"She is a devil," Bianca said.

"Only to the uneducated peasant. You know better. The commrach are just another people upon this earth. Strange, yes, but mere flesh. Mortal as any."

"I have never known her like," Bianca said. "Monstrous, a woman with a sword, by God. And her eyes, they crush my heart with their freezing stare."

"You are quite safe, my love."

"And to wear men's clothes. To roister in taverns. And that… that other thing. With whores. That any woman should desire *that*…"

"You worry too much."

Bianca said nothing. She bit her lower lip in a way Lucandro had never seen before. She drew up her nightgown and closed her eyes.

"Let's begin, my husband," she said.

FOUR

Furious, Lucandro seized the commrach by the back of her neck and marched her down the lamp-lit corridor, his guards and Bianca in tow. The commrach ceased struggling and simply laughed.

"The statuette didn't impress, I take it?" she asked between giggles. "Oh, do tell, sweet duke!"

He marched her faster. "I told the cardinal something wondrous had happened, that the pilgrim statuette had taken on a heavenly sheen. That the servants and my wife and I had all *marveled* at it."

The pointy-eared bitch hooted with laughter.

"And when I led him through the doors, Lucandro said, "and showed him… he looked at me like I was mad, pitiful. The statuette was as cheap and ordinary as ever."

"Worse," Bianca added, striding beside them. "Dull as dirt."

"What can I say?" the commrach replied. "My kind's touch can improve a statue, absolutely, but it barely lasts two nights."

"Why didn't you tell us that?" Lucandro demanded. "And don't say 'because we didn't ask'."

"Because you embarrassed me. Now I humiliate you. I give what I get."

He tossed her against two locked double doors and she winced. He pressed his forearm under her chin and held her there.

"He would have spoken for me, the cardinal. The miracle of the lamb happened here, on my land, centuries past. He would have spoken for me to all my peers. My brother-in-law would have lost all right to steal from me. There would be no war. Do you understand? No bloodshed."

"Oh dear," the commrach said. "Best give my sword back and hire me."

"Your sword lingers upon my desk." Lucandro sneered. "Without your touch. It dulls, becomes the blunt weight it always was."

"Give me my sword," she demanded. "Give me my freedom. And, for the love of your putrid god, *give me some bloody wine!*" She bared her sharp teeth and her breath smelled of strawberry.

Lucandro pressed his forearm into her throat and she winced.

"Open this door," he told a guard.

He did so and the commrach fell backwards onto a pine floor.

The air in the hall was all wood polish and dust. It was the largest room in the southwest wing, large enough for revels and banquets, its timber wreathed in gold leaf from pillar to vault and its walls a deep red. At its center stood a life-size statue of pewter and bronze.

Conzansi Il'Lunadella, the old duke of Ribot. Lucandro's father. His likeness stood there in full armor, the sigil of Il'Lunadella repeating a hundred times in a pattern across the bronze tabard, his golden and noble face staring out from the silver bascinet helm. The artist had rendered him in a fighting pose, sword outright, readied to lunge or parry.

For a few breaths everyone stared at it.

"So much silver," Lucandro said. "A fortune father should have spent on his war."

"Runs in the family, I suspect," the commrach said. "Anyway, I thought you said splendid art stops war."

"A duke of Mancua can offer war with one hand and splendor with the other. The trick is knowing which hand to use when." Lucandro circled around the supine elf, his boots thumping the pinewood floor, while Bianca watched from the doorway. "I have kept this project before you hidden from view, the artist confined to my land. This statue would have been an embarrassment to my father, had anyone known he had commissioned it as men died for his crest. His timing was all wrong. Better to tell the world that I commissioned it, say, two years ago, before the new troubles had begun."

"I see," the commrach said. "You want me to feel your papa up." She waggled her fingers and wiggled her eyebrows, and Lucandro decided he would slice off both when her usefulness was over.

"In two weeks' time," he said without rancor, "all the noblemen in this realm who truly count will visit our home. They will listen to mine and my brother-in-law's arguments and adjudicate. Yet, before they do, I shall offer them our estate's finest wine and lead them to this room."

"Oh, so you *do* have wine? Could've fooled me…"

"They shall see the glory of the father and the devotion of his son. They will recognise that I, not the Duke Balanetti, am the finer soul and better man. The day will be mine. That, beast, is the edge that art lends politics."

He took a deep breath. He booted her in the belly.

"Lucandro!" Bianca said, and she made toward the demon on the floor.

Lucandro gave his wife a look both fearsome and gallant, and Bianca could only tremble before it. He gazed down at the commrach.

"You will use your race's power to make this statue resplendent, to make it shine above all others, above the reasoning faculties of men. You shall do so every day for two weeks and an hour before my peers walk in this hall and see my father in pewter and bronze. That is why you still live, beast. That is your point." He shoved the flat of his boot against her spine. "Understood?"

Bianca stepped forward again. "Please, my love. This is not like you. You hurt her. She'll need her strength."

His wife had a point. Lucandro drew breath. He stepped back and studied the blade of his father's statue, its blunt tip readied for a winning lunge that never came in life. "You feared her a week ago, Bianca."

"I did," she replied. "I do. But she is a woman, Lucandro, delicate beneath her manly affectation. And I think… she could find it in her to be good. To find the love of God and his pilgrim."

Lucandro laughed.

"My sweet silly thing," he told Bianca. "I shall have her tied to a chair whenever she is not working and you can read from the holy book to her."

"Oh shit…" the commrach muttered to the floor.

"You see, commrach?" Lucandro said. "My wife is the true torturer, not I."

FIVE

Wine flowed at the speed of congeniality, which is to say neither miserly nor flagrant. Some sixty noblemen, the worthiest of Mancua, were sat about the long table in the old hall. A pleasant summer night. The scent of the cypress trees drifted through the opened windows and all talk was politely avoidant of the impending debate.

"This statue," said portly Duke DiMalfo, sat beside Lucandro at the table's head, "come, friend. Tell us what it depicts."

The other nearby nobles awaited their host's response, all grinning.

Lucandro smiled. "Gentlemen, permit my reticence. When you enter the hall in the south-west wing for our discussion, then you will see this work of art. And I shall see your faces, friends."

"Very well," DiMalfo said, and he and the others chuckled. He lifted his goblet. "To our host."

They toasted him. Lucandro made a brief glance toward the far end of the table, where his brother-in-law sat. His enemy looked back at him and just as quickly looked away. Did he know himself the loser already? Surely. The wine in Lucandro's mouth tasted sublime.

"My lord." It was Dulenci, his head guard.

"What is it, Dulenci?" Lucandro kept his smile before his peers, but he was rattled by this unorthodox intrusion.

"Your lady wife, sir. She wishes your presence in the southwest hall. Urgently."

What was Bianca still doing in there? She had been teaching the commrach of God and his pilgrim all week. The commrach was to be taken from the hall mere minutes before the noblemen entered, so as to ensure the statue be imbued to its very limit. Had something gone wrong? He had to know.

"Wait here," he told Dulenci. If he were to leave this room with a guard accompanying him, the noblemen would talk.

"Everything fine?" the Duke DiMalfo asked.

"My wife," Lucandro explained with an indulgent chuckle. "She weeps and worries over her husband and brother at odds."

"Go see to her," DiMalfo insisted. "We here can keep ourselves occupied, as only men drinking the finest wine can!"

The men laughed and Lucandro arose and bowed, almost catching his ceremonial sword against the arm of his chair. He made for the southwest wing.

<h2 style="text-align:center">SIX</h2>

He heard laughter behind the double doors. Sanzo's. His boy. Fear seized him.

Lucandro threw the doors open. The she-devil was leaning over Sanzo, showing him something. Bianca, beside them, looked on indulgently.

"Step away from her!" Lucandro bellowed at the boy. He strode toward the two women. "She is meant to be bound when you are here, Bianca. There is meant to be a guard!"

"Please, my love," Bianca said, "she has improved Sanzo's toy. That is all."

He grabbed the toy soldier from Sanzo's hand and flung it across the hall. Sanzo ran out of the room.

"You have gone too far," Lucandro told the commrach. "Too far!"

"She is good now, Lucandro," Bianca protested. "The words of the holy book have cleansed her very spirit."

He slapped Bianca. It echoed against the painted walls.

He had never hit her, not until this moment. She stared at him aghast, as if this betrayal of his was even a tenth of hers. She clutched her cheek and wept.

"You let her touch our *son*?" he said, hissing the words. "Talk to him? This demon?" He went to slap her again, but she ducked round the back of the statue.

By God. The statue was astounding. His father's face was alive, as if caught in some moment between breaths. Lucandro stared in wonder.

A fist cracked his nose. Lucandro stumbled to one side and righted himself. He drew his ceremonial sword and swung toward the attack.

The commrach ducked and swerved with each strike, inhumanly swift. She laughed her contemptible laugh.

"Give me my sword, coward," she said. "Prove yourself."

"Bitch." Hot blood ran down from Lucandro's nose onto his tunic. "How shall I explain this wound to our guests?"

The commrach ran to the side of the statue. She, his father, his wife: all were stood in a line, all looking at Lucandro. Judging him. He felt dizzy, the lamps above bright as suns. He would need to sit down after he killed the elf.

She was grinning at him, that grin that seemed to know something no one else did.

Lucandro lunged at her. His sword hit nothing.

Something jabbed his stomach and he froze. Looking down he saw the tip of the statue's sword. It had pierced his doublet. Had he stepped another inch, his lunge a fraction more powerful, he would have impaled himself.

"You sharpened it," he said. "With your power." He looked up at the commrach, but she was not looking back. She nodded to someone behind him.

He felt a shove against his shoulder blades and his father's sword slid in, passing through his belly and out the small of his back. There was no pain. Not yet.

"Told you it would work," the commrach said.

"With a little improvisation," Bianca answered. She walked around Lucandro and met his gaze, her face as kind as only the gentlest wife's could be.

"Your brother," Lucandro said. He coughed blood, hot and dark. "You betrayed me, Bianca."

"No, my love," she said. "My loyalty to your house is greater than you know. You would have lost a war against my brother, as did your father." She looked at his statue and shook her head. "And this ploy in silver and bronze… it was as flawed as your father's stratagems. Oh, my sweet hypocrite, my 'man of peace,' you never comprehended your own foolishness, never saw the joke you were to your peers. But now, when they see Sanzo's father dead by his own hand, the nobility will vow to protect the boy and his suffering mother. My brother will lose all honor if he lifts the banner of war. House Il'Lunadella will survive, my husband. It will prosper."

God's mercy. She was right. Everything would be fine now, their son safe. The pain began to make itself known in his gut. Lucandro winced. "The commrach's idea, yes?"

"Your wife's idle whim," the commrach answered. "Uttered a few days into our conversations." Her supple arms drifted around Bianca's waist. She began to place soft kisses upon her neck. Bianca murmured and closed her eyes. She smiled with pleasure.

"Kyra showed me my fancies could be real," Bianca said. "She is nothing if not… convincing."

Lucandro laughed. He simply had to. The world was as absurd as it was bitter.

"Damn it, Bianca," he said as warm darkness took him. "Be a good host now. Bring our guest here her wine."

No More Barbara, Only Bubbles

Angela Sylvaine

Barbara Ann "Bubbles" Johnson lingered over the coffin of her mentor, scowling at his amateurish painted face, the white cake cracking to reveal deep wrinkles beneath. The mortician had tried to replicate the arched eyebrows, diamond eye accents, and wide, smiling lips Pop was known for, but they didn't have the decades of practice the master clown had. And they hadn't used the special makeup Pop's widow, Catie, delivered into the casket after saying her tearful goodbyes; makeup Barbara expertly extracted, tucking each palette into her billowy sleeve before bending to grip Pop's rigid body in a tight hug. He still smelled of sage, but there was an odd sweetness that spoiled his familiar scent.

Sleight of hand was her specialty, a skill she perfected in her quest to become Pop's protégé, and maybe why he'd eventually agreed to take her on. Perhaps he also felt some debt to her for taking every one of her baby teeth, starting with the first at Jackie Johansson's birthday party when Barbara was just six. Lucky for her, it was a "whole class invited" party.

The tight elastic at the wrists of her dress held her pilfered treasure secure as Barbara mingled with the other mourners, who weren't mourning much. Clown funerals were known for laughter and silliness, a fitting tribute in death to what the entertainers had been in life. She was sprayed by more than one squirting rose, fell victim to Loopy's hand buzzer, and accepted an impressive balloon peacock from Magpie.

Bubbles and Pop were the company's most popular duo- a jovial green-haired giant and his spritely polka-dotted sidekick. They'd even been recruited to go on the road with the big top, and Barbara thought she might finally escape, but Pop refused on behalf of both of them, insisting he performed no more than once a week.

She broke down when he told her, her makeup running under rivulets of tears. He didn't apologize, just pulled a chair close, wiped her face clean, and reapplied her base makeup with his own special blend, one he'd never before shared.

As he slicked the thick white cake over her skin, a pleasant flush blanketed every inch of her skin. The feeling spread, grew, until a powerful confidence she'd never known formed a bright hot flame in her stomach and burned outward.

"You've been holding out on me," she said to Pop as she stared at herself in the lighted mirror.

He stood, wincing as he did more often in recent days.

"What's in it?" The question she meant to sound casual came out as a demand.

Pop reached into the small, hidden side pocket of his striped jumpsuit and extracted a smiley face coin purse, unzipping it to reveal a handful of tiny teeth mixed in with bits of dried sage.

She sucked in a breath. "Baby teeth." The loose tooth trick was a favorite. He'd point a finger at the gathered crowd of children and call forward each one who had a baby tooth beginning to wiggle.

Little Barbara herself had felt the tingle of her own tooth as it seemed to respond to his beckoning finger. In her mouth one minute, clasped between his white gloved fingers the next. He'd called her special and rewarded her with a rainbow bundle of fake flowers that ended up in the trash that same night. Over the next year she saved each of her baby teeth in an old pickle jar, easy enough since no tooth fairy or any other mythical giver of gifts had never visited her house. She brought that rattling jar to Pop, crashing a party that was not 'whole class invited' and earning a rainbow banner of scarves so long the bulk of it created a bulge beneath her mattress where she kept it hidden.

"Pop," she said, her voice sharp. "Why do you still have those?" At the end of each children's party, he made a show of burying them in the family's garden, a tradition to ensure good luck to the children. Luck some kids, like Barbara, sorely needed.

He didn't answer, just gave her a painted-on smile and said, "Finish up. It's showtime."

The children adored Bubbles even more than usual that day, riveted to her every word and command. But Pop didn't let her use his special makeup again, and while the effect partially carried over to her next performance, by the end of the month she'd faded back to her normal self. A good clown, unique and lovable, but not extra special.

All she'd ever wanted was to be seen and loved. That's why clowning meant so much to her. The day of their next show, she arrived at the company's dressing rooms ready to confess to Pop what this job meant to her and beg him to share more of his special blend.

Instead, she found his body lying half in, half out of the bathroom. He was nude from the waist up and white cake covered him, the empty palette on the floor beside him and no other makeup in sight. She pocketed the palette before calling 911, thinking she could scrape out any remnants with a Q-tip, then sat beside him and cried. Pop, the only one in the whole world who really cared about her, was gone.

Shaking off the memory of her mentor's lifeless face staring up from the bathroom floor, Barbara extracted herself from the funeral, her skin itching to don the makeup, though she had no gig that day. Sitting in her car, the balloon peacock in the passenger seat, she pulled the pink palette from her sleeve. The color wasn't one Pop used, nor was the baby blue. He stuck to bold primaries.

He'd made the pastel paints for her, must have wanted her to take them. She knew now he was very sick in the months leading up to his death, hardly able to eat and plagued by muscle weakness and bone pain the doctors couldn't explain. Even still, he'd taken the time to make *her* colors, to let her know how much she meant to him.

She turned the palette over, noting a markered note not to exceed once per week application, then opened it and slicked the paint over her lips. As the concoction sank into her skin, her lips plumped and tingled, signaling it was not your average makeup. She pressed her lips together but could feel no grittiness to signal the inclusion of ground baby teeth.

A knock sounded at her window, startling her, and she saw Mr. Emory, owner of Parties Plus, staring at her through the glass.

She rolled down her window halfway, and he said, "Was hoping to talk before you left."

His eyes strayed to the palette in her hand. Did he know she stole it from Pop's corpse?

"What is it?" she asked.

"I'm sending Taffy and Peanut to your gig this weekend, and I'll work on subbing in for the rest until we can find you a new partner."

Heat flushed her body. "You can't do that." Knowing she'd get to be Bubbles for just one day was all that got her through each week.

"I can't?" His brow furrowed and he tugged at the collar of his dress shirt, as if it were too tight.

"I'll do them alone, it'll be fine." She felt her words leap from her tongue on spider legs and crawl into his ear.

"Oh. Right. It'll be fine." He stood and gave his head a little shake.

"And I want to go full time," she called after him, gripping the top lip of the window with both hands. "Work every day."

"Every day. Well, we don't have work every day." He raised one hand, pressed two fingers to his temple.

"As many as I can, then. Okay?" The pilfered makeup hung heavy in her sleeve, clanking against the glass.

"Okay." He winced and turned away. "As many as you can. Okay," he said again, and walked away, weaving a bit.

She tugged the rest of the palettes from her sleeve and used her bare fingers to smear white over every inch of her face and neck. A rush of warmth flushed her skin from her scalp to her fingertips. "Thank you, Pop," she whispered.

From that moment on, there was no more Barbara, only Bubbles. She arrived home in full paint, something she'd never done before, knowing it would trigger her father's wrath. And it did, until she commanded him to stop laughing, then to stop breathing.

With a very Bubbles giggle, she told him to start breathing again and he did. He stayed in his room after that, leaving the rest of the apartment to her.

Bubbles dressed each day in her makeup and polka dots and brought joy to every party or event, earning tips larger than anything she'd ever gotten before. And because she was generous, she spread that joy for free through the aisles of the grocery store, the pumps at the gas station, and the McDonalds drive thru lane. At night, she carefully wrapped her face in cloth to hold the paint tight to her skin, to ensure every molecule absorbed into her pores so that nothing went to waste.

She knew the makeup wouldn't last forever, so she tried the tooth trick herself, and, of course, she was a natural. Bubbles deftly slipped countless baby teeth from children's mouths and displayed them with a flourish before bestowing the giver with a wonderful prize. Maybe one of them would save up a whole jar for her and become her protégé just as she had with Pop.

The paint proved harder to make than she expected, though, and she wasted several dozen teeth on failed batches that had no effect beyond coloring her skin. Most of her original supply from Pop was gone by the time she received the box, a gift from the grave.

His widow dropped off a few things for Bubbles, and there was no more makeup, but there was a smiley face coin purse. Empty of teeth but still smelling of sage. Pop's secret to good health and good luck, he'd always said.

Bubbles arrived at the birthday party for little Sofia Harrington intent on restocking her supply. Though there were almost forty children in attendance, they were a bit too young, only one of them responding to her beckoning finger and yielding teeth.

But Bubbles, when she'd been Barbara, had helped her own teeth along, hadn't she? She would lie in bed and grip them with her fingers and force them back and forth until she tasted copper.

After pulling a rabbit from a hat, a feat the kids always loved, Bubbles returned to the tooth trick. This time, she didn't wait for anyone to respond to her beckoning finger. She pointed at a child in the front and simply demanded his tooth break free and come to her.

It did, though a little bloodier and more tear-drenched than was usual. Several more followed like that, until one of the parents noticed the group of pale-faced children seated on the grass clutching a stuffed animal or balloon, red running down their chins.

"Losing baby teeth is perfectly natural," Bubbles said, making eye contact with each parent and giving them a soothing smile. Her head pounded from the effort, and she could feel the makeup thinning on her skin, begging for a touch up.

One of the rewarded kids stood and came over to the group, dragging his new teddy bear by the arm, and said, "I don't feel good." He proceeded to vomit blood-tinged birthday cake at her feet.

Bubbles decided she had enough teeth for her next batch and grabbed her case before excusing herself, not bothering to soothe the wave of anger directed at her as she ran to her car. The family was sure to give her a poor review, but she could take care of Mr. Emory when she saw him.

She only drove a few blocks before pulling over to plaster her face with a new layer of paint, her racing heart calming as she leaned back against the seat and felt the concoction work its magic. The palette was the last of the white; as she replaced the lid over what remained, she calculated her supply would only last another day, maybe two.

But there was nothing to worry about, she knew now what she'd done wrong. The new teeth would work. Maybe even better, since they were so freshly unrooted. Back at home, she crushed the teeth and combined them with finely ground sage before blending the concoction with the paint in an old pickle jar, for luck.

After letting it set, she stood before the bathroom mirror and spread the mix over her skin. The texture was much grittier, but she'd have plenty of time to perfect the mix in her next batches. Bubbles closed her eyes and waited for the rush of warmth, the thrum of power.

It never came.

She opened her eyes, saw herself in the mirror. Not Bubbles, just Barbara, looking ridiculous with her face smeared white.

"No," she screamed, chucking the jar at the mirror and sending a spiderweb of cracks through the glass.

"Hey," her father's voice boomed through the wall, then went quiet. He'd forgotten for a moment that there were consequences to treating her like that now.

Or there had been. Barbara's reflection twisted, a collection of shards barely held together.

Her body shook and she wrapped her arms around herself. She couldn't go back to what she was, had to figure out how to be Bubbles again. Forever.

"Please, Pop, help me," she whispered, clenching her eyes closed. His voice drifted through her mind, through her memories.

"You're special, Barbara," he'd said, that first day when he'd taken her baby tooth. And later too, he'd always told her she was special.

"That's it," she said, opening her eyes and dropping to her knees to fling open the cabinet beneath the sink.

The magic couldn't be done with just any teeth, they had to be special. Why hadn't she seen that before?

Grabbing the toolbox from the back corner, she placed it on the dingy linoleum floor and flipped back the lid. She pushed aside the hammer and the file and the screwdrivers, finally finding the pliers.

Barbara stood and leaned over the counter to get close to the cracked mirror. She opened her mouth wide and clamped the pliers onto a back molar, figuring the more tooth the better. Bubbles' eyes sparkled back at her in the reflection. This time would work for sure.

The Brightest and Most Remarkable

Ren Hutchings

The strange books in the Library of the Mages, Jossley supposed, must have something in common with mushrooms. He remembered reading somewhere that mushrooms could speak to one another across distance; that they were separate organisms, and yet they were also *one*, linked through an unseen network that wove through the earth beneath the forest.

Likewise, the pulse of magic at the heart of the Library was a living thing, and the books were all connected to it. There were thousands upon thousands of them, linked by some invisible root system, those twining tendrils of enchantment that wove through every parchment and sheaf and spine.

Despite all the dangerous magic that crackled and hissed in the bones of this building, Jossley had always felt at home here, ensconced in the Library's labyrinthine corridors and vaulted rooms. And he still remembered every bit of the awe he'd felt on the day the Eldest Professor first took his cohort around for their campus orientation.

"Don't be alarmed if you see something unusual," the Professor had told them. "The Library might be a bit temperamental until it gets to know you. But just watch your step, mind your magic, and study diligently. Prove yourself to be the brightest and most remarkable… and the Library might take a liking to you. And then, there will be no limits to the knowledge it will grant you."

As all the newcomers soon discovered, the books were capricious, appearing and disappearing from the shelves without warning. They often switched places or changed titles, and some even had covers that shifted color with the seasons. Jossley had once spent the better part of a week scouring the shelves for a greyish-blue tome he'd referenced the previous autumn, only to discover that it had turned a verdant spring green, sprouting new vines of gold along its spine.

Certain staircases and doorways would only show themselves to the Library's favorite scholars, and the geometry of the building ebbed and flowed like an ever-changing tide. Some of the more elusive wings had been known to vanish for entire decades before someone was deemed worthy of perusing their shelves again. To enter these ancient halls was to submit oneself entirely to the Library's harsh judgment.

It wasn't that the Library was *malevolent* exactly, but there were trials one had to endure before its trust could be gained. Jossley had seen more than one student injured when a door suddenly slammed on them. Almost everyone in his cohort had taken a mysterious tumble on the curling staircases. And he'd lost count of the number of times that a heavy tome had catapulted itself from a high shelf, hurtling directly into an unsuspecting student's head.

But an encounter with a flying book or a mercurial staircase wasn't even the worst of it, for there had always been whispers of far more terrifying fates. The Library had been known to trap students for hours or days in its stone passageways when a door suddenly sealed itself behind them. And it was rumored that some archivist mages in the days of old had been swallowed into the stacks, never to be heard from again.

None of that should trouble *the brightest and most remarkable,* Jossley always told himself. He'd taken the Eldest Professor's words to heart, and he had endeavored to live by them. He was a brilliant student, a promising mage and a distinguished academic. A shining star, even among the ranks of his prestigious cohort.

Jossley had come to understand, over time, that the Library *needed* the students—that it called out to them for some very specific purpose. Perhaps the books were actually more like flowers than mushrooms, he mused. Perhaps they needed the mages to pollinate them, carrying traces of magic from one tome to the next. Whenever he ran his finger over the words in an open codex, he imagined that some spark of its enchantment, and the knowledge within it, now rested upon his fingertips.

Do new books grow here? he wondered. *Do the words inside them merge and change along with their covers? Do they learn from one another? How many more hidden secrets does this ancient building hold?*

Jossley would have done anything to show the Library of the Mages that he was worthy, that he deserved all the knowledge it contained. But despite his near-perfect academic record and his ever-increasing proficiency at spellwork, there was another student that the Library had always favored more. No matter how hard Jossley tried, he could never quite measure up to *Hedge*.

Hedge had the makings of a truly exceptional mage, the kind of once-in-a-century talent that put Jossley's own exploits to shame. On top of that, Hedge was a relentless scholar, the type who seemed neither to eat nor sleep if there was research to be done. He spent most of his free time exploring the Library's shifting halls, drawing ever more elaborate maps and formulas to untangle its puzzling floor plan. Whatever spells Jossley could do, Hedge could always do them just a little bit better, and he never missed an opportunity to show off under the Library's watchful gaze.

The bitter truth was that Jossley probably wouldn't have been half the scholar he was if it weren't for Hedge. Many of Jossley's best research papers had referenced obscure codices that Hedge had dug up, or scrolls that he'd deigned to let Jossley have a quick look at before he released them back into the Library's vaults.

Whenever Hedge rolled out the ladder and sent it sailing down the stacks, Jossley hurried along in the ladder's wake, examining the shelves it had just passed over for the flash of some rare new title. And inevitably, something useful would appear. The most elusive books and scrolls seemed to flock toward Hedge like birds to the main character of a fairytale, and the Library's magic sang sweetly for him.

One day, the two of them had both been searching the upper floors for a particularly rare scroll when they'd discovered a newly opened passageway in one of the stairwells. Well, that is to say, *Hedge* had discovered it, and he had oh-so-magnanimously invited Jossley to explore it with him. Probably because he wanted Jossley to go in first and check it for traps.

The new stone arch had opened up like a hungry mouth, and it had a door so low that they both had to duck to get inside. Jossley's heart had been pounding, his palms sweating with nerves, but he didn't dare show any weakness when Hedge was standing right there. Jossley needed to show the Library who *really* had the courage to seize greatness. And so he'd grabbed a hanging lantern from the wall of the stairwell, and he'd bravely barged right into the dark chamber that lay beyond the arch.

"Oh, come *on*. Are you a mage or not? You don't need that, mate," Hedge had said, looking at Jossley's lantern with a mocking laugh. Hedge had already summoned a little orb of light with a quickly hummed illumination spell, and he was holding the glowing sphere aloft in one hand as he followed.

Jossley pretended not to hear it, but he raged silently at himself. Why hadn't *he* thought to use an illumination spell? Surely the Library was equally unimpressed with him. He rushed onward into the room, grateful that Hedge couldn't see how his cheeks flushed with embarrassment.

But Jossley had soon forgotten about his mortifying misstep, for inside the small chamber was a cache of lost scrolls that instantly captured his attention. Some of them hadn't been spotted in years—and a few hadn't even been cataloged yet!

Jossley and Hedge had spent several long days going through their finds together, and Jossley was so enthralled with the arcane knowledge they'd just unlocked that he could hardly bring himself to keep any grudge against Hedge. He'd aced his next research paper, and damn it, he was *proud* of it—even though he was sure that Hedge's grade would be a little bit higher.

On the last day of term before graduation, most of the students had taken off right after their last lecture, eager to get into the sunshine and to start the rowdy celebration in the campus square. Jossley had considered joining them; he'd even rolled up his sleeves and loosened his tie for the occasion. But as he crossed the campus grounds and passed under the shadow of the Library's great spire, *something* called him back. And instead, he took his familiar route up the great stone stairs, pushing open the ornately carved door and entering the vaulted lobby.

Inside, the Library was much quieter than usual. It was not only the absence of sound that struck him—no flick of pages, no creak of wooden floorboards—but the magic itself seemed subdued, as though the whole building held its breath. He stepped softly through the lobby, passed through the lower floor reading-rooms, and climbed up to his favorite section, where the bookshelves curved in a great spiral up the spire. He closed his eyes and inhaled deeply: the familiar scent of ancient paper and stone, and the unmistakable tang of magic.

Then, the rattle of the rolling ladder broke through the silence, and Jossley looked up with a start. It was Hedge... of *course* it was Hedge.

He was flipping nonchalantly through a book with one hand, the other one cradling the half-dozen volumes he already had stacked on his arm. Only a mage who knew he had the Library's favor would dare such a precarious feat, knowing how quickly that ladder could jerk away from beneath him.

"It's bad luck to stand under a ladder, don't you know?" Hedge drawled, peering down from his lofty perch. "What are you doing down there, mate?"

"None of your business. I can stand where I please," Jossley shot back, averting his gaze from Hedge's obnoxious smirk. He fixed his eyes on the nearest bookcase, scanning over the spines on the shelves. "I think my luck is just fine, thank you very much. I'm going to—"

He trailed off, his mouth suddenly going bone-dry. For on the shelf right in front of him, sitting diagonally over the top of several other books, was a slender, leather-bound journal. It was stuck haphazardly into the bookcase, as though someone had neglected to return it to its correct place and had simply set it down there.

There was a thick layer of dust upon it, a mass of cobwebs stretching from one corner to the wall of the shelf, as though it had remained undisturbed for a very long time. If someone *had* set this book down, it must have happened decades ago, long before Hedge or Jossley had even been students here.

Jossley's heart pounded triple time. Talk about luck! He chanced a quick glance back up at Hedge, but Hedge had already lost interest in him. He'd turned back to the open book he was holding, muttering some spell quietly to himself as he read.

Jossley looked back at the shelf, wondering if the journal would have disappeared in a blink. But no, it was still there. Old magic radiated from it, so strong that Jossley could feel it burning against his face. Surely Hedge would perceive it momentarily, if he were paying any attention at all—

Jossley reached out and seized the book, slipping it silently from the shelf and hiding it under one edge of his jacket. A puff of dust filled the air, and he stifled a cough.

"I've got to go," Jossley choked out. "See you in the campus square, if you're going to the party!"

Then he turned and bolted from the stacks, clutching the fold of his jacket, his white-knuckled fingers gripping his precious cargo.

He knew exactly what he'd just discovered, and he could scarcely believe it. This must be the *Librarian's Book*. It was the rarest of all the Library's ancient tomes, a journal said to have been handwritten by the Librarian himself—the nameless mage who'd founded this place more than sixteen centuries ago. The book hardly ever showed itself, and the Eldest Professor said that it could only be opened by a mage of extraordinary power.

Even the Professor herself had never actually read its contents. She claimed to have spotted the book twice in her youth—but alas, she said, it had disappeared from the shelf both times before she could grab hold of it.

"What does it look like?" the newcomers always chorused, wide-eyed and eager after hearing of the legend. Of course, they all soon realized what a futile question that was in a place like the Library. "You'll know it if you see it," was all the Professor ever said in reply.

Now, Jossley ran further up the spiral staircase, heading to the top of the spire. There was a small study room up there, and he shouldered open the creaking door and hurried inside, locking it behind him. He laid the ancient journal out on the wooden table, brushing the remaining dust and cobwebs from its cover with the palm of his trembling hand.

There was no title inscribed upon the front. Indeed, there was nothing on it at all except a bright, star-shaped crest—the logo of the old Archivists' Guild, embossed into the leather. It glinted with gold leaf that had withstood the hands of time. There had once been a name embossed beneath it, Jossley thought, just below the star. But the letters had been scratched out of the leather, obscured by what looked like sharp claw-marks.

Jossley shivered with sudden dread, but he was not deterred. Far from it; he was more certain than ever that he was about to do something of singular importance. Like every other student, Jossley had eagerly searched the shelves for the Librarian's Book the whole time he'd been here, and he'd even dared to imagine that *he* might be the next mage to hold the legendary journal. But the bitterest parts of him had always been grimly certain that if anyone *did* manage to locate the book, it would surely have been Hedge.

And yet… somehow, the Library had chosen *him*. Here at last was the proof that *he* had been deemed the better of the two mages. Irrefutable evidence that he, Jossley, was the brightest and most remarkable.

Taking a steadying breath, Jossley pinched open the cover and leafed delicately through the journal's thin pages. The text inside was handwritten, each page filled from edge to edge with thick scrawls of ink the color of midnight.

There were spells and alchemical formulas, diary entries, descriptions of rare magical herbs, and lengthy annotated bibliographies of lost arcane works. In some places, the passages had been struck out and revised; in others, further calculations had been added in the margins. Jossley identified at least five different dead languages, glowing with pride at how proficiently he could translate them all.

This was a record as old as the Library itself. These were the words of the founding mage, right here beneath his fingertips. His breath caught in his throat as he skimmed through page after page.

Then a moment of doubt suddenly seized him. Had the Library *really* chosen him? Or had he simply snatched up a boon that had been destined for Hedge? The question needled at him. Hedge had been *right there*. The book had appeared under Hedge's ladder.

But no, Jossley reassured himself. If Hedge had been meant to have it, then the journal would have appeared on the higher shelf, next to Hedge's hand. Instead, it had revealed itself in the very place where *Jossley's* hand was resting. And, he reasoned, unlike the Eldest Professor's tale, it had not vanished when he reached out to take it. This triumph was wholly and entirely his own.

Yes. That's right, said the book, speaking in a low whisper that curled like smoke into Jossley's awareness. *It is all yours to take. Is this not what you've been working so hard for?*

Jossley startled back, nearly knocking the book off the table. Did the Librarian's journal really just *talk* to him? In all the time he'd spent working with all manner of enchanted books, he had never encountered one that could speak.

"What *are* you?" he asked, his voice shaking. "How is it that a book is talking to me?"

You should know by now that the books here are only vessels, said the voice. *You are not speaking to a book, but to the greater whole.*

"Are you... are you the Library, then?" Jossley gasped.

A chuckle like distant thunder rumbled from the stone walls. *In a manner of speaking,* the voice whispered. *They once called me the Librarian... but now I am more. I am not one, but many.*

Jossley thought again of the mushrooms, of their invisible communication network, of their whispers in the forest dirt. *Like mushrooms?* he wanted to ask. But all he could do was nod wordlessly.

We are everything, and we know everything, the voice went on. *We are every book and scroll that has ever rested in these hallowed halls, or ever will. We are every spell that has been cast here. We are outside of time. We are one with the knowledge.*

At once, the study room had grown very cold. The pages in the journal fluttered wildly, as if some ghostly hand leafed through them, faster and faster until the scrawls of midnight ink all blurred together.

You will become part of something greater, much more than a mage or a scholar, the voice chanted. *All the knowledge we contain will be granted to you. And in return, you will bind your magic to the Library. It will make a fine addition to our collection.*

At last, the journal shuddered and went still again. When it came to rest, it was open to a page almost exactly in the middle. There was some poem or incantation inscribed there in unfamiliar runes, the small, dense shapes closely packed on the parchment. Some archaic language that Jossley had never seen before.

Do you pledge to strengthen and repair us, to feed and grow the collection? the voice asked. *Are you ready? Do you agree to follow in the Librarian's own footsteps?*

"I do! I am!" Jossley cried out. His words echoed with surprising volume, a hoarse and triumphant shout that sounded strangely like more voices than one. "I will!"

Then he looked back down at the book, at those runes he couldn't read, in that language he didn't know. And as he squinted down at the page, the runes shifted, warped and reshaped themselves. They took on *meaning...*

…and suddenly, Jossley could understand them quite easily. He laughed in jubilant disbelief as he took in the Librarian's neatly-formed words:

I am one with the knowledge,
and the knowledge is me.
I give myself over in my entirety.
All that I am, I give to the whole.
The knowledge will consume me,
I will become one with all that is known—

Already, more new information was flooding into Jossley's mind, like a river freed from behind an exploding dam, like the rush of spring thaw from something long frozen. How simple it all seemed, understanding the deep spellwork and old magic that had been far beyond his comprehension this morning!

His veins were still thrumming with the euphoria of victory when he became aware of another student standing in the wide-open doorway.

Hedge was here, smirking in his familiar fashion, sauntering into the room. But there was something otherworldly in his grin. A glint of too-shiny sharp teeth. A stare like something older than it should be.

And then Jossley remembered—*he had locked that door behind him.*

"Welcome to the Library," Hedge said in a voice like dried leaves, his whisper a hiss of escaping smoke. "I think you'll like it here."

Jossley slammed shut the leather journal, the ancient pages inside crumpling under his hand.

He stared at Hedge, and Hedge stared back.

And all of a sudden, Jossley was dreadfully unsure of everything. Had he *ever* seen Hedge anywhere outside the Library?

He tried to picture Hedge sitting in the dining hall, but the image came up blank. Surely, he must have seen Hedge at least once in the dormitory corridors, or sitting beside him in class, or somewhere on the campus grounds—

Panic was rising in Jossley's throat. How had they first met? It wasn't in a lecture hall, or in some extracurricular orientation. No, it was—

Here.

In the Library. Jossley had been holed up in the spire for hours, looking for some obscure tome about lithomancy. He'd been just about to give up the hunt when he'd turned a corner and nearly run right into someone.

A tall, dark-haired young student with sharp and serious eyes, a pair of thick horn-rimmed glasses perched precariously on the end of his nose.

And there, clutched between his hands, was the exact book Jossley had been looking for.

"Excuse me!" Jossley had blurted out. "I was just looking for that book. I need it for my paper on lithomancy. Do you mind if I have a quick look?"

"No worries," the student said in a peculiar drawl, arching one dark eyebrow. "Take it, have a look. It's not like I can't find more where this came from." It was not generosity, but something more like arrogance that flashed in his smile as he held out the book to Jossley. "You can call me Hedge, by the way."

Now, Jossley snapped out of his reverie, and Hedge was standing across the table from him with that same self-satisfied grin on his face. Hedge's eyes were darker than a starless night—not a color, but an absence. As if all the light in the Library had been swallowed into them. As if Jossley himself could drown in that fathomless well of power.

At once, the study room turned upside down, and the whole world began to drip like molten candlewax. Jossley tasted copper in his mouth. His breath came in short, frenzied bursts. Was this a dream?

"It's you!" he shouted at Hedge, a thundering accusation. His voice was a crack of lightning. "*You're* the Librarian!"

So are you.

Jossley was weightless, floating down through the spire. As he descended, the space grew smaller and smaller. The spiral of bookcases was closing in on him, surrounding him.

He was disintegrating, and the Library was consuming his magic. Like the mushrooms consumed all that fell to the forest floor.

You will be one with the knowledge. You will know everything we know, wield the power we wield. Is that not what you wanted? It was. It will be.

The Library creaked and heaved, the great ribs of the building expanding and contracting with surges of pulsing magic. Jossley looked down at his hands, and scrawls of ink were crawling upward from his fingertips. Long lines of words were winding up his arms like vines, unfurling small gilt leaves as they climbed.

"Stop!" Jossley shouted. "Wait!"

We have. We did. We waited a very long time for you, for someone of your talent. The brightest and most remarkable.

Jossley's body was dissolving into a mass of bright particles, a cloud of fireflies, a beam of light spiraling into the dark. He had become paper. He had become a dried flower, pressed between the pages. He had become a swirl of ink. He had become pure magic.

He had become a *thought*—

And then, quite suddenly, the Library was right-side-up again. Bright sunshine was streaming onto his face through the stained-glass windows. The bookshelves no longer dripped like melting wax, and the stacks looked perfectly ordinary again—in as much as an enchanted library could ever be called ordinary.

Jossley blinked. He was standing at the top of the rolling ladder in the spire, in the very aisle where he'd been speaking to Hedge earlier today.

He exhaled with relief. A dream, of course it was. It wasn't the first time he'd fallen asleep while pulling an all-nighter in the Library. He was damn lucky he hadn't plummeted to his demise from this ladder.

But as Jossley shifted his feet and looked around, he noticed immediately that something was different. He could *see* that shimmering root system, all the delicate tendrils of magic that wove through the Library and connected everything. He could *feel* the well of enchantment that they all drank from, the pulsing heart of the Library.

We are every book and scroll that has ever rested in these hallowed halls, or ever will. We are every spell that has been cast here. We are outside of time. We are one with the knowledge.

Jossley was a part of it, and it was a part of him. His own magic stretched into everything, threads of it woven through every spine and stone and shelf in the Library.

He started to step down the ladder, but the moment he moved, the enchantments surrounding him flexed and flickered. He felt the entire

Library shift with his unsteady movement, the aisles and bookcases vibrating like the connected strands of a spiderweb.

A large hardbound codex shook loose from the top shelf, and before Jossley could reach out to catch it, it tumbled over the edge. He heard it clattering down on the other side of the bookcase, its metal bindings knocking against the wood as it fell.

A moment later, there was a loud chorus of startled shrieks from somewhere below. "Whoa!" "Did you see that?" "Where'd that book come from?" "What *was* that?"

Jossley peered breathlessly over the top of the bookcase. A dozen first-year students were standing down there, crowded around the Eldest Professor. They were all wearing crisp green student blazers, star pins gleaming on their freshly-ironed ties.

"Nothing to worry about. Don't be alarmed if you see something strange in here," the Eldest Professor said, waving her hand with an unconcerned hum. "The Library can be a little temperamental sometimes until it gets to know you better."

The students huddled even closer together, linking arms as they tiptoed a little further down the aisle. They walked like they were daring each other to brave a haunted house, their frightened eyes as wide as saucers.

Only one dark-haired boy had dared to step slightly ahead of the others. There was an incongruous, awestruck grin on his face as he stared up into the Library, peering up toward the spire through his thick horn-rimmed glasses.

"Just watch your step, mind your magic, and study diligently," the Eldest Professor said. "And if you prove yourself the brightest and most remarkable… the Library might yet take a liking to you."

The Wisher of Waffle House

Chris Panatier

Stephen's belly churned as he contemplated the glob of whipped butter sitting proud and taut like an unpopped zit atop his pancakes. He'd very intentionally asked for no butter because he hated butter in all forms, and most of all ping-pong sized dollops of it served on breakfast food. Ian, Stephen's recently deceased husband, had loved the stuff: deliver unto him congealed milk in a crimped paper cup and he was yours forever.

Which gave Stephen's present conundrum the feel of a cosmic joke—as if Ian had pulled the strings from somewhere to prank his widower. Ian had been a master of taunting his mostly humorless husband until laughter was the only response—and it usually worked. The man's life's work had been the heavy lifting of turning Stephen's frown upside down. Staring at his pancakes, he felt the loss of Ian anew. *Fucking life*. It had left the butter, but taken the man.

He swiped the wet sphere of fat from atop the stack and let it plop onto the small saucer holding his side order of sausage. Then he felt bad because the butter symbolized his dead husband.

"Fuck!" he hissed, lightly hammering his fist on the table. Heads in the neighboring booth shifted in his direction, then back to their own plates as Stephen mouthed apologies. "Sorry," he added, for the sake of the butter.

Waffle House. Breakfast. The location of their first date—or to be more specific, the place they'd eaten after their first date. Stephen wasn't a fan. He was too bougie and finicky for dives and greasy spoons. For Ian, though, it was a place from his childhood. His dumb face lit up every time they slid into the almost-clean booths, while Stephen's germaphobia had him speed-pumping the sanitizer. But he'd been smitten by Ian, and even kept his opinions to himself when Ian suggested it become a yearly tradition. *Yes, of course we should do that,* Stephen had said.

Today was their fifteenth anniversary, their fifth spent apart. Stephen could almost hear Ian laughing, wherever he was, as he watched his husband dutifully carry out their tradition while hating every butter-sheened minute. And hate it Stephen did, but only because of how fresh the loss felt when he stepped into the place and sat down across from his husband's colossal absence.

Truth be told, he was tired of grieving. Time was supposed to make things better. It hadn't.

The waiter returned, a free-spirit type with green eyeshadow, black nail polish, and an apron made to look like a Dalek from *Doctor Who*. Stephen read her nametag. *Kelli*. She eyed the butter.

"Oh my gosh, you asked for no butter. I'm so sorry. I apologize. I'll get you a new stack, alright?" She reached for his plate with a tattooed arm.

"No—no, that's alright," said Stephen, smiling wide but with his mouth closed like he always did—a habit he'd had since his adult teeth came in crooked. Teeth that Ian, of course, loved 'for their Dickensian character.' "It's not a big deal," said Stephen, making a show of slathering the pancakes with syrup. "Nothing a little sugar can't cover up, right?"

"Okay. Sorry again, those will be on me."

Stephen waved his hand. "Nonsense." Hoping to change the subject from pancakes, he pointed to her forearm. "I like your tattoos."

"Ah, yeah?" She turned her arm up as if checking to see if she still had them.

He pointed to a cartoon dragon flexing its bicep, which was tattooed with a classic silhouette of a woman. "What's that one?"

"The dragon with the girl tattoo. Get it?"

He chuckled. "That's hilarious, actually."

"Thanks, dude."

Ian had a tattoo. A delicate outline of a bird on the back of his middle finger. *A bird on his bird.* Funny guy. Ian had wanted them to get matching birds, but Stephen had been a stick-in-the-mud. Now he regretted his churlishness. There was no redoing the past. He mused, "I wish I had a tattoo."

"It's never too late," said Kelli, darting off for the kitchen.

He felt a lump in his throat. Ian had really wanted him to get that stupid tattoo, but Stephen had been vain about his beautiful, unmarred skin. And for what? How Ian ever stayed with him—

He tried clearing his throat, but the object was stubborn. It wasn't a lump of sadness at all.

He grunted. The thing didn't budge. It wasn't phlegm and it couldn't be food. He hummed loudly to break it up. Something solid. Substantial. He realized then, with a surprising degree of serenity, that his airway was blocked.

He wasn't about to involve the Waffle House staff or the other customers. He wouldn't suffocate and be the guy who died a pancake death at the Waffle House, memorialized forever as a meme. *Memorialized—oh no!* He couldn't drop dead in the Anniversary Booth! He lurched from the table, determined to zombie shuffle outside where he could die in the parking lot like a normal person.

The thing wasn't stuck, though. It was moving. Up and up his throat. He braced against the table, urging it to make its way fast before he passed out and went headfirst into breakfast.

The object climbed, hitting the back of this throat, then his tongue, and finally, with a rush of air, the cavern of his mouth. He sat back into the booth, then calmly brought his hand to his face and let the thing roll out into his palm, then hid his hand in his lap.

He scanned the room. No one was watching. Down in the shadow of the table, he opened his fingers.

An egg. Small. Blue and speckled. Was it robins that laid those? He wiped it clean with a napkin and brought it into the light. While tiny, it had enough weight to let him know there was something inside.

He dug into his jacket pocket and found his phone, switched on the flashlight. Back under the table he pressed it up against the egg, trying to make it glow like a jack-o-lantern. What did they call that? Candling?

But this egg didn't glow. It seemed solid, totally opaque. He leaned down and got close, trying to make out anything that might be inside. Nothing presented itself. No baby bird fetus. No eye spot. He shook it. Nothing.

He pocketed the phone and quickly, surreptitiously, tapped the egg on the side of his plate. Some of the shell broke away—far more easily than that of a normal egg. It was like the candy shell on an M&M.

Kelli appeared holding a second plate of pancakes. "I brought these just in case, okay?"

Stephen cleared his throat. "No, really, I'm good."

"Look: I feel bad about the butter. And they make these things by the ton back there. It's no problem."

"These right here are enough. Please, it's okay."

"Maybe you change your mind. And these are fresh." She set the plate across from him. Stephen's mind briefly flashed to Ian, grinning wide as he relished his good fortune in bonus flapjacks.

"Sure. Okay," said Stephen. "Thanks."

Kelli's eyes flicked to the egg. "Hey, is that one of those Cadbury eggs?"

"Um, yeah—well, not Cadbury, but something like them, I guess."

"You usually bring along your dessert for breakfast?"

"Not especially," he answered. "I found it in my pocket."

"Mm, pocket treasure. I'll refresh that coffee!" She galloped off.

Stephen eyed the egg, then leaned over and sniffed it. Smelled like chocolate. That cheap, waxy kind just like from Easter. He imagined Ian, seated opposite, saying *Go on, you big baby, eat it. You know you're curious.*

So he did.

It tasted like it smelled, an unremarkable piece of grocery store candy. But also: what the fuck was going on?

Kelli zigged around the counter and through the tables with the coffee pot. Stephen held out his mug in an effort to speed things up so she'd go away quicker and he could try to understand his life.

She tilted her head as the mug filled. "Oh, you're very silly."

"Hmm?"

"No tattoos, huh? Very funny."

"What?"

She leaned over and peered at the fist holding the mug. "Oh, I get it. A bird on your bird. You flip somebody off and it's a double bird with one finger. Very *meta*."

He mumbled after her as she moved to the next table.

He put down the mug and held his hand wide. There it was. The thin outline of a bird on the back of his right middle finger. "No. What the fuck. What the fuck is this?" He mashed his thumb down and rubbed, expecting it to smear away or to disappear entirely. It didn't.

He dipped his napkin in water and shrank down in the booth while trying to scrub the bird off his finger. It didn't come off. Didn't even fade. He bent over and inspected it. Legit. A real tattoo. "What in the hell?" He tried to act normal, but in all truth, he was quickly going insane.

Okay, he thought, *how had this happened?* He broke down the preceding minutes. He'd complimented Kelli's tattoos, reminisced about Ian's. Then expressed regret that he hadn't gotten one too. No, no—he hadn't done that. He hadn't just expressed regret. *No: he'd wished for a tattoo.* Literally said, *I wish I had a tattoo.*

And now he had one. He popped his cheeks with his palms and reassessed. The bird remained. Was he some kind of Waffle House genie coughing up wish eggs? *Okay,* he thought, *okay, fuck it.* Only one way to truly know. So he made another wish.

The second lump was much smaller than the first, barely choking him at all. He spat it into his hand, small and plain brown. It looked like a hummingbird's egg, barely the size of a Tic-Tac. A tiny egg for a tiny wish. He tossed it in his mouth, chewed, and swallowed. Then he watched as a perfect ball of butter emerged from the center of the pancakes sitting in Ian's spot.

"Ohmygodohmygodohmygod."

Make a wish and he would cough up the egg that granted it.

Was he hallucinating? Was it some sort of drug flashback? There had been a time. He looked around the restaurant. "Ian?"

Kelli walked by and stopped, eyed the previously unbuttered pancakes, and scrunched her brow. Stephen shrugged.

Stephen speed-walked to his car and called in sick to work. At home, he locked the doors and drew the shades over the windows. He washed his hands, changed soaps, and rewashed. The tattoo remained. He compared it with pictures of Ian's. It was identical, except that Ian's had been on his left hand with the bird's head angled to the right. Stephen's was on his right hand with head angled to the left. A matching pair.

He paced on the area rug Ian had picked out, then resolved to try again. It had only happened twice—something like that could be a weird coincidence. Three times would be a streak. Undeniable.

He stood in the center of the room and stared at a bouquet of dead flowers on the kitchen table. Then with a sorcerer's flourish, he threw his arms wide and wished them back to life.

He cleared his throat to make way and waited. But there was no lump, not so much as a layer of phlegm. No egg. He let his arms fall to the side. Maybe he was going crazy. Maybe there was no Ian. Maybe he was becoming Ian.

Or maybe it was a matter of location.

Stephen cursed under his breath as he slid into the booth the following morning. Oh, Ian would be laughing his ankle socks off right about now. Waffle House two days in a row. But maybe the joke was on Ian—he'd had to wait until after he was dead to get Stephen to do it.

Hoping to get on with things without having to first order any food, Stephen quickly tried to decide on a wish.

"Didn't expect to see you two days in a row!"

It was Kelli. She'd snuck up. Coffee was pouring before he could say no.

"What'll it be? Or do you need time to peruse our extensive menu?" She drew her hand over the laminated page like a game show host revealing a prize.

"Coffee is all for now, actually. Thanks."

"'Kay, just lemme know." And she was off.

Stephen swiped the menu back and forth over the table. Ian used to do that all the time, and it had driven Stephen nuts. Now here he was doing the same thing. God, he missed him.

Okay, a wish. No more parlor tricks. This time, it would be a wish for answers.

I wish I understood what is going on.

A lump, bigger than before, worked its way up. For a moment Stephen thought it might get stuck, but it pushed fully into his mouth. He didn't bother spitting it out to examine it; just chewed and swallowed. Then immediately, his wish was granted. And the answer was:

Location, location, location. *This* Waffle House. Its significance to Ian meant that the afterlife was close—closer than in any other place. Being nearby let him communicate—but only in the medium of the afterworld, which apparently was wish fulfillment. Ian could bundle them, send them across—but only if a wish was made in this one special place. The wish delivery system was customizable, with the eggs being an obvious Ian flourish. It was a breakfast place, after all, and Stephen's husband wasn't going to let a little death get in the way of his never-ending quest for thematic continuity.

"I don't want your magic eggs, you prick. I want you," Stephen mumbled.

His heart jumped a little. Was there a limit to his ghost-husband's powers? What if he wished…bigger?

Stephen eyed Kelli as she moved down the bar, cleaning up the dishes from a trio that had just left. He made a wish—a big wish—and an egg soon followed. He chewed and swallowed as quickly as he could. It was a lot of chocolate for one morning.

Kelli bussed the last plate and stopped moving completely, as if she was a computer glitch, frozen on the screen. Then she gasped and looked around. Stephen tried to appear uninterested.

Beneath the plate was a pile of bills. Kelli gathered them together and shuffled them from one hand to another, counting, but Stephen already knew the number. Ten thousand dollars.

It had worked. Ian could deliver on the big wishes too. Stephen knew what he wanted to do next. He even thought he could feel Ian encouraging him. *Go ahead,* he imagined hearing. *You can do it. What is it you want more than anything in the world?*

Stephen took a deep breath. *I want you. That's my wish. I want you back.*

A sensation of fullness began deep within his chest and moved upward, swelling into the base of his throat. But quickly, there was trouble. The egg was massive. And of course it was. Resurrecting someone wasn't the same as asking for ten large!

As it edged slowly up and cut off his air, Stephen chastised himself for his idiocy. He straightened his torso and tried to relax, to give the wish an unmarred path out and into the world. It had to be the size of a real chicken egg! Bigger, even. There was no way he was getting it out. He was going to choke on the wish and be just as dead as Ian!

Fuck!

He flew from the booth, hands around his neck, mouthing silent pleas for help. He spun around. Where were all the customers? Kelli was in back on the phone, telling her mother how someone had tipped her ten thousand dollars. He stumbled to the counter, propping himself up on a stool and slapping at the cake stand, trying to make it crash to the floor. *Kelli, turn around! Look and you'll see me dying!*

Dying! Dying! He was dying!

Then a pair of arms wrapped around his middle, came together at his belly button, and smashed in toward his diaphragm. It was the hardest he'd ever been punched in his life, but the egg blasted up his throat and into his mouth. He doubled over and gagged it out, letting it fall to the floor broken in a puddle of bile and phlegm.

Coughing, sucking air, he experienced a bright and sudden clarity. He saw how stupid, how greedy he'd become. He'd let his grief for Ian get the best of him. Grieving was a long process and he'd tried to cut corners. Bringing back the dead never worked out anyway! Catching his breath, he felt his heart stop pounding, and spun around to thank his rescuer.

"Morning, Stephen," said Ian. "I knew you hated Waffle House, but I didn't think you hated it *that* bad."

"Ian?" Stephen smashed into him, pulling his body close, becoming one with his warmth. And he was warm. And as real as he'd ever been.

Stephen's eyes filled with joyous tears. The rest of the world seemed to vanish. He was too happy to think about anything else. "Want to sit in our booth and have anniversary breakfast? I know it's a day late, but who cares?"

"That'd be my favorite thing in the world," said Ian.

Kelli came around, winked at Ian, and took their orders. For Stephen, two eggs and toast. For Ian, a large stack with extra butter. When the food came, Ian made a show of coating every inch of his pancakes, and for once, Stephen didn't care. He welcomed it. Buttered pancakes were back. They were back forever.

They ate and talked just like old times. Stephen told Ian he'd been trying to be less of a curmudgeon. Ian told Stephen what Heaven was like—but the words sometimes didn't make much sense to Stephen. Ian's vocabulary was different, occasionally slipping into a strange vernacular, like he was using a new language when describing the afterworld. Something about the exchange bothered Stephen, but he couldn't put his finger on it.

Kelli topped their coffees and they clinked mugs. "Happy anniversary, sweetheart," said Stephen.

"Happy anniversary, darling," said Ian. "And many more."

Stephen put the mug to his lips, but something made him stop. He returned it to the table and looked across to Ian. "I never ate the egg."

Ian swallowed a gulp of coffee and gently set down his mug. "You didn't."

"But you came back. How, if I didn't eat the wish to make it come true?"

"I'm sorry, love. Your wish didn't come true."

"But it did. I wished to have you back! You came and you saved me!"

"I didn't come to you, Stephen. You came to me."

"What?"

He took Stephen's hand. "I wanted to come back." Ian's eyes flicked to the bar, where a scene unfolded quietly, like a TV show playing with the sound off. Kelli shooting around the counter, seeing a body on the floor—Stephen's body—and screaming, yanking her phone out and dialing 9-1-1, then rolling him over and starting CPR.

"No, I—" said Stephen, standing from the booth, which was lit in a twinkling golden light. "But you came. You did the Heimlich maneuver and saved me."

"I didn't, Stephen. I welcomed you here in the only way I knew that would spare you the shock of what really happened. I'm so sorry." His face was drenched in tears.

Stephen took him into his arms to feel him, how real he was. "I'm actually dead?"

Ian nodded against Stephen's shoulder. "You made an impossible wish. I didn't know there were impossible wishes. And I didn't know the cost of asking for the impossible to come true."

"It's not your fault. I knew better. The eggs got bigger with the wishes. I rolled the dice. I missed you too much."

"Heaven is Hell without you here," added Ian.

Stephen looked around. Everything faded to black—all but the solitary booth, bathed in a numinous glow.

Ian gestured to it. "Should we finish our breakfast?"

They slid into the booth on the same side together. Ian gobbled his pancakes. Between bites he said, "I'm sorry you're dead."

"I'm glad we're dead together. The food tastes the exact same."

"Well, get used to it. It's only Waffle Houses here."

"Seriously?" said Stephen.

Ian winked. "Eat up."

Under Damnable Eaves

James Bennett

"My nurse had long been tempted by a wicked spirit: but this day it was evident how she was possessed of him."

—The Private Diary of Doctor John Dee

London, 1590

There is something in the house that shouldn't be. Avis learns this on her third night at Mortlake when she hears the peculiar keening of the wind and marks the dampness on her cheeks, rousing her in the east wing servants' quarters. The night is calm as far as she can tell. The mullioned windows sealed. What reason can there be for the rain to fall inside? There's naught remarkable to the manse itself, the old place by the river. 'Tis a rambling residence behind high walls of red brick with a thatched, sagging roof, an overgrown garden and an orchard stretching to the bank of the Thames. At this hour—which must be past midnight—the neighbouring spire of St Mary's fails to assure the lass that all is good and godly under these eaves. Perhaps she's dreaming; overwhelmed by the business of watching over three neglected (and impish) children. Or the legend of its owner praps, spinning a haunting from her wonder—for here dwells none other than the royal mathematician, tutor and magician, the esteemed Doctor Dee.

"Heed me well, Mistress Follywolle," Matron Barwyk told her when they'd first rattled into Mortlake in the carriage, dispatched from the city by the physician Giffard, their employer. "Remember that this is a house of science. It won't do to go starting at… shadows. Perform your duties and speak when you're spoken to."

Then, while the matron rapped on the door with all the force to wake a giant, the lass had thought that the pox would prove the worst of her worries. But science cannot account for the small black cloud under the rafters, speckling her bedclothes with rain. Nor the little flashes of lightning that illuminate the room, the cramped space rumbling with the miniature storm. By its radiance, she marks that the adjacent bed, the one reserved for the housemaid Ann, is empty. Where can she have gone? The matron will bellow and flap should she come bustling from her own chamber, startled by the uproar and finding her charge missing. Even though Avis hasn't taken to the pale, downcast girl with whom she shares a room, she knows Barwyk's moods well enough for it to see her onto her feet, keen to seek the lass out.

"Ann? Are you about?"

Only the cloud answers her, another illogical boom. On an ordinary eve, Avis would never have thought to go wandering into the house, for such has been forbidden after dark. But matters seem far from ordinary and fain to be out from under it, she hastens into the parlour, shoeless and without a lamp.

Avis is in the library when she hears the weeping, faint under the gale. The gloom makes tracing its source troublesome. High shelves line the chamber, most stripped bare. She's heard that during the Doctor's travels in Europe, some of his pupils had ransacked the house, making off with valuable tomes on strange rituals and long-lost tongues, along with several scientific instruments. The scant furniture suggests monetary straits, though it's neither the evidence of theft nor penury that arrests her, trembling there in her nightgown. Some of the few remaining books—leather bound incunabula, crumbling pamphlets, the odd scroll—are afloat in the space, their gold-leafed pages fluttering like the wings of absurd, indolent birds. Remembering Barwyk's advice, Avis steals a breath and knocks them out of the way as she goes. A fresh copy of Spenser's *Faerie Queene,* a dogeared *Doctor Faustus* and even one of Dee's own, the *General and Rare Memorials Pertayning to the Perfect Arte of Navigation* with its righteous claims of royal conquest and empire. Forging her own passage through the library, she comes to the door of the study at the far end, detecting, with heart thudding, the origin of the sorrowing.

Oh, but Barwyk would see her whipped if she caught her here, kneeling with an eye pressed to the keyhole. But Avis doesn't tarry long.

Once she's spied the scene on the other side of the door, lit in the glow of a hearth, the lass is off and running. Fleet she goes into her quarters, accompanied by tears of her own.

Shuddering, Avis pulls the blanket over her head and storm and books be damned.

The morrow affords Avis no time to investigate further. She knows better than to ask questions. Did she imagine the whole affair, some nightmare brought on by her unfamiliar lodgings? And Ann, she finds, has returned to her bed, tousled, clothed in her shift, but too dour for Avis to risk pressing the girl. The house, it seems, has returned to the expected, no thunderhead in the room and the books in the library scattered on the floor, several smeared with mud. Barwyk appears not long after dawn to urge the lasses to their duties. The master, she says, has been taken abed, his aches and pains, the cramps in his legs a regular occurrence. 'Tis why Avis is there, she's reminded. Madam Dee is occupied with the newborn Madimi and the two-year-old Theodore, the latter confined to his crib due to ague and a bloodshot eye, and under the fastidious care of the matron. Someone must watch the other children.

"Pray no tardiness, Follywolle." It's plain that the matron, hands on her considerable hips, already foresees cause for scolding. "Break fast swiftly and go at once to the nursery."

There are three of them awaiting in the chamber at the rear of the house. Arthur, the eldest at eleven years, seems the most aware of her lesser position and declares upon sight of her that he wishes to play brickbats in the garden. Rowland, aged nine, chuckles behind his hand, a muss-haired conspirator. Michael, the four-year-old, clings to Avis's skirts from the off, plainly glad of attention in the bustling house. Neglect shows in their ragged garb and, eager to start on a happy footing, the lass consents to the jaunt outside, ignoring Arthur's triumphant grin.

For an hour or so, all seems pleasant enough. The older boys amuse themselves by chucking stones at the garden wall, Avis wincing at the noise and praying that the neighbour, the lordly Sir Herbert, is not at home. Michael decapitates daisies and chases after bees, giggling in the August sun. All is well with the world. At least, the war with Spain is elsewhere, privateers hounding treasure fleets in the Atlantic and the great statesman Raleigh having sent a ship to the newfound colony on Roanoke Island, there to answer reports of tribal hostilities. None of these matters concern a young nursemaid in Mortlake, but the memory of last night's prying forbids Avis much ease. Why had Ann stood there in the study, naked, weeping and daubed in glyphs? What was the strange mirror that the old man, Doctor Dee, had sat hunched over at his desk, staring into a circle of blackest glass? It had been no more than a glimpse, some bizarre ceremony after dark, but enough to enlighten Avis to the fact that all is not proper in the house.

"*Ow!* Watch where you throw, harecop!"

"I never! I -"

"I give not a fart, Rowland. Don't—"

Another thwacking sound shakes Avis from reverie and returns her attention to the children. At once, she's up and running, scooping Michael up from the grass. There's no time to linger, question the marvel unfolding by the wall. Instinct propels her forth, calling to the brats to follow her.

"Quickly now. Into the house."

Arthur, bloodied, looks at her wide-eyed. Rowland requires no encouragement. Avis yells at the eldest boy, then cries out when a sharp object bites into her shoulder and at terrific speed. Somewhere, she hears glass shatter. One of the parlour windows, she thinks. The sky above remains clear and blue. St Mary's looks on, impassive.

"God's wounds! Hearken at once!"

Avis had promised herself that she wouldn't raise her voice at the children. The moment demands it.

Followed by the boys, she hurries for shelter, the lot of them pelted by stones.

Matron Barwyk is most displeased. Nor is she inclined to heed the babbling of a nursemaid, trembling beside her in the kitchen. Arthur and Rowland shiver and sob, the both of them bleeding from several parts. Michael stands gawping, shaken. While Barwyk dabs at the boys with a damp rag (and none too gently), 'tis plain that she's vexed at having been dragged away from her duties, and by a fool of a lass who cannot even mind three children in a garden. When Avis attempts to mount a defence—for who could foresee an invisible assailant, let alone withstand such an assault?—Barwyk thrusts a tray into her hands, one laden with bottles and a warm bowl of ale.

"Take the old man his possets, for midday is nigh," the matron tuts. "Knock thrice on the chamber door and then withdraw. Speak to no one."

If Avis thinks it the worst of the strife, she's soon disabused of the notion. Upstairs, outside the bedroom in question, she all but drops the tray at the door to hearken the quarrel behind it. Shoulder smarting, she places the medicines on the floor, a fist raised and frozen. Should she dare intrude?

"… naught but an addled old fool," a woman, Jane, is saying. "Did not Kelley tell you to forgo dabbling with the glass? Look what you've brought down upon us."

Mumbling answers this, gruff and perhaps a little ashamed. Jane, a spirited if sullen woman, seems to possess the fire to fight; she's at least a score of years younger than her husband.

Dee parries his wife from the bed.

"Then find the fitting spell and close it," snaps Jane. "You swore to keep the shadow at bay. Would you risk our younglings, even after we've acquired the maids? The bargain was meant to spare us and restore you to health. Oaf."

Further mumbling. Harsher this time.

"Angel, my arse. Your Maherion is no angel. Why, the milk sours and the halls are far from sound at night. Shadows stalk the stairway. Paintings fall. Why, did not Rowland near drown in the river last month? And only this morn I found the babe on the floor, plucked from her crib and knocking her head. There is something in the house that shouldn't be!"

Avis, privy to the thundercloud, the books and the flying stones, could unhappily confirm this. All is not well in Mortlake. But 'tis not her place, she knows, and the old man is grumbling again.

"I can see that Ann ails." Jane sighs, her exasperation at its height. "Wickedness is upon her. Oh, how you've erred in the exchange. Prithee amend it or I and the children shall be gone!"

There's cursing then. And footsteps, heading for the door.

Before Madam Dee can reach it, Avis turns and hastens down the stairway. Sooner face Barwyk than risk discovery.

Aye, sooner face the fires of Hell.

September comes around before Avis marks any further oddities. Aside from the ones she's grown accustomed to, that is. The cold patches in the house at night. The way that the shadows pool in places, shifting and thick as tar. On occasion, she seems to catch figures in the corner of her eye, darting this way and that, their serpentine tails weaving. Their eyes, pinpricks of ruby, tell Avis that they're not mice. Candles do not behave as they should, snuffing or leaping at unexpected moments. Smells come and go, midden-sweet and sulphurous. And on some nights, she wakes to find Ann absent—not that she wishes to follow the girl again. Instead, she remembers how much she needs the shillings (and any future appointments); there's an ailing mother and a house to keep in London. In light of that, Avis presses her face to her pillow and does her utmost to see naught at all.

But doubts linger. "Acquired the maids" strikes her as a strange turn of phrase. As does "Maherion" (there's no servant in the house of that name). "Angel," she thinks, is to be expected; the rumours surrounding the Doctor claim that he converses with the seraphic realm, drawing on the wisdom of heaven for omens and prophecies, though there are just as many who call him a fraud. Plays in the city have begun to mock and scorn magicians. Despite the Queen's favour, the old man is not as well-regarded as he once was. Still, 'tis a mystery. And one that her duties, the washing, the cooking, the minding of children (two of which have decided that a lass her age holds no authority at all and lead her to the feet of apple trees to harangue them in the branches far more often that she'd like) leave her little time to dwell.

Then, one afternoon when Barwyk has summoned the mites for their monthly bathing, Avis wanders outside for a breath and encounters the curious Ann. The lass, garbed in a frock that's seen better days, is sitting on the edge of the well by the orchard. Her hair, lank and fair, hangs in her face. Even when Avis draws near, giving an innocent whistle to announce her presence, the girl keeps staring at her hands.

"Good morrow, Ann. Is it not a pleasant…?"

The paint on the girl's skin, whorls of ochre and gold, checks Avis's greeting on her tongue. Ann is studying the glyphs, it seems, symbols on her palms and wrists that bear no resemblance to any letters Avis knows.

Like a startled rabbit, Ann's head snaps up at the intrusion.

"He'll not have me, I tell you. I shall never be his."

Despite the crawl of gooseflesh and the force of her words, Avis continues, her arms spread in consolation.

"Oh, Ann. Of what do you speak? Tell me what vexes you, I pray you."

"Pray all you like. It'll not save you."

"Save me from what?" But Avis suspects 'tis a *who* and finding no idle talk in the girl, she presses her enquiry, keen to unravel the riddle. "Do you mean the Doctor?" The memory of Ann stood naked in the study, weeping well after midnight, adds queasiness to her discomfort. "Perhaps we should speak to Matron Barwyk and -"

Ann is weeping today too. Tears streak her ashen face. Like a crack in the day, she gives a laugh, shrill and full of scorn.

"He'll not have me, do you understand? *Never!*"

With that, and a morbid grace that permits no intervention, Ann shoves herself backwards, swift over the lip of the well.

The following days hold drudgery and gloom. Whatever shadow lies over the house dwells in Avis now too, a black flood seeping in through the cracks and her fears adrift upon it, all she knows as solid and true. Matron Barwyk, of course, had much to say about the mishap in the orchard. Thank the Lord, the girl was saved, albeit narrowly. Hearing Avis scream, Barwyk had come running, holding her skirts, her cheeks aflame. And Dee himself, plucked from his books in the study and hobbling across the sward, his long-robed and bony form leant precariously over the well to drag a waterlogged and shivering maid from the depths. "Wicked creature," he'd spat, though whether he'd meant the lass or otherwise, Avis could not say. Then, as Ann had spluttered on the ground, how the old man had shaken his newly appointed nursemaid, barking questions into her face that held the sting of blame.

"What did she tell you?" and, "Why not stop her?"

Avis, wide-eyed and sobbing, found she had naught to tell him. It had been left to the matron to prise the old man away from her, Dee coughing and trembling, and lead him to his bed. No one had asked how Avis fared. No one spoke of it later either. The tedious routine of the house had continued with barely a hitch for a good two weeks afterwards.

Then, on a Friday, with the matron seemingly satisfied that Avis grasped the tasks required of her, Barwyk had collected her pay and returned to London. Whether due to another position or from distress was never made clear.

"We thank you for your service," Jane had told her on the step. "For bringing us the girls as requested. Pray bring us more, if need be."

The matron, keen to embark the carriage, had given a grunt in return, the matter plainly onerous, some necessity the cause of which Avis couldn't determine. *Aye, acquisitions,* she'd thought, though why the word should hold such a timbre of dread was beyond her. All Barwyk had left her with was a stern instruction to watch over Ann now as well, a command that had come down from the Doctor. Without so much as a fare-thee-well, Avis had found herself alone in the house. And any relief she might have felt soon evaporated when she'd glanced at Ann's wan and expressionless face, the girl sat slumped on her bed as usual.

At night, the shadows thicken. Birds unlike any Avis has heard squawk in the trees outside. There are footsteps too, thumping on the floorboards in the parlour, long after all have gone abed. Avis, shivering under her blanket, dreams of flaming ships and great circles of black glass, the echo of laughter through empty halls.

There is something in the house that shouldn't be. And she is one of them.

'Tis the second to last night of September when Avis awakens to chanting. In the stillness of the room, the wind howling afresh outside, she sits up and rubs her eyes. Ice creeps into her veins when she marks the strangeness of the words—Latin, she thinks, or something much like it—and their loudness, resounding over the gale, is enough to drag her upright. The bed beside her, she sees with a jolt, lies empty. Ann has gone to the study again. To whatever ritual unfolds there.

Wickedness is upon her.

Avis herself would never have followed, adopted her habit of sinking under the blanket and rocking herself back to sleep, if not for the presence in the room. For a moment, she thinks it a cat, though Dee claims he is not fond of the creatures. Small, slick and ruby-eyed, it watches her from the top of the cupboard. Does she catch the flick of a tail, slender and arrow-tipped? The glint of moonlight on little teeth, each as sharp as a razor? The lass does not tarry to investigate. Even as the thing leaps and scuttles, favouring the shadows, Avis slips into the parlour and the library beyond. The books, she finds, all lie open on the floorboards, their worn pages impossibly ablaze, the gilded illustrations, the complex diagrams, the strange, crabbed letters aglow with some unearthly force. Breathless in the radiance, a spectre compelled to the source of its summons, Avis makes for the study door.

Oh, but she'll have an end to this. Unravel the riddle even if the sight puts out her eyes! Muttering a prayer, Avis kneels to peer through the keyhole, repressing a cry when the portal creaks open a degree, affording her a view of the room beyond.

The maps on the walls, the trinkets on the shelves, the gleam of a bronze armillary sphere—none of these visions compare to the chaos awaiting her. At his desk, the Doctor sits, hunched over and bellowing his charms, his frail figure shaking in his robes. 'Tis plain what spurs his commands, dread and panic trembling in his voice. Before him rests the mirror, the polished circle of obsidian, into which the old man barks. The speculum, that damnable eye, has far exceeded the bounds of its shaping. Shadows coil from the relic, thick and weaving into the room. The tendrils lick the shelves, the scrolls and the relics there, around phial, globe and skull. Lamps flicker in the brume, their flames far too long for their wicks, each tongue blue and crackling. Some, Avis spies with a quickening heart, blacken the beast suspended from the rafters, a stuffed, scaled animal from some distant land that she will never see.

But it is not the only one suspended. In the middle of the room, naked, glyph-daubed and moaning, the maid Ann hovers. Borne on the air, her toes a foot off the rug, she spreads her arms to the invocation underway. Under her locks, all wreathing as if submerged, her eyes are white, rolled up in her skull. Foam speckles her parted lips, her senses lost to the spell. The symbols on her limbs, her breasts and brow, shine with the same effulgence that Avis encountered in the library. The shadows from the glass seek Ann as a focus, the evident draw in the study, twisting like serpents about her, swathing her flesh in black.

Avis gasps, sinks down in the doorway. Who can say what business is afoot, arcane and sinful? Or what the Doctor is about, whether striving to seal the power in that lightless portal or invite it, the unfathomable words blasting from his throat. *Oh, how you've erred in the exchange.* Rumour has been given flesh, dashing all doubt aside. But 'tis then that the snippets Avis has gleaned in the house threaten to slide into place, chilling her to the bone. The girl, Ann, has been employed for more than mere sweeping and dusting, hanging here and anointed like an offering, a fact too stark to deny.

Nor does she owe the girl salvation, an obligation to risk her own neck. Nevertheless, the sight appalls her. Fright draws her gaze once more to the mirror, the brimming mouth of black. In the depths of the glass, a surface that reflects naught of the room, Avis spies the unmistakable ripple of flame. And she meets the gaze of the eyes within, holding the fury of the same. Madam Dee, she knows, has spoken true. Whatever lurks there, whatever waits, it is no angel.

Maherion.

Calling on the Lord above, just as the Doctor calls to the darkness, it is sheer mortal terror that forces Avis onto her feet. With a cry, she crashes into the study, lunging for the airborne girl. Before she can think to check herself, reckon on the danger, Avis grabs for Ann's legs and yanks her from the gyring shadows.

"Nay! Nay! Foolish wench!"

The old man's outrage rings in her ears as Avis scurries for the parlour. Events in the study had unfolded in quick succession, a fraught, frantic blur. The girl, Ann, had spluttered and vented a wail, shaken from her godless trance. She'd fallen from the air like a windfall apple, one as much ripe as poisoned. Then, in a flash, Ann was on her feet, bolting from the chamber. Smoke coiled, reaching but empty-handed. Distantly, deep in the glass, a tremendous roar had shaken the room, a voice filled with the fury of the pit. The pained echoes of denial. It proved enough to spin Avis on her heel—she'd not tarry to face the magician—and pursue Ann into the house.

"Wait, blast you. We must away."

Aye, away, thinks Avis. *Away from these hellish shadows and the evils they hide.*

Through the library she goes, her lungs fit to burst in her haste. The books, she sees, are all aflame, miniature braziers on the floor. Pillars, bright, splutter from the pages, singing her frock, her hair. Shapes, dark and slick, cavort about the room, leaping from chair and chest, swinging on the drapes. Nevertheless, the Doctor gives chase, stumbling in her wake.

"Come back here, scullion. Come back at once!"

Avis will not heed him. Instead, she ducks down a corridor and bursts into the kitchen, the room a cavern of darkness and stone, the night pressed against the windows. Here, panting, she slews to a halt, pots clanging from the table. Bruised, shaken, Avis feels naught of it when she spies her quarry. The poor lass, Ann, stands shuddering in the gloom by the stove, her eyes orbs of alarm.

If Avis has come to her aid, the girl seems not to gauge it. Nor does she thank her. Moonlight flashes on the blade in her hand, a carving knife doubtless recovered from the surface behind her. At her would-be saviour's approach, she lashes out, slashing the air. She'll not let Avis draw closer.

"Swore it, I did," she says, with the same wild glee as she had in the orchard. "He'll not have me. Ever."

"Ann!"

Too late, the warning comes, the plea raw in her throat. Suspicion lingers between them, along with a throttling dread. And the two of them have never been friends. She laments it then, the fact of it. Perhaps there was more she could've done. A kind word. A squeezed hand. But the girl had seemed so distant. So... *lost.*

Maddened by fright, whatever sorcery she's been subjected to, Ann gives Avis a grin.

Then she brings the blade to her neck. Draws it across her throat.

Blood sprays, splashing on the tiles. The knife clatters, spinning across the floor, a judgement at Avis's feet. Her strings cut, the girl slumps, a ragged sack spilling its goods, the bright crimson stuff of her.

A ritual by her own hand.

Outside, the night is chill. The wind plays havoc with the orchard. St Mary's looks on unmoved. Ahead, the trees weave a riddle, the Thames glittering beyond, a strew of a thousand silver pieces. It reminds Avis that she's in her nightgown, her feet bare, exposed to thistle and stone. Her flesh prickles, a matter that does not belong to the weather. Where can she go from here? Giffard, she knows, will hear no ill of his illustrious client. And Barwyk brought the lasses here, rattling into Mortlake in the carriage. There's naught to suggest the matron's collusion in such strange, diabolical acts. Naught to disprove it.

Shillings aside, the threat of penury in London, she also has the children in mind. Wayward or no, a lingering sense of duty draws her gaze up to the windows, the mullioned glass betraying no sign of wakefulness despite the uproar in the study. Can Avis rightly leave them behind, proud Arthur, chuckling Rowland, the flower-stamping Michael and the babes? God will not look kindly on such…

Her hesitation costs her dear. The old man emerges from the house, his shadow falling over her. Wheeling, she finds him mere steps away, his tall, thin form atremble and his cap askew.

"What have you done?" says he.

He raises his palms. The leavings of Ann, she sees. He has blood on his hands, and in more ways than one. And she'd ask him the same, the purpose of his ritual, the shadows in the house and the black glass, but such knowledge, she thinks, will bring its own terrors. Avis has seen enough this night.

There's another shadow then, falling over them both. A figure between the trees.

"A curse upon thee, conjurer. A vessel was promised me, one of flesh and bone. I had me a mind to go walking, explore the lands hereabouts. How they reek of plague and sin. All ripe for the reaping." The shadow sighs, his disappointment plain. "Alas, the exchange has failed."

'Tis the same voice, Avis marks then: the same hollow timbre from the study. Vaporous, flame-eyed, a man regards them. Dressed he is in gentleman's garb. Or perhaps the idea of them. Wings of shadow enfold him, shifting. He is more smoke than present; the matter, she thinks, of his arrival.

"'Twas not of my doing! The lass, this meddlesome shrew, she -"

"No matter," Maherion says (for despite her dread, Avis knows it is he). "I shall keep the gifts in my keeping. And there are yet bantlings sheltered under yon roof."

"Nay! Spare the children, I beg you. Was that not our agreement?"

Dee near sobs, his hands clasped, begging the darkness that's come for him.

Then, a spark glimmers in his eyes and they fall again upon Avis.

"Look, lord! Look! Another I've procured for our trade."

The old man reaches out, his hand closing upon her—a clammy gesture of ownership as if she's naught but a prize cow brought from the market for slaughter. There's a truth in that. A bitter one. 'Tis enough to spark a need of her own. Slippery as it is in her grip, Avis is glad of the knife. Thank the stars that she plucked it from the kitchen floor, from the scene of self-destruction. And she gives no thought to kindness nor sin as she plunges the blade into Dee's arm.

As the old man crumples, Avis is away, plunging through the grass under darkened boughs. If the shadow, the daemon, thinks to give chase, then he either lacks the power or the will. Hastening towards the river and the road, she tells herself she mustn't think of the children. The night demands that she look to herself and her mortal soul with it. There is something in the house that shouldn't be, and she'll not fall foul of it.

Into the darkness, Avis goes, away from the shadow of those damnable eaves.

Thirteen Lies

Anne Corlett

It's Thursday when I come face to face with the first lie.

Well, not exactly the *first* lie. I mean, I'm not saying I'm George Washington.

Just the first one that's stood in my hallway, *judging* me.

I don't work Thursdays. Well, technically I work from home, but everyone knows what that means. You can't blame me. There's something interminable about Thursdays. They don't have the righteous martyrdom of Mondays or the false-summit cheeriness of Wednesdays. They're the post-apocalypse of the working week. The zombies have been and gone, the casualties counted, and everyone is hanging around waiting for someone to tell them what comes next.

I've never told Dan about Thursdays, which gives me a lovely, illicit slab of me-time—eight decadent hours to please myself, without feeling like someone else is thinking I should be doing something more constructive. This Thursday involves a quick—well, quick*ish*—shopping trip. I get the tube back around lunchtime, gritting my teeth against the infernal screeching that's the Bakerloo line's main feature, and trying not to think about last night's row with Dan.

A distraction comes in the form of a plastic pot being shoved in my face and rattled vigorously. I twist away from the sour tang of coins that have been grubbed from hand to unwashed hand and perform the traditional swift eye-flick, assessing the situation without engaging in anything that might encourage further overtures. The situation is an old woman who looks like she's got lost on her way to some sort of hippy commune, what with her weird knitted poncho, peaked hat and crooked walking stick.

She rattles the pot again, more insistently this time.

"Sorry." I drop my gaze to my phone. "I've got no money on me."

She'll move on now. The rules of tube engagement are clear.

Request. Refusal. Retreat.

She doesn't move.

When I risk another look up, she offers me a toothy grin. "Liar," she says, in a high sing-song voice. "Liar, liar, pants on fire."

A clammy feeling makes its way down my spine. I shoot a swift look around the carriage, but everyone is doing a convincing job of not noticing what's going on. That's London for you.

"Can you leave me alone, please?" I try to sound brisk and assertive. "I told you, I can't help you."

She tilts her head and regards me, eyes bright in her wrinkled face. "No." She says it contemplatively. "But maybe I can help you."

"I don't need any help." My voice sounds loud in the otherwise silent carriage. A woman a few seats along glances my way with a frown, but yanks her gaze away when my head starts to turn towards her. No help there, then. "I'm fine."

The woman stares at me for a long, sweaty-palmed moment, then shrugs and moves away towards the end of the carriage. I cast a furtive look that way, then blink. We're the front carriage. There's nowhere she could have gone, but there's no sign of her. I stare for a moment, then mentally file it away in the bulging Weird Stuff I've Seen in London folder. Not for the first time, I'm glad we live a bit further out, where everything is normal.

When I get home, the first lie is in the hallway, wearing my face and clothes and flicking through my post.

"Oops." It drops my bank statement. "I thought you'd gone out."

I find my voice. "Who the hell are you?"

"I'm you." There's a distinct note of *who the fuck do you think I am* in its voice and the lift of its eyebrows. "Working Thursdays. I'm just off to the office now."

I look the lie up and down and find that I'm struggling to be as shocked as I should be. Maybe some part of me always expected it to show up sooner or later. After all, they do say your lies come back to haunt you. Or is that your bad deeds?

Christ, there's a thought.

The lie grins, flaps its arms and makes a half-hearted *woooh* noise. It's my turn for a *what the fuck* expression.

It has the grace to look embarrassed. "Back to haunt you? Oh, never mind." It covers its faux pas with a glance in the mirror as it settles one of my bags on its shoulder. "Right, I'm off."

I block its way. "You can't go to the office. My boss thinks I'm working from home."

The lie shrugs. "Should have thought of that, shouldn't you?"

Then it sidesteps me and is gone.

I stand still, staring at the closed door and trying to process what just happened.

Except it didn't, did it?

I feel a lift of relief. Of course it didn't. Just like the weird old woman on the tube didn't disappear into thin air. I'm just tired and stressed and I had a funny moment. I'll set myself to *in a meeting* on the office system, and have a nice long nap.

The lie gets home just before six.

It chucks my bag on the table before helping itself to a yoghurt and sitting down with my magazine.

"Oh, don't mind me," I say from across the table. The shock of its arrival is swift-fading. Clearly, I never actually believed my own story about stress-induced hallucinations. I eyeball the lie. "Did anyone notice?"

It shrugs, not lifting its gaze from *The Importance of Honesty in Intimate Relationships* "Hardly."

I jump guiltily at the sound of a key in the door.

The lie gives me a look of cool appraisal. "Worried?"

Before I can respond, Dan appears in the doorway. He stops, his gaze flicking between the two of us. "What…" He breaks off, stares a bit more, then closes his mouth.

I make a swift decision. We need to ignore the lie. If we don't feed it with attention, it will disappear, back wherever it came from, and we can forget this ever happened.

I get up and sidle over to initiate an uncharacteristic hug. "Good day?"

Over his shoulder, I see the lie raise its eyes heavenward and disappear behind the magazine again.

"Um, yeah, it was…alright." He extricates himself. "Look…" His hand wafts in a vague gesture. "What…um…"

"It's nothing," I say brightly. "Everything's fine. Don't worry about it."

"Worry about what?" The second lie wanders in and opens the fridge. "Are we out of milk?"

"You said you'd pick some up," Dan says to me, his gaze locked on the lie.

"I'm sure I did." I know I didn't, but it's hardly our biggest problem right now.

The second lie pours itself a glass of wine, then attempts to sit on top of the first lie, who shouts and smacks it with my magazine, then shoves it onto the floor, where it sits, sipping its wine and smiling peacefully.

"Who are you?" My *ignore it and it will go away* plan didn't factor in the lies multiplying. What are they? Gremlins? "What the bloody hell is going on?"

It looks up at me with an air of faint surprise. "I'm you," it says. "And nothing's going on. Why?"

I can see the dawning of suspicion in Dan's eyes. Before he can shape a question, there's a noise like a bomb going off, and the third lie crashes through the door, losing its grip on an armful of bottles. They explode all over the floor, firing milk and shards of glass everywhere. The first lie gets up and storms out, yelling about needing some peace after a hard day at work. The second lie just sips its wine and ignores the milk trickling down its face. The third lie mutters something that sounds like *not my fault.*

"Who are you?" I ask for the third time that day.

"I'm you," the lie said, clearly surprised that I need to ask. "I bought milk."

Dan turns and gives me a long, level look.

Shit.

⌁

It was the old woman on the tube.

I reach the bedroom wall and turn back the other way. I've almost worn a groove in the carpet with my pacing.

I don't know how or why but it's the only explanation. She's put a bloody curse on me.

I make another turn.

Why me? All those other people in the carriage, and none of them noticeably falling over themselves to put money in her pot. Why pick on me?

There's a noise in the hallway, and I move to the door and crack it open, just in time to see the third lie disappearing on another shopping trip. It's been out half a dozen times already, returning with vast armfuls of what seems to be everything I've ever forgotten to pick up at the supermarket, all the time muttering resentfully about things not being on the list.

A furtive check of the flat reveals the other two lies sitting at the kitchen table, ignoring one another. Dan is in the sitting room, staring unseeingly at something on the TV. Unsurprisingly, things were a little strained after his encounter with the lies, despite me working hard to get him on board with plan nothing-to-see-here.

As I return to the bedroom, my phone buzzes with a message from James from work.

Where are you?

My stomach twists. Shit, I completely forgot.

Let's clear something up before the Anti-Fidelity Fairy gets any ideas. I'm not having an affair with James. We did have a bit of an on-and-off thing before I met Dan, but we're just friends now. And it's not as though we're sloping off alone for secret assignations. There's a whole group from work. It's just that most nights out end up with the two of us staying for one more, then sometimes one more for the road, and at the time it feels fine, but then I wake up the next morning with a cold squirm in my stomach about something he said, or the way his gaze held mine, or just the whole close-quarters, conspiratorial *feel* of it, and when Dan asks who was out last night, somehow I never mention James.

Sometimes, it's just easier not to tell the whole truth, because the truth sometimes looks much bigger than the thing it's about. Like that thing in cartoons where there's a huge, menacing shadow on the wall, but thing casting it is just a tiny mouse. Some people will always see the monster, not the mouse.

I stare at the message. I can't tell him I'm sick in case he saw the first lie in the office today.

Shit, sorry, I type. *Double-booked myself. I'm out with the girls.*

The reply comes almost immediately. *Come join us later?*

Sure. I'll message you. I've just pressed send when the door opens and the fourth lie walks in.

It stops when it sees me. "Oh. It's you."

I'm better prepared this time, and I look it right in the eye. "Yes. It's me. And you are?"

"You." The lie strolls over to my wardrobe, and starts pulling out some of the bags I've stashed there, ready to be drip-fed to Dan. *What? This old thing?* "Going out with the girls."

My stomach clenches. "Shh," I hiss. "If Dan hears…"

"I know," the lie says, sympathetically, still rummaging in my wardrobe. "Tricky, isn't it?" It takes a top out of a bag. The label is still attached. "This was *how* much?"

"It was reduced," I say, automatically.

The lie brightens. "Bargain."

There's a high-pitched buzzing in my ears as I close the bedroom door on the lie and head through to the kitchen. Dan making dinner with his back to the third lie, who is performing an inventory of the fridge. The second lie is still at the table, smiling at nothing, while the first lie is nowhere to be seen.

"Um…" I search for an opener.

"Something smells off in here." The third lie wrinkles its nose at the vegetable tray.

"It certainly does," Dan says.

I laugh uproariously.

He turns and gives me a questioning look.

"Sorry." I stop laughing. "It's just that…"

"…you're just so *funny*." The fifth lie appears from behind the fridge door. Stepping close, it gazes up at him, stroking his arm.

Dan stands very still, his gaze locked with mine.

A distraction comes in the form of the first lie wandering in and sitting down at the table. "I've done that presentation."

"Great. Have a gold star." I turn away, extract a glass from the cupboard and pour myself a dangerously large wine, just as the fourth lie appears, bright-faced and floaty in one of my recent purchases.

It strolls over and picks up the glass. As it takes a sip, a slosh of red lands on the front of my dress.

"Oops," says the first lie.

"That old thing?" The sixth lie wanders in. "It was in the sale."

The fourth lie grins and takes another slug of wine. "Don't wait up," it says, as it sashays out.

Dan stares after it, then turns to look at me.

"No," I say. "It isn't…I mean, I didn't…" I tail off, unable to think of a safe explanation that won't trigger the arrival of another lie, waving a diary full of conflicting social engagements. "Look, I…"

But Dan is already turning away. "Never mind."

The rest of the evening passes in a tense sort of dance, as the lies wander about the flat and I try to avoid them. I go to bed early, but I can't sleep. Dan follows a little while later, and we lie side by side for a little while.

"Do you want to talk about it?" He addresses his remark to the ceiling.

I roll onto my side, presenting him with my stiff back. "I've got a headache."

On the other side of the wall, I hear the seventh lie open the medicine cabinet and begin to rummage.

By Saturday, I'm about down to my last nerve.

Two more lies have joined the party, and it's getting distinctly crowded in the flat. I should probably be thankful that the third and sixth lies are out so much. The latter is decimating my credit card, returning from its constant shopping trips with armfuls of bags, all blazoned with garish *SALE* announcements.

"But it was *reduced*," it whines, if challenged, wide-eyed with incomprehension at everyone's inability to recognise a bargain. The hallway cupboard is bulging at the hinges, and piles of cropped trousers and cold shoulder tops have formed in the corner of the spare room, like sartorial stalagmites.

If it discovers Vinted, I'm done for.

Not that anyone can get at the computer, with the eighth lie in permanent residence in the office. If I stick my head round the door, it covers the screen and hisses at me to leave it alone. Yesterday, I waited until it came out to use the bathroom, then slipped in. The lie had installed a webcam and a ring light, and I tried not to think about what it might have been up to with those. When I stabbed at the keyboard, feeling like an intruder in my own home, I was infuriated to discover that it had changed all the passwords.

While I'm almost at screaming point, Dan has gone entirely the other way. He's perked right up over the last couple of days. At first, it was obvious that he was trying to make the best of things, but now he genuinely seems to be enjoying himself. Well, things aren't working out too badly for him, are they? The ninth lie has cleaned the entire flat, sorted through the pile of unopened post, done all the laundry and cancelled that TV subscription I never got round to dealing with. He only has to wonder out loud if we have a particular snack and the third lie rushes out to get it, while the fifth lie keeps dragging him into empty rooms, from which he emerges adjusting his clothes and looking faintly dazed. The last time it happened, I positioned myself outside the spare room door, and when he came out, he found me there, tapping my fingers on the wall.

"Sorry." He didn't sound all that sorry. "It's just…"

He broke off. The fifth lie had slid out of the room and was engaged in groping his arse.

I raised my eyebrows. "Am I interrupting something?"

The lie gave him a sideways smile and slipped off to the kitchen. Dan hesitated, shrugged, then followed it, leaving me grinding my teeth in the hallway.

He's in the kitchen right now, making daft jokes, playing to the crowd. The crowd are squashed round the table, tittering like a chorus of particularly sycophantic birds with the exception of the seventh lie, who is clutching its head and shovelling in another dose of paracetamol.

"We're going to need a bigger table," Dan says with a grin.

Judging from the chorus of glee this elicits, it's the funniest thing the lies have ever heard.

I ignore them and open the fridge to find about a thousand bottles of milk and nothing else.

Slamming the door, I pick up a notepad to make a list.

"We need bread," Dan says.

"Pizza," suggests the fourth lie.

"Condoms." The fifth lie collapses in a fit of self-titillation.

"I'll go," the sixth lie offers.

"Christ." The seventh lie lifts its head from its arms. "If you go, we'll be eating Poundland spam for the next month." It looks at me. "Painkillers."

Smothering a profanity, I head for the door, where I collide with the first lie, holding a copy of my CV.

I move swiftly, whipping the page out of the lie's hands. "I don't think so."

The lie folds its arms. "What's the problem? I'm just considering my options."

I make a suggestion as to where it can shove its options, and stomp over to the bin, just as someone runs past the window. The tenth lie gives me a cheery wave and disappears along the street, arms pumping, feet pounding the pavement.

"What…" I break off, suspicion dawning.

The *Hobbies and Interests* section of my CV confirms that yes, I apparently am training for a marathon.

"Everything okay?" Dan says from the table, where everyone is shuffling and scraping to make room for the first lie.

"Fine." I stalk through to the bedroom to pick up my phone.

I've had enough. I'm going to find the old woman. I'll put a few pounds in that bloody pot of hers, get her to undo whatever hocus-pocus she worked on me, and that will be the end of it.

The ninth lie intercepts me in the hallway. "Your mother called. I took a message. Do you want it?"

Oh yes, I just manage to bite back the instinctive response. *That will improve my day.*

I don't know where sarcasm falls on the spectrum of truthfulness, and I definitely do not need a version of myself skipping about the place like something from a musical, singing about the joys of mothers.

I tell the lie to shove the message in the same place as the first lie's options, then walk out of the flat and slam the door.

I spend the rest of that day underground. I ride the Bakerloo line from one end to the other, then switch to the Northern line, then the Victoria. A couple of times, I think I glimpse the old woman on another platform, but by the time I get round there, she's long gone, if it was even her at all. Once, I was absolutely sure I'd seen her a few carriages along, but when I jumped off and sprinted up the platform, there was no sign of her or anyone looking like her. As the day wears on, I start to hear things— mocking laughter right at the edge of hearing, and the faintest suggestion of a sing-song echo.

Liar, liar.

By the time Monday comes around, I've hardly slept, constantly woken by the comings and goings of the more nocturnal lies. There are whispers in the hallway, outbreaks of smothered sniggering. Doors *snick*, not furtively enough to evade my overactive hearing. My mother has left three messages. I haven't replied. No more lies have shown up, but the existing ones show no signs of moving on, instead bickering and jostling for position in the world that was once mine.

Unable to face work, I call in sick.

I think we can safely say I didn't think that one through.

As I ring off, the eleventh lie steps out of the bathroom and throws up on my feet.

"Sorry," it groans, clutching theatrically at the door frame. "Stomach bug."

Within half an hour, four of the lies are down with it, and two others are complaining that they feel sick. The ninth lie seems immune and wanders about, trying to jolly the others out of their nauseous slumps, until the seventh lie tells it to fuck off. There's a minor scuffle when the first lie decides it's going into work anyway, and I have to practically wrestle it to the ground with the assistance of the third lie. The sixth lie uses the distraction to slip out of the front door, and when I check the sideboard, my wallet is gone.

Abandoning the lies to their moaning and heaving, I spend another day chasing ghosts around the underground. When I get back, the ninth lie is on the phone.

It covers the handset and whispers "It's your mother. She thinks you're ignoring her. She's very upset." It takes its hand away to make soothing noises, then covers the mouthpiece again. "She wants to come over."

My stomach twists at the thought of my mother here, seeing the lies. That would be eleven more sticks for her to beat me with. *You should stand up to her*, Dan used to say. *You're an adult. You don't have to worry about what she thinks anymore.* But it's not that easy. Not when you spent your formative years trying not to let her see anything she wouldn't like.

"Tell her..." I try to find a safe excuse. One occurs to me. It's not exactly convincing, but then beggars can't be choosers. "Tell her I'm training for a marathon."

Another day passes. Finding the old woman has become my only obsession. Those echoes are constant now, the glimpses more frequent. It's probably a test. If I keep looking, don't give up, I'll turn a corner in the labyrinth of some underground station, and she'll be there, waiting for me.

Back home, I'm barely through the door when my phone beeps with another message from James. He's spent the last three days text-nagging me to meet up with him, until the mere sight of his name on the screen is enough to tip me into a murderous rage.

It feels like you're avoiding me. If I've done something, at least tell me to my face.

I grind my teeth together. *It's not you, it's...*

"Me," finishes the twelfth lie, reading over my shoulder.

"Shit." I jump about three feet in the air and accidentally press send. "What the bloody hell are you playing at?"

As the lie begins to sob theatrically, my screen lights up.

It's what?

For fuck's sake.

Me, I type furiously. *It's me. I'm sorry. Now please stop messaging.*

"It's all my fault," the lie wails. "Everything is always my fault."

"Oh, give it a rest," I snap, which causes the lie to collapse on the floor in a paroxysm of sobs.

This can't go on. I've got to do something, but I can't do it on my own.

Stepping over the twelfth lie, I head for the sitting room, where I find most of the others squashed together on the sofa, or lolling on the floor. There's one of those daytime TV programs on, where someone swears on their child's life that they've been faithful, does a lie detector test, then spends the rest of the show screaming that it's a set-up before confessing in the last five minutes. The lies seem to like this one—there's almost always at least one of them watching it.

"Where's Dan?" I ask.

The lies shoot each other shifty looks and don't reply.

I turn and stalk down the hallway to the bedroom, shove the door open and stride in with all the indignant confidence of the wronged. Dan is lying on the bed, eyes closed, a blissful expression on his face. Two of the lies are cavorting on top of him in an improbable burlesque display of legs and lips and tangled bodies, all to a chorus of incoherent endearments.

Stalking over, I grab the nearest lie—three? four?—by the scruff of its fluffy basque and drag it off the bed.

"Out." As I shove it towards the door, the other lie—definitely five—squeals and makes a big show of covering itself up. "Out," I repeat.

It scowls at me and doesn't move.

Dan clears his throat. "Um, maybe you better..." He tails off, jerking his head towards the door.

As the lie stomps out, the bedspread trailing around it, I kick the door shut behind it, and turn to Dan. "This can't go on."

He pushes up on his elbow. "Hang on a minute…"

"No, not that." I waft my hand in the direction taken by the lies. "Well, yes, that, but all the rest as well. I…" I tail off, looking away. I have to do this, but it's hard. I'm teetering right on the edge, and it wouldn't take much for me to pull back.

From the bed, Dan says my name, his voice low.

I shake my head, pressing my lips together. "I'm fine."

The door opens and the second lie looks in.

"Fuck off." We say it in unison.

The lie withdraws, and I turned back to Dan. "Look, I love you." We both hold our breath, but no lie appears. "I really do, and I'm so sorry. I'm going to put this right, but I need you to listen."

"Okay." There's tension in his eyes, but something else that gives me hope.

I move to the door, so that everyone can hear. "I don't work Thursdays." There's silence from the other end of the hallway. "I owe two grand on a credit card you don't know about." A couple of lies appear at the sitting room door. "I always tell you everything costs half as much as it actually did." More lies press into view. There seem to be as many of them as ever. I push on. "When I…"

The doorbell rings, cutting me off.

"I'll get it." Before I can stop it, the ninth lie is at the front door, pulling it open.

"Oh, so you're alive." My mother steps past the lie, then stops, staring at the others, crowded together in the sitting room doorway, then at me. Something flickers in her eyes—something almost guilty. She knows, I realise. About the lies. Not the ones listening at the sitting room door, but all the others I learned to tell to protect myself. Then her face hardens. "What have you done now?" She folds her arms. "It's always something with you, isn't it? It always was." There's something moving behind her, the thirteenth lie already beginning to take shadowy form. I curl my trembling fingers inside my palm. "I gave up everything for you. *Everything*. I made sure you worked hard at school, made the most of all your opportunities. I took you to museums, to *stately homes*. Nothing was ever enough." The thirteenth lie is growing clearer. It smiles, waiting for me to give it life. It knows I will, because I've done it before, over and over. *Get it over with*, that smile says. *Then everything can carry on as it always has.* My mother jabs a finger towards me. "Admit it," she says. "I was a good mother, wasn't I?"

The thirteenth lie's smile widens. It takes a step forward. The lies are moving closer too, intent upon the unfolding scene.

I open my mouth, then close it again as Dan steps up beside me and wraps his hand around mine. I look up at him and find him looking back at me, his gaze steady. As I look back at my mother, I feel a sudden loosening, like something that's been knotted about me for years untangling and falling away.

"No," I say. "No, you weren't. And you're not."

In the silence that follows, I can hear the thudding of my own heart. Then the world blurs, and when it comes back into focus, the lies are gone, and there's only my mother standing in the hallway. Except it's not my mother. It's someone else with a wrinkled face and bright, knowing eyes. A familiar phrase echoes, but the sound is softer, almost gentle.

Liar, liar.

As it fades, the old woman smiles, and then she's gone, like the lies, leaving Dan and me alone.

My heart is still beating hard, but I feel lighter than I have in years. As Dan slides his arms around me, I lean back against him. We've got a lot of talking to do, but there's time for that. For now, it's just the two of us, without the whisper and jostle of all the lies.

"Are we okay?" he asks quietly.

"Yes," I say, and it's the truth.

Hex Education

Alice James

"Eye of newt, and toe of frog,
Wool of bat, and tongue of dog,
Adder's fork, and blind-worm's sting,
Lizard's leg, and owlet's wing,
For a charm of powerful trouble,
Like a hell-broth boil and bubble.
Double, double toil and trouble;
Fire burn, and caldron bubble."
— William Shakespeare

The senior research wizard threw up his hands. His ornamental staff flew into a pile of crucibles, bounced off a startled junior druid, and came to rest somewhere under a lectern.

"What do you mean, you lost the wolf? I told you to take it for a walk and put it back in its cage."

I made a murmur of protest, but he interrupted me.

"No, don't make excuses. We're halfway through testing that new synthetic wolfsbane, and we need to submit at least one more peer-reviewed scroll before the end of solstice term! How in Merlin's name do you expect this fraternity ever to get tenure if you go releasing the test subjects willy-nilly?"

I tried to squeeze in a word, but he just held out a hand, angling the palm to my face.

"I said no excuses. You 'lost' two owls last semester, not to mention that basilisk whose hissing glands I was Botoxing. Much more of this and you can find yourself a new supervisor."

I twisted my hands together. They were stained with feverfew and newt's blood. I didn't even like killing the newts; dosing the wolf with synthetic bane had been excruciating. I'd taken it four miles into the centre of the forest and left it near a herd of plump moon deer. The scent of lemon balm and pine had been intoxicating. The two owls had been pleased to see me again.

"I didn't mean to let it go," I whispered.

A lie. I'd taken off its harness and broken the impoundment charms. I'd crushed them to powder under my feet.

"I'm sorry," I said, even more quietly.

I wasn't sorry. The wolf had pricked its ears up and sauntered into the undergrowth. I'd wanted to follow it. I felt my eyes well up.

"Oh, by Morgan's hat, don't start snivelling. Just go down to the Dean's office and order in a replacement wolf. Get a nice big one this time. And say we need it by full moon; I'm not losing funding over this, damnit."

He clicked his fingers disdainfully. The staff flew back to his grasp, and he caught it in his long, elegant fingers. Hard grey eyes, set under sculpted brows, stared into my soul for a moment... And then he turned and flounced out of the room in a swirl of cloaks and expensive robes.

I trailed back to my bench and looked down at the potion I had been making. For my thesis, I was attempting to find a cruelty-free alternative to some standard potion ingredients. A jelly of angel hair ferns, raspberry root and mallow blossoms made a perfectly serviceable substitute for eye of newt; frog toes could be easily replaced by euphorbia lobes sliced up with an obsidian blade and seasoned under moonlight with a syrup of belladonna and white baneberry. I was struggling with anything that would come close to the potency of wool of bat, but I thought that one would be the hands down winner if I managed it. I mean, goodness only knows you don't get much off a single bat, and getting them to keep still whilst shaving them is an absolute bugger.

Also, they bite.

"You shouldn't wind him up, you know."

It was the junior druid who had been quietly watching me get my dressing down. He wasn't in my research group, but we shared the hedgerow lab through some kind of funding agreement. I envied him sometimes. He always seemed to have a row of happy baby trees in front of him. No one ever asked him to go down to stores for a jar of dog tongues. Still, it could have been worse. I'd lasted only a week with my original supervisor; she'd specialised in the power of entrails in forecasting the future. She sacked me after I threw up on her scholarship student's viva exhibit of cat guts and koala spleens; potentially highly influential in seer-guided investment management, but two days fermenting in a lab cauldron and they had an even more profound effect on the olfactory senses. And my stomach, apparently.

I wasn't sorry about that either—in my opinion anyone who thought kittens and koalas were appropriate potion ingredients had it coming— but the druid was right. I wouldn't get a third supervisor in a hurry.

"Sometimes, I want to give it all up and just go home," I said miserably. "But, you know, I wanted to be the first person in my coven to graduate from uni. Get real mage status. Not be just another hedge witch."

The druid didn't reply immediately. He was sprinkling pigeon dung onto some shiny banyan saplings. He talked to them constantly. Sometimes he sang to them. I knew full well that he left the radio on for them on his days off.

"There's nothing wrong with being a hedge witch," he said. "Everyone needs love charms."

I felt my shoulders slump.

"Yes, but these days they want them in a fancy bottle," I said. "With a posh wax seal and an endorsement from an influencer on TikToccult."

He patted my shoulders.

"Fashions come and go," he said. "Maybe you can be the next big thing."

Maybe. My preliminary scroll was through its first round of reviews. I had my own SpellCast now and we were growing more subscribers; "The Vegan Witch" had a small but dedicated group of followers on heX (formerly known as Glitter). I picked up a banyan leaf and swirled it in my fingers.

"Are you going to go and sign him out a new wolf?"

I looked up at the druid. He had a smidgen of moss stuck to one cheek. He smelled slightly of pigeon dung. He was still a million times more endearing than my supervisor. I would rather have hung out with him than all the master wizards in the university.

"No," I said eventually. "He can get his own sodding wolf. That synthetic wolfsbane is a snare and delusion anyway. The wolves are only sickening because he doesn't give them enough exercise or natural light. He has no control group, and his experimental process is shoddy."

The druid laughed.

"Well then, perhaps you'd like to join me for lunch?"

I brightened up.

"I'd love that. But we have to feed the basilisk first. I let it go in the cistern beneath the Department of Sigils and Binding Runes."

"And no one's noticed?"

"You know academics: it's often said that they wouldn't notice if there was a basilisk right under their noses, and it turns out that's really true."

He put the radio on for the banyans before we left.

A Puff of Smoke

Dennis K. Crosby

Wallack's Theater, New York City—June 30, 1880

"Magic isn't real," said Alex.

"So you don't believe in it?" asked the magician.

"Have you seen the state of this world?" asked Alex with a sly grin. "Why should I?"

"Because it believes in you," said the magician, pointing to Alex's chest.

Following the gesture, Alex looked down and reached inside his jacket for the inside pocket. From it, he retrieved a bank note. Unfolding it, he saw that it was, in fact, the bank note he'd signed moments ago. The very same note the magician had taken from him and subsequently burned by candlelight. It carried no sign of molestation. Not so much as a carbon smudge.

The crowd around them erupted in astonished applause.

"Well done, good sir," said Alex, over the roar. "A little sleight of hand? Perhaps some misdirection?"

"Or, it could just be magic," said Adelaide.

"You know, you could be biased," said Alex wryly.

The trio shared a laugh, and before long, Alex joined the rest of the crowd in applause. He'd heard stories about Herrmann the Great, and, as far as showmanship went, he was indeed impressive. The magician and his wife Adelaide delivered a wonderful experience to the men and women in attendance at Wallack's. With a week that included the deaths of three former U.S. senators, people needed a distraction. The novelties of electric streetlights, railway systems, and such were titillating, but there was still much to understand about them. And while some considered those things to be magical in their own way, nothing beat a performance by a true practitioner of the art.

"What *is* your name, sir?" asked the magician.

"I actually share your name," said Alex with a slight bow.

"Ah! How wonderful," said the magician. "Then you are clearly a man of good taste and lineage."

"Questionable on both. But I appreciate the compliment."

The trio laughed again before Alex respectfully excused himself. His spot was immediately filled by scores of people wanting to meet the magician and his lovely wife, who also served as his assistant. He admired how the duo performed their show on the theater floor as opposed to the stage, giving attendees the opportunity to see everything up front—to be a part of the magic. The city, and the country, needed to believe in…something. Fifteen years removed from the Civil War, and the land was still very much divided. Still healing. If ever there was a need for magic, it was now.

Alex moved away from the crowd, just out of sight, but close enough to keep an eye on things. He pulled out a cigarette and put it between his lips while searching for his lighter. He patted his pockets, both on his pants and jacket, but found nothing.

"Dammit," he whispered.

Stepping further into the shadows, away from the crowd, Alex whispered a single word: "Incendio." The end of his cigarette began to glow red-orange. The colors grew brighter as he inhaled. After a short hold, he released the smoke from his lungs and watched the crowd through it. Within that haze, his adversary was revealed.

"Time for some real magic," he said to himself.

The cigarette fell to the ground. He stamped it out. Then Alex Frost vanished into thin air.

Three Days Earlier

"I'm sorry. You did what?" asked Alex.

"I…okay, look, maybe it wasn't the smartest move, but—"

"Not the smartest move?" Alex said loudly, before remembering they were in a restaurant with no empty seats. He acknowledged the many faces staring at him and mouthed an apology. Turning back to his dinner companion, Alex whispered, "You hid the Tears of Nyx in the baggage of a magician's assistant?"

"I had to get them here without detection. What better way than to hide them among the eclectic items of a performer?"

Alex had known Marcus Shelby for a couple of decades. Their run-ins weren't frequent, as Marcus lived across the ocean. Originally from Virginia, Marcus fled the states at the start of the Civil War. He told Alex that he'd opposed it, and how that was unacceptable in his family. He could have left for the North, he'd said, but the whole war, everything about it, left him heartbroken. So he left the continent altogether. Alex first encountered him in Seville, Spain. The adventure they shared had opened the door to a world Marcus could never have imagined.

Magic.

Sorcery.

Witchcraft.

He'd learned about things that went against all he'd been taught in school and church. Things that spoke to a world in which true evil existed. Marcus had admitted to being terrified—but only at first. His terror turned to curiosity, and that curiosity turned to passion. Before long, he had become the foremost authority on magic and the occult—at least among humans. And he found a different way to fight against injustice. Among men like Alex, magic wielders, Marcus was the ultimate ally in the battles that took place in the shadows. Battles that made the Civil War and similar campaigns look like minor skirmishes. Eventually, Marcus became known as the Concierge.

"It was not ideal, I admit," began Marcus, "But under the circumstances it made the most sense."

Marcus bore the scars of a man who'd battled evil, both metaphorical and real. His youthful look and southern charm misled many about his age. The only thing about him that spoke to his forty-five years was the weathered look in his eyes. Most saw it as maturity, or the sign of a learned and well-traveled man. But Alex knew the truth. The chiseled jawline kept slightly warm by a well-manicured beard, and smart brown hair with only a light dusting of gray, served as a mask for a man who was weary. Despite that weariness, though, Marcus continued, and Alex had trusted him every step of the way.

He was resigned to trust him now.

"We go back some time," said Alex.

Marcus acknowledged him with a nod.

"If you say that was the only way…the *best* way, then I am inclined to trust to your instincts, even though I may not like it. My apologies for the way I reacted."

"Thank you, my friend," replied Marcus. "Believe me when I say I understand your concern, and I likely would have responded similarly, were I in your shoes."

Alex raised his glass, and the pair made a light clink with the respective libations. Scotch for Marcus, a taste acquired during his year in Edinburgh, and for Alex, absinthe, because his real and metaphorical demons had razor-sharp claws.

"I still can't believe the Tears of Nyx actually exist," said Alex. "Imagine, if the legends are true, the powers of the first known goddess at your disposal. The power to create. To destroy. To change the very fabric of reality. We cannot let them fall into the wrong hands."

"Agreed," said Marcus.

"You're certain they're here, then?" asked Alex.

"Yes. Herrmann and his wife are here this week for a series of shows at Wallack's Theater."

"On Broadway?"

"Mm hm…and Thirteenth," added Marcus.

"It should be no trouble, then, to get the Tears while they're on stage," said Alex. "I'd like to do it sooner, but it's not as if they're practicing real magic, so there's no fear of activating the stones and alerting the Society."

"Still, it might be nice to—"

Marcus froze mid-sentence.

"To what?" asked Alex.

It took a few beats to realize that his friend was not at a loss for words, but *literally* frozen. The same was true of all the patrons in Delmonico's. Alex took a deep breath, maintaining his calm. The unexpected had been a constant in his life since his death and subsequent resurrection during the Battle of Trenton.

He felt the buzz of energy in the air. The sensation tingled his second sight. It meant that not only were the people in the restaurant frozen, so too was time itself.

"Reveal yourself," he said.

A portal manifested to his right, and a woman stepped through. Long reddish-brown curls cascaded around her shoulders. She wore a tailored jacket, black with crimson trim atop a long black skirt, trimmed in kind. Her green eyes glowed bright until the shimmer behind her dissipated. The smile on her face was pleasant, but Alex wasn't fooled. The woman behind it was sinister. Deadly.

So it had been throughout the centuries.

"Greetings, Alex. It's both pleasing and distressing to see you again." she said.

"Morgan le Fay," replied Alex.

"You wound me," said le Fay, feigning sadness.

"How's that?"

"You say my name with such…disdain."

Alex gave a half-hearted smile and stood up from his table. He walked toward her, trying to hide his fear. They'd worked together once. Their respective objectives had been in line. That wasn't always the case with Morgan le Fay and…well…anyone. He'd witnessed her power, and was certain it was only a small fraction. Simple spells. Elemental controls and such. Things that he had been proficient in by that time. His power had grown since then, but he was still no match for her.

Few *living* souls were.

"My apologies," he said. "I can assure you, I meant no disrespect."

"Hmm. I wonder," she replied.

Alex thought about the sheer power it took to stop time the way she had. He wondered how long she could maintain it. Would it weaken her? Could he take her down?

"Tsk tsk, Alex," she began, "you're scheming. I can see it in your eyes."

In a blink, she stood inches from him.

"I am simply curious about…all this," he said, waving his arm toward the frozen scene before them. Doing his best to remain calm.

"I wanted privacy."

"We could have met later."

"I was feeling impatient," said le Fay.

He smiled back. Despite her power and duplicitous nature, he'd always enjoyed their banter. Alex Frost was, in general, a calm individual. There was a fire inside, though. The product of his environment, to be sure, but he'd learned to temper that after several incidents had reminded him that he was not always the biggest fish in the pond. Unlike many of his contemporaries, he'd learned humility. Dying can do that to a man. It had been a hard lesson, but it stuck. Still, managing his temper had been one thing. Managing his fears? Well, that was something else entirely.

"What were you—"

"Why don't we get to the point, Alex," said Morgan. "I know the Tears of Nyx are here, in this city. And we both know what the legends say."

"That they are the very essence of the goddess Nyx—the embodiment of night and mother of primordial forces."

"Mm…yes. And to possess them, to bind with them, is to know limitless power. The power of an original god," said le Fay.

"I don't—"

"If you are planning to secure them, I need you to know that it is my intention to liberate them from you. And I'll do so from your corpse if necessary."

Alex felt his throat close. He loosened his collar, as if that would help. Dread and urgency covering him like a dark cloak. He felt himself lifted in the air.

"You are here, having dinner with the Concierge. I find it hard to believe you don't know the stones are here. I do not wish to cause a scene, but I will tear this city apart for them. So gather them. Bring them to me. And save countless lives. Including your own."

Darkness began to cloud his vision. As he felt his consciousness leave, a sudden rush of air, followed by the smack of a solid surface, brought him back to reality. Alex lifted his head from the floor slowly, allowing the pain to dissipate. He looked up at a smiling le Fay.

"Do I have your attention, Mr. Frost?"

Alex nodded.

"Good. I'll see you soon, then," she said.

She shimmered out of view and the restaurant came back to life.

"…get it done sooner…than—uh, Alex?"

Marcus' confused look matched that of the people looking down at Alex as he slowly stirred. He got to his feet and took a seat. He returned Marcus' dumbfounded gaze, grabbed his drink, and finished it in one swallow. When he put his glass down, he stared at it for a long while, before making eye contact with Marcus.

"We've got problems," he said.

After they spoke, Alex insisted on walking Marcus back to his hotel. Marcus declined, and Alex acquiesced, but thought it was best to follow his friend anyway. Morgan le Fay was about, and that did not bode well for anyone.

Not more than three minutes into the walk did le Fay appear.

As she and Marcus sat on a nearby bench, Alex aligned himself with the shadows of trees. Tapping into his own magic, he closed his eyes and spoke a single word, "Auditus." Immediately, his hearing was augmented and focused on the conversation between the sorceress and the Concierge.

"I could kill you right here, right now, and no one could do a thing to stop me," said Morgan.

"You could," said Marcus.

"And that doesn't frighten you?"

"It does."

"So your calm is a façade," she said, with a hint of satisfaction.

"Not so much a façade as the realization that while you *can* kill me, you won't."

"And why not?"

"Because you need me," said Marcus.

"You think?"

"You are searching for the Tears of Nyx. It stands to reason that if you're here, talking to me, you either believe I have them, know where they are, or have a line on their whereabouts."

"Frost spoke to you?"

Marcus nodded.

"Perhaps you're right, Mr. Shelby. Perhaps I won't kill you. But I can do things to you that would make you wish I had."

Alex shifted at the threat. He needed to get Marcus out of there. He thought of some spells that could help in the immediate. A cloaking spell. Maybe the faux death spell. He took a step from the shadows, and then Marcus spoke.

"I don't think that'll be necessary at all. There's no need to torture, maim, or kill me. You magic wielders strut around with all this power and no real clue how to use it…and honestly, it amuses me. Maybe you're different."

"Maybe?" asked Morgan, rhetorically.

"Fair," said Marcus. "You *are* different. Perhaps this world would be better if the Tears were in your hands. The power to reshape things as you see fit. Bring order to chaos. Right the wrongs. Would you do that?"

"Maybe," said le Fay, with a grin.

"Look, bottom line, I'm a broker, and most importantly, I'm human. I can't match any of you in a fight. What I *can* do is ally myself with the person who can have the greatest impact on my well-being, both now and in the future. If that's you, then perhaps we can do business."

Snap!

Alex turned at the sound behind him and found a dog. The animal stepped on a brittle twig as it sidled up to him. A stray. Not dangerous. Alex turned back to the scene on the bench only to find that Morgan and Marcus were gone.

"Dammit, Marcus! What have you done?"

After an hour of searching, Alex gave up and went back to his hotel. Concerned. Angry. Confused.

"Illumina," he said when he walked in.

At once, several candles came to life, bringing day to night…and form to the figure sitting in the chair near the window.

"Where the hell have you been?" asked Marcus.

Wallack's Theater, New York City—June 30, 1880

Alex reappeared backstage. He scoured the crowd from behind the curtain and searched the area where he'd seen le Fay. His mind raced with thoughts and scenarios about best ways to get out of the theater with his life and the Tears of Nyx.

While he had second sight, the ability to see things outside of, or influenced by, the concept and flow of time, Alex could not see the auras of other magic wielders. To compensate, he'd procured a special herb from a shaman he'd met while out west. It was a blend of tobacco, some other naturally occurring green herb with jagged leaves, and peyote. Once rolled, they were soaked in a sacred extract. When lit, and the smoke inhaled, the result was the opening of the Third Eye, and through the exhaled smoke, the aura of another Magic Wielder would become visible. The intensity of the aura was directly proportional to their power.

Le Fay's aura had been the brightest thing in the theater.

"Damn," Alex muttered under his breath.

The stones were a gateway to powers that no one should possess. In her hands, it would be a recipe for destruction—in this world and the next. Getting those stones to safety was imperative. And if he couldn't do that, he'd do the next best thing.

Destroy them.

"Hey," said a voice from behind. "Is she here?"

Alex's concerns about Marcus' involvement in this madness flared up again.

"She's here. She's hiding among the crowd. Looks like you were right. She followed you."

"Nothing like a walking worm on a hook, eh?" said Marcus, walking closer.

Alex said nothing. None of this sat well with him. He was older than he looked, well over a century. A byproduct of the magic that brought him back from the dead. In that time, he'd seen the best of the worst of humanity. And in all that time, he encountered few who gave him as much hope for the future as Marcus Shelby.

Now, he wondered if that hope was misplaced.

"We're clear on what's next, yes?" Alex asked, turning to his old friend.

Marcus nodded.

"Good. Give me a minute to conjure, then you're off to it, yes?"

Another nod.

"Careful out there, my friend," said Marcus.

"You, too."

The two men shook hands; then Alex moved back to the curtain. He pulled it slightly to allow an unobstructed view of the scene unfolding. Herrmann had the audience captivated with more tricks. Astonished faces, gasps of wonder and delight, and general feelings of happiness made him a little sad about what he'd have to do next.

Allowing his energies to build, Alex spoke words that helped augment and direct his power. He repeated the spell three times, and half a beat later heard the first scream as someone saw the lion he'd manifested from nothing. Another scream overshadowed the first as the second lion appeared. Chaos erupted when a third lion leapt from the stage to the theater floor where the attendees stood and sat around Herrmann the Great and his wife. All it took was one person to run in fear and…

There it was.

Frenzy.

Bodies running everywhere to escape three mighty lions let loose.

Alex smiled.

"You're up," he said.

When he looked back, Marcus was already gone.

Amid the screams, and bodies pushing and shoving their way out of the theater, a lone woman stood. She had a smile on her face, but Alex didn't know if it was one of satisfaction, amusement, or annoyance. Aligned with Marcus, she must have known this was coming, so she was likely going through the motions. On some level, Alex expected this. *Unexpected* was what he saw in the center of the theater floor. Stepping from behind the curtain, Alex walked onto the stage, and as the last patron ran from the theater, he snapped his fingers.

The lions vanished in a puff of smoke.

There was, of course, no look of shock on the face of Morgan le Fay. Even if she were not aligned with Marcus, she would have recognized those animals as an illusion. Instead, the look of shock lay solely on the faces of the magician and his wife, clearly unable to move despite the clear desire on their faces.

She compelled them to stay. Damn!

"Please, join us," said le Fay.

To save time, but also, and probably more importantly, to demonstrate some power, Alex vanished from the stage and reappeared on the theater floor opposite Herrmann and Adelaide. The fear in their eyes gutted him. His lion illusion was meant to empty the theater and leave only *him* with le Fay.

"Let them go," said Alex.

"Deliver the Tears of Nyx," said the sorceress.

"I don't have them."

"I wasn't talking to you," she countered.

Alex followed le Fay's gaze toward the stage and found Marcus standing there. He took the steps at stage left and walked to the center of the floor to join everyone. The obstacle course of chairs strewn here and there delayed him, adding to the tension in the room.

"Alex," said Marcus.

Alex said nothing. Offered nothing. Just stared at his old friend.

"Do you have them?" asked le Fay.

"They weren't where I'd left them, but eventually…yes," replied Marcus.

"What is this about? If it's money you need…please…let my wife go, and I'll give you anything you want," said Herrmann.

His plea was met with laughter by le Fay.

"This isn't about anything as trivial as money, magician," she said. "This is about the power to reshape the world. This is about *real* magic."

Herrmann looked dumbfounded.

"My dear girl," began the magician, "Magic is not real. It's sleight of hand. It's illusion. It's—"

The magician stopped speaking when le Fay rose in the air. Lights swirled about her. The sorceress launched fireballs and conjured a dragon. Unlike the lions Alex manifested, this dragon was real and hellbent on destruction. Le Fay lowered herself to the ground. The dragon took root behind her. All around them, portions of the theater burned, and her laughter echoed throughout the great hall.

Alex closed his eyes, mouthed a short spell, and the fires were suffocated. A growl from the dragon caused everyone to jump.

"Your power is noted, Lady le Fay," said Alex, attempting to appease her ego with formality. "Please…"

He gestured toward the dragon, and after a sigh of annoyance from the sorceress, the creature shimmered into nothingness.

"I…I…can't…," stammered Herrmann.

"Well, we can," said le Fay. "So hold your tongue while real magic wielders talk."

Alex gestured to the magician and his wife to remain calm. His non-verbal cues assured them things would be okay.

"They don't need to be here for this," said Alex.

"They stay! Since your friend here has betrayed you, he's not likely to work as leverage. Them, on the other hand…"

Alex turned his attention to Marcus. Their eyes spoke. In a language developed over a couple of decades, they had a deep conversation.

"Don't be so sad. There are greater things in life than friendship. And in the new world, you'll be better off. Besides, you'll outlive him by centuries, so…best to forget him now," said le Fay with callous disregard. "Now, do you have something for me, Mr. Shelby?"

Marcus reached inside his coat and produced a small black felt bag. He released the cinch and poured the contents into his hand. Out tumbled two blue iridescent stones with white clouds of liquid swirling inside. In the presence of magic wielders, the orbs glowed and hummed.

"Ah…ah…HOT!" screamed Marcus, quickly placing them back in the felt bag.

"Those aren't meant for mortals," said Alex with a sneer.

With an outstretched hand, Alex called upon his power and willed the bag to fly from Marcus' hand to his. Out of the corner of his eye he saw le Fay conjure a fireball and launch it in his direction. Bag in hand, he dove out of the way, avoiding one volley, then threw up a magical energy shield to protect himself from the follow-up attack. The sorceress was relentless, but his shield held. Blow after blow hit his defense and pushed him back. Finally, they stopped. Alex took the moment to mouth a spell and conjured his lions once more. They were not illusions as the others had been. The three felines converged on le Fay. With her distracted, he pulled a celestial black onyx dagger from a sheath at his back. According to legend, it was the only thing that could injure immortals. He hoped it would do the same to their relics. He mouthed a second spell, and the dagger transformed into a smith's hammer. He rolled the stones onto the floor and raised the hammer high.

"No!" screamed le Fay, all but confirming Alex's hypothesis. She had to know what he held in his hand.

"Oh my god!" shouted Marcus, who dove for the magician and his wife, tackling them to ground to shield them.

Alex brought the hammer down and whispered a spell as he did. The hammer shattered the stones, and the resulting explosion sent him flying back into the chaotic maze of chairs around them. His conjured lions vanished. The sorceress, too, felt the backlash of the explosion.

Minutes passed before the chaotic scene calmed. Alex, feeling soreness in his extremities, stood slowly. Marcus helped Herrmann and Adelaide to their feet. A scream startled them all as le Fay sprang to her feet, ready to fight.

"What have you done?!" she screamed. "I'll kill you!"

"Wait!" shouted Marcus.

"You dare?" she spat.

"If I may," began Marcus, "while he has thwarted your plans here, he is still useful in the magical world. And, I might add, difficult to kill."

"Then I will take pleasure in trying," said le Fay, stepping forward with intent, a fireball in her hand.

"Or!" exclaimed Marcus, holding up one finger dramatically. "You could leave him, loathe him, and take possession of the thing you've sought for centuries."

Le Fay stopped in her tracks and extinguished the flame in her hand. Alex relaxed his stance and looked from Marcus to the sorceress.

"Marcus, no!" said Alex.

"Silence!" shouted le Fay, snapping her fingers, causing Alex's mouth to seal shut.

Adelaide yelped and buried her head in her husband's chest at the sight of a man with no mouth.

"Let this end," said Marcus. "No good can come from harming anyone here. Take this information and fulfil your greatest desire."

Marcus extended an envelope. It vanished, only to reappear in the hands of le Fay. She opened it. She smiled. Sinister laughter echoed through the theater again.

"I'll see you again, Frost," she said. A threat, more than anything else. She vanished seconds later.

As did the seal on Alex's mouth.

Hands on his knees, he took deep breaths as he looked around at the scene before him. Standing at full height, he looked at Herrmann, then to Adelaide, and finally to Marcus.

"And you thought it wouldn't work," said Marcus.

The two laughed and then embraced one another.

"Are you okay?" asked Marcus.

"Yeah. Sore, but okay. You?" asked Alex.

"About the same."

Then, the friends turned to Herrmann and his wife.

"Please accept my apologies," said Alex. "I hadn't expected her to keep the two of you here through all this."

"I…I…don't understand what's happening," said Adelaide.

"That woman was Morgan le Fay," said Marcus.

"Like…from the—"

"The very same," finished Alex. "Some portions of those stories are fictitious. But what is real is the fact that she is a sorceress, and one of, if not the, most powerful Magic Wielder alive. She was after something called the Tears of Nyx. Stones imbued with the power of the goddess Nyx herself. They grant unlimited power to anyone who possesses them."

"We suspected her aim was to destroy this world and recreate one in her image. So we devised a plan to trick her into thinking I would secure them, turn on old Alex here, and give them to her," said Marcus.

"I, in turn, would intercept them and destroy them," finished Alex.

"Magic is real? I…I…can't believe it," said Herrmann.

"You should. Because it believes in you," said Alex with a smirk, gesturing to the magician's chest.

Confused, Herrmann tapped his jacket, felt something, then reached inside. A felt bag emerged from his inside pocket. He opened it and poured the Tears of Nyx into his hand.

"But…I watched you destroy these," said the magician.

"You watched me destroy forgeries. You felt the shockwave created by a spell I cast that activated as soon as my hammer came down. All an elaborate ruse."

"If she's as powerful as you say, how could she not see through that?" asked Adelaide.

"What's the greatest tool in a magician's bag?" asked Alex.

"Distraction," said Herrmann.

Alex nodded.

"So, the lions? The chaos you created by snatching the stones. All designed to—"

"Keep her distracted," finished Adelaide.

Alex winked.

"Incredible," said Herrmann, handing the bag to Alex.

"What now?" asked Marcus.

"I need to keep these somewhere safe. Or...*with* someone safe," said Alex.

"You got someone in mind?"

"Yeah. A guy I met out west recently. A marshal. He's...seen some things. Not afraid to get in the fight and protect those who can't protect themselves."

"Sounds like a good man. When do we leave?" asked Marcus.

"How about now?"

The foursome talked for a bit. Then, satisfied that the Herrmanns were okay, both Alex and Marcus shook hands with the magician and his wife.

"It's been a pleasure," said Alex. "Keep people believing in magic. Magic brings hope. And we'll need that in the coming days."

Herrmann nodded.

Adelaide followed suit.

Alex waved his arm; then he and Marcus vanished in a puff of smoke.

The Crumbs of My Body

Renan Bernardo

Content warning: effects of hunger; suffering; descriptions of dead bodies.

My body crackles. Brown crumbs run down my sides while my carapace splinters and pops out. It disintegrates from my arms, legs, and torso like bark falling off an ancient tree. I stagger along the forest, my knees trembling without the carapace's firmness. I try to force myself forward just a bit more. The bag upon my shoulders rolls over, scattering roots, tubers, fruits, rocks, and ores all over the turf. I try to force some weight on my knees, but they give in. I fall, face to the ground.

"No…"

I crush the damp earth between my fingers. Failure. My legs return to what they were. I can't stand up. Not without the carapace. *You're weak.* How many times did I fall, always thinking I could do a little more, walk a bit further? I've been pushing myself farther since I fled Iuquira, turning my gaze away from the Husk Decay that ripped through Abati's body. And since then, I've been walking, falling, and standing, over and over, following my body's cycle as the carapace breaks and regrows.

I choke a scream, turning it into a sigh before it alerts some animal.

Sun rays streak through the trees and blind me for a moment. I cringe and roll over, belly up to the sky. I'm just a naked, unhusked Root Boiler stranded far from home. Even my name doesn't fit me: Juruaru—"god" in the Iuquira language. But if gods existed, they wouldn't fall.

I snatch a lilac fruit and a coiled black root that dropped from my bag, glaring at them as if those parts of nature could be blamed for the forest's sterility. I'd already insisted on blending more and more of those items—roots, herbs, flowers, fruits, meat, plants—adding even rocks, wood, sand, and ore dust to the mix, in the vain hope of infusing something novel, of finding out whatever can sate our hunger. But I'm certain that all the remainders of my bag are unfit for anyone's belly, as useless as the rest of the forest. I throw the lilac fruit and the root aside.

The besprinkled slivers of my husk lie on the soil, scattered amidst the ingredients. I grasp a handful and crunch them in my mouth. They quickly dissolve, running down my throat. Warm, invigorating. It always ends this way, in the certainty of my body, my crumbs. The only thing that can sate me.

A breeze carries dandelions into the clearing, sunlight turning them into golden dust. Leaves waltz around them. When one dies, one sprouts seeds. Abati could be part of those flying flowers. Grains of her whole. Listening, watching. I imagine the dots mingling and tainting the thin air with Abati's turquoise-painted face, her body covered in beads and feathers, carrying a bow, a quiver of arrows, her dose of scorn. She would laugh at me and take me back to the Iuquiras.

"I'll make edible food someday, Abati…" I whisper to the wind, to her.

Something ruffles through the stilt palms. My muscles tense, but there's little I can do without the carapace serving as my armor and legs.

A bulky shade stretches along the trees. It won't be anyone I know, not this far.

Singing voices build up across the clearing. Canticles—melodious with an edge of dissonance.

"Fill our guts," the voices sing in unison. "Save our children."

No, not a song. Supplications and appeals to gods, prayers for edible food.

A trio stops when they see me lying on the ground. White-clouded faces, slim bodies, ropes and clubs in their hands. Memuines, the old enemies of the Iuquiras, who live isolated in the far reaches of the forest. I'd truly gone far this time.

A slim woman steps forward and unfolds a rope from her waist, her lips curling in a grimace. She raises her club and before I can say anything, she pounds my head.

The bonfire in front of me burns its last flames. A thin strip of smoke rises from it. When it threatens to extinguish, a breeze flares it up again, making the wood crackle. A cacophony of children's wails mingles through the dozens of voices of the people gathered around me, all at a safe distance, as if I'm some kind of evil spirit. They're all rickety, huddled in groups of five and six. Their okas—straw-built conical homes— surround the village and occupy most of the clearing. They're all battered by inclement weather, some completely dismantled. Behind them, the sickly odor of carcasses and rotten meat leaches through the air—the few edible dregs of the forest.

An old man approaches me. Their chief. His bones protrude from his body. His skeleton seems carved out of his blemished, scarred skin, his ribs like bony totems yearning to be set free. His name is Tuia, as I'd heard someone say.

"What are you doing in our lands?" he says. His voice is barely a thread, but decisive. He stops before me without the same apprehension as the rest of his tribe.

I stare at the fire and twist the rope around my wrists. Tight. At least they know they don't need to tie my legs.

What would Abati do? She'd have the right choice of words and the suitable amount of scorn to deal with the enemy. She'd talk her way out of that rope and back home. I have nothing but the truth.

"My name is Juruaru. I'm a Root Boiler." I don't know if the Memuines are familiar with the term. "I infuse, mix, cook, and research herbs, flowers, roots, and even rocks, sand, and other things in a quest for eatable food."

"Food?" a woman says, eavesdropping on the conversation and approaching us. She coughs and stoops over me, etching the aspect of a corpse.

"You know how to make food?" Tuia crouches next to me. The brewed smell of the forest's last promises exhales from his mouth. Fruits, plants, and meat that don't fill up bellies, things they'd kept rationed and stocked for the last five full moons since the forest stopped providing.

"I try to," I say again. "I experiment with ingredients, but haven't been successful so far."

"You're well-fed." Tuia scans my face. One of his hands slides along the feathered club corded to his waist. The other one cups my chin. His fingers are rough, his nails absent. He plucks my lips to see my teeth. I taste bloodied earth. "Tell me where you find food."

"I don't need to——"

He whacks my face with the bones of his hand. Other skinny warriors crowd around us, moved by Tuia's courage. Disgusted faces with clubs, bows, and spears. Some wear stretchers in their lips, others have bird's beaks around their branchlike necks, and most have their cheeks caved in their faces.

"We rescued you," Tuia says, hands fisted. "We've been sucking the last of what we kept. You know how to make food; you will make food."

Tuia's fingers enfold the club's handle before I say anything. I flit my eyes to the bonfire again. A thin black strip rises from the last birch barks.

"I can try..."

"You'll start now." Tuia tries to dig his fingers into my shoulders, but it's just a pat.

He moves away with the others.

Every morning, Tuia brings a bowl of ingredients to the oka where I'm assigned, darting fierce looks at me. Every morning, the tint on his face seems whiter. I use walking staffs to move from side to side, mixing and infusing with the Memuines' rudimentary pestles and bowls. My carapace slowly expands each day, discreetly shrouding my legs, provoking itches at night, gently shredding the hairs around my body. And when the sun sets, Tuia inquires me about my productions. I offer him mixtures that range from savory root soups to bland herb-filled tubers. I tread the safest path, creating only what I know to be safe, not risking iron dust, rocks, or any other dangerous ingredients. But I can't make anything capable of allaying the hunger in their sons and daughters.

Voices through the ages tell that more than ten thousand cycles of the moon ago, an uncountable amount of armored frogs leaped from a river. They came when the Iuquiras needed them most: when famine reft all our villages, shrinking our people, laying bodies all over the forest. The Voices utter that the frogs scattered through the woodland, leaving their edible armor behind as an act of mercy. My tribe doesn't believe in gods like others, so the Voices tell that the frogs were just an amendment of nature; a requital for the lands, trees, and tribes we tended to over the years. You give, nature gives back.

Ten sunsets after my arrival, Tuia stands at the entrance of my oka, casting a lanky shadow across the soil.

"You have to do it for us." It's an order that sounds like a plea.

"I will." I can share bits of my body with them, but without his comprehension, it's useless to explain my carapace won't disentangle from my body whenever I want. If I try to rip out a piece, it'd be like plucking out my skin and muscles.

Tuia nods and leaves, limping across the outgrown grass toward the center of the village like a walking shadow.

Abati's lessons bounce in my mind when I resume my work. Shunning her intrusive voice has proved useless. When she'd explained to me about the frogs, we were atop the boulder in the middle of Iuquira River. I'd noticed some brown grains of her carapace scattered around the spot where she was sitting. That had been the first sign something was out of place. She used to be all smiles, laughter, and the healthy scorn that only masters know. With her, I floated from nervousness to gratitude; from anger to love. But that day a shadow had lingered over her, not unlike the one that hangs over Tuia, like some ancient spirit whispering your fate in your ears.

A grating cough sounds outside the oka. Tuia leans on a tree and gasps for air. A man escorts him somewhere out of my sight.

They won't resist much longer. Time passes, the Memuines die, and my compounds won't save anyone. I'm soon to be alone among corpses.

The thought makes me shiver. I drop the pestle and raise my hands before my eyes. My fingernails are oversized, but in a few days, my carapace will grow, break them, and envelop my fingers. I have food in me. I am food. It isn't nearly enough to placate the Memuines' hunger, but perhaps the Iuquiras can help.

Some lessons you can't grasp. Do you want to join us with the enemy? The Abati in my mind rebukes me, the one who survived.

No. But they need us.

I hobble with the walking staffs to the bonfire at the center of the village. Now it blazes with intensity. Tuia is next to it, sitting on the soil with the woman named Oria beside him. His eyes are closed. His head's down, chin softly rubbing his chest, as if sleeping or in a trance. Oria wipes the drool that runs down his neck. One of Tuia's hands rests on a volume wrapped in tapir leather. Oria gently raises his face, forcing him to look at me. He clamps his teeth, and his hands grasp for the club that's no longer at his waist. White reigns over his cheeks. Not the tribe's paint.

"I have a proposal," I say.

"What do you—" He closes his eyes and spits. Oria puts a hand over his chest and forbids him to speak further.

Putting aside my staffs, I sit on the soil, face to face with Tuia and Oria. My knees snap as the carapace adjusts itself. Oria frowns at it. It's reaching my pelvis, and soon it'll be expanding across my belly and back.

"My people have ways to provide food." Apart from Tuia's protectors, the rest of the tribe seems too engulfed in their own troubles to perceive me. Weak men and women remain in their okas and close to bonfires. Some of them have risked themselves into the woods in a desperate search for nutrition, and now their relatives and friends stand guard at the edge of the clearing, eyes vigilant and hopeful.

"Who are your people?" Oria says.

"I'm from the Iuquiras." I gulp.

Oria stands, almost tumbling to one side. Her thin breasts sag against protuberant ribs. "Shapeshifter!"

"Will you listen to me?"

"To a filthy creature? Everything you produced so far was lies, Root Boiler." She hisses, losing her balance and kneeling before me. I help her sit, but she shoves my hand off. Still kneeling, she lifts up the tapir leather that covers the volume next to Tuia. It's a man's corpse. Skinny like all the others, the man's eyes bulge from their sockets. Scars clot on his belly as patterns wrongly painted then hastily amended by unskillful hands. "Tuia's son. He was perishing, and his friend tried to slash his guts to fill with plants, herbs… even stones."

Something gets stuck in my throat. Air, or the stench of rottenness pervading the diminishing village. I lower my head to avoid the inquisitorial eyes of Oria.

"So, yes. We are desperate, shapeshifter. I will listen to you."

I look at her face. I hadn't been able to save Abati when the Husk Decay tore through her. I couldn't save myself from weakness and rejection when she told me to go away. *Let go of me!* What made me think I could do anything for an entire tribe?

"Let me go and I will come back with my people. We can help to feed you, and then we can work together in growing edible food."

"You're coming back with an army." She points a finger at me.

"For what?" I look around the clearing. They know the only thing that will remain is the wind to shake the okas and rattle the bones.

Oria glares at me, teeth biting her cracked lips. Tuia moans and curls his arms around his legs. She pats his back.

"I won't tell the rest of the tribe that you're a shapeshifter. Go to yours and come back with something for our bellies."

With time, the Voices utter, we became the frogs. The carapace grew around our bodies, covering us from feet to fingers; from legs to chest; all over our faces, except for mouth, nose, and eyes. Finally, five full moons ago, when the forest's animals and fruits completely stopped providing sustenance after years of ever-diminishing sources of nutrition, the Iuquiras already had their bodies to protect themselves from hunger. We had transformed into our only source of food.

Three sunrises after our conversation, I ask Oria for permission to leave. It's when my carapace will be half-grown and capable of making me walk. She consents.

By the end of the first day, a heavy rain chastises the tribe. The okas resist, but not the people. I sit inside my oka, protected, trying to mute those wailings that are still loud among the downpour. Will the Memuines still be there when I come back with the husks of my tribe to share? There's nothing I can do but wait for my shell to sprout and walk me home.

I focus on the raindrops outside. Each one of them a single entity, a minuscule deity of its own. When one dies, one sprouts seeds. Each of those drops, you. Drops of the whole. I close my eyes.

As time passed, more and more Iuquiras hadn't grown fully developed carapaces. They became weaker, loosening from the body, and the diseased sometimes needed to partake in the remains of others. But the Iuquiras' bodies demanded the covering that wasn't there. Every time parts of our husk peeled off before the right time, the carapace ripped throughout the body in a frenzied attempt to fill vacant space. It was fast enough to hurt—to destroy. It expanded within, tearing the skin, pricking the brain, twirling the thoughts.

This is not forever, Abati had said on the top of the river's boulder, sliding a hand across her elbow's carapace, hard crust peeling off of it. *Nature will get it back someday. From all of us.* She'd never told me she suffered from the Decay, but only rain could hide the trail she left behind.

A scream echoes outside my oka, waking me from my thoughts. Amidst the haze, a man tumbles, seeking protection. He tries to run, but his feet trip on the muddy soil. He tries to balance himself. The windy rain knocks him down.

I stand, supporting myself with the staffs, and walk out. The man's face is turned down. He gurgles in a puddle, arms not strong enough to save himself, not even to push away from the water.

The man spasms.

Not enough time.

I discard the staffs and run, using the scarce strength the carapace provides in its incomplete shape. My knees bend as my cloistered feet wade through the wet soil. I touch the ground and push up, barely balancing myself.

I sprint. Faster. Legs flailing, toes numb, clinging to the ground and sinking into it.

I'll fall. I know I'd fall. I fell before. *Some lessons you can't grasp*, the Abati in my head echoes the dead one.

The man is drowning in hunger and mud.

"Get up!" My voice quivers. I'm just a few steps from him.

He squirms like a worm unable to dig its own hole. I reach for his shoulders, but the carapace breaks before I can touch him. My body crackles. The carapace collapses. I join the man onto the ground as he emits a last, suffocated gurgle.

Some lessons I can't grasp.

Silhouettes surround me. I close my eyes as the rain taps my nape.

"A shapeshifter," someone hisses.

In the end, I wished I was strong to withstand the tears, to devise ways to ease Abati's suffering. On her last day, the sunlight had illuminated her face, bringing out sulky eyes and fissured, tottering lips that tapped the carapace swelling up from her chin. She had stepped away from me when I tried to hold her hand. Brown chunks were scattered all around her.

I'm dying, and you're the one trembling. You're weak. Let go of me. Get away!

Her words had tasted like the worst of my mixtures, but I lingered, watching her mingling with the shadows, sitting in a corner while her carapace extruded from her skin. First slowly, then…

"You're a monster," Raoni says, one of the two skinny guards that protect the entrance of the oka with clubs and stones. They'd dragged me there thinking I had done something to the drowning man. "The gods will punish you." He scratches his neck. Blood runs down his gaunt collarbone. His eyes keep locked on my legs as I don't need the walking staffs anymore.

"I am not." I haul a chunk of the carapace taking over my thighs. It peels off, but not without pain. I gasp. "This is food." I take a bite and offer it to them.

"You mock us, shapeshifter." His hands close around his club, but he isn't able to brandish it against me. "Be quiet."

When silence sinks, he glances behind his back. Moans vent through the village.

"You need it." I pull another loose piece. Cramps and spasms rush through me. A bolting pain strikes my right leg as if an arrow has pierced it.

"I said—" Raoni kneels down, using both hands to avoid the fall. His partner can barely move to help him.

"You're weak and dying." I insist, extending a handful of the bits. "Eat it."

The man clasps the remains of my hand, taking them desperately into his mouth. His partner furrows. As Raoni chews the new food, I snatch more pieces, ripping them out of me as if they're just leaves. Raoni widens his eyes, leaves the club behind, and stretches his bony hand. I give him more.

His partner kneels down beside him, begging for the chunks. I feed him too.

Three other villagers appear at the entrance of the oka and join the begging. Soon, the oka is surrounded by a flock of survivors.

"I have to stop," I say after distributing handfuls. The carapace is a half-moon just below my chest. Soon the pain will flow as it tries to grow back, winning my body, following the order of things. I have to stop, but I keep feeding them.

Crumbs of the carapace scatter across the soil but disappear quickly while hands grapple for them. A woman jostles against the villagers, knocking two of them to the ground. Oria.

"Please." All the pride she once held is now vanished under swollen eyes and bleached cheeks. "Give us."

Tuia comes next, a haggard shadow. His osseous arms stretch out, hands wide open. His eyes catch mine, livelier than anything else, gorged with regrets and yearning. I shred a fair piece of me and hand it to him, making sure no one else snatches it up. He tumbles, elbows fraying the earth, but manages to lift the food into his mouth. He chews it rapidly.

I rive, split, divide myself into pieces, into grains of a whole. Over and over again.

The cries of the survivors diminish. The ones in my head get louder. Every crack, a remembrance. Every bolt of pain, a recalling of the carapace piercing Abati. Her sour voice echoes through my head as the faces before me darken. *Let go of me.* Her screams drown in my shriek of pain. I'd tried to fold her in my arms when the husk ripped through her belly, legs, and arms. To keep her intact somehow. I pulled the thorn-like bulges of the carapace, but it only intensified her pain. I rested her on the ground. Her body twitched, fingers clenching the air, searching for something to hold on to, but finding nothing, not even me. Someone touched my shoulder in the end, asking me to leave, saying there was no way out—that was the Decay. So I obeyed and avoided her last arduous breath. I couldn't be there. I'd saved the last crumbs of my sanity and ran into the woods, to the hills ahead, to the unknown.

My eyes adjust to the oka. The images of the night I fled from my tribe vanish from my mind. The rainstorm is but a drizzle now.

Hands reach for me. A lot. I'll be torn and eaten alive.

Tuia opens the way among his people and approaches me with infusions and water bowls.

My vision blurs with enervation, but there's relief and gratitude in the hand Tuia puts on my forehead.

"You're saving us," he says.

Elephant in Winter

Jenny Rae Rappaport

Bess was late to the river.

So late, so very late, that they were already lighting the dusk-lanterns when she got there. Henry would be on the ice by now, his anger stewing despite the chill in the air. But the baby had been colicky again and Meg-down-the-street had been delayed coming to watch him, and really, today was just a terrible day.

It didn't matter how lovely the lanterns were with their tiny glass bowls and steady flames, each one a defense against the twilight-darkness of the midwinter day. It didn't matter that she wanted to stand on the frozen river and watch them, wanted to lose herself in them, wanted to think a thought just for herself and no one else. It didn't matter because there was no time to stop, and so, Bess went on.

She rewrapped her scarf around her neck and tied her skates on at the river's edge. One step after another, her blades biting into the ice, and then, she was flying towards the Frost Fair, the wind whipping against her face. It would be months before the sun made its slow climb above the horizon and the river warmed to life. Months more of magic and movement, of spells cast from the midst of fatigue, and Henry, always Henry, like a lodestone turned the wrong way.

He was waiting at their tent when she arrived, trying to placate the line of impatient children. They wanted the animals and the animals needed her, and Bess knew how it was. But Henry didn't care, had never cared, and his fingers were rough when he pulled her through the canvas door, crowding her against the elephant.

"My skates—" she said.

"You're late," he said, and the way his eyes darkened was a warning she knew all too well.

"The baby—"

"Make them move."

His hand twisted on her arm and Bess took a deep breath before she wrenched herself free.

"Mat is your son, too."

"I would think so."

"You could take an interest."

"When he can talk. And hold a wrench."

"When he's useful in the shop," Bess said, trying and failing to keep the bitterness from her words.

When he could putter around behind his father, when he could learn to repair the intricate gears, when he could one day be trusted to craft the clockwork animals himself—only then would he have value. The knowledge was ice in the pit of her stomach.

"Yes."

Her fingers itched to smack the smug look from Henry's face. But that would lead to trouble and if this marriage had taught her nothing else, it was that trouble was best avoided. Through sleepless nights and silent breakfasts, trouble haunted them both, working its way into the seams, and ripping them apart from the inside out.

It was better to say nothing than to say the wrong thing.

"We're going to lose all our business to the fools running the ninepins stall," Henry said, taking a step closer. "I need you working sooner."

"I couldn't leave Mat," she said, the cold elephant pressing against her back. "Meg was late."

"Then find someone else to watch the brat."

Another step, just one more, and he was close enough that if she was a different woman, she could wrap her hands around his throat. But she was tired, so dreadfully tired, like a miasma that swirled around her and never let go. And Mat was at home and there were the animals to tend to, and it was safer—it was always safer—to fold her hands together and nod.

"Work," he said, his voice cutting into her like a quiet knife.

Bess said nothing, was nothing, until he turned his back and stomped off to deal with the customers outside.

Animals packed the interior of the canvas tent. The elephant against her back was crammed next to the peacock who stood watch over the silent lion. Clockwork animal after clockwork animal, all of them crafted from copper and coils and Henry's skill in the shop; an entire menagerie made to impress and dazzle and bring in extra income. They were waiting for her now, and for one brief moment, Bess thought about refusing to make them move. But even they deserved their bit of life; even they deserved the chance to make their way in the world, to have their moment of freedom before everything within them wound down, yet again.

She bent down to remove the skates from her shoes, carefully untying each one before she tucked them into an out-of-the-way corner. There was barely enough room to move inside the tent, let alone skate. Every winter was the same: the long week spent setting up the tent frame, securing it on their piece of the Frost Fair, bringing the canvas and the covered lantern and the animals themselves. All of it, just to earn a tiny bit more coin.

It was simple, at the core of it. One spell, one way of animating them, if only for a few hours. One moment, one phrase, in a language that her grandmother's grandmother had brought with her to this frozen place so long ago. One skill that made her valuable to the world, to Henry, to everyone who wasn't her. One thing that she had learned as a child and that had served her alone ever since. There had been no need of a dowry, no need of anything that her family couldn't afford to spare; the spell had been enough for Henry, enough for Bess in the moments when he had charmed her into this marriage with a smile and a laugh.

Enough, when now nothing was enough, except perhaps the feel of the baby in her arms when she was awake enough to enjoy it.

Bess leaned her forehead against the elephant's cold copper side and whispered the words. It was a spell of life, of new things and awakenings, that was as out of place at the Frost Fair as she was. But there was an energy to it that she knew; it was the same as the pulse that had beat through her when Mat had flutter-kicked inside her belly, his tiny fists a constant reminder that she wasn't alone in the world. She let the spell fill her, envelop her, as the drumming music of her heart became the song that brought the animals to life.

The elephant's trunk was in her hair, its heated breath a snort against her ear. Bess wanted to stay with it, to let it tangle her curls while she leaned against its solid, dependable warmth. The life within powered its copper body, its gears ticking away in a rhythm that threatened to lull her into complacency.

It was so tempting to close her eyes, to give in to the sleep that she so badly needed, to take back what motherhood had stolen from her in the dark of night. To let the elephant watch over whatever remained of her dreams, in this cramped place of frost and fiery copper hearts.

But the other animals were stirring, and so Bess forced herself to move, forced herself to exist. The tiger and the lion were stretching in the confined space, their metal paws clanging against one another. The tiger leaned over and licked the lion with its metal tongue, earning a batted paw in return. The peacock let out a screech to wake the dead and for one moment, Bess wished that she could scream with it. But the pony in the corner needed a gentle hand against its mane, and the elephant snorted in her ear again.

"Wait," she told it, wiggling her way towards the clapping seal, who was eagerly smacking its flippers together. There was an order that they needed to follow, a way of maneuvering everyone out of the cramped tent with a minimum of fuss. Bess squeezed past the lion and the tiger, scratching each of them gently between the ears, to the sound of their ticking purrs.

She would be here the next day and the next, making them line up obediently, making them take the children outside on their backs, making them be something that perhaps they did not want to be. The animals were just as helpless as she was, just as confined in their roles as any other creature in this land.

And yet.

The elephant's trunk wrapped around her waist as she passed near it again.

"You're impatient today," she said, trying to free herself.

The elephant tightened its trunk and drew her closer. Another snort, another bit of breath, and then, the elephant lifted her up. She clung to its ears, sliding against the surface of its back.

"You don't have your saddle yet," she told it, which earned her two snorts in a row. The world moved underneath her as the elephant pushed its way past the other animals, clanging against them.

Outside, Henry's voice rose in volume, and Bess could hear him selling the children on this ridiculous ride, extolling the virtues of sliding across the frozen river on the animals' backs. Charging them more and more pennies, even when he knew they couldn't afford it, spurred on by avarice and anger. Making them line up next to the side of the tent so that he could practically steal from them, day after day.

In another world, in another lifetime, it could be Mat out there, clutching his pennies for a ride. If he had a mother who didn't know the crucial spell, if he had a father who didn't build the animals themselves, if anything in his young life was different. But no, he would be expected to grow up and continue this, whether he wanted to or not. No matter what else life might have to offer.

"Let me down," she told the elephant, pressing into it with her heels. "Now, please."

It finished walking to the tent door before it reached up with its trunk and lifted her down in front of it. Bess felt it push against her, its trunk curled behind her neck, and somehow, she knew. That the door to the tent would open this way in her hand; that Henry would be standing there, in just that spot. That if she whispered the word, said one small yes, that she could cast a different sort of spell.

She let the elephant run.

What's Left Behind

D.K. Stone

Thursday

Tonight wasn't the first time the ghost had visited, but this was the first time Isla knew it was there *before* it appeared.

She woke in the dark with her heart pounding. Frowning, she tried to pinpoint what had woken her, but there was only the subtle sense of awareness. The lights were off. Door closed. Still, the feeling remained. What had changed since she'd crawled into bed? Was there a slight hum to the air? *Maybe.*

Isla took a shaky breath. Froze. There, under the layers of home, waited a familiar odor: leather, sandalwood, sunshine. The last dregs of sleepiness evaporated as a shiver ran through her.

Logan was back.

"Go away," Isla whimpered. "I don't want to talk to you."

The thud of boots crossed the floor. *Surely*, Isla thought, *someone will hear!* Her parents slept in the bedroom next door, her brothers downstairs. The sound neared. Stopped. The bed dipped down at her hip. It was a weight—a *real* one—and she knew if she opened her eyes what she'd see: Logan alive. Wanting to talk. (The ghost *always* wanted to talk.)

"Hey Isla," he whispered. *"You awake?"*

His voice was so real, so alive, that she almost answered.

The specter bumped her hip, his touch prickling the skin like frostbite. Had it been a year ago when he'd last tugged her hair? That was the day when he'd caught up with her in the parking lot, teasing her about spending all her free time with Caleb, his brother. He'd joked that she'd had no time for him anymore.

If this *was* in her head, like the psychologist insisted, she had a damned good memory for details. Right now, it felt all too real.

"Isla, listen to me. I need you to wake up." Dead fingers shook her shoulder, chilling her to the bone. She squeezed her eyelids closed.

"Isla, stop fucking around. I know you're awake."

He tugged her hair—hard—and Isla yelped, opening her eyes.

The ghost grinned. *"Knew you were faking."*

Isla's heart twisted. She hated how fucking *real* he looked. "Get out of my room," she said. "I don't want to talk to you."

Logan scowled and the air dropped ten degrees. *"Isla, listen. I need to tell you something about Caleb."* He leaned in, and her fear returned. The dead boy's face flickered like water. Logan's summer tan disappeared, a deathly pallor replacing it, eyes glittering and serious.

"This is really important," he hissed. *"You have to remember this time. There's going to be a storm tomorrow. Caleb's going to—"*

Isla began to scream.

Friday

Meg and Isla were on their way back from the 4H meeting when taillights appeared in the distance. A truck sat idling by the gate outside Isla's family farm, its interior dark.

"Slow down, Meg," Isla said, yawning. "I think someone's stuck."

"One of your brothers hit the ditch?"

"Don't think so." Isla squinted. "Taillights are wrong."

"Your dad?"

"No. It looks more like…" A passing vehicle backlit the truck's driver and the cowboy hat he wore. In a flash, she knew. *Caleb.* The exhaustion she'd been fighting since the nightmare had woken her the night before was gone in an instant.

"Looks like what?" Meg asked.

"Drop me off here."

"Why?"

"It's Caleb."

"Caleb?!" Meg's car shimmied on the icy road and Isla regretted speaking.

"Pull over," Isla said. "I promised I'd bring him his math homework."

Meg snorted. Their rural school had exactly fifteen students in twelfth grade. Meg was one of them. She most certainly knew there *wasn't* any math homework to give, but she still dutifully pulled the vehicle to the side of the road. Best friends did those things.

"You want me to wait?" Meg said dryly. "You know… if things *don't* go well with Caleb and his missing homework?"

Isla put her fingers on the door handle. "Don't be like that."

"Like what?"

"Don't judge me."

Meg rolled her eyes. "You know, if I was the one getting out in the dark to go talk to my ex, you'd be saying the exact same thing."

Isla glared.

Meg sighed. "You want me to wait or what?"

"No," Isla said. "I'm fine. But thanks for dropping me off." She pushed open the door and the wind banged it against her knuckles. "Don't, um… don't tell anyone where I went, okay? If my parents call, cover for me."

"Sure… but—"

"What?"

"Be careful, Isla."

"I will."

"And if you need anything, you text me. All right?"

"Got it."

Meg pointed. "You should hurry. Reverse lights just flashed. Caleb's getting ready to—"

Isla slammed the door before Meg finished, but she knew what she'd been about to say: *Run.* The breakup had been messy for many reasons. That was one… Logan's death another. After the funeral, Caleb had cut her entirely out of his life.

No explanation given.

Isla strolled up to the passenger's side of the truck, half-blinded by blowing snow. Behind her, Meg's car eased back onto the range-road and drove away. She tugged open the door. "Hey, Caleb. What's—" Her breath caught like she'd been punched. Her ex's face was blotchy, eyes rimmed red. "Jesus! Are you okay?"

He shook his head: *No.*

She crawled into the cab. "What happened? You look like you've been..." Isla caught herself before she said 'crying.' She'd said *that* at Logan's funeral too. It hadn't gone well.

Caleb rubbed his eyes on the sleeve of his coat. "D'you have time to talk?"

"Sure. What about?"

He shifted the truck into first and eased off the clutch, pulling the pickup onto the icy road. It wasn't until they were driving past the farm, snow blurring the windshield, that he finally spoke.

"Had a huge fight with Dad tonight," he said. "I'm leaving home, and I'm never going back..."

For an hour, they drove without direction, meandering from one gravel road to the other, a thread of conversation filling the truck's cab. The quietest tracks were in the north, and Caleb followed those range roads into barren farmland. Drifting snow moved ghostlike across the road's surface, hypnotic in its undulation. Outside, the wind dropped as the snow began in earnest, scattered flecks of light shining in the darkness.

Though they hadn't talked for months, there now seemed an endless stream of things to say. It was a relief, but Isla felt like she'd been blindsided. Layers of grief wrapped Caleb, and she wasn't sure how to help. This wasn't the same young man who'd run off at his brother's funeral, then refused to take her calls or texts.

"...and so we kind of just... live with each other," he said. "Dad does his thing. I do mine. Nobody talks about Logan at all." He paused. "It's hard."

"You talked to anyone else about this?" Isla asked. "A counsellor?" For a moment, the dream of Logan's ghost was at the surface. She shook her head. "Your mom, maybe?"

"I can't. If I call her, Dad will—"

Caleb turned to look at her just as the wheel hit a ridge of ice. Everything happened at once. The truck lurched sideways. Isla screamed. He pumped the brakes, but the vehicle was moving too fast on a layer of melting ice. With a roar, the truck careened off the road.

"You need to wake up, Isla. LISTEN! Caleb's going to die if—!"

Isla swam out of the darkness, heart pounding.

Her head ached, her chest—where she'd been thrown against the seatbelt—on fire. The cab seemed abnormally dark, the only light coming from the single headlight not buried in the snow drift. It cast a sickly band of illumination out onto the snowy landscape, grazing the top of a submerged fencepost. Beyond it, darkness swallowed the world.

With a groan, Isla unbuckled. "Caleb?" She gasped as she caught sight of him leaned over the steering wheel. "Caleb, wake up!" She shook his shoulder, fear sharpening her senses. They were alone. Crashed. Caleb wasn't moving, and the storm was getting worse. Suddenly the nightmare about Logan felt like a premonition. "Caleb!" she snapped. "CALEB! You've got to wake up!"

He groaned as his head lolled to the side. "Wh-what happened?"

"We crashed."

"But..." He rubbed his face, hissing as he hit the gash on his temple. He jerked his hand back, staring at the blood on his fingers. "You all right?"

"I'm fine. Just bruised." She squinted out of the window. "It's snowing harder now." She shivered. Her winter coat, mittens, and knit hat were adequate to get her from the bus to the school, or from Meg's car to the house, but they weren't meant for deep cold. "We need to get your truck back on the road."

"Got it." Caleb reached for the ignition. "Must've stalled when we hit the ditch." He turned the key.

Nothing happened.

He swore and tried again.

"What's going on?" she asked.

"Not sure. I, um... Just gotta take a look."

Caleb flicked on the hazard lights, then reached down, popped open the hood, and opened the door. Icy wind filled the cab. Stepping out, his cowboy boots sank knee-deep in a drift.

Inside the cab, Isla listened to Caleb's distant swearing. Every once in a while, he popped back into the vehicle to try to start it. Eventually Isla's nerves got the best of her and she climbed out after him, following his path around the front of the truck to where Caleb stood staring down into the engine.

"What's up?"

"Not sure. It'll turn over but the engine won't catch."

Around them, snowflakes fell faster, creating a thin veil of grey that hung between the truck and the road.

"If I had a flashlight," Caleb said, "I could—" He spun. "Hey! Do you have your phone with you?"

"Yeah."

"Can you shine it here—" He pointed into the engine. "I want to check something."

Isla reached into her pocket, but it was empty. She turned around, searching the ground. As she stepped backwards, her heel hit something solid.

"Oh, no!"

Isla picked up the phone, cradling it in her hands. The entire phone was bent. It wouldn't even turn on.

"What is it?" Caleb asked. "What's wrong?"

She turned the phone around. The screen was smashed into a thousand pieces, the back of it twisted into a 'V'. "I stepped on it."

"Crap. I'm sorry."

"It's okay." She shoved the destroyed phone into her pocket. "I'm going to go sit in the truck, though." She shivered. "Temperature's dropping. I'm already cold."

"I'll help you in."

He reached out his hand. For a few seconds Isla stared at his open palm, as if deciding, and then she took it. Her fingers were chilled, and shivers ran through her as she stepped through the slushy snow. Again, the memory of the ghost flickered in her mind.

"Thanks," she said. "You should warm up too."

Caleb nodded and climbed in beside her. "It's still warm in here. You should be okay in a few minutes."

Isla wrapped her arms around herself. "You don't have your phone, do you? My parents don't know where I am."

"Sorry. That was part of the argument. My phone's locked in Dad's safe."

Isla groaned. "I should have told Mom where I was going. She's gonna be so pissed."

"But Meg knows we're together, right?"

"Yeah, but that's no help."

"It's not?"

She promised not to tell. And since it's Meg… she'll keep her word."

"Least we're not out in the storm," he said. "It's not warm, but it could be worse."

"Yeah. Someone will come along eventually, right?"

"I'm sure they will."

Isla stared out the passenger side window. Snow had begun to pile up on the outside. "Fuck!" She suddenly turned back to him, her mouth a slash of worry.

"What?" Caleb asked.

"We're out way past the Nielson farm," she said. "They don't plow here. Hardly anyone except Mr. Pearson drives these roads at all."

"When I came this way, I didn't—"

"I'm not blaming you. I'm just saying it the way it is. No one's going to find us." She nodded to the storm. "At some point, we're going to have to walk."

Saturday

By noon the next day, it was clear: No one was coming to help them.

The radio announced that all roads were closed between Choteau and Great Falls, all drivers advised to stay at home. With the closure, the chances that someone would see the vehicle in the ditch had dropped to nil. That was the least of their problems. Even huddled together, the truck was impossibly cold. Isla's feet ached, her hands trembling. Outside, each fence post was silver with frost, a foot of snow covering everything as far as the eye could see. Even the truck had disappeared into the drifts.

Caleb pulled his cowboy hat down as low as it would go. "You ready?" he asked.

"Uh-huh." Isla nodded and wrapped a torn piece of seat cover around her face like a scarf. Caleb had another piece of it around his neck. It wasn't much, but it would have to do.

"Good," he said. "Then let's go."

He pushed open the door and a gust of arctic air howled past as they crawled from the safety of the truck. Isla's shivering redoubled.

"So what's the plan?" Caleb asked.

She straightened her shoulders. "We walk until we reach a farmhouse with a phone…"

They trudged, side by side, into the endless field of snow. The wind had died down, but the cold was infinitely worse. Isla's lungs ached, her cheeks and forehead prickling. The seat cover scarf they'd destroyed was effective, but without a cowboy hat to hold it in place like Caleb had, the strip of fabric kept slipping down below the edge of her hat. First her nose was exposed, then her cheeks and ears. Isla pushed the front up, only to have the flap on the back of her neck untucked.

"Wait," she said. "I've got to fix this."

She pulled the scarf from her head to redo the wrapping and the frigid air splashed her face. It felt like diving into a mountain lake. With numbed fingers, she slung the fabric around her head-first, lacing the loop around her neck. The scarf flapped loosely in the wind. It took two tries to get the end inside her collar, another to tuck it tightly enough to stay in place. A faint warmth bloomed over that part of her skin, but the rest of her neck was still freezing.

The wind tugged it loose and Isla swore. She grabbed it again. "Come on…." The frayed fabric flapped out of her grip, its motion drawing her attention toward the horizon. Her heart lurched.

A dark shape waited in the field.

The figure was backlit, a jagged black cut-out of a man against the bright snow. His limbs hung limp as a puppet, his shoulders hunched, the fabric of his coat and pants dangling as if tethered too loosely together. It was a man or, perhaps, a scarecrow. With the sun behind him, Isla couldn't actually tell. There was an unnatural stillness to whomever (or whatever) it was. A single detail caught her eye. The figure wasn't so much standing there as *hovering*, a foot above the drifts.

Logan.

The figure twitched as the name passed through her mind. It lifted its head with a marionette's jerk and Isla took an involuntary step back. She wasn't asleep! And yet, here was her ghost again. She opened her mouth to scream—

"What the hell?" Caleb said, interrupting her thoughts. "What is *that?*"

Isla turned. "What?"

"Do you see that?" Caleb rubbed his eyes. "That... That guy over there?" She followed his pointed fingers to the distant figure. "There's somebody in the field."

"You see him too?"

At her words, the wind rose in an angry gust and the surface of the nearest snowdrift swirled. Sparkles of ice blinded her. When the snow had settled again, the field was empty.

"I swear to God," Caleb said, "I saw someone standing there."

"I did too." Isla's voice was shrill. "Who was it?"

"Don't know. Someone." Caleb swallowed hard. "He kind of looked like he wasn't really there."

Isla's stomach dropped.

"I know, it's stupid." Caleb scrubbed his hands over his face. "It looked like he was sort of floating, or something." He turned to her. "Could you see who it was?"

Isla opened her mouth and closed it again. There was no good way to say it was Logan, not without starting a fight. Caleb would run. He *always* did. His brother's death was an open wound.

"I couldn't," she said. "Could you?"

He shrugged. "I dunno. It just looked like some guy." He squinted out at the field again. "But it could have been a shadow, I guess. Fuck. This is creeping me out. I *did* see something, Isla. I swear I did."

"I-I did too. I'm worried, Caleb. It... reminded me of a nightmare I had."

He frowned. "About what?"

Isla didn't answer. Beyond the now-empty field, the afternoon sun was low in the sky, shadows stretching out in blue bands before them. Another gust of wind blew a swirl of snow.

After a long moment, she spoke. "What if the guy in the field was a warning?"

"About what?"

"I don't know." She bit back the words she wanted to say: *I saw your dead brother, Caleb. Standing right there. In that goddamned field. He was watching us.*

"Nah. We're both overtired," Caleb added. "We barely slept last night. Haven't eaten, and we've been walking for hours. With the sun, and the shadows, and the lack of sleep, our brains are playing tricks on us. That's all."

"I guess," she said, feeling like she'd somehow lost an argument. "Sometimes when I wake up at night, I see stuff."

"Like what?"

"Stuff." She frowned. "Nightmares. Things I can't get out of my head." She turned to look at the horizon. The empty field stared back at her. "We need to keep moving. It's getting colder."

"Got it. Then let's walk."

Sunset came early, and soon a brilliant glimmer of light lit the snowy horizon from one side to the other, pink and orange against a backdrop of blue. If Isla wasn't so exhausted and cold, she'd appreciate the beauty of it. As it was, she barely took notice of the sky. Caleb had been silent since the moment when they'd seen something in the field. It left her uneasy.

Why is Logan here now? Why can Caleb see him too?

She kept her gaze on the snow-covered field on which they walked, barely noticing where they were going. An urgency had taken hold of her, a realization that death was coming if they didn't find shelter.

The sunset bled into bruised brown and indigo before Isla looked up again. Her breath caught. There, on the horizon, shone a twinkling star.

"A porch light!" she cried.

Caleb turned so fast he stumbled. "Where?"

"There. North side of the field." She pointed. "Whose farm is that?"

"Not sure. I think we must be near the Old Pearson place." Caleb changed direction, heading straight toward it. "Let's go!"

Isla took two steps and nearly went to her knees. Her core was warm, her back sweating under her coat, but the feet attached to her legs had grown wooden in the last hour. They no longer seemed to follow her instructions.

"If there's a light on, we've got power," Caleb said, marching forward. "And if there's power, there's probably people."

"Safety," she panted, tucking her hands under her arms. She could barely feel her fingers. "Heat."

"Even if we got to break into that house, we're gonna be warm." Caleb whooped as he walked faster. "We're home free!"

Isla squinted as they struggled across the field. Without the light they could barely see where they were going, but she knew the area *should* be familiar. In her mind's eye, the summer previous flashed to life. She, Logan and Caleb, swimming on a scorching summer day. There'd been trees by the reservoir, but as for other landmarks, she couldn't remember. Beneath her feet, the rolling prairie flattened into a smooth expanse of snow.

"Caleb?"

He walked faster, stretching the distance between them: ten feet to twenty, then thirty.

"Caleb, wait!"

He glanced back. "What?"

"Where are we?"

"Dunno." He shrugged. "North of Deep Creek Road somewhere."

He turned back, walking faster. Isla scrambled to follow, but her feet were numb.

"Yes, I *know* that," she shouted, "but *where* on the road, exactly?

He didn't answer.

"Caleb, slow down! Where ARE we?!"

He was forty paces ahead of her when he finally stopped. He tugged his scarf down so she could hear his words. "The Pearson place, I think. Not sure."

Isla's eyes widened. "But the Old Pearson place is next to the reservoir."

"No," he said. "That's more east, toward the—"

With a crack, the ice hidden beneath the layer of freshly fallen snow broke and Caleb disappeared, leaving only his scarf floating on the top of the black water.

Isla dropped to her stomach, spreading her legs and arms out to even her weight. Between one heartbeat and the next, awareness of their situation appeared fully formed in her mind: *They were on ice, not land.*

"Help!" she bellowed. "Someone HELP us!"

Somehow in the last few minutes, the two of them had accidentally wandered onto the ice-covered reservoir. The weather had been hovering close to freezing for weeks and that meant that the ice was no longer thick enough to support them. Caleb, the heavier of the two of them, had just broken through. He was underwater. Drowning.

This is what the ghost was warning me about!

Isla crawled forward as Caleb's head broke the surface. "Quick!" she said. "Grab the edge!"

He went under again.

This time he didn't come up. Isla wiggled toward the toothy mouth of broken ice, stopping whenever she heard it cracking beneath her. She reached the open edge of the pond, grabbing for the floating piece of fabric. Water soaked the arm of her jacket as she tugged the fabric toward her. Unraveling from his neck, it came too easily.

"No!"

She tossed the torn seat-cover onto the ice beside her and reached into the blue-black water. Her fingers numbed at once, pain radiating up her arm into her elbow as she sloshed back and forth through the open water. Her fingertips brushed something soft.

"Caleb!" she gasped.

His hair swirled beneath her fingers as she wiggled closer to the water's edge. Beneath her, the ice cracked again and she spread her legs as wide as she could. She clawed through the black water until she brushed his hair a second time, then his face, and eventually the solid shape of his shoulder. He was under the ice, his body almost directly below hers, separated by a thin frozen layer. Isla's fingers tightened into a vise and she pulled him to the surface.

"Got you!"

Caleb's lips were blue, lids half-closed over sightless eyes as he surfaced. He coughed once, then went silent.

"You are NOT going to die on me!"

She dragged him up but stopped as the sound of the ice groaning like an animal filled her ears. She was too far out and the ice too thin. Pull again and they'd *both* go under.

A flicker of movement in her peripheral drew her attention. Isla gasped. There, right next to her—so close she could reach out and touch him if she wanted—crouched Logan. He was down on one knee on the jagged edge of ice, looking as real as the day he'd died. Isla stared, one hand holding Caleb's head above water, her body spread-eagled across the fractured ice.

"I warned you."

"Wh-what?!"

Logan's gaze jerked up and their eyes met. *"You need to get him out. Caleb's dying."*

Isla couldn't move… couldn't breathe.

"Stop wasting time!" Logan barked. *"Get him OUT!"*

The ghost's shout freed her. Isla looked back to the silent boy floating in the ice-choked water. How many seconds had passed? *Ten? Twenty?* Either way, there was no more time to lose! She tightened her grip on his coat and dragged Caleb forward with frozen fingers.

"Hold on," she whispered. "I've got you."

Isla planted her elbow and shifted her weight backwards a foot. With a crack, a new section of ice gave way and her free arm went up to her elbow into the water. She flattened herself and scuttled back another foot. Her arm—stretched flat against the ice and snow—ached with cold, but her clawed hand on Caleb's jacket tightened into a death grip.

"Got to spread my weight out," she panted. "Stay with me. Okay?"

Caleb's lips were slack, eyes closed, his shoulders half in and half out of the reservoir. A trickle of water poured from his mouth.

At the edge of her vision, the ghost waited and watched.

"He's unconscious," Logan said.

"I know that!"

"You're running out of time."

With a swear, she shimmied back another foot. The ice cracked again. "Just need the ice to be a bit thicker…" She wedged her elbows under her and heaved. This time she got Caleb's shoulders and torso out of the water, and then she felt the ice under her hips dip with a groan. Water soaked her jeans. She froze.

"Hurry!" Logan bellowed. *"He's not breathing anymore."*

"I know that!" she cried. "But I can't get him out without falling in myself, and then—"

"He's DYING!"

With a roar of frustration, she slid away from the newly-spreading web of cracks, one hand on Caleb's coat. "Hold on," she panted. "Almost there." When she was back from the edge, she pulled again. The back half of Caleb's body bobbed and lurched. Soon his whole torso was out, then up to his thighs, then his knees. She could feel Logan's ghost waiting at her side, but didn't dare look up. She needed to focus.

"Almost… almost."

Isla hooked her fingers under Caleb's armpits and pulled hard, hoping to winch him out of the water by force of will alone. There was a long moment where something *else* flickered in her periphery. It distracted her at the same moment that the ice beneath her broke free. Isla's face and chest went under. The shock of cold dislodged her grip. Caleb disappeared under the ice.

Resurfacing, Isla scrambled backwards, choking as she tried to catch her breath. Her fingers raked through the water, desperately searching for the hint of fabric—anything!—to grab onto. "Caleb! Hold on! Caleb—"

"It's okay."

With a jerk, Isla looked up. Two ghosts waited next to her. They floated, rather than stood on the water's edge.

"No!" she screamed.

"It's okay," Caleb's ghost gave her a sad smile, one she knew too well. *"You tried."*

"Don't die!"

Logan frowned. *"It's over."*

"Please," she begged. "Wait! I can get him out."

Logan slung his arm over Caleb's shoulders in a gesture so familiar, so brotherly, Isla was momentarily blinded by tears.

"Please wait," she begged. "Don't leave me. PLEASE!"

She rubbed away her tears, but when she could see clearly again, the specters had faded and only the shimmer of ice and darkness remained.

Around her, the storm raged.

Celebrated Manifestations of the Weary Modern Woman

Khan Wong

Imani couldn't believe she had to deal with this shit again. "It doesn't work like that," she explained to her boss for the umpteenth time. "Illusions fade. That's just how it is."

"Your job is to leverage your powers for the benefit of our clients." Jennis Rumer was the city's queen of P.R., fixer extraordinaire for the moneyed set of Generation Turbo, and landing a job at her boutique agency in San Francisco was a bright and floofy feather in Imani's cap. It had turned out to be a careful-what-you-wish-for kind of thing.

"I can give him a boost, but he has to make the most of it with his own effort—"

"They pay for magic so they don't have to make their own effort."

The view of the bay outside the window offered a brief distraction from another tiresome discussion of the unreasonable demands of Jak Toniq, superstar rapper and producer, caught with his pants down, again. An affair with yet another barely legal fan had come to light, only this one had gotten pregnant. Jak Toxiq was more like it. That blue water promised a beautiful oblivion under its shimmer.

"Can't you just keep the charm going on an ongoing basis, in perpetuity?"

Imani looked away from the window. She had more than once fantasized about throwing both Jennis and Jak out of it—a daydream she couldn't indulge for long, given her powers of manifestation. Not that a random thought could do that; there'd have to be a ritual and everything.

"What you ask would require me to remain in trance, chanting and channeling, until he drops dead or I do. I wouldn't be able to sleep, or eat, or have a life—"

"I'm not paying you to have a life."

"You're not paying me to drop dead either."

Jennis rolled her eyes. "Don't be dramatic."

"And anyway, if I do as you ask, I wouldn't be able to do anything for any other client. You really want Maxine Hargrove's botched face lift all over the feeds? Or for everyone to hear Stella Rue's real singing voice? Not to mention the Governor's—"

"Okay." Jennis cut her off. "Point taken. But that doesn't change the fact we need to come up with a solution for Jak. Today, 4 of-the-sun. Strategy meet. Be ready to present."

Imani smiled and nodded, exuding the strongest aura of competence she could muster. In such moments, she imagined her brown skin shining with her inner light, glowing from her heart right down to her perfect mani-pedi and the amber cloud of her hair.

"I know you can do it," Jennis said. "Go make some magic."

Imani seethed with frustration on the walk back to her office. Her co-workers buzzed about the breakroom, or else they focused on the screens glowing on their desks, tap-tap-tapping away amidst arrays of potted plants and succulents. A few colleagues paced behind glass walls, taking calls in their own offices, their strategizing silenced to her ears by privacy wards. Everybody and everything irritated her. She contained it until she shut her door, at which point she let loose a low moan of anguish. Okay, maybe she *was* being dramatic, but not that much. This wasn't the first time, and it wouldn't be the last: their clients were all such entitled motherfuckers. She had known what she was getting into when she signed a contract with this firm, had wanted it, had manifested it, but the reality of the people she served—most of them, anyway—was much more challenging than she had imagined. Live and learn.

She lit a candle at her altar, a spray of bright pink ranunculus beside it. One of the blossoms shone through the flawless, double terminated quartz hovering above a mirrored disc. A good grounding meditation always helped in moments like this, opened her perception to the cosmic threads she had a talent for weaving. Her gaze into the crystal's translucence was the bridge her conscious mind flowed across to become the crystal, so she could perceive reality through its facets.

The first manifestation performed for Jak Toniq had been simple: an affair with a music producer's wife erased from the minds of the parties involved, witnesses and all. These included a couple of session musicians, a janitor, the wife, and Jak himself. Built into that charm was a stipulation that the lovers would experience no attraction to each other should their paths cross again. It worked until the sexting scandal with a prom queen. The girl in question was a legal adult—but—for Jak, at the age of thirty-two—still inappropriately young. She was about to go public with the photos when the second manifestation by Imani resulted in the girl tripping at a ferry stop and dropping her phone in the bay, photos lost, and everyone moving on. His future behavior was the karmic collateral for this manifestation—no teens, no adultery, take no for an answer. The compact was simple: be on your best behavior, or else. This third time was else.

This third time, he impregnated a nineteen year-old, someone he had traded private messages with since she was seventeen, and Imani thought this one would be trickier, with more blowback to contain and potentially a third party involved. Did the claimant want to keep the baby? She should find that out. Jak and the girl hadn't had physical relations until she was of legal age, but still. This was by far the toughest knot she'd been asked to untangle.

Yes, she could cast a charm over the Governor's influence-peddling scandal so that the media and the public's attention just didn't stick—but if the Governor had not actually changed his behavior afterwards, it would have come back in the news with harsher consequences for him. Sure, she could manifest a lucky break for an artist or entrepreneur—but if that person didn't follow up with diligent effort and bring their A-game in whatever field they were in, nothing would come of it. For such hopeful people, she could open a door, but that in itself guaranteed nothing. Still, it was more than what a lot of people got.

Illusions were trickier. Illusions never lasted. Case in point: socialite Maxine Hargrove's botched face-lift. Yes, Imani could cast a glamour that made Maxine glow with youthful vivacity, her unfortunate misshapen left brow and cheek protrusions veiled from the perception of all onlookers; what they saw was her imagined perfect self. But the glamour didn't last long, six hours tops. And so, with a combination of limited public appearances and Imani's handiwork, Maxine could still have a semblance of a life, with nobody but her personal assistant and select staff members at the firm ever knowing her true appearance. But that meant Imani had to be called in whenever there was to be an outing. She had even travelled to Europe with Maxine for various royal weddings and billionaire birthdays. All billable hours, of course.

Oh, but Jak. Fucking Jak. This latest incident was the third time around with an unscrupulous dalliance, and the second with the exact same scenario, and she was getting weary of that man's perversions and peccadilloes. She'd really rather not deal with him at all, but alas, her contract didn't allow her to decline the work Jennis assigned her. In some ways, it was an easy task. She'd just cast the same charm she'd done before. Although, would it actually be easier this time? There was a pregnancy, and he'd allowed his own bad behavior to undo the previous workings. There'd be more blowback, both publicity-wise and karmic-wise, this time.

She let out another groan of frustration and opened her eyes. This meditation was not working at all. There were still a few hours before the strategy session, so she got up, threw on her cape, and headed out to get some air.

The firm's office was at the top of the Transamerica Pyramid, whose distinctive shape proved to be the perfect conduit for broadcasting arcane energies through the aether to effect mass changes. Illusions like that which was cast for Maxine could be done in a home or office, but workings such as those the Governor required, or what Jak Toniq wanted, needed amplification. At the base of the pyramid, just outside, stood a redwood grove that was a favorite spot of Imani's for lunch, and tea, and space.

The day was warm, and the plaza crowded with people lunching and taking breaks from the offices in the area. An LED screen flashed with Jak Toniq's face, advertising his upcoming show at the arena. An illusionist worked his wonders on the small stage, making a circus of balloon animals do choreographed dance routines to a remix of a Jak Toniq track; a young woman clapping at the front of the stage wore a Jak Toniq shirt. Could Imani not get away from him for a moment? A few vendors had set up pop-up stands, peddling jewelry, and crystals, and divinations. As she walked by the latter one of these booths, someone called her name, "You! Imani Renwick!" For a moment she trembled with a chill, despite the warmth of the day.

Behind a table with a placard reading *Alana Z *** know your future* sat an unassuming and petite young woman draped in a shawl, her hair in a loose bun stuck through with glittery hairpins. Her gaze was intense and seemed to exert a gravitational pull. Who the hell was she?

Imani walked over warily. "Do I know you? How do you know me?"

"The spirits bade me beckon you."

Although she herself could not connect directly with them, Imani was well aware of the spirits that hung about sometimes. Anybody with any type of magic experienced a sort of buzzing shiver in their presence, even if they couldn't see or hear them.

"I have a message for you." Plus, when mediums have a spirit in them, their voices go all weird, like Alana's was now—spaced out, with a low rumble, somehow echoey.

Their gazes locked and confirmed for Imani that the medium was not the one behind those eyes at the moment. Those eyes shimmered with the glazed, distant look of the possessed. Plus, the presence whose chill she felt was clearly not native to the body it spilled out of. Imani took a seat on the stool in front of the spirit-woman's booth.

"Your lesson is your exit, and your exit is free."

Upon the utterance of these words, the speaker-spirit exited the medium, the latter's frame giving a slight shiver as she came to. She yawned, then gave her head a shake. The eyes that now blinked at Imani had a different light behind them than they had before. The light of whoever this Alana actually was. The shiver-inducing presence was gone, and the woman's own presence was much lighter than it had been just a moment before.

"Did somebody talk to you?" she asked, then took a sip of water from a bright green bottle. "Must've been urgent."

"Do you remember anything you say when that happens?"

"Not mostly, no." The shake of her head was apparently weary from answering that question every time.

"Well, you—the spirit—said 'your lesson is your exit and your exit is free.'" Imani held out her hands as if offering a special gift. "Any idea what that might mean?"

"Does that make sense to you?"

"It does not, hence my question."

Alana chuckled. "I see. Well. Let's start with: what do you want to exit?"

"What—?" The question stumped Imani with the audacity of its obviousness.

"I get the feeling it's why you're out here now." In addition to channeling spirits, this woman's talents obviously also included intuitive insight. It was a common talent, which was annoying. Who needs so many random strangers knowing what existential crisis you're going through at any given moment? But useful in this moment, it turned out, however unsettling.

"My job is being a lot right now."

"You need to work for someone you respect, and not just admire." A cloud drifted, revealing the sun, which illuminated the whole section of the plaza where they sat. Alana's hairpins glimmered brightly, like a cluster of stars winking on.

"How can you admire somebody you don't respect?"

The intuitive shrugged. "It seems to me that admiration can be about worldly accomplishment, but respect is about character. Greatness in both areas often overlaps, but they don't have to."

Huh. Imani had never really thought about it like that.

At the side of the table sat a wooden box, from which Alana pulled a stack of cards that she placed between them. "Shuffle and ask a question."

Without a second thought, Imani picked up the deck. "How do I get out of my contract?" After a few shuffles, she reassembled the deck and set it back down.

Alana drew a card. "Queen of Mirrors, reversed. Someone with a fierce intellect, but calculating. Always seeking the most advantageous position for herself, which sometimes benefits others but sometimes not. Reversed indicates the exertion of control."

Next card. "The cross-card, the challenge, is the Prince of Gems, also reversed. Someone of privilege, but it is squandered on foolishness. Ego-driven and selfish."

Next card. "The Queen of Flowers. She represents liberation, the celebration of one's own authority. In this positioning, she suggests that getting out from under the control of the Queen of Mirrors will require bringing the Prince of Gems to some sort of justice."

Imani looked at the spread—the mirror queen's haughty beauty reflected at multiple angles, her back to the viewer. The young man, bare chested though his neck was laden with strands of jewels and a large ruby pendant, about to step into a fire. The flower queen sitting on a tree stump surrounded by tall birds-of-paradise, a field of wildflowers behind her. Imani saw how these cards applied to her situation, but wasn't sure what she was supposed to do. How could she bring Jak Toniq to justice?

Alana watched Imani contemplate the cards. She let a moment or two of silence go by before asking, "Do these cards make sense to you?"

"Yes, though I'm still not sure what to do."

Alana tapped the Queen of Flowers. "You must do what it is in your power to do. What only you, in this situation, can do."

So—a justice that only she could bring. Another manifestation would be demanded, this she knew. How could that bring justice?

"Thank you," Imani said as she reached for her wallet.

"Oh, no charge," Alana said as she gathered up the cards and rejoined them to the deck. "Not when spirit brings you to this chair."

Imani stood and thanked her; it was time to get back to the office and figure out just what the hell her plan was. She had three hours. Three hours to bring justice to the Prince of Gems, who was obviously Jak. Sometimes, the spirits just hit you over the head with that stuff, didn't they? But what would justice mean in this case? The previous two times, as part of the working, Jak had made private contrition to the parties involved. Nothing public. This time, he'd have to publicly own up to his actions and withstand the judgment that was bound to come. He'd bounce back afterwards, and it would be like nothing ever happened—nobody would think about it again. He could make the same promise to curb his behavior, but what good did that do last time?

Then it struck her that Jak wasn't the only one involved in this mess. His wasn't the only life affected, and thus, in the interest of justice, his needs and consequences weren't the only ones to be considered.

The girl on the other end of the video call looked bored more than anything.

"Hi, Bianca, I'm Imani. I—"

"You're the magical makes-problems-goes-away lady Jak's got on retention."

"Retainer—"

"Whatever." The girl was pretty in a casual, bohemian way. She wore her hair in twin poofs atop her head, one green, one pink. The colors looked fresh. *"I'm only taking this call 'cause my lawyer said I should. I can tell you right now, I don't want to help that asshole."*

"I want to see how I can help you—"

Bianca scoffed loudly and rolled her eyes. *"You help rich people cover up their crimes and scandals. Why the fuck would you want to help someone like me?"* Imani had read the file: daughter of an Army veteran who took his own life. Mother eked out a living in service jobs before eventually becoming a paralegal. Bianca recently graduated high school and was working as a barista.

"I want to help people like you, not people like him. But I went for money and prestige over purpose. Living in this town is expensive, you know?" San Francisco had always been a town of booms and busts. This latest boom happened to be magic, and like every boom, it made the rent too damn high. She hadn't planned on being this open with the girl and wondered if it was a good idea, even as her words tumbled out. Something told her Bianca would respond to realness, so she went for it. "What do you want from life, Bianca?"

The girl looked stunned at the question. From her expression, Imani imagined she wasn't used to her wants or not-wants being considered.

"If you mean, like, a 'career' or whatever, I wanted to get an industry cert in VR game design. But I can't do that and take care of a kid. My mom will help, but still…"

"Does that mean you've decided to keep the baby?"

Bianca nodded. *"My friends think I should give it up or get a…you know. Like I think women should be able to choose, but my choice is to have this baby and take care of it, like my mom did me."*

This girl should have more help than just what her mother could provide. And certainly, Jak should be on the hook for something.

"Would you want to go to VR design school if you could swing it?"

Bianca laughed—genuine mirth cracked her grumpy façade. *"I mean, yeah. No duh. But there's no way. Especially with a kid."*

"I think we can take care of that."

A highly skeptical look jabbed right through the screen. *"With whatever you're going to do for Jak?"*

"It'll be part of the working."

"What does that mean?"

"It means he has to make an offering for restitution."

"And you just get to decide? Will it hold up in court?"

"The law has nothing to do with it. We go with magic rules for this part. In order for the manifestation to work, the client has to offer a sacrifice, the nature of which is determined by the situation they wish to disappear. And since I am the Weaver of this manifestation, yes—I just get to decide."

"So he has to do what you say?"

"If he wants to get the results he's hoping for? Yes."

Bianca nodded as she took this in. *"Okay. What you got in mind?"*

They took the meeting in the conference room, its soundproofing reinforced by a charm by one of the building maintenance mages. Jennis at one end of the table, while Imani took a corner seat beside her. Jak took the other end of the table, his agent on one side, his business manager and publicist on the other.

"Things are getting real bad for me out there," Jak said. He leaned back in his chair, hands clasped across his belly. His shirt was open nearly down to his navel, loops of diamonds glinting on his waxed chest. He kept his sunglasses on. "I thought your spell or whatever was supposed to keep my rep clean."

"It's a manifestation," Imani explained, patiently as she could for having repeated herself so many times. "Your follow-through is key to it working. I can magic the problem away, but you have to change your behavior for it to stick. Getting a teenager pregnant doesn't really accomplish that."

"What did that bitch say...?" Jak turned to one of the men beside him, his manager or agent, Imani wasn't sure which. They were both new.

Jennis cleared her throat and caught Imani's eye. "Try not to be too confrontational," she had said before the clients arrived. So much for that.

"The young lady in question is a legal adult," the agent or manager replied.

"Be that as it may," Jennis said. "We have a course of action that will clear Jak's reputation and keep him in the good graces of the public and the law. Imani, why don't you tell us about it?" Jennis put on an expectant face; she was no doubt curious what Imani would say, since there hadn't been time for a pre-meeting briefing.

"Repentance, responsibility, restitution."

"Say what now?" Jak leaned forward, rested his crossed arms on the table in front of him.

"I can craft another manifestation for you," Imani explained. "But as you should know by now, you need to sacrifice too. To repent, you need to publicly acknowledge wrongdoing. To take responsibility, you must pay for the care of this child until they are a legal adult—"

"That ho needs to just get rid of it. I'll pay for that."

"Miss Shura has indicated she wishes to keep the child."

"That's her choice, not mine," Jak said. "Bitch just wants my money."

"Stop using that word," Jennis said, her voice calm but firm.

"What did you say?" Jak raised his sunglasses and rested them on his forehead, then stared Jennis down across the table.

"Stop referring to women as bitches or your contract with us will be terminated, and you can find someone else to take your case. Though, I doubt you will after what is now your third scandal. Besides, there's no manifester as celebrated in our industry as Imani, so good luck with that. It's not hard, Jak. Just don't say bitch. Or ho."

Imani suppressed a smile. Though Jennis had asked for no confrontation, Jak's blatant disrespect was apparently a step too far.

"Fuckin hell," Jak grumbled, clearly exasperated. "Fine. But why do I have to pay child support now? Why do I have to make a public statement? I didn't before."

"You didn't before because you swore to the aggrieved party, and to the staff you have apparently fired, to change your behavior, to not do it again," Imani said. "That promise was key to the magic working. When you broke your promise, you broke the magic. And now, because it is the third time, there's a higher price to pay—"

"I'm already paying your fee!" Jak bellowed.

"We do pay handsomely for the services of this firm," one of Jak's entourage said. That one was the business manager, definitely.

"The fee you pay this firm grants you access to its services," Imani said, amazing herself with how calm she was keeping her voice. "But magic has a cost too. An energetic cost. A karmic cost. This time, because you broke your previous compacts, you have to pay a higher cost. The public statement and atonement is one. The child support is the other. It's not so much the money, it's the accountability. It's taking responsibility, however minimal, for the life you created out of carelessness."

"This is fucking bullshit," Jak said. "Why doesn't she have to take responsibility?"

"What the hell do you think raising a kid is?" Imani stared Jak down, unblinking. "I mean, you could marry her instead." She would never in a million years wish that upon the poor girl, but she knew what Jak's reaction would be.

"Fuck that," he said. "Child support and I don't have to have anything to do with her?"

Imani nodded. "That's how it would work. Yes."

"Can I craft the statement, or does he have to do it?" the publicist asked.

Imani cast her glance over to the earnest young man. Was this his first big time client? There was a kindness and understanding in his eyes that she hoped Jak wouldn't quash. "It's fine if you craft it, but he has to deliver it." She pointed at Jak.

"I'll make it sincere," the publicist said.

"Yeah, you do that." Jak sat back in his seat, slipped his sunglasses back down and drummed his fingers.

"And restitution?" The new business manager blinked at her over the table's glossy glass surface. "The repentance is the public statement; the responsibility comes in the form of child support. And the offering for restitution…?"

Imani smiled. This business manager paid attention. She liked him. "The offering for restitution is tuition and the required equipment costs for an Industry Certification of Virtual Reality Game Design."

Jak burst with laughter. "No way. She—"

"It's what she wants to do, which you would know if you ever talked to her like a person."

Thunderheads gathered behind Jak's eyes, and Imani could see the calculus going on in his mind. He didn't want to help Bianca get ahead, but doing so was the lock on the treasure chest of public forgive-and-forgetfulness. "All right. Yes. A statement, and child support, and school stuff? Is there anything else?"

"Just be more careful who you stick your dick in," Imani said.

Jennis let out a snort, then quickly regained her composure.

Jak couldn't even hide his smirk at that. "Let's do what we gotta do and make this go away."

The discussions went more easily after that. They set the timetable for the public announcement, the drafting of the child support agreement: a one-time payment of $1,800,000 which, amortized over the course of eighteen years, amounted to five thousand dollars a month. Finally, a one-time payment of $100,000 to support Bianca's pursuit of industry certification, at current tuition and market prices. They also reserved the ritual space at the top of the pyramid for a midnight working.

Jennis was thrilled at the outcome, though there was one other piece of this working that she wasn't too happy about.

"If he breaks the compact, I'm breaking my contract too."

Jennis bristled when Imani presented this clause after the client meeting. Imani hadn't mentioned it to the client because it had no effect on his business. "One has nothing to do with the other," Jennis rightly declared. She'd been sitting behind her desk when Imani brought it to her. Let it be on her turf. Imani would have the upper hand anyway.

"I can no longer put my talents to use for people who won't make good faith efforts to keep their end of the bargain. This is the third manifestation on behalf of Jak, for the same damn thing. If he breaks it again, that's it. I'm building it into the working. If you don't like it, fire me."

Jennis well understood if she fired Imani, it would require a severance payout, and then she'd have nobody else who could effectively do the working for Jak, one of her biggest clients, and then the firm would be in breach of contract.

"If Jak keeps his word, then we have no issue," Imani said, even as she understood, all too well, that both of them knew the chances of that were slim. Still, there was a chance.

"Very shrewd of you," Jennis had said finally. Imani thought she detected grudging respect.

Imani was proud of herself. It was indeed shrewd of her.

Six months was all it took. And this time the accuser was not some anonymous girl, some groupie, some fan, or somebody's assistant. This time it was a famous actress, and the assault took place at the after party for some awards show. He had comforted her, won her over with flattery, then got her alone in the library of the mansion and used the laughable line "Books make me horny." Allegedly. Unlike the others, this victim had her own fame and her own resources, and she was not having it.

The magical compact thus having been broken, Jak Toniq's fall from grace was spectacular as the media, his detractors, and even his fans turned against him. They burned his merchandise in the streets and made viral videos of themselves deleting his music from their playlists. He would await trial in jail.

Imani got her exit. Freed from her contract, she parted ways with Jennis and opened her own shop. She hired Alana to offer intuitive services a couple days a week, and set up a cute little nook in the newly acquired storefront for that purpose. Maxine Hargrove followed her to her new practice, as did a couple of smaller clients, but the Governor stayed with Jennis. Which was fine with her—she didn't have the resources for transmission-level manifestations on her own anyway. Besides, she'd lost her taste for working with the celebrity class and major public figures. A lucky break here, enhanced attractiveness there. Normal people stuff, that's what satisfied. Helping dreams come true, as she had for Bianca. Not covering up celebrity scandal.

"Come check it out," Alana said, poking her head into the back office where Imani was having lunch. This was worth interrupting a salad for. When they got out to the curb, Imani turned to face her shop. The gold lettering gleamed with promise.

IMANI RENWICK: Bespoke Charms & Manifestations

"How does it feel?" Alana asked.

Your lesson is your exit and your exit is—

"Free."

A wood carving swung gently over the door, intricate and graceful: the Queen of Flowers.

Words Are for Those With Promises to Keep

Jonathan Maberry

Celeste came into the garden before the sun had risen above the trees.

There were shadows in a dozen shades of purple and lavender draped across everything. The trees that embowered her garden were filled with songbirds, their many voices somehow blending into a concert that made sense if she did not try too hard to listen. Meaning crept into the back of her thoughts and whispered secrets filled with subtle promises.

It made her smile.

Smiles were so rare these days.

These weeks.

These months…

She stood on the flagstones in bare feet. The stones were damp with cool morning dew and there was a smell of seawater in the air, even though her house was far from the ocean. It was like that sometimes. Scents from faraway places found this place.

Found her.

Shared with her.

Reminded her of those times when sadness was even further away than the sea.

All around her, the flowers were coming awake, stretching their petals like arms reaching out with a morning yawn. A trellis of pink and white roses climbed in a graceful arc over the flagstone path, and the morning's first bees drifted sleepily from one to the other.

Along the fence wall were the pleated green folds of lady's mantle, and here and there were the chartreuse flowers. The white flowers of the thornless benenden, cousin to the blackberry plants, thrust upward with joy at the new day, and pale blue delphinium revealed their yellow hearts. A caterpillar sat dozing atop a tulip bulb, and hummingbirds flitted among the orange poppies.

The garden shouted in all its voices and colors. It whispered and nattered and sometimes, it sang.

Celeste stood there, cradling a cup of tea between her palms, watching the morning light pour its colors into the day. There were so many shades of green, from the lush grass to the leaves of sycamore and oak and maple. Scents rose from mint and thyme and rosemary, alchemizing a potion of enchantment in the air.

She remembered laughter in that garden. And peace. Real peace.

Long ago.

Andrew dozing in his hammock with Rufus sprawled beside him, all four legs straight up and bushy tail hanging over the side, swishing away flies. Wagging for the fun of it. A Bluetooth Bose speaker sitting somewhere out of sight, picking random songs from a playlist compiled over years but subject to no discernible structure. That was Andrew. One cut was Yo-Yo Ma playing Bach with introspective melancholy; another was Pink Floyd singing to the mad and broken ghost of Syd Barrett. Like that, from mood to mood, tone to tone, meaning to meaning, allowing the shuffle function to have its own fun. Andrew used to smile as he slept.

Though, Andrew sometimes only pretended to sleep so he could watch her. Celeste had become aware of it over time. Sometimes she danced among the flowers for herself, sometimes for Andrew. Sometimes for no one at all. His music and her dance, and the audience made up of flowers and bees and stray cats and babies on blankets.

Andrew's shadow was all that remained of him.

Cancer had stolen everything else. His laughter. His warm hands and warmer heart. The kind tolerance in his eyes. The smile that seeing her ignited on his face.

Gone.

Wasted down to a scarecrow.

Turned to dust.

The ashes carried away by the bright waters of the little stream at the back of the garden. She remembered watching the dance of strange little colorful fishes moving as the ash fell.

He was gone, taking his smiles and his games and his music with him.

Caleb and Angie were gone, too.

Not cancer. Nothing so slow for them. The car that ran the red light smashed them out of her world in a heartbeat. Alive on one side of a fragile moment, and on the other side…things that needed to be zipped into bags and taken away by grim-faced men and women in uniforms.

Gone, though.

Gone as completely as Andrew.

Their ashes had floated on top of the gurgling waters of last autumn. She had stood on the bank, clutching her blouse in white fists, screaming at the stream that took her babies away.

To some faraway land where cars did not steal innocence.

Where cancer could find no foothold.

Where the cruelty of life did not leave her broken and robbed and alone.

And the colored fish swirled and swam as if in celebration of the ashfall.

Above her, strung from fifty arms of the intermingled trees, wind chimes of wood and bamboo, metal and glass tinkled in the air. Never too loud. Never intrusive. Always in tune with her mood and her thoughts. Celeste looked up and saw that the first rays of sunlight sparkled on the shiniest pieces and were transformed to rainbows as they passed through edges of glass. She had begun hanging them after Andrew died. Now it was the wind who played for her, and when she danced—those rare times she danced now—it was mostly her swaying in whichever direction the wind pushed her. Eyes closed, hoping to catch a glimpse of Andrew, Caleb, and Angie in her personal darkness.

Sometimes they were there.

They always seemed far away, though. And they always seemed to be beckoning her.

How odd, that those daydreams always ended the same way…with her husband and babies swimming in the stream with the fish. Small, like the fish. Quick and elusive, just like those fish.

Celeste walked deeper into the garden.

A green turtle watched her from the bank of the run-off that led from her property down to her stream. She could hear the gurgle of the water as it tumbled over stones on its way south. On impulse she stooped to set her cup down on the path and then followed the runoff through the trees. A mockingbird flitted from branch to branch, regaling her with borrowed songs learned in a hundred places. A sound made her turn, and she saw a rabbit vanish beneath a clutch of soft orange echinacea.

It made her smile. Another of those rare smiles. The stretch of her mouth felt odd against the resistance of tear-streaked cheeks.

The runoff widened as it spilled into the stream and Celeste stood on the bank, her toes sinking into the mud. Sunlight had found the water and it glimmered on the ripples. She saw a flash of silver and realized that it was a fish.

Then there was another flash. Orange this time. Then green and blue. Those fish dancing in the cool water.

That made her smile, too.

Celeste moved to where the trunk of a fallen tree hung out over the edge of the water, and sat down. She shifted over to let her toes dangle in the water. It was colder than she expected, but nice, because the day was going to be hot. She loosened her bathrobe to let the breeze caress her throat and chest and thighs. The mockingbird perched on a branch directly above her, continuing its songs.

A second fish swam by. And after a moment, a third followed.

Celeste leaned down to look and saw her reflection in the rippling water. Dark rust-red hair falling down her shoulders, her eyes filled with so many questions. She felt that somewhere, somehow, deep inside she was changing. Becoming someone else. Leaving behind the person she had been all these years.

Sometimes on days like this, she imagined that her grief was a stain and that the breeze and the running water could wash it away. Or…maybe that they would wash her away, leaving the stain behind.

Those were good daydreams. The soft caress of morning wind that was sweetened by every flower over which it passed. The gurgle of water and the sparkling ripples, as unique and quixotic as the shapes that fire made. Celeste held the image in her mind as she closed her eyes. How lovely it was to feel wind and water move through the person she was now—a person she was sure was not her true self. This version of Celeste was the journey, not the destination. That was the only thing that made sense to her.

Two more fish shot past, and one of them brushed against her ankle.

She did not jerk away, and that surprised her. Celeste stared down into the water as more of the brightly-colored fish went by, hurrying on toward...

Toward what?

She found that she actually wanted to know. As if there was somewhere for the fish to be that mattered. Not just to them, but to her.

The sun rose higher, pushing shadows across the span of the stream and for a moment the crisscrossed shadows looked like a maze. A labyrinth. It troubled her because it reminded her so much of her life. Not always, but the way it was often enough. Things to do, things to be, things to need. So many problems to solve and puzzles to navigate every single day.

Celeste paused, head cocked to listen. Had she heard Andrew's music? Or was it the laughter of the twins?

The more she strained to hear, the less she heard.

She felt a fresh tear break from her eye and roll down over her cheek.

Was it grief? No. There was joy in her life, too. There were things she loved about who and what she was.

Then what was it?

The fish swam past her. Five of them. Ten. Dozens.

They came from somewhere and were heading somewhere, but as they passed her, they looked so...free.

Free in the moment.

Free to be what they were, without condition or expectation or demand.

Pieces of silver flitting through a sunlight stream on a summer morning.

A second tear fell.

She watched it strike the surface of the water at the exact moment another fish went past. She hadn't seen the fish coming and for a moment fancied that the tear had become the fish. A stupid idea, she told herself.

She watched that fish swim away.

Free.

In her mind, she heard Andrew call her name. And then that high, sweet, untroubled laughter of the two children. There was no pain in those sounds. There was no gasping, scraping, desperate struggle against cancer. There were no screams of shock as headlights rushed at the car and filled the world with darkness.

His voice. Their laughter.

She opened her eyes and looked around, genuinely surprised to see no one. Not her husband. Not her children.

There was only the forest. Its magic was not in bringing back what was lost. The magic of this place was always that it came from somewhere and went somewhere and paused only to leave its sweetness and its promise. Perhaps an invitation.

It was why she had poured out those precious ashes in the stream. In this stream, where the orange and blue and silver and green fish swam with such freedom. With joy.

Once more she closed her eyes. She spoke the name of her husband. "Andrew…"

She said it over and over. Seven times seven she said it, though she did not know why it needed to be said that precise number of times. It felt right.

Then, she spoke Caleb's name. Him next because he was eleven minutes older than Angie. Seven times seven as the water bubbled past and the fish leaped and played in the current.

Then Angie's name. Angie, not Angela. She was an Angie from the moment Celeste first held her. Angie. Seven times seven.

Saying their names in order to let them go. To free them from the chains of her grief. Weeping as she did so, seeding the stream with those tears.

Then, she said her own name. Celeste. Speaking it the way she spoke the names of the lost ones. Her husband and children. Those beautiful souls who deserved to be free and joyful.

When she was finished, she sat for a long time on the trunk of the tree.

An hour later, when the mockingbird flew away, there was a pale blue bathrobe folded neatly over the edge of the trunk.

And there was a dark rust-red fish swimming in the rippling, tumbling, sparkling water, with the other fish all around.

It, too, swam fast and swam free.

The Smiling Dead

Guido Eekhaut

Mr. Donetz stares at me with that vacuous look all father's patients have. He does not really notice me, and I wonder what he sees. Perhaps I don't want to know. I don't want to know what he sees, what he thinks, or even where he is. I have not entered father's practice out of my own free will, but rather to bring him some urgently needed towels. Otherwise I would not think of bothering him while he is working. I'm in no need of nightmares, thank you very much.

I hastily deposit the towels on the chest of drawers against the far wall and turn around so I don't have to look at Mr. Donetz's face. Too bad, really, since he's always been nice to me. He had a shop selling tobacco, newspapers, books, magazines, lotto forms, paper and pencils. I went there regularly: a magazine, a book. He also sold candy. Always a kind word for the children, and for me as well. A man all alone, never married.

Murder, in his case. The police want to question him. Dad isn't too happy about that. It's his job, waking the dead, but when there's a criminal investigation involved, he thinks it's all awful. Sometimes, he fears that the killer will break into our home to prevent the deceased from informing the authorities of his identity. By burning the body, for example. My father can't do anything with burnt bodies. He can't bring them back to life if they're too badly damaged, not even for a few minutes. He succeeds only with people whose brains are still intact. A couple of hours. Enough to offer relatives one last conversation, or the police a testimony.

Mr. Donetz was murdered. Steel rod through the heart. He may have seen his attacker, that's what police are counting on. Chief Inspector Massart, who is leading the investigation, is the one doing the counting. A grim, gloomy man, square jaw, dark hair, maybe forty. I do not like him. The feeling is probably mutual. He is accompanied by a young woman whom he introduces as Hamblin. No rank or anything. She must be a cadet, and he behaves like she is. Just orders her around and lets her do the chores and jot things down and stuff. They were here yesterday, but Mr. Donetz didn't have much to say about anything yet.

It is difficult to adapt. For the dead, I mean. They realize they are dead, and that their return is only temporary. Most of them are upset, which is quite understandable. One moment you're alive, the next they wake you up with the message that you're actually dead but you can still play the game of the living, at least for a short while. It's really cruel, when you think about it. I think it's cruel.

But hey, it's what my dad does, and it's what other people pay him for. A final goodbye, an interrogation. Sometimes, a dead person is requested to address a meeting or see some friends one last time, but that is rare. Some are awakened with the request to sign some documents, which is illegal. I'm not saying it doesn't happen, but if discovered, there are severe penalties. Insurance companies are not happy about it, and neither are the tax authorities. My father keeps himself at a distance from such practices.

When Chief Inspector Massart and the young woman arrive, Mr. Donetz is sitting at the table in father's workspace. In principle, a dead person cannot leave the room. There are a few exceptions. However, no one wants the dead to roam the streets. People are sensitive about that. Some say you don't notice, them being dead and all, but I'm sure you can.

The policeman asks my father and me to leave them alone with the victim. That's the term he uses. Victim. Those civil servants surely lack imagination. Father lays his hand on my shoulder, and we retreat to the kitchen. We drink coffee, eat a pastry. He doesn't talk much about his job. He talks even less about his feelings. He already knows I won't succeed him. He doesn't really want that to happen anyway. He wants me to do something meaningful with my life. Something creative. He doesn't want me to deal with death.

The two policemen reappear after twenty minutes. Hamblin stashes her booklet in her purse. Massart looks gloomy. "Thank you," he says. "He can sleep permanently now, if nobody wants him." And that's it. Result or not, they won't inform us. It is part of the secret of the investigation. But they certainly have no further questions; otherwise they would ask to keep Mr. Donetz alive.

Father lets them out. "Now, you go upstairs again," he tells me. "I'll finish things here." It means he will be occupied part of the night preparing Mr. Donetz for the last trip. No idea what that involves, and he won't tell me. It's partially a matter of confidentiality, and he does not want me around, handling the dead body. Whenever he retires, machines and manuals will go straight back to the Guild, as they are very strict about guarding their professional secrets.

Grandmaster Adelbert has already asked my father if I don't want to get into the trade. But father keeps that door firmly closed. The Guild will have to do without me.

The next day Mr. Donetz's body is collected by a hearse. Three taciturn and solemn men handle the body, packed in a black bag, and that concludes this chapter. Mr. Donetz is now where all the dead should be.

Three days later, a young woman is brought in. Father forbids me to enter his study, not even to bring towels or his lunch. He holds the door tightly closed. I've learned not to ask questions when he's clearly not willing to answer them. But soon enough, and through gossip, I discover who she is: The Lady Landsheer. She's not just anyone, as can be deduced from her title. She's firmly related to a wealthy family of steel magnates, who own a number of factories in the southernmost part of the country.

As father is the only practitioner of his craft in the city, every single case has to pass through him, for as much as someone wants to resurrect a deceased. No police are involved this time, it seems, as her death is attributed to natural causes. Well, in so far as a car accident can be considered natural. Anyway, the police do not need to question her. The request comes from her parents, who want to speak to her one last time, a final word. They want closure.

Closure? Creepy, if you ask me. Of course, you don't ask me anything, but that's not the point. The whole thing about raising the dead and so on always seemed bizarre and unnatural to me. Our ancestors would have hanged a man like my father, if not worse. But what he's doing is considered science now, and so it is all right.

The Lady Landsheer was twenty, in the prime of her life when she was alive, but now she's as dead as all the others, and rather damaged on account of the accident (I read some details in the paper this morning). So no, I don't need to see her, thank you very much.

Or do I?

Why can't I see her? Usually, father does not forbid me to see the patients; he's never as strict as now. Sometimes I just walk in, and he never really chases me away. He does now. Does he fear I will see too much of myself in this young lady, a little too much as her fate is concerned, the horror that can befall an innocent young lady? Is he afraid I might identify myself with her? He need not fear: I don't drive an expensive sports car during the night along the poorly lit roads around the city. You challenge fate, and sometimes fate decides you've gone a tad too far. In her case, the trip ended up against a tree.

And now she's in father's infamous room.

And what do her parents want from her?

I can't really ask her, can I?

But I'll take a chance. I wait for the night to fall heavily over the city, father sleeping his innocent sleep, and I sneak downstairs. His practice isn't locked, never locked, he's counting on my common sense (which I conveniently left in my room). I have a pathetic electric torch, but that's all I need to find my way around the house. And I know the layout of his practice. Won't bump my toe against anything.

She lies on the table in the middle of the room, the altar of father's magical powers, with a white sheet draped over her. Need any more clichés? I expect her to sit up when I enter.

But she doesn't. He keeps his patients in a sort of artificial sleep until he needs them fully conscious. Otherwise they would be difficult to handle.

Two windows are set high against the ceiling, each with milky white glass. They let in some light, which does not contribute anything to the atmosphere. I think of old movies, a horror cabinet, zombies or mummies.

Carefully, I pull the sheet away, and at once I am captivated by the girl's beauty. The accident left her head and shoulders as well as her breasts intact. I leave the rest covered. What I'm revealing is almost otherworldly. The milky light caresses her skin, her hair.

I switch off my torch and bend over her. I'm jealous of the flawless skin, the shiny hair. She has long eyelashes. She has full lips, which look red even now. A beauty, even now. Too bad she disappears underground in a day or two. The worms won't admire her.

Oddly enough, she is smiling. Never seen that on a dead person before. Mr. Donetz never looked peaceful, but then he was conscious. He knew how the cards had been dealt.

I wonder if Miss Landsheer is dreaming. It seems as if she is dreaming. As if she has a pleasant dream. Can the dead dream when they are in this state?

For a moment, I consider a kiss. For a moment I consider kissing those full, sensual lips, pressing against them a firm kiss, feeling them yield, feeling as if...

She moves. I should not be surprised: sleeping people move. And like them, the sleeping dead find themselves in the dark universe of their own thoughts. Anyway, that's what I assume. In our dreams, we are all the same.

She opens her eyes. The Lady Landsheer's eyes open, and she glances around, and then notices me. I am, of course, shocked, at least for a moment, but she seems to find my presence quite logical, and certainly acceptable. As if she were expecting me.

I back away a bit. I realize I might have gone too far in my curiosity, and as a consequence of my presence, my father might lose his license.

She is sitting up. "Are you his daughter?" she inquires. "Are you the daughter of the man who...?"

I nod. I am the daughter.

" Why," she asks. "Why did he bring me back?"

I don't know how father handles these situations. How he reacts when his patients inquire about the reason for their resurrection. How much does he explain? Or does he keep them fully in the dark concerning the motivation of those willing them back? Do they even want to be resurrected? Have they left anything like a will, and could they have objected to this procedure?

I assume not. I am not really familiar with the legal aspects of this case, but I seem to remember that no one can take *a priori* legal action against resurrection, which only official authorities are allowed to do, at the request of family or a judge. This seems unnecessarily cruel to me, bringing them back and having them realize their life is over, and that the added time will be short-lived.

But that's not for me to judge.

" Your parents," I tell her.

A disturbing sound originates deep from her ravaged body (the part I cannot see, and don't want to see). I assume laughing is difficult for her, given the accident. Under the sheet, her body seems to have taken on a strange shape. She notices me looking and quickly pulls the sheet up again, over her breasts. "I don't want to see them," she says.

" All they want is to say farewell."

" You say farewell to the living," she says, "not to the dead. The dead do not fare well."

Such is true, in a sense, but that's not how surviving family members see it. Anyway, hardly anyone knows how to deal with death, and with the dying. Very few people can do that.

She sounds hurt and bitter. This is obviously a problem family. I suddenly wonder if the accident was an accident, but that's not something I will discuss with her. She's more than upset enough as it is.

" It should be forbidden," she says. "There should be laws against it."

That's right, so many things should be forbidden, but here we are nonetheless, with a civilization that can't even leave the dead in peace.

" I just dreamed about death," she says.

That calls for an elaboration, but I'm sure I don't want to hear how the dead dream about death. As far as she is concerned, the whole situation is not only nonsensical, but also abhorrent.

" Can you help me?"

Help her? What does she mean?

I know what she means.

"My father has his professional duties," I tell her, cowardly hiding behind my father.

"I don't want to do this," she says. "And you can make all this go away."

You should have handled your accident differently, I think, at once realizing this is grossly unfair towards her. But it is true: she could have made certain not enough of her body would have been found to allow resuscitation. Then, not even my father could not have helped her parents.

But as things stand…

She lowers the sheet again. "This is what I sacrificed," she says. "This is what I left behind. What I ask from you is merely a small act of pity."

I realize she is right.

The fire is extinguished quickly enough, but father is devastated. The damage is minor, however. He will have to buy a new table and replace some instruments, but the Guild will surely compensate him. The police will want to know how the fire started, but I've been careful. Some of the substances my father uses are very flammable, under the right circumstances. Even a man as experienced as my father sometimes proves to be a bit careless.

Chief Inspector Massart has already visited, with his assistant trailing along, almost like a zombie. They find no proof a crime has been committed. Not for now, at least. I keep my fingers crossed.

Lady Landsheer's parents are angry and horrified. They are being denied a last grand gesture, a last conversation, a last opportunity for catharsis. My feeling is they should have tried harder when their daughter was alive. But of course, I don't know who's to blame for the family problems. Maybe she was an insufferable bitch.

For my part, I now realize I urgently need to depart from my father's house. Find a job somewhere, preferably in another city. Something creative, something that opens doors. I've seen enough of death.

Blue and Pearl, Green as the Sea

Helen Glynn Jones

"Did I ever tell you how I got this scar, the one under my eye?"

Sara shook her head, spraying cleaning solution onto a soft cloth. "No, I don't think I've heard that one." She always saved Leon's room until the end of her shift, so she could take her time. The rest of the staff thought him quiet, but she knew differently.

"Well," Leon said, his voice a wispy quaver, "it's a rather good one."

"Your stories do tend to be," she said, wiping the cloth across the small wooden table next to his bed. His gnarled hands were dark gold against the white sheets, his bald head spotted with age. He was her favorite resident at the care home even though, like a mother with her children, they weren't supposed to have favorites. But all the staff did, laughing over lukewarm coffee and slightly stale biscuits in the cramped breakroom, sharing what they'd done or seen or heard. Perhaps it was a way for the residents to be remembered, when so many of them seemed to be forgotten. It was a sad thing, she thought, lifting his cup to wipe underneath before putting it down again, that "out of sight, out of mind" seemed to be a family motto for so many of those she looked after.

Leon was watching her, his watery gaze still deep blue, even though the rest of him was faded, like a photograph left in the sun. "Are you ready?"

"Go on, then," she said. "Tell me."

"You see how it's shaped like a star?"

"Yes." She had noticed, but thought it a remnant of some youthful folly, like a faded blue tattoo almost lost in the folds of skin under his eye.

"That's because it's from a kiss. A mermaid's kiss."

"Oh now, come on," she said with a smile, moving over to the shelving unit. She started lifting each small ornament, wiping it carefully before putting it back. "There are no such things as mermaids, surely." This was one of the reasons she enjoyed his stories, for all that she found them ridiculous. They were full of magic, mythical beasts and enchanted treasure, lands accessed through hidden portals, opal skies and glittering seas. There was not much magic to speak of in Sara's own life, in the days spent cleaning and caring, the nights spent alone in her small flat.

"There are," he said, "and don't let anyone tell you otherwise." He started coughing, a deep rasp in his chest. Putting down her cloth, she went to the trolley by the bed and poured him a glass of water from the jug, handing it to him.

"Now, don't get yourself all worked up," she said. "You know what the doctor said."

His hand gripped her wrist, hard, shocking her into momentary silence. His eyes met hers, and for a moment they seemed filled with stars falling, with endless seas, and she caught a glimpse of the handsome young man he had once been. "Let me tell you," he whispered. "It's the last one, I promise."

"The last one? You'll never run out of stories to tell me, surely?"

He said nothing, just held her with his starlit gaze until she nodded, strangeness curling in the pit of her stomach.

He let go of her wrist. "I wore a younger man's skin in those days," he began. "Everything where it should be, my hair dark as a raven's wing." He huffed out a laugh. "And I loved the sea. Every day. I would take the fishing boat out with the rest of the crew, catching a thousand fish, ten thousand fish, a hundred thousand fish or more, so the deck was awash with scales and the bow so low in the water, it was a wonder we made it back to shore."

Sara swallowed, picking up her cloth once more, the feeling of oddness lingering like mist curling at the edges of her vision. She shook her head as though to clear it, focusing on her task. It was just another of his tall tales, that's all. She would listen, as she always did. "That many fish?"

"Indeed. The sea was alive with them, shimmering in the waves, so thick in parts we could walk on water if we were fast enough." He laughed again. "That's what I was trying to do, the day I met her."

"Walk on water?" She laughed, feeling more like herself. She moved over to the wardrobe, wiping down the door, opening it to check the clothes inside were tidy. "You must be joking."

"I swear it, on my sainted mother's grave," he said. "So there I was, lowering myself over the side of the boat, the fish churning and splashing like a great rippling silver carpet. I had my net in hand and my sturdiest boots on, and I stood on the back of the great shoal and felt the power of their mass rolling through the soles of my feet. I dipped my net once, throwing the fish on board, then again, then a third time. But then the net grew so heavy I couldn't lift it, dragging me down through the shoal and into the deep blue waters below." He coughed again as though reliving the moment, taking a sip of water before continuing.

"Why didn't you let go?" She finished the ornaments and moved along to the pictures on the walls, wiping the timber frames.

"Oh no, I couldn't let go. That net had been woven by seven maids from their own hair, each strand finer and more delicate than the last, yet together stronger than steel. It was a great treasure, it was."

"Oh, now I know you're having me on. A net made from the hair of seven maids? Give over." She laughed, thinking he'd do the same.

But Leon just stared at her, a line creasing the age-spotted skin between his brows. "Everything I tell you, everything I've ever told you, is the truth." Spittle flecked his lips as he struggled to sit up, his hands sinking into the mattress. Feeling sick, as though she'd somehow broken something fragile, Sara hurried over to help him, raising the back of the bed and rearranging the pillows behind him.

"I didn't mean—"

"It's the *truth*," he said again. "I thought you knew that... I thought..." He started coughing again, bent forward with the effort. Sara passed him the water, her hand gentle on his back, her heart hurting. He'd never minded before, when she'd tried to poke holes in his stories. Simply doubled down, insisting the dragon really did guard the gold, that magic lurked in hidden folds across the world for those eager and willing enough to find it.

"Shall I get the nurse?"

Leon, still coughing, shook his head. "S'all right," he croaked. "Don't mind me."

"Leon, I'm s—" The pager at her waist buzzed, insistently, interrupting.

"You go now," Leon rasped, waving her away. "Go on. Someone else needs you."

"But…"

Leon closed his eyes, leaning back against the pillows, the scar beneath his eye more visible, like a violet against his pale skin. Sara stared at him, her throat tight. The pager at her waist buzzed again, like an angry bee. With a sigh, she collected her cleaning supplies and left.

The next morning was gray. Rain ran in rivulets down Sara's windshield, blurring the red brick and cupolas of the old Victorian house as she pulled into one of the staff parking spots. It would have been a grand place once, stained glass above the door and patterns in the brickwork hinting at former grandeur. Sara turned off the ignition, but didn't get out of the car. Her head felt heavy, her eyes sore. She rubbed them, remnants of her restless night still swirling in her mind. She'd tossed and turned, dreaming she was searching for something precious but didn't have the right key to open the door, and each time she'd tried, waves had crashed around her, pulling her out to sea. She'd woken with the smell of salt in her nostrils, her vision clouded as though sea mist filled the room.

She leaned forward, resting her head on her forearm against the steering wheel. Stuff and nonsense, that's all it was. Remnants of the strange story Leon had told her. She huffed out a small laugh. Fish so plentiful a man could walk on water, held in a net woven from the hair of seven maidens. Honestly, he should write a book. Maybe she'd suggest it to him when she saw him today.

Enough of this. She had work to do, and amends to make. She hurried into the house, rain leaving dark spots on the crisp blue cotton of her tunic, beading on her sensible black shoes. The place smelled as it always did, a mix of air freshener and gravy and the mild sting of antiseptic, the dark halls seeming even more so with the gray day outside.

"Hoo, it's a wet one out there today!" Agnes, one of her co-workers, nodded to Sara as she entered the break room, hanging her bag on the peg.

"Shockin' weather. Ah well, at least we're indoors. You on another double shift?" Agnes seemed to work at the home every hour she could. She was saving for a house, she'd told Sara once, and needed every penny she could get.

"Yep, day and night. You want tea? I've just boiled the kettle."

"Ah, thanks. Can you pour two, please?"

"Two? You got a date?" Agnes cackled with laughter as she got the cups out, dropping the teabags in and pouring the boiling water on them.

"Hah! Fat chance of that." Sadness pierced her at the truth in her words. "No, it's for Leon."

"Leon?" Agnes frowned as she stirred the tea, adding sugar to Sara's. "Why not get him one from the canteen?"

"Oh, you know those cups are too small."

"What'd you do?" Agnes brought the teas over, putting them on the scratched laminate table. "Break one of his ornaments?"

No, just his heart.

It was ridiculous, and she knew it was, to think that way. She'd done nothing wrong. But she couldn't help remembering the hurt in Leon's eyes, the way he'd coughed and coughed. The way that he, like so many others in the home, was simply waiting for death, alone, their voices no longer seeming to matter. She was the only person he shared his stories with. It wouldn't hurt her to let him tell them without poking fun, for once. Maybe she should offer to write them down for him, a record of who he was.

She had something in her purse for him, a slice of lemon cake, made last night. She knew it was his favorite. He didn't mind the cake from the canteen, but he could never resist her homemade version. That was one thing her mother had done for her, at least. Taught her to bake a decent cake. She tried not to think of all the things her mother hadn't done, the myriad ways she'd let her daughter down before departing the world, not least of which was mortgaging the family home to the hilt in order to pay for holidays and fur coats and whatever nonsense she wanted for herself, while seemingly content to let her only child scrape by.

She didn't share any of this with Agnes. The other woman would probably think she'd gone mad. "Oh, nothing. It's just a bit of a dull day and I wanted to cheer him up." She tucked a bottle of cleaner under her arm, stuffed a cloth in her other pocket, then picked up the tea, opening the door with her shoulder to leave the room.

"Well, mind you don't go giving anyone else ideas," Agnes called after her, humor in her tone. "I don't want to be lugging mugs of tea around all day."

Sara headed along the hallway, climbing the curving carved stairs to the second floor. There was a lift, but it was supposed to be for residents, not carers who didn't want to carry a couple of mugs upstairs. Besides, she could use the exercise.

The light outside changed from gray to gold, sun finally breaking through the clouds as Sara made her way to Leon's room. The door was ajar, and she knocked before entering, placing the teas on the small table next to the bed. "Good morning!"

Leon was lying there, almost as she'd left him the day before, frail against the white pillows. He was staring into the distance, a faint smile on his lips. He was also, Sara realized as she got closer, humming something.

"Leon?"

He kept humming, the swaying lilt of the song awakening something in Sara, flickers of memory, a sense of crashing waves and locked doors that would open if only she spoke the correct words.

"Leon!" Her voice was sharper than she intended, and the old man flinched, turning wide eyes to her. She fought down a burst of irritation, smiling instead, though her heart was pounding. She'd thought he'd gone, she realized, slipping into that strange twilight world the very old often inhabited just before death, where they saw loved ones and spoke of parties or times long past. She realized she very much didn't want him to die.

"Oh. It's you." His gaze turned down.

"Who else would it be?" She kept her tone gentle, still regretting her hasty words from the day before. "Thought I'd come in to see you, first up. I might like to hear the rest of that story, if you want to tell it."

Leon dragged his hand down his face, trembling fingers catching the slack flesh of his cheeks. His arms were bare, the faded blue tattoos on his forearms visible. "What story was that, then?" he asked.

But Sara wasn't fooled. She'd seen the flash of mischief in his eyes as he'd lifted his hand. She grinned. "Something about a net made from the hair of seven maidens?"

"You sure you want to hear the rest? Didn't seem as though you were interested." There was a proud tilt to the old man's head, though his gaze slid to the mug of tea, gently steaming.

"Oh, you go on now. You know I love your stories. Even thought about writing some of them down for you. Plus, I brought you this." Sara pulled the cake from her pocket, unwrapping the napkin around it.

Leon's eyes widened; then he chuckled, the sound throaty. "Go on, then."

Sara relaxed. She knew she had him. "So, what happened next?"

"Where were we?" His blue gaze was sharp, and Sara knew he was testing her.

"You'd just been dragged down, in your maidenhair net, surrounded by fish."

"Ah yes, so it was. Ha! That was an experience." He was distant for a moment.

Sara took a sip of her tea. Footsteps passed the room, then paused. With a start, she remembered she was supposed to be working. If the shift supervisor, Mavis, saw her, she'd have words to say, and Sara didn't need that. She hastily put down her mug, pulling the cloth from her pocket and spraying it with cleaner as Leon began to talk.

"So down I went, riding the net and the shoal of fish as though they were a chariot, my lungs feeling like they were about to pop. Then I saw her."

He paused, and Sara realized he was waiting for her response. "The mermaid?"

"The mermaid. First her face, pale ivory in the gloom. I thought it a mask at first, a dead man's caul, some witchery come to take me. Then she smiled, and her teeth gleamed like pearls. She had the net in her hands, smooth slender fingers curved through the knots. It was she who had pulled me down. 'Let it go,' I said, but she shook her head, laughing all the while, hair greenish brown around her."

"But how could you speak, all the way down there?" Sara moved over to the window, starting on the slats of the blind. They were dusty, and she swiped them methodically, all while Leon's words wove magic in the room. She could almost see the swirling blue depths, the fierce beauty of the mermaid, feel the ache in her lungs.

"I used the last of my air, words forming in bubbles above my head before fading away. We floated there together, staring at each other. Then she put her hand on my arm and, all at once, I could breathe. I could hear her in my mind. 'I like your net,' she said. 'And I wish to keep it.' 'But it's mine,' I said. At this she frowned. 'Every day you take what is mine. Should I not get something in return?'"

Sara raised her eyebrows. Sliding the cloth along the last of the slats, she pulled the blind up, letting in pale sunshine. "What did she mean?"

"Well, it was the fish, of course. Turns out she was some sort of sea shepherdess, the shoal of fish her flock. Each day she'd bring them to our part of the ocean, and we'd come with our boat and take part of them away. Of course we hadn't realized what we were doing." He huffed out another laugh, the bed creaking as he moved, reaching for his tea. Sara went to help him, raising the back of the bed a little further and handing him the mug.

"So how did you escape? And why did she kiss you?"

"Well…" His voice trailed off and he winked at Sara. "Why do you think?"

"Oh, don't tell me you charmed your way out of it."

"I was a charming fellow in those days. You don't get a net made from the hair of seven maids for nothing, you know."

"So what did you do?"

"I pulled the net closer, meaning to trap her in it, but she was too fast for me. With a flick of her green tail, she had me trussed up like a caterpillar; then she towed me away, the shoal around us all slithering scales, like a great cloud. I could see the hull of our boat getting smaller and smaller, and I thought I was done for, truly I did."

Sara shook her head. "Well, I never."

"She took me to a little island, a rocky outcrop way out in the sea. We all steered clear of it on account of the rocks below the surface like sharks' teeth, ready to tear the hull of your boat. She pulled me onto a little bit of sand, towering rocks all around us, the murmur of the sea in our ears. Then she unwrapped me."

"Unwrapped you?"

"Completely, if you get my drift."

"Oh, Leon," Sara laughed, moving over to one of the pictures on the wall and wiping the glass.

He chuckled as well, the sound unexpectedly rich. "Like I say, I was a charming fellow. So there we were, her about to have her wicked way with me when there was a shout from the ocean, and there I saw the head and shoulders of a noble-looking fellow, all silvery hair and beard, holding some sort of trident, bobbing in the waves. When she heard the shout she flinched, pulling back. Our eyes met, and she leaned in and kissed me. I think she meant to get my mouth, but I turned my head, and she got me just below the eye. Turns out mermaids are venomous, y'see."

"They are?" Sara realized she'd been cleaning the same picture frame for far too long and went on to the next one. "You never hear about that in the fairy tales."

"I swear on my blessed father's reputation it's true," he said, a twinkle in his eye. "Before she slipped between the waves, leaving me half-unconscious, she put a shell in my hand to remember her by. Blue and pearl it was, green as the sea. Told me all I had to do was listen, and it would lead me back to her. I resolved that I'd see her again, one day, and finish what we started, but I never did."

"You didn't? How come?" Sara put her cloth down and went over to the table, picking up her tea and taking a sip.

Leon's blue gaze was distant. "Life, I suppose. It shifts, like the sea, one minute the current taking you away, then the next a change in the wind and you're dead in the water."

"What happened?"

"The land called me, magic whispering in the pages of a book handed to me in an opium den taking me away from the waves. And by the time I surfaced I'd forgotten about her, apart from the scar under my eye. It wasn't until much later, when I was an old man, and I found the shell among my things, that it all came back to me. And by then it was too late."

"It's never too late," Sara whispered. There was an ache in her chest, silver-sharp.

"Aye, it is." Leon sounded resigned, leaning back against the pillows. "All stories come to an end, one day." He sighed, a sound like the distant sea.

"Sara?" Agnes stuck her head round the door. "Sorry to interrupt. It's just, Mavis is on the warpath and there are three more rooms we need to finish."

"I'll be there in a sec."

Agnes nodded, then disappeared.

Sara turned back to Leon. He had his eyes closed, his hands, frail and gnarled, resting on his chest. There were crumbs from her cake on the bedding, and she gently brushed them away. Leon smiled, just a touch, as though he knew she was there.

"It's never too late," she whispered again, the magic of his story curling through her, the yearning in his voice. She'd speak to the supervisor, see if perhaps they could organise a day trip to the seaside. It wouldn't be the same, but it would be something.

Footsteps approached in the hallway outside, and Sara, with one last look at the old man, hastily grabbed her cleaning supplies and went to find Agnes.

The next morning, more lemon cake in her pocket, Sara knocked on Leon's door. She'd spoken to Mavis about the trip, the supervisor surprisingly receptive to the idea, saying something about the salt air doing the residents good. She couldn't wait to tell him. But when the door opened the room was empty, the bed made up. Someone came up behind her and she turned to see Agnes, looking somber.

"Where's Leon?" She knew, though. Knew it in her bones.

"Died in the night, he did. I'm so sorry," she said. "I know he was one of your favorites."

Tears came to Sara's eyes. "Was it… did he?"

"It was quick enough. Peaceful, in the end."

"Were you with him?"

Agnes nodded. "It was funny, though."

"What was funny?"

"Well, when I went in to check on him, there was a smell everywhere, like the sea, you know? And he gave me this, said it was for you. Said to tell you that there was still magic in the world, if you knew where to look. Said that you needed to continue the story. The next thing we knew, he'd gone." She dug in the breast pocket of her tunic and pulled something out. "Here."

Stunned, Sara held out her hand. Agnes dropped something in it.
A shell, blue and pearl, green as the sea.

Kindling

Somto Ihezue

In a moonbeam far, far from ours, or perhaps raying towards ours, or in a distant, distant breaking sky, or maybe in this very light, there was a girl who lived in a young forest, and her name was Forest.

Forest lived here with the trees: the udara trees, mighty, the becoming of giants, reaching high, splitting the sky. The baobabs, two thousand years old; ten thousand years old; immortals. The banyans whose branches broke bread with their roots. Forest lived here with the kudu whose horns touched and bent wind. The wildebeest, wandering, wandering, wandering. Forest lived here with her kin, her sailing fathers and mothers who swallowed suns; her brothers with bodies of tarnished trinkets, and sisters who held rain. Forest lived here with the spirits of her kin, her grandparents chiseling bone into ice, and her great-grandparents, who stood ten feet tall.

Once, a piece of Forest was carved into the bark of a dying Iroko. In that carving, Forest's hair was scattering vines. In that scattering, tangerine seeds sprouted here. In that sprouting, earthworms burrowed there. And Forest's hair was a forest baring its teeth. And the body of Forest's body was honey badger hide. It was tilapia gills. It was turtle shell. And the hair of her skin was green, green grasshoppers. It was falling leaves. Her nails were mountain shards. Her tears were rainfalls. Her voice was morning. Her legs were gazelles. Her hands were prayers. Her breath was wind holding wind, and her eyes, her eyes, they saw.

One day, fire came for the forest. It ran through the trees, and they learned to die. It found the creatures, all mighty and small, and when fire met their fur, their sheening fur patterned by a thousand years, gods, and children, their fur went from holy, to sacrifice, to nothing.

And Forest screamed, *Keep your burning from my trees.* And the fires did not listen. They came; they came *cackling*, they came *crackling*.

And as farmers grew maize, Forest grew fear. And this fear was hers, living in her edges, blooming with her tangerines. Forest hid in a hole, and listened, and saw as the fires came for her fields and basins. And when the fields and basins fell, the fires came for her. To see what the fires did to Forest, hold a candle to your tongue.

In all that burning, a flame-keeper reached out their hand. *Come, take my hand.* Their hands were coal.

What of my udaras and my kudu? Forest shrank deeper into the hole.

Let us find shelter first.

What of my father? What of my sisters?

They are gone to a place where nothing can harm them.

Forest knew not this stranger, whose skin was fleeting embered diamonds. Her mother had said, *Be wary of strangers.* Where was her mother now?

So Forest took the stranger's hand, and the stranger walked through fire. And their hands were warm. Not the warmth of fire, but of a fireplace.

What about me? Forest asked. *What will happen to me?*

The flame-keeper chose silence. The flame-keeper chose words. *Do you want to go on a journey?*

A journey? To where?

To quench fire.

And Forest touched her hair. There were no vines. There were no tangerines. Only ash, trailing behind her, only ash, ash, and something scorched. Her legs were no longer gazelles, and Forest would never run again. She would never pray again.

I want to quench fire. It was not an utterance. It was a wanting. *I want to quench fire.*

And Forest and the flame-keeper set off to quench fire.

In their journeying, they found clay piled high by a child. And the flame-keeper said, *Clay, you have birthed ten thousand cliffs, and you have quenched fire before. Tell us how to quench fire.*

And the clay piled high said, *If I tell you how to quench fire, what will be left of tomorrow?*

Let tomorrow fend for tomorrow.

Why have you brought a child on this journey?

Forest is a child, and Forest is many things.

Who is burning you, child? The clay piled high touched Forest.

You know who burnt her.

I do not ask who burnt her, I ask who is burning her.

I do not know, Forest said, and her footprints were gravestones.

Only fire can quench fire, the clay piled high spoke their last.

And the child and the flame-keeper carried on. In their carrying, they found a raindrop lifted by an ant. And the flame-keeper said, *Raindrop, you have birthed ten thousand seas, and you have quenched fire before. Tell us how to quench fire.*

And the raindrop lifted by an ant said, *If I tell you how to quench fire, what will be left tomorrow?*

Let tomorrow fend for tomorrow.

Why have you brought a littling on this journey?

Forest is a littling, and Forest is many things.

Who is parching you, little one?

You know who parches her.

I do not ask who parches her, I ask who is parching her.

I do not know, Forest cried, and there were no tears. Her eyes were seabeds cracked open.

Only fire can quench fire, the raindrop lifted by an ant spoke their last.

And the littling and the flame-keeper waded on. In their wading, they found a breath sealed in a jar. And the flame-keeper said, *Breath, you give life, and you have quenched fire before. Tell us how to quench fire.*

And the breath sealed in a jar said, *If I tell you how to quench fire, what will be left of tomorrow?*

Let tomorrow fend for tomorrow.

Why have you brought a gentle thing on this journey?

Forest is gentle, and Forest is many things.

Who is poisoning you, gentle thing?

You know who poisons her.

I do not ask who poisons her, I ask who is poisoning her.

I do not know, Forest exhaled, and her breathing was smoke, and her breath was soot.

Only fire can quench fire, the breath sealed in a jar spoke their last.

Stories. They were all Forest had left. The stories her mothers had lent her. Of children who began where infinity ended. Of a broken spirit who loved a spirit. Of Zaram and Kiki chasing fireflies. Of porridge, untethered things, and rabbits. Three sisters fledging into doors and anchors. A daughter who became war. A city, a desert, and all their dirges. And Forest held tight to these stories, else they fall through her fingers.

I once saw a fish love a bird. Forest gave the flame-keeper a story.

A fish cannot love a bird. The flame-keeper gave the story back.

Why?

One is for the oceans. One is for the skies. Where would they live?

And Forest chose silence. And Forest chose words. *On the horizon.*

Where is your mourning?

It is here. I want to be elsewhere.

Where is elsewhere?

On the horizon.

What will you find on the horizon?

Home.

Home will come after mourning.

I want to go home.

Home will come after retribution.

I want to go home.

Do you know what happened to your kin spirits when fire reached for them?

I want to go—

Do you know what it means for a spirit to learn death again?

I want—

Let me show you.

And the flame-keeper showed her, and Forest screamed, and screamed, and screamed, and all her kin screamed through the cracking in her being. And in their screaming, hands—desert hands, frail hands, cindered hands—reached for Forest's throat and snapped her in half. And in their screaming, Forest learned to die again, and again, and again.

Forest would never scream again. And her mourning returned. Her retribution returned.

Teach me.

What is there to teach?

If the clay piled high, and the raindrop lifted by an ant, and the breath sealed in a jar, if they will not tell us, then you must teach me.

What is there to teach?

How to keep fire.

And what will you do with kept fire?

I will quench it.

You must know there will be pain.

Hold a candle to your tongue.

And the flame-keeper held a candle to their tongue, and they knew Forest would weather this pain, and any that followed. So the flame-keeper taught Forest. He took a fire petal and nestled it in her open palms. And the petal danced, a dance gentle, a dance wild.

It feels like a heartbeat.

Because it is alive.

And the flame-keeper led Forest to a volcano's brimming mouth and said, *Eat.* And Forest ate, and her teeth blackened to charcoal. Up to a mountaintop and said *touch*, and Forest strained and touched a comet, and her fingers thawed winter. Into a storm, and said, *Drink.* And Forest drank a lightning bolt, and when she spoke, it was in tongues aburning.

In time, where there was once ash, Forest's hair became wildfire.

When will I be ready?

Tomorrow.

When will tomorrow come?

Today.

And what will come after today?

Let today fend for today. Now, we must quench.

And Forest stood still. She stood there. In all the fire she was keeping, and the flames touched her silence.

You hesitate.

If we quench fire, what will… what will happen to you?

Let me fend for me.

And Forest stood still. In all the fire she was keeping, and the flame-keeper touched her silence.

You cannot waver now.

I have wavered since the moonbeam.

Who is burning you?

And the flame-keeper chose silence.

And Forest chose words. *You touch nothing. You hold nothing. You shrink away. Your hands are sheathed. You run, not fast enough. Your shadow frightens you. Your breath is labor. You loathe your footprints. You never walk through a village. You are something on the run. A flame-keeper on a journey to quench fire. Who is burning you?*

I touched you once.

Once.

And I will never touch again.

Why?

Do you think yourself the only one marked by fire? Do you think grief was spun just for you? Come and see.

And the flame-keeper tossed Forest into the Big Burn. And Forest saw child fires merge into glowing whirlwinds, roaring louder than all the wars she had seen. She watched the Lost Crew perish at Setzer Creek. She watched whole towns packed into carts, fleeing with only gin and wedding rings. And like the flames had besieged her, they besieged Bitterroot, Cabinet, and Clearwater. They laid waste to Kaniksu, Kootenai, and St. Joe. Forest knew those forests, and now she knew the candles beneath their tongues.

And the flame-keeper shoved Forest into Black Thursday where one million sheep had died. This is what they said of the fires, they said *it wrapped the country in a sheet of flame—fierce, awful, and irresistible.* They called it *rushing fire,* for it ran like water. The fires didn't just burn timber, they peeled lands back to bone. Forest heard no bird calls, only bark bursting, black rain falling, and the sea a kettle steaming. No one lit a candle that night.

And the flame-keeper dragged Forest into Daxing'anling. The Black Dragon. It did not come from the sea, but found birth in the larch trees, *eating, eating, eating* its name. And its flames leapt across borders like fallow spirits. Something in the fir trees exploded like cannons. The clouds became ink over Heilongjiang—shadowed snow *falling, falling, falling* where fire had not claimed. *A digger dropped a match.*

Remember your mourning.

And Forest held her candle, and Forest remembered. No more questioning. No more hesitating. Forest reached out with her fire petal and the flame-keeper reached out with his. And when their burning met, someone wailed on the horizon, and a thousand eyes looked back. Blink by blink, their fire petals thinned, until all that was left was nothing.

In that nothingness, these are the things that followed: Sunlight blazed its last. Heat fled the earth. Ice and frost took hold of grasslands and choked them. Hell, once fable, became a lie. Lightning did not come before thunder. Eucalyptus pods broke their last, and koalas went extinct. The Bronze Age and the Iron Age fell lost to the ages. Storytellers and children gathered no longer around campfires. No more shadows. The ash trees bled. Dreams ebbed, and memory faded away.

And all the fire, in all the hearths, in all the kitchens, in all the fireplaces, all the fire held up by warriors standing guard. All the fires flickered out.

What is happening? Forest turned to the flame-keeper and no one was there.

What have you done? It was the clay piled high.

I— we only meant to quench fire.

And you have. It was the raindrop lifted by an ant. *This is the quenching of our kin.*

I do not understand.

Your companion was our kin. It was the breath sealed in a jar.

No, they were a flame-keeper.

Oh, child, fire has no keeper. Fire cannot be held. Only fire keeps fire.

We held hands. We held fast. They were here.

And now they are gone.

My spirits… My siblings….

Yes. Our kin burnt your kin.

Why?

Littling, that is what fire does.

But know this, though we scourge, and the raindrop lifted by an ant became a tsunami, *we also tend.* And the tsunami became a babbling brook through a desert.

Though we break things, and the clay piled high became an earthquake, *we also nurture.* And the earthquake became loam in a famine, and from the loam came a breadfruit.

Though we bellow, and the breath sealed in jar became a blizzard, *we also whistle.* And the blizzard became a breeze teaching a sparrow hatchling to soar.

Even you, forest girl, what happens when your trees fall? What happens to the nest of raven eggs once held high and safe in its branches? What happens to the colony of termites that breaks its fall? The questioning came with the voice of many and Forest clasped her ears.

I am not on trial!

We are all on trial.

I do not shatter things!

We all shatter things.

I—

Hush, child, the clay piled high brought a finger to her lips. *When a tree falls, where does it go?*

Come, come and see. The raindrop lifted by an ant touched her pupils.

And Forest saw. She saw a tree crashing through a forest. She saw its fruits nourishing the ground critters that could never reach high enough. She saw its leaves yellowing into the soil. She saw its seeds scattering.

And what comes from scattered seeds?

Forests.

Forests.

Forests.

I don't know how to change this. Forest held the candle. It was not lit. It did not burn. Still, the pain held on.

Yes, you do. You are wrestling trees. You are tempests, impalas, blacksmiths, and carpenters. You are batik and raffia, terra-cotta and weavers. You are Kalahari and all her oases, apologies and blessings, boys with petals in their hair, salt and crescent moons. You are pebbles turn to stone turn to mountains. You are Kunle, Bambi, Jide, and Chizaram. You are Emeka, Ugochinyere, Ifesinachi, and Wole.

Who are they? Forest asked.

Don't you remember? They are your siblings teaching themselves to run. They are coconut-headed children leaping into the horizon, holy and scattered in a wild place. They are screams turn to laughter turn to song. They are the names you will not burn in. They are scorching alive. They want to go home.

And Forest remembered, and she let the candle fall through her fingers. And Forest started fires.

～

And ten thousand years sailed by, and in those years many fires came, and many fires went. The sun blazed its first. Heat seeped into the earth. Ice and frost let go of the grasslands, and they inhaled. Hell, once lie, became fable. Lightning came before thunder. Eucalyptus pods broke again, and the koalas came back. The Bronze Age and Iron Age were found in the ages. Storytellers and children gathered around campfires. Shadows. The ash trees bloomed. Dreams ran free, and memory held on.

And in those years, Forest waited. She waited and waited, and on a sunbeam far, far from ours, or perhaps raying towards ours, or in a distant, distant mending sky, or maybe in this very light, a boy came catching, a boy who kept young fires, and his name was Fire.

What is this? Fire said, burning, burning. *I should not be on this horizon.*

No. Forest held the boy.

Why have you brought me back?

Because we need you.

That is not enough.

Because I need you.

A forest cannot care for a flame. Where would they live?

Here. They would live here.

Remember your mourning. Remember your bluejays, how the flames came for them. Remember the grief in their singing.

And Forest chose silence. And Forest chose words. *But they sang. They sang.*

No. The boy tore away, running, running. *We cannot live here. Look at the mark I leave.* He pointed to the place where she had held him, where their skin had met. It had charred and blackened, the smell of burnt grass taking to the air. *See. See how everything I touch dies.*

I see it. I see it. Now, so must you. Forest held onto Fire. At the char, at the ash on her skin, she brushed it all away, and something came, a blade of grass, it came sprouting.

Fire stopped. He looked at the lone green grass. He tasted its air, and it was of unripe mangoes and elephants. He touched it and touched a hare's fur. He listened, and it was breathing. Fire stared at the blade of grass, and the blade of grass stared back.

What is it?

It is what kindles from you.

Rat King

Ian Green

A rat king is a horror. A dozen rats at least, tails entwined, bodies facing outward, a clock of teeth and fur. Overcrowded, the ragged pink of their tails writhe and knot and fuse, and they become a new thing altogether. The other rats defer to their liege and fetch sustenance. Where one is stupid, a dozen together begin to ponder, and they are...more. There is some quixotic alchemy of energy, an arcana of teeth and tail. The rat king thinks thoughts beyond its sum and sends these thoughts out. It demands obeisance. In a nexus of sewer pipes, an abandoned cellar, a forgotten ledge, a rat king may form; when it is found, the revulsion is profound. Death comes with swift blows, boot and stick. Humanity cannot abide a pest, but this reaction is a visceral thing beyond simple disdain. A rat king is a horror.

The rat king is something more again.

You are never more than six feet from a rat in London, it is said; this is of course true. They move unseen below, alongside, above. Always there. Hidden in wall, floor, and roof. *Scratch.* In every direction, they propagate, indifferent numbers overruling trap and poison. London has layers below glass and steel, below stone and wood. In the underground, there is a world of warrens and nooks, hidden shelters for whiskered faces, discarded fast food and lost packed lunches sustaining a million million mouths. Amongst that thick intrusion of tunnels, amongst and above and below and around and within, endless miles of pipes connect the city to the river, two thousand years of plumbing woven like endless hot pink tails latticed and knotted and fused. Stink and waste and water.

There are rat kings in London and around the world in any city of note, but *the* rat king, who sits above all others, lives in an old pump house in the East End. It has no comparison; a simple clock of teeth and nerve is as nothing. A rat king might access the arcana of the occult, the naturally obtained magic that is deemed paranormal by the myopic observer. *The* rat king is more. Its puissance is unmatched. The principle is of course the same: rats wriggling in the dark, pressured and close, and a twisted tail becomes a joining, and on and on. *The* rat king is made of more. If you ask the right Thames Water employee as they stare sullenly at the filthy river and smoke and blink in the pale light of day, they might tell you a tale.

Beneath Roman London, squalid in the shit of centurions and slaves, the first rats came. Before that, there were *rats* of course, but these new rats were different; fat strong Europeans, flocking to opportunity. They came and they flourished and they hid and they stole, and one day a few twisted together and these rats fattened on olives from the old world joined, a rat king, a simple clock of teeth and fur, thinking, projecting its will through the natural arcana of massed neural tissue. They joined beneath a Roman bathhouse that stood not so far from what would later be Tower Hill, nestled in a wet spot hidden from prying eyes and hands. They grew still through necessity, and they grew clever by odd proximity, and they grew old through the mysticism of rodent rituals no human will ever ken. The other rats fed them. Not so unusual in any time or place, but this time, the clock did not stagnate or fall to ruin. No Roman cudgel stroke fell. No battered slave took note. They sat and grew fat and one day, a thirteenth rat nestled in the centre of the clock face, and then a fourteenth.

The Romans never found the rat king. When one member of this rodent coven fell to old age, disease, a fresh rat would press, would writhe, would make itself part of the greater whole. The presence they exuded through whatever preternatural paranormal mechanism the rat king had accessed allowed them time, and with time came knowledge, and with knowledge came scope. Humans always judge animal intelligence against a human bar, setting tests that are not apposite. The rat king grew smart, for a king of rats. It grew smart in the way a rat can be smart, and it grew potent in its effect on the world around. The mechanism does not matter- is it a quantum fluctuation, to affect the neurobiology of a passing creature merely through force of will? In this epoch, perhaps. In another it was magic. In another it was simply the world.

And so on. Through ages dark and light, through war, through industry and endless change, through plague and flood and fire. If physical danger loomed, their stupid and obedient followers would drag, would chew through wood and wall, would pull and strain, and would ensure the safety of the master meld. What the running rats knew, so too did the king.

A note: of course king is the name because the patriarchy has long ruled on matters of nomenclature. The rats were male, were female, were young, were old. No gerontocracy or sex-based hierarchy here. Monarch would suit better, or council perhaps, but for our purposes king will suffice with this caveat. There is a question of memory- how does the rat king remember, when its constituent members ever change? It is the ship of Theseus, but plank and sail and rope are tooth and fur and tail. The materialist view would be that memory would be impossible, perhaps- but then, the materialists weep when the rat king makes them dance to its vermin tune, when the visions come.

Eighteen, nineteen centuries. Twenty? Time is a loose concept, to a rat. London went onward as it does, peaks and troughs of people, but always rubbish, always waste and shit and scraps and dark and water beneath the surface. The sewers got bigger. In the plagues, the rats grew still and learned a deeper fear, but the rat king survived, always. The rat king moved. The rat king grew and so grew a legend amongst the human sewer workers, this sphere of teeth and shit and beaded eyes; one said a hundred of them at least, roiling and screaming in his very mind, in a language that was not language, in a voice that made no sound but could be felt in dreams forever more. Another claimed the rat king was two dozen at most, an oddity but no more. Almost any human or creature that came close would be chased away by swarms of vicious rodents. The rat king grew, and the rat king learned, and the rat king influenced. It sat under Parliament, it sat beneath Buckingham Palace. Ever it moved, so slow and careful, in search of somewhere perfect.

Other rat kings were found, those simple affairs so loathed, but endlessly excused as an oddity by those that saw them live, or explained as the japes of taxidermists when the dead were displayed. Never did a human set eyes on the true rat king, that ultimate presence.

How stupid is the stupidest man? How clever is that cleverest rat? It is unclear who the first human follower was. The arcana of neurobiology- the entwinement of quantum particles- the dance of memory, be it material, or held elsewhere. Regardless, by whatever name or mechanism, the mage-craft of the rat king was potent. In time, perhaps a handful of simple souls at any given day would fall under its psionic sway. The destitute, addled by life and circumstance and the cruel hammers of commerce. Others too broken by the world to heed the revulsion the rat king normally instilled, able to hear a deeper message beyond. They would not know, of course, but would feel a compulsion to leave a certain food in a certain place, to divert a certain pipe a certain way. The sewers grew more elaborate. The rat king thrived.

Blessed Sainted Joseph Bazalgette, Victorian engineer of great renown, was the servant most high. There is rapture in service, even when it is done without understanding. Not a stupid man. Not easily influenced. The rat king had to swell its own numbers and focus all of its energy, and relocated beneath his Hampstead House for many years. There it sat, unmoving, and at night when Bazalgette dreamed of a unified sewer for all of wonderful London, it was the rat king below that pushed those images to the fore. To impact the dream of another- the practitioners of the black arts with no tails and blunt teeth would turn green with envy if they understood the depths of the rat king's capacity to dream. It felt his mind as he inspected, as he dug his preliminary tunnels. It felt him, and it saw a mind of water and stench and stone and numbers. It felt opportunity. Bazalgette got to work, and London's rivers and sewers and waste became organized. Beautiful.

The Greenway now runs from Stratford out, out to the deep east where the tidal Thames leaves a tang in the air. It is a cycle path, a walking route, a simple raised bed of grass and asphalt. It crosses streets and cuts through estates, and small trees cling to its verges. Local teens do what local teens do wherever there is a dark space away from prying eyes, and vagrants take shelter in its borders, fence and hedge blocking the intrusion of the wind. They seek peace.

The Greenway, however, was a sewer. Bazalgette's finest, a vaulting tunnel of shit and stink and brown water leading away from the dense East End. A great idea, he thought. There is a pump house there, halfway along. Of course, now it sits purely as an object of architecture; the modern sewerage is run from a sleek building cosseted by trees in the pump house grounds. Bazalgette is long dead, and Thames Water runs a tight ship.

But...

Below the pump house, down past the storied brick and vaulted stonework, down just above the guts and piping of a century of city, there is a room not on any plan. Bazalgette built it, and hid it, never sure why, but so sure that he must, though he often felt...an aversion even as he worked. An unnamable disgust. The room cannot be accessed from the pump house, but there are some grates, some pipes. It is an oddity, safe and secure, dry brick and soft earth.

The rats of London pay pilgrimage to this spot with their news and tales, things they have sensed and heard and had no language for, but the rat king understands. The rat king sits resplendent, and grows, and dreams anew.

Ace of Diamonds

Cynthia Pelayo

"The card trick is simple."

I felt an ache in my chest.

"It is?" I asked. I felt frozen in place, mesmerized by the man in the middle of the train station platform.

Some days there were musicians here in this very same spot. In fact, most days here stood someone, singing, or playing an instrument. In front of them they'd have a sign, reading 'Please help,' with an open container of some sort in front of them dotted with a few coins or crumpled up dollar bills. Today, the preferred method was a digital pathway of some sort, name one of the multiple means of transferring currency across imaginary lines.

Sometimes, all of this felt imaginary, or maybe imagined.

My train went by without me. I was distracted because of him, the man seated here at a card table dressed in a black suit. No, not black suit, a tuxedo.

I wondered if I would stop for one of those tarot card readers, and I chuckled to myself.

The man looked up at me from the cards he was shuffling, and almost as if he'd read my mind he said: "You don't look like the kind of man who would pause for a tarot card reader."

"I don't believe in any of that," I said. I found it all silly, subjective. All of this about the symbols, knives or swords or whatever, queens and coins, pentacles, was it?

"But this you do?"

Maybe. At least, I wanted to believe in the probability of something. I remembered being a kid and watching stage magicians on television, the old-fashioned kind who would appear on late night talk shows. I miss those days, when simple things seemed like magic. When life just felt like it was possible and fresh and new. I wanted that feeling again, but no matter how hard I tried to reach for it, I just couldn't conjure up that sensation of possibility, that things could be wondrous, that things could be all right.

"You missed your train," the man said, his eyes darting over to my knuckles.

Yes, they were a little bloody and raw. I shouldn't have punched that brick wall again and again. I moved my hands behind my back and held them there.

He patted his tuxedo pocket. "Need a Band-Aid?"

"Nah, I'm good."

For a moment there I thought he was really going to produce a Band-Aid. What would be the coincidence there? Maybe this whole night was just a big string of coincidental things, one right after the other, moving from positive to negative.

I realize now that there was no sign at his table, no method of payment with which to tip. There was just this man in a tuxedo, a card table with a white sheet over it, and a deck of playing cards.

"How much?" I finally asked, more so for my own amusement, or validation, because everything has to have a price. And really, what could I afford right now anyway? I'd lost my job. I was at risk of losing my house. I was too scared to even log into my bank account.

"How much for what?" he asked, perplexed.

I pointed a hand to the table and quickly held both hands behind my back again. "For this."

He cut the deck of cards in two halves and faced each half out to me; both hands held the Nine of Clubs.

"I'm not sure what you're talking about. I'm just seated here, practicing my card tricks."

I looked from left to right. The platform was completely clear. I looked overhead to the train tracker. Another one would be coming in a few minutes. It was surprising no one else had joined us since the last train passed, but then again it was later in the evening, and that's why I picked this time.

My head still ached from the shouting. Shouting at myself in my living room. Shouting at myself for having set aside so much for a job that now I see …. didn't care. How could they just let me go like that? I gave them thirty years of my life. Thirty years. How many company holiday parties did I attend? How many birthday cards and baby shower cards for co-workers did I sign? How many company lunches did I have to sit through while someone droned on about "strategy," "new normal," whatever new corporate buzzword they'd picked up that week which just translated into "sell more"? I gave them thirty years and Human Resources approached my desk; told me I was being laid off and that was it. I left my computer behind, family pictures I'd decorated my space with, because I didn't want to be seen walking out with a box stuffed with the symbols of 'Hey, that guy got laid off today.'

I missed so much time. My kids were already off at college. My wife spent most days volunteering at the art museum. Everyone had their own life, their own friends, their own joys, but me. All I had was a job that I'd abandoned them all for, which I now regretted.

"Think of a card," he says.

Easy, I thought. Ace of Diamonds.

The man in the tuxedo placed one deck on top of the other. "Do you think you'll miss your next train?" He began shuffling. There was something sort of smooth and hypnotic about the way he did that. A blur of movement, the edges of the cards flashing white as they bent and snapped back into place.

"Probably not," I say, focused on how the cards cascade down in a waterfall-like motion, as the halves collapse into each other.

The man nods, holding the completed deck together in both hands.

"Train accidents can be permanent," he said.

I ignored him.

"Are you a magician?" I asked.

He lifts the top card on the deck and shows it to me. An Ace of Diamonds.

Maybe it was luck, I think, and he continues looking at me, waiting for my reaction, and finally I say, "Sure, fine. It was Ace of Diamonds."

He smiles. Still holding the card out to me, he says: "I suppose that depends on which type of magician you're inquiring about. Are you asking me if I'm someone with magical powers, like say Merlin, like a sorcerer, a warlock?" He shrugged. "Who knows? If you're asking me if I'm a person who performs magic tricks for entertainment, I guess I'll ask you then … are you being entertained?"

I guess I was, and without saying anything, the man dropped the card back atop the deck and began to shuffle. The deck bent and breathed in his hands. Cards danced together, halves interleaved with a soft, ticking flutter.

"I've had many names throughout the years," he said, continuing his work. "Dedi, Acetabularii, later on, John Henry Anderson, Alexander Herrmann, or Herrmann the Great, lots of others, many, many others, some you may have heard of, some you may not have heard of. But maybe think of me like these cards." He continued shuffling; the deck was broken, spun, reassembled in a blur. His fingers moved like the hands of a clock sped up, deliberate and precise. Every single movement, every single shuffle seemed aimless, smooth, and elegant.

"What you're seeing is the deck of cards being broken apart, placed together, flipped around, but it's still a deck of cards, no matter what, no matter what time or place." he said.

In the distance a faint clatter grew of the approaching train.

"I'll ask you once more," he said, continuing his movements. "Are you going to miss your train again?"

I thought about it, and why did I even stop here in front of this table? Did I even really want to jump in front of that train? I lost a job, so what? I'd probably lose my house, yeah, sure, who knows? My wife loves me. I love her. Now, I have time. Maybe she and I could do more things together. Maybe I could volunteer at the art museum with her. Maybe she and I could spend some weekends visiting the kids at college. Maybe that was magic, time, and I just needed to realize I finally had it.

The magician tapped the final stack against his palm, and lifted the top card again, Ace of Diamonds.

I smiled to myself. Maybe all I needed was a magician to show me that redirection didn't have to be a bad thing.

The train pulled into the station with a gust of warm air and a metallic sigh. The magician gave a half-smile, tucked the card back in, and then stood and gave a bow. I responded with applause.

As the train left the station, I realized how late it was. My wife was probably worried.

"I think I'll go home now," I said, and walked down the platform, and up the stairs. I didn't want to turn back, scared that he wouldn't be there, scared that he was just maybe my imagination. I just wanted to keep believing in what I saw, in what I experienced, and so I just kept on walking, walking until I got home, walking until I entered my house, walking until I went up to bed and found my wife there peacefully asleep, and an ace of diamonds card on my pillow.

Beneath Scorching Sand,
Above Metal Sun

KC Grifant

Another day—*another day*—with the sky arching endless blue above us, cold and sharp as we lay the tracks. I struggled to keep count of the time; too much had passed. I could see it in my callused and scarred hands, far too weathered for someone only of 20 years.

Abel Yao, you are Abel Yao, I told myself, pushing my long braid back under my wide straw hat. Not "*Worker.*"

One more month.

Workers directed small horse-drawn carts next to us while we removed the rails and placed them parallel. Bolting, spiking, hammering–again and again–the sound of the sledgehammer driving the spikes and securing the rail to the bed echoed inside my head. My ears still rang long after we had returned to our makeshift temporary campsite, crammed into stinky tents.

In the morning, my thoughts trickled along despite the deep aches that had taken up permanent residence in every inch of my fiber: I was a fool, the worst thing. My father undoubtedly would laugh, incredulously and cruelly, to see me bound in servitude this way.

"Abel Yao, are you a smart man or are you a fool?" Father would ask me while he nailed papers holding the names of the cursed in our basement. They were the names of those whose souls he temporarily snatched to do his bidding—the souls that helped keep us safe in our home in the Far Isles. I swore, despite his threats, I'd never be like him.

And I wasn't. He would never be trapped this way, doing the bidding of other men, men who desperately sought to make this a place of "civilization." The land was thick with monsters and thieves, but still, the foremen worked for powerful families who wanted to create a railroad within this region, dubbed "South Bowl." I sailed far to escape home—escape *him*—with the idea of seeing new lands a fire in my heart. But I was tricked into what I thought was a temporary contract with good pay; instead, I found myself trapped in endless, grueling labor under a glaring sun. Wandering monster herds might undo months of work. Oldcomers that lived here long before sometimes visited, amused or annoyed at our efforts, while a few of us traded our meager funds for teas and food beyond the stale biscuits and jerky that we ate day in and day out. The hammering in my head grew louder with each passing month, haunting my sleep.

"You signed a *contract*," the lead foreman, Crocker, would snarl, raising his pistol when the man, a pale-flecked fellow with a shock of rust-colored hair, dared to challenge him. "It's *illegal* to break out of your *contract*." The man blathered a protest and Crocker beat him down.

"Should've known better," one of the workers muttered in disgust as we all turned away.

At first it had been manageable, though grueling work. In the mornings and evenings, I'd sip tea with others from the Far Isles as we eyed the other group of workers from the North Isles, a dozen men who talked rapidly in a way different than I was used to, making it impossible to understand them half the time.

Many spoke in my homeland's language, some talking to me when they first had questions and then falling into the moody distant silence of those too weary, too broken to talk.

"You owe two more years," I had explained to one of the men when he inquired about a small square of paper the foreman had given him.

"How is that possible?" he asked me. "I'm supposed to be done."

"None of us are done," I said, more bleakly than I meant.

Later that night the man had argued with Crocker. They beat him. He resisted. They shot him. I watched them carry his body away, an example for the rest of us.

After that, I kept to myself.

Still, I missed having someone to talk to. I read the same worn book each night, a history of the world before the monsters took over, jotting my notes and questions on the pages and longing for more information.

As time passed, and my contract kept extending due to some obscure rulings, the hope of finding more books grew fainter.

You have it easy, Crocker and the other foremen would remind us with a faintly veiled threat. *You should see how some of the other camps are run.*

"Learn to be powerful, or you will always be dominated," my father would say. He had more in common with the foreman than me—he wielded power over others, never the opposite. But I was nothing like him, and never would be.

A few more months, I had told myself over the years, though I knew it was a lie, one I needed to keep myself from going mad. They would always find another reason to extend my debt, some imagined misstep. And they worked us harder and faster—sometimes for a bonus; they were promised if we laid down track faster.

But now I knew, only one month remained. I had overheard how many miles we had left. I heard the more energetic chatting of the other men. We were nearly done with the railroad line. There would be no extensions.

One more month.

That night, like hundreds of identical nights sprinkled across the long years, the cloud arrived just after midnight, sneaking in between the tent flaps as a fist-shaped condensation of gray, a cluster of wispy tendrils like fog captured in a glass. Waiting.

"No," I said to it, the prickling stillness waking me while the other men slept, heavy as logs after the day's work, all but dead to the world. "Tell him I don't want it. Not then. Not now. Never. I'll be out of here in a month, so he can stop sending you."

Sometimes the cloud—a possessed soul that my father summoned— took a few minutes to slip back out; other times it fled almost immediately. The fury would grip me: *Now* he cares about my life? *Now* he wants to help, once I am hundreds of miles from the dark cloud he had put over his whole family?

I'd turned over in my bed, listening to the men snore, some groan with shuddery breaths long and pained. When my eyes finally closed against the darkness, I bade away visions of my childhood that would flint in.

The sickening sweet swirl of incense.

My mother and brothers and little sister at the dinner table, downturned faces and stubborn juts to their chins of those determined to ignore what lay before them.

The scrawled names of townspeople on torn paper, nailed to a wooden pole.

My father's fingers pressing into my shoulder, urging me to chant.

When sleep came, it was too heavy, too mercilessly short, before the day came again.

At dawn, three new men came, stumbling out from the packed wagon, blinking and stiff as they took in the desert around them.

"Greet your kinsmen," Crocker sneered at us from under his large-brimmed leather hat. "We're going to finish the track in double time for a bonus, so I want y'all on your best." My gaze caught one new worker, pale with jet black hair. He wore a stained work shirt, red handkerchief around his neck over his bony limbs. But it was how his gaze darted, quick and open, taking in his situation in a split second, that had caught my attention. A scholarly sort, I guessed.

In the evening, I spotted the man heading into one of the sleeping tents with his bedroll. From his first day of railroad work, his fair skin was badly burnt, the nervous energy that had animated his movements before squashed out of him. He moved stiffly and hunched. When he came out, I offered him a chipped mug of tea warmed over the small campfire.

"Howdy." Harston nodded at me and looked at the tea quizzically. "We've been baking like a toad's hide out here. Why would I want to feel hotter?"

"Helps starve off whatever afflicts them," I said, nodding my chin toward another tent, where several of the North Isle men groaned and expelled the contents of their stomachs. "I'm Abel Yao."

"Harston." He accepted the drink and settled onto the crude log across from me, pulling out a small notebook from his pocket, and began writing. His pen fumbled in his bruised fingers and he grimaced.

"A letter?" I asked, despite myself.

Harston shook his head. "Writing tall tales. I've been in this damned contract for two months now, coming from an east mine. Storytelling is a solace."

"Tales of...?"

He shrugged. "Mythologies retold. Worlds unlike ours. What might exist out there in the sky." He glanced upwards.

"I prefer learning about the world as it is," I said. "There is more to be studied than can ever be accessed by one man. Why does one need fantastical make believe?"

"It's like..." Harston paused. "Like opening invisible gateways into other realms, where you sense what one might be doing in another life, and you are transcribing it. It's like magic."

I shuddered at his last word. He cast me a questioning glance, which I ignored.

Over the next few days, we talked more, and I found the hammering in my head subdued when I spoke with him. After all this time I had almost forgotten the feeling of a friend. More than that—a rare meeting of the minds. I tried to keep his spirits up even as he grew desolate under our stark conditions.

"One more month," I told him. "That's all you have to bear."

Then one night, he stirred next to me.

"What is that?" Harston hissed. I turned to the entrance of the tent, expecting a drunken worker looking for a fight, but it was the cloud again.

"Most people can't see a possessed spirit without some training in the magical arts," I whispered, puzzled. I stared hard at the cloud. "Go. I bid you."

It disappeared a second later and Harston stared at me, mouth agape.

"Strange," I mused. "You are exceptionally perceptive, so perhaps you can spot the subtle. You would likely do well in the magics."

"Magic..." Harston trailed off. "You...?"

"Not me," I said hastily. "At least, not really. My father studied intensely after our cluster of towns gave way to a controlling power-hungry minority that sowed discord." I had been too young to remember much. My parents' hushed frantic conversations about who in the village had turned. Mother wiping angry tears, Father's eyes growing hard after something unspeakable had happened in town.

At Harston's stare, I continued. "I was 6 or 7 years old. I knew something terrible had occurred, but they wouldn't tell me what. Now, I think it was a massacre in town. My father became reclusive, leaving for long periods and returning with ancient tomes, saying he needed to protect us from harm."

And he did. He learned to temporarily steal souls and use them to do his work of seeking out ancient demons. He'd extract and bind the demons to do the darker work of siphoning power to himself, work I wanted no part of. I blinked away visions of scrawled names of doomed souls on papers in the basement, of the shadowy otherworldly figures that would appear in the corners.

"But now he sends spirits here," I said. "Trying to get me to draw upon his power to escape. But I will never be like him; I've seen what this magic can do. It's unpredictable, dangerous."

"You have access to all of that power…" Harston's eyes widened. "And yet you stay here?"

He looked at me, not just in shock but in something that shook me more: confusion. As if I were too pathetic, too feeble-minded to do what needed to be done.

"You don't understand." My neck grew hot. "Magic is erratic. It chewed at my father's soul. Little by little, until he was a shell of himself."

I remembered Father smiling once, long, long ago. After he sank more into his magical practices, he never smiled again. Nor Mother, for that matter.

"Abel, please. To speak plainly, we will die here," Harston said. "They'd keep us here as long as we can work. I can't survive this much longer."

"Be patient," I said. *One more month.* "You wouldn't ask me if you'd seen what I had seen."

"I've seen enough here," Harston all but snapped back, and found himself, his dark eyes growing weary. "You're correct. It's not my right to ask."

"Indeed," I said, turning over in my bedroll. It had been a mistake to befriend him.

I managed to avoid Harston for the next two days, until I heard a ruckus at dawn. I stumbled out of the tent along with the others, shivering in the desert cold. A batch of workers came, this time a dozen, pouring out from the packed wagon.

"Why are they bringing new men?" I whispered, more to myself as Harston came to stand next to me. "We're almost done."

One of the workers overheard me and shouted, "Yeah, why ya got more workers here?"

Crocker glanced at his comrade with a smirk that made my heart plummet like a dropped ball of steel.

"Well," Crocker said, smoothing his giant gray handlebar moustache. "We got a new mining operation we set up 'bout, oh, 50 miles from here. In need of some good labor. And a few of you qualify."

"No," I whispered, my body tensing to jerk forward. It wasn't *fair*. But it never was.

My swollen fists clenched, wanting to lash out, but my mind wheeled me into focus. Of course they'd keep us, their free labor, indefinitely.

Harston was not as calm, his face pale despite his sunburn. "You can't imprison us longer!" he hollered.

I put a hand on his arm instinctively. I could see Crocker was in a mood, restless, waiting for someone to unleash his pent-up tension, but it was too late. Harston had caught his attention.

I winced as Crocker smashed his pistol into Harston's face, causing him to stumble. Crocker shoved him backwards, and his foreman joined in the kicking as Harston groaned, curling up protectively. Usually the foremen stopped any beatings after one or two blows, so the men could still work, but this time they didn't.

They were setting an example to the new men, I realized, all of whom watched in quiet, hooded horror.

"You'll kill him!" I jolted forward before a foreman grabbed me and slammed his fist into my stomach. I tried to suck in air as pain radiated like a web from my gut, but all the strands pulled me into myself, allowing no room to breathe. I doubled over, the sound of Harston's guttural moans the only thing keeping me from collapsing.

"Please, stop," I managed. "He's new, he has years of work in him."

Crocker glanced at me and kicked Harston's huddled form one more time before holding up a hand.

"To your stations!" Crocker bellowed.

Many more months. The thoughts buzzed, sluggish in my spinning head as I watched two men heave Harston up to his feet and drag him to his tent.

Many, many, many, many, many—

That night, I sat close to Harston, who had been curled on his bedroll all day, panting slowly, trying to help him sip tea when he roused. I turned away from his face that had ballooned up, like a bunch of grapes had bubbled up under his skin.

As he slept, my comfort thought of "one more month" turned to ash, leaving my mind blank, scrubbed out.

"What…is it…" Harston croaked from between split lips in the dead of night, jolting me from my half-sleep.

"A cracked rib, at least," I said quietly. "Bad bruising. Maybe worse. Try to sleep."

"I can't take another day." His eyes fluttered but stayed open. He lifted a trembling hand to the tent flaps, and I already knew what he spotted.

The cloud hovered, a faint mist that watched. Waited.

I looked back to see Harston's beaten face, a sight that sent a chasm down my center.

"Enter," I commanded the spirit.

The cloud rolled over the ground like a fog. A sigh of a breeze sent a shiver along my spine before it swept into the figure nearest to me. Harston.

"Come back to your father," Harston's voice said as the spirit traveler spoke my father's wishes and turned Harston's eyes white and blank as a fresh snow.

"Never," I said. "Just show me how to get out of here. With him."

"Paper," Father's minion hissed between Harston's swollen lips.

Harston's bruised fingers twitched. I handed him his charcoal pencil and opened his journal to a blank page. Though Harston's eyes remained closed, his hand scribbled across the paper.

"Your grimoire," Harston's voice rasped. The breeze rose again as the cloud tendrils slipped back out of the tent.

"What was *that?*" Harston's eyes flew open with a gasp as the spirit left him. He lifted the pages to show what my father's traveler had sketched in a script. I flinched at the sight of the handwriting I wished I could burn from my mind. That, and the memory of how Father'd lash out at me until I learned how to read his arcane language.

"How to summon a demon," I said numbly.

"The demons help us, like guard dogs," Father had told me. *"This is how we stay safe. In control."*

As I scanned the text, I could nearly sense it—one of the many demons my father had captured and buried, a safety backup should he need to evoke destructive power. A distant crack echoed below, as though lightning ran far beneath the shifting sands.

Harston's face grew more alert by the second, and he propped himself up with a wince. "Abel, please. Let's escape. What is your hesitation?"

"Magic is fickle at best. It can affect one's soul, one's *mind*, for the worst," I said. I tried not to think of the light and laughter draining from my father, leaving him a husk of himself. I pushed away memories of Mother's hushed angry tones, the deep wrinkles along her mouth that never disappeared. Little Sister's scarred hand.

But they were free, I reminded myself. Father, despite his flaws, had kept them alive.

"I can't survive here another day," Harston murmured. It was the first time I heard true desperation lace his voice. "Please."

I nodded as something in me sagged. I would take it—this demon my father promised—rather than spend another second here waiting for death, mine or Harston's. I pulled out my dull two-inch knife and held up Harston's notebook.

"Let me do it," Harston said. "Translate, and I will speak them."

"It's not just reading the words," I told him. "They must be infused with a force, an emotion. It takes practice."

I quietly spoke the words, channeling my hopelessness, my anguish from the last day, the last few months, *the years.* The pages gleamed faintly like moonlight, the dusky hues pilling from the pages as if they were made of pure gold. Harston stifled a gasp at seeing it but forced himself quiet. Behind us, one man shifted but kept snoring, his body heavy in sleep.

My shaking hands, all bone and calluses, tried to hold the page steady as I read. Something far below us was tearing open with every word: one of the portals. They were what Father called "the membranes" that kept the demons in check, like cocoons encasing caterpillars.

As I chanted, my head seemed to balloon into the sun, even though it had set long ago. The world inverted—a dark star slid under me, the sands shifted overhead. I was being buried alive by black light and glittering sand.

"Abel!" Harston's voice urgently whispered. His hand pressed my shoulder. "Focus. Listen to my voice. Let me help."

"I can do it," I muttered. I could feel it there, the unspoken force that we called magic—an ancient stirring as the membrane holding the closest demon began to rip. I paused to slice the top of each of my fingers on my left hand and let the blood stream onto the scribbled words. I spoke the last line, but the membrane wasn't fully open, the spell was failing.

Foolish, weak

"Something's wrong," I whispered. "It's not working…"

Harston took the knife from me and sliced the tops of his fingers before I could stop him.

"It's too much," I protested, watching his blood stream over the words. I sensed the membrane ripple and rip completely. The tear released a burst of stored power that went straight into my chest, humming in my spine, the back of my neck.

I was lighter, cooler. Empty, as though my fears and the dozens of invisible weights across my shoulders had slid off. Is this how Father had felt when he evoked magic?

It was intoxicating.

"Such force!" Harston's eyes were wide, too wide as he sat up straighter. I realized whatever power stored in that broken membrane had fed into him too. His eyes flared with light and he stood with the ease of a man in perfect health. A wind started to swirl, stirring some of the men from their deep sleeps.

"What is this magic?" Harston marveled.

"I don't know," I stammered. "My father didn't say anything about this. But it would reason that the binding membranes that hold the demons have their own power and perhaps ricochetted into us. As I said, magic is fickle, wild."

"But it *worked*," Harston said. "I feel so strong, like I could fight ten men at once." He started to laugh but broke off when the demon appeared.

A being larger than a man stood between the flaps of the tent. Maggot-colored and hunched, it took on the shape of a bull on its hind legs. The demon shimmered in and out of vision, a horrific sight that made me want to rush backwards, shut my eyes and never open them again. Harston stiffened, frozen like a prey in the sights of a predator.

"You summoned," the demon growled, its voice trailing in and around my head like a slither. Before we could speak the wind grew stronger, the men around us starting to wake.

I steadied myself, remembering how my father would command the demons. *I'm the one in charge.*

"Free us from this place," I demanded.

The demon smiled, a hideous grin full of far too many teeth. "Your soul," the demon fixed his eyes eagerly on us. "Your human souls have fresh magic on them. Give me a taste, for your freedom…"

"I don't bargain with demons," I retorted and lifted one of my glowing hands. "My words have bound you to my will."

"Your father's words bound me," the demon replied. Reddish winds around it kicked up and the other men began to wake up and mutter. They couldn't see the demon but could surely sense the *wrongness* in the air as they stared at me and Harston.

"Your father could hardly contain me," the demon continued. "You, little sorcerer, cannot. A taste of the magic in your soul for your freedom."

I yanked Harston back. "We have to control it!"

"How?" Harston stood next to me, helpless. "I feel the power inside, but I don't know how to use it–"

"*Weak*," one of the men hissed next to me suddenly, with the blank eyes of the possessed, as another of Father's stolen souls arrived. The man grabbed my knife and used it to carve words into his arm. "You're *weak*. Harness the demon," the man muttered my father's message. "Use what I taught you."

I grabbed the man's bleeding arm and read the words.

"You won't trap me again!" The demon roared. A vortex of wind blasted out from its mouth, a seismic shock that tore our tent to shreds and sent everyone but me and Harston back dozens of feet. I fought to stand upright, the newfound magical strength inside me like a pole.

"Is it a tornado?" one of the men hollered.

"Get back!" I yelled at them.

"Abel!" Harston shouted. "It's too powerful!"

"I need an object to bind the demon, subdue some of its power so we can control it." I scanned the mess and grabbed Harston's blood-soaked journal. Father had always said that words of a spell had to be infused with an emotion, the rawer the better. Before, I had used desperation. Despair. This time, I summoned the fury that filled me all too quickly.

Harston stood next to me, and I felt his rage swell next to mine—at being captured, at the injustice of it all, at the feeling of being a thunderstorm trapped in a glass bottle. Our mingled blood on the journal's pages amplified our emotions, looping invisible threads around the demon. It bellowed and charged at us.

I spoke the final sentence I had seen on the man's arm.

The journal shook in my hand as the magical threads emanating from it enveloped the demon entirely. The demon's furious roar echoed in my ears, a fractal pattern of an inhuman scream. As it disappeared, another blast shot out. Not wind, not heat, but something else: a mystical force that radiated from me and Harston like an earthquake: the aftershock from binding a demon.

The book in my hand burned hot.

But the demon was contained.

"Abel…" Harston's voice choked in the sudden silence.

Then I could see, finally, what devastation the demon–*we*–had wrought under the moonlight.

The men —*the men*—

All the tents around us had blown apart from the force of the binding spell. Objects lay in a wide circle as far as I could see under the moonlight. It took me a moment to understand what I was seeing.

Body parts. Scattered, limbs torn from the blast lay around us in a massive circle.

All dead, the foremen and the workers.

"No," I choked. I was on my knees before I realized it, staring. *They are simply unconscious*, I tried to tell myself despite what I saw. *Some of them are intact. Some of them might be alive.*

"Abel!" Harston hauled me to my feet. "We must go."

"What about…the…" I trailed off.

"There are no witnesses." Harston shook me. "Do you understand? We must lock the demon forever and never speak of it. Never let anyone unleash it. The book…look!"

Harston's journal vibrated angrily in front of me.

"It won't contain the demon for long," I said, and brushed off my tattered clothes. "We need to find a place to bury the demon where it will never be found. Not by my father. Not by anyone."

Harston nodded and pointed west. "We have to go now in case anyone comes at dawn."

I walked next to him, ignoring the sensation of molten metal fused to my bones, my insides hotter than any sunbeam. My soul hummed, shone, too bright. I'd have to untangle how to use this new power later. For now, like my father, I would learn what magic I needed to keep safe. But unlike my father, I would never hurt anyone again—I swore it silently under the swollen, sinking moonlight. Even if it killed me.

The Gift

Mya Duong

"She went fast. She wasn't in pain." Cecelia said, crumpling up tissues and unfolding them again. She looked up at all the sympathetic eyes staring back at her. "Mom loved having everybody together—her friends and family. Maybe not this way."

"We understand, Lia. Whatever we can do, please let us know."

A chorus of nods followed the words of endearment from her mom's coworker. They had all been good friends, weathered the company and all the ups and downs over the years. Births, marriage, divorce, kids, even restructuring.

Maria looked over at the pair talking in the corner. "It was nice of your dad to come. She never said anything bad about him. Always wanted to make sure you were taken care of." Maria followed Cecelia's pained eyes.

"The divorce was eighteen years ago. Dad has always been there for me. And Aunt Susan has been great." Cecelia turned away when they both caught her longing stare.

Cecelia's dad walked toward them. Aunt Susan kept a questioning eye on Maria before breaking away and heading outside. Maria followed shortly afterward.

Cecelia's dad hugged her. "It was a nice service, and the reception—you really pulled it together under the circumstances. Mom was always proud of how you were able to manage."

"I had help. This was something that just needed to get done," she said flatly. She thought about why he had said managed, *like this was another task at work.*

"I meant how strong and brave you've been dealing with your mom's illness. And knowing the next steps in your life…"

Cecelia paused. She looked at her dad like he had sprung another head, his words of riddles and moving on to the next phase of life. Grief really does make a person say random things, she thought. "Sure, Dad. There's a lot to settle now."

Six months later

Cecelia opened a storage box that she had kept from her mom's house. Something compelled her to retrieve an item from this box even though everything had been packed and stored. Even the house had already been sold. She pulled out a peculiar and ornamental box.

"Aunt Susan, do you know where Mom got this box? It's so cute. I don't remember seeing it at her place."

Aunt Susan's eyes widened. She blinked a few times. "You only found this now?"

"Well...yeah. I don't know why it wasn't in the garage with the rest of her things. I knew I needed something from this box."

Aunt Susan took a drink of water. "Then I guess it was time for you to find it."

"Find what?"

"Let's see if anything is inside. Maybe your mom put something in there."

Cecelia opened the hexagon-shaped wooden box. A stream of mist poured out and evaporated.

"That was odd." She reached inside. "Nothing. Maybe Mom just liked the box. I'll keep it on my dresser."

Aunt Susan reached for the artistic box. "May I?"

She examined the outside, turning it at multiple angles. She placed two fingers in the box and made a circular motion. Aunt Susan's face flushed. She quickly removed her fingers and closed the box.

"Aunt Susan, you look red. Are you sick?"

"This is definitely for you."

Cecelia shook her head. "What's that supposed to mean?"

"Let's sit down, and I'll tell you."

They both moved into the kitchen and sat at the table.

"First, do you feel different? Like more energy or something feels off?"

"No, not really. Maybe a little tired after everything."

"Hmmm." Aunt Susan brushed her hair away from her face. "Any random thoughts calling out to you? Any surges of strength or a keen sense of awareness? Do you feel like you're glowing?"

Cecelia raised an eyebrow. "What are you getting at?"

"I don't know how to say this." Aunt Susan paused. "My sister—your mother—came from different stock—a particular line."

"Ancestry?"

"No. More like a special type of people."

"I'm not following."

Aunt Susan swallowed more water. "Lia, we've been given the gift of magic. Some of us were chosen. I'm not sure why or how, but we have it. Now, you have it. But I guess it hasn't quite manifested."

Cecelia looked at her aunt. She laughed. "Okay, I know we've been under a lot of stress and mourning Mom. But come on...*magic?*" She shook her head and laughed to herself. "Look, it's the afternoon, but hey, we can polish off a few glasses of wine and joke about this absurd theory."

Aunt Susan rolled her eyes and frowned. She placed her palms out and closed her eyes. Two balls of fire formed on her hands. She let them simmer.

Cecelia jumped from her chair. *"What the he...! How* did you do that?"

"One of my parlor tricks. Although I was younger than you are when I manifested." She doused the flames with water. "Your mom, too. She manifested before I did. Since your dad isn't like us, that might explain the delay."

Cecelia's mind whirred. "Does Dad know?"

"Yes. They've always remained good friends. He found out your mom was...different. He knew it was part of a plan. He accepted it. That's why he could move on without any guilt."

Cecelia shook her head. "They never fought. They always seemed patient and observing. Supportive of each other and of me."

Aunt Susan looked at her phone. "We can talk more about our kind another time." She looked in the direction of Cecelia's room. "I'm not allowed to tell you, nor do I know the details of how and when you'll manifest to your full level. That fancy box in there? It holds the key. Only you can experience it."

"What do I do?"

"Everything as usual. It'll reach out to you." She grabbed her purse. "Good luck, my dear. I wish you a joyous journey and some answers."

❧

"Her sign came."

"Are you sure? What happened? Did the process start?"

Susan shook her head. "Not yet. Her mom's box appeared."

"Then it's time she knows."

"She'll know." Susan clasped her hand around her friend's. "Maria, she's on her way. It's what JoAnne predicted."

Both women appeared hopeful, despite an air of sadness.

❧

"Okay, box. Do your thing. Show me what you've got."

The rest of the afternoon and all evening, nothing stirred within or around the wooden box. Cecelia waited and waited.

Frustrated, she left her bedroom. She went into the kitchen to make herself some dinner. As she was cleaning up, she jumped.

"How did it get here?"

The magic box sat on her kitchen island. Glowing.

Cecelia hesitated. She slowly reached for the box, fear and thoughts of burning herself weighed on her mind.

The box sprang open. White and yellow light jetted out, then a smoky grey mist formed. Cecelia stepped back, looking around for a weapon. She grabbed a broom.

The mist danced as it grew and grew in front of her eyes. It reached life size. Cecelia gripped the broom tighter, pointing it at the mist. The mist cleared and an image formed.

Hair the color of flames, and stark yellow eyes that stared back at Cecelia. She inched the broom closer to the image.

The stranger flicked her fingers, and the broom released from Cecelia's hand.

"Is this how you greet me?"

Cecelia swallowed, her voice hoarse. "I...I didn't know what to expect. I thought you might hurt me."

"Is this what they told you?" the strange woman inquired. "I could, you know, but that's not why I'm here."

Cecelia straightened. "No, I was told to expect something. I didn't know who or what."

The mysterious being scrunched her hair. "You get what you get." She scrutinized. "We have a lot of work ahead to complete your training. How you'll manifest."

"How I'll become who I'm meant to be?"

"Basically." The magical being paused. "I'm Ezram. Let's just say I'm your guardian. I'll be helping you along the way. But first, you must pass the five-stage rule. You'll receive wishes—with limitations—and unknown scenarios. I can't tell you what order they'll come in or what they'll be."

"Okayyy. That's pretty vague. I guess I'll just handle it."

"We will see." Ezram moved around the kitchen gracefully, her long, shiny maroon gown gliding across the floor. "I'll need to change." She flicked her fingers, and modern sporty clothes replaced her gown. She looked in the decorative mirror. "That'll do."

"I'm ready for my lesson."

"Oh, Cecelia. Only the powers can tell you if you're ready, and if you'll succeed."

"You already know my name." Cecelia appeared weary.

"I already know much about you." Ezram grabbed her wrist, then flicked her fingers.

In seconds, they entered a café in the city's downtown area. The afternoon bustled with people coming and going, the city alive on a spring afternoon.

"What are we doing here?"

Ezram gave her a perplexed look. "Getting coffee, of course. You think I don't need the extra energy?"

"I...wasn't sure if you even ate."

"I don't really need to, but it smells good, and the props fit the stage." She ordered black coffee and a latte for Cecelia. "Can you pay for this? I don't have any currency."

Cecelia frowned. "Good thing I grabbed my crossbody when you whisked us away." She paid the clerk. They grabbed their drinks and left.

"Where to?" They started walking down the street, unsure of their direction.

"We just go as the day takes us."

Cecelia remained quiet, thoughts of a new world, the new metamorphosis she was embarking upon, and what she'd become filled her mind. She tossed her empty latte in the nearby garbage.

"Have we been this way for a long time?"

"For a very long time. Your family line is long, stretching across countries, even before the United States was formed."

"That's a long history. I'd like to research more—" Cecelia looked up and waved. "That's Maria, a friend of Mom's." She sped forward. "Maria!"

Maria turned her head, smiled at them, then raced ahead.

"Maria?" Cecelia grabbed Ezram's wrist, and they bolted down the sidewalk.

They turned right, then left, and right again. They ended up in an alley.

"Maria, wait for us!"

Maria stopped but kept her back to them.

"I thought you heard me. Why are you running away?" They stood waiting for her to respond.

Ezram nudged Cecelia. "Now is the time where you need to decide what's your best course of action. Will this be a wish or a response?"

"What do you mean?"

Maria turned around. "Yes, listen to your guardian." Her voice was lower and stranger than normal. "Who are you looking for, Cecelia?" The image of Maria changed before them. A creature with menacing eyes, horns, and sharp teeth growled at them.

"Ahhh! We need to run!"

Ezram grabbed Cecelia's arm. "We don't run. You *need* to decide."

"How? What...what do I do?"

"What does your mind and body tell you?"

Cecelia's frantic mind thought through this dilemma despite her heart racing. Yet, something compelled her to act. "I...I want it to vanish. It isn't Maria."

"Good. Now make it happen. Push that will." Cecelia demonstrated with her arms out as the creature across from them positioned itself to charge headlong.

Cecelia chanted, "*I want you to go away. I want you to disappear. I want . . .*"

She pushed her arms out with a force she didn't know she had. "*Vanish!*"

An invisible energy zapped the creature across from them. In seconds, it fizzled away, leaving behind smoke and steam.

"I did it! I actually used my powers!" She hugged Ezram. "I can do this."

Ezram stepped back, straightening her clothes. "That's a start. You responded well." She eyed her seriously. "One wish used. You must complete all tasks in two days."

"Two days. Hmmm."

They moved out of the alley and into the open. Something safer, for now.

"Did Mom master her magic right away?"

"I was told she was a fast learner. Details are between her and her guardian. You must remember, each person has her own path. You started out later because only one parent had the gift."

I'm a hybrid, Cecelia thought.

"One or both parents, it doesn't matter. It's in your line."

"Then how did you become a guardian?"

Cecelia's phone rang. It was her boyfriend.

"*Hey, I'm at the restaurant on Tenth and Central Avenue. Meet me there for a late lunch.*"

"We need to go. You can meet my boyfriend, Marc."

They sped through long streets between tall buildings. Downtown remained full of traffic and people everywhere. In no time, they reached the restaurant.

"We've only been here once. It wasn't his favorite."

Marc sat at a table. He waved to them.

"Marc, this is Ezram. She's with me for a few days, a...distant relative."

They greeted and shook hands, neither one friendly toward the other.

"You look different. Your hair is a different style. When did you do that?"

He hesitated. "Today."

He had already ordered food. They ate, only saying a few words.

"I thought you were seeing your parents this weekend."

"I changed my mind. I wanted to talk to you about a few things."

"Oh? What's up?"

He took a deep breath. "I've been thinking a lot. I feel my life is going a different direction." He took a drink of water. "I think we need to take a break. I want to break up and move on." Marc continued to eat.

Cecelia put her fork down. Her face heated, and a frenzy of raw emotions swam inside her head. "What? When did you decide this? I thought you were happy," she choked out. Ezram patted her hand.

Several heads turned their way; sympathetic eyes followed her.

"I've thought this through. I'll move my stuff out this week."

Cecelia forced back tears. "Why are you doing this? We need to talk about it."

"I've made up my mind. You'll see that I'm right."

She shook her head. "Check, please." She moved from her chair like a zombie.

Marc paid for the meal, and they left the restaurant.

Cecelia gathered her thoughts. "I don't understand. You just talked about our future a few weeks ago. This isn't like you."

Marc appeared bored. "It's who I am. I don't want to be tied down." He rolled his eyes.

His face started to shift. His dark hair turned white. Marc gave her a crooked smile. In moments, a tooth elongated from the front of his mouth.

Cecelia jumped back. "You're definitely not Marc."

"What gave it away? My stellar personality?"

"Now you must decide," Ezram cautioned. "Because your heart and head can't be in conflict."

"You're not winning any contests today." Cecelia gathered her magic. She pushed out, *"I wish you were gone!"*

Fog and steam rolled off the creature, but he remained standing.

"Not as good as you think." The creature raised his arms and threw a ball of energy at her.

Cecelia jumped out of the way.

"Use your will!" Ezram hastily instructed.

Anger filled Cecelia's body. She gathered her magic and thrust it at the creature. This time, it was a direct hit. He vanished into the unknown. Smoke and steam lifted from where he stood.

"That was too close."

"You'll do fine, if you know how to separate what's real or not."

Cecelia looked at her hands in awe. Nerves and questions, and some doubt wrapped its arms around the anointed student. They left the restaurant. They walked for some time down the long streets in silence.

After picking up some water at a local market, they stopped at an open space.

"Let's sit at the park and we can discuss your progress."

"Will I be encountering all these *choices* in the future, or is this just a test for my initiation? I wish Mom would've told me some of this."

"My dear, she couldn't. It was your path to follow just like it had been hers."

"I miss her so much. One minute she was healthy and energetic, and the next, she wasn't. Gone. Just like that. So fast." Cecelia slumped over on the bench.

"We can burn out fast. It's unclear why some people live a long time while others fade into the afterlife. Your mom was a shining star. But she knew her time would come soon. Sooner than she wanted," Ezram explained, her understanding eyes directed at her distraught pupil. "The hope and focus are on you. She would want this; more importantly, you should want this. It's who you are."

Cecelia took a deep breath. Confidence filled her lungs. "I don't want to fail, not only for her, but for myself. I want to believe I can be that person transformed." She stood up. "I know I can do this."

"That's what you need to conquer your remaining tasks. You have natural instincts in—"

The ground shook, nearly knocking Cecelia off balance. She grabbed the bench. "We can't be having an earthquake, can we?"

"That is a predicament."

A gentle shake erupted again. People around them stood still, fear gripping their sense of safety and security.

Small rocks began to fall from the sky. The hard objects hit a few people and cars nearby. People shouted and scrambled, taking cover.

"Let's get out of here!" Cecelia rushed ahead as Ezram formed a cover over them.

"How can I stop this? This is too much! It's more than I can handle!" They stood protectively inside a store with others wondering if the end of time was near.

"Are you so certain about this? Your limitations?"

They watched as bigger rocks arrived and small ones continued to fall at random places, colliding with bikes, cars, and buildings.

"We're all going to die!"

"We'll be trapped and crushed!"

"It's the rapture! We'll all be judged. Repent! Repent!"

They moved to the other side of the store. "What am I supposed to do? If I can't stop this—fail this test—then it's over? I don't know if I *can* be that powerful person. What if I'm not worthy to belong?" Regret and despair filled Cecelia's mind.

"Is your value placed on how powerful you can be or what kind of magic you can conjure? If we believed that, it would be endless wars and rifts throughout our world. Our kind would cease as a whole." Ezram gently touched Cecelia's face. "You're much more than the idea of being insignificant. Even the smallest voice or the least known person can have the greatest impact. That is your power."

Cecelia absorbed everything Ezram just said. She never believed she would amount to anything more than just living day to day, a simple life with rewards and challenges. She never wanted that sense of greatness.

"It's okay if I don't conquer the world. I don't need to. I need to live and believe I'm more than a dot in the matrix."

Cecelia took a deep breath and slipped out the front door. "Can you show me how to bring up a shield?"

Ezram demonstrated for her. "That should protect you against falling objects."

Cecelia stood away from spectators' eyes. Larger rocks collided with the ground. The rocks slowed their movement and sped up again. It was chaos personified. She didn't recognize the city she lived in.

"I'm glad you're here with me. I couldn't do this alone."

"And so, you won't be."

Cecelia closed her eyes. She chanted in her mind until the words spilled out into the open. "Make the rocks stop falling. I wish for all the destruction to go away. Return the city back."

A glow and a surge seeped out of her and whisked across the perimeter. Smaller rocks began to move upwards as larger ones slowed down their descent. Soon, they too moved away from the ground. Bent and destroyed objects started to reform themselves and return to their original shape. The magic moved quickly and efficiently, lifting all the debris and stones from the earth.

"What's happening? Everything's moving backwards."

"We're saved! It's a miracle!"

The sky cleared to its previous state of sunshine and brightness, and the air was no longer thick with fine particles, as if nothing had disrupted the day. Time moved back.

"I did it," Cecelia huffed. She collapsed back against a brick wall, her mind drained. She closed her eyes to slow the fatigue driving her down.

"You used a large amount of your magic. Here, let me help you." Ezram guided Cecelia to a nearby bench. She produced a bottle of water and gave it to her star pupil.

Cecelia gulped down the water quickly. "I'm so thirsty."

Ezram produced another bottle. "It takes the water out of you." They waited quietly on the bench until Cecelia regained herself.

"You've had quite the eventful day. I can say with certainty that you did well today. Your quick reaction and your resolve enabled you to make clear choices. And sometimes, you'll need to make those choices despite your own desires."

Cecelia gazed at the downtown area in front of them. "It is a beautiful day."

"And tomorrow, you'll conquer the rest of your journey."

They returned to Cecelia's home; a long sleep awaited after the surprising and exhausting day. She turned around. Ezram managed to disappear without a trace. Cecelia thought she went back inside the box.

$$\backsim$$

Cecelia tossed and turned that night. Visions of menacing eyes and horns and sharp teeth flooded her dreams. The ground under her feet shifted upside down until everything stood from the ceiling. People she recognized crossed into her sleep. Cecelia reached out to them only to have Ezram appear with a disapproving nod. Cecelia then faded into a hazy, visionless slumber.

$$\backsim$$

Cecelia woke up to the smell of food. She jumped out of bed, freshened up, and headed for the kitchen. Standing there, Ezram prepared a feast at the stove.

"Good morning. Did you sleep well? I've made breakfast," she gushed.

"I can see that. Didn't know you could cook."

"There're so many cooking shows, they made it easy."

"Easy." Cecelia looked at the pancakes, toast, eggs, bacon, and fruit set in front of her. "You've got quite a few choices here. I hope you're going to help me."

An alarm went off from the oven. "Oh, the muffins are done," Ezram cheered. She took out the puffed dessert and poured some coffee into a mug, giving it to Cecelia. "Eat. You'll need all the energy for today."

"Great. Looking forward to today's disaster."

Ezram took a sip of her juice. "You did well yesterday. We must face our challenges with an open mind and a willingness to succeed. You *must* believe you can conquer this."

"And if I don't?"

Ezram took a bite of her pancake and poured herself some coffee. She savored the drink. "There's always another day."

Cecelia studied her. "Seems like that could be a long wait."

After a long pause, Ezram placed a muffin on her plate. "Eat up. Today is here. Tomorrow, we don't know."

They ate breakfast in silence with a million thoughts and questions lingering in Cecelia's mind.

"Where to?" Cecelia drove down some familiar streets.

"Turn here, then turn there. Keep going down this street," Ezram directed.

They passed her old high school and headed for a strip mall, which had been renovated years ago with a completely different exterior.

"Let's go inside and look around." Ezram led them into a gift shop. "I need to buy someone a card."

"Will you be needing some cash again?"

"Oh, no. I found ten dollars on the kitchen table."

As they looked through the cards, a familiar face passed by, which caught Cecelia's attention.

"Let's stay focused, shall we? What you seem to see might not always aspire to be."

A loud commotion, more like an argument, came from the front of the store.

"What's going on?" Ezram didn't respond as Cecelia angled her head toward the front of the store.

"I said, give me whatcha got! Make it quick. I don't got all day."

"They're being robbed! We need to call the police!" she said in a low, frantic voice. She pulled Ezram to the side so nobody would see them.

"Normally, yes, we should call the authorities. Taking on a potential threat could be dangerous."

"And?"

"And this could also be another test."

"Could. Maybe. Still a threat. Test or not, I don't want to get shot." Cecelia eyed the front of the store.

The clerk cautiously handed a zipped bag to the assailant. He grabbed the bag, put it and the gun down at the counter. He took a cigarette out and lit it, then took a few puffs.

"Criminals usually don't spend time smoking while robbing a place." She inched forward, motioning for Ezram to follow. They walked on the side of the store to stay hidden, hoping to sneak up on him.

"I was wondering when you'd come up," the assailant said, and took another puff. He turned to face them.

Cecelia froze, startled by his awareness.

"A new protégé, Ezram? Seems like there're enough of you walking this earth."

"Not enough, unfortunately. But your people seem to show up frequently."

"I can make this easy on all of us and eliminate extra work." He waved the gun around. The store clerk took a step back. "Don't call for help," he ordered.

"Not so fast, Melcore. You've got a debt to pay."

"You ruin all the fun." He took another puff and made a ring formation. "I miss this."

"Did you ask this guy to come and teach me a lesson?"

"I don't get to choose. Your training comes from somewhere else. We've known each other through the years."

"Well, let's move this show along." Melcore pointed the gun at Cecelia.

The clerk whimpered and ducked. Cecelia's heart raced along with fury in her blood. She narrowed her eyes as determination took over.

"Melcore, let's all calm down before we do anything reckless," Ezram advised.

"I don't do impulsive. I'm always in control and know when something gets in my way. In fact, I don't appreciate *you* telling me what the rules—"

Cecelia pushed an enormous amount of power at Melcore. He disintegrated before he could pull the trigger, his gun turning to dust. He cursed at them through faded words. She stared at her palms, her newfound powers finding their home. She noticed the cigarette butt on the counter.

"What just happened?"

"I wasn't sure how much of this was real, but I didn't want to take any chances. You can get up now," Ezram said.

The clerk stood up and looked both ways. "Where did he go?"

"Changed his mind. Here, your cash. And I'll pay for this card." She handed the clerk the zipped bag and the ten-dollar bill.

She took the change as the store's door opened. Cecelia looked up, her heart stopped, her mouth agape. Her eyes turned wide with disbelief.

"Mom?"

JoAnne smiled at her daughter. "I see you're in good hands. Just a final step."

Cecelia rushed over and put her arms around her mother, tears streaming down her face. "You're really here. I've missed you every single day." She gripped her mother tighter.

JoAnne waited a few moments before releasing her daughter. "Lia, you're almost there. Not too much longer. You'll understand everything."

"Why didn't you tell me? I would've understood."

"You know why. We can't. You must find your own way, with a little help." She looked over at Ezram.

"She's a fast learner. She gets it from you." Ezram handed the card to Cecelia. "It's for your mom. A little reminder."

Realization hit Cecelia. "Your birthday is this week."

"Put it next to the box if you'd like."

"How could I forget? So many things have happened."

"You didn't forget. Your learning is your priority. This is your life now. Embrace it."

"But I can't without you."

JoAnne looked at her daughter thoughtfully before opening the door and walking out into the sunshine. They followed her.

"Mom, please stay. Find a way."

"It's your time now." JoAnne started to walk away.

"Stop!" Cecelia pulled in her newfound powers and directed them at her mom. "I command you to stay!"

The magic caused her mom to fade in and out.

"Lia, it doesn't work that way."

"I wish for you to come back!"

JoAnne continued to fade in and out.

"Return to us!" She sent another wave of magic.

JoAnne reached over to her distraught daughter. Cecelia looked at her hands, frustrated. She looked up at her mom. "I just want you back."

"I'm always here." She touched her daughter's hand, and something sparked between the two of them. Light, joy, surprise, hope, and all the memories they'd shared passed from mother to daughter.

Wisdom.

Cecelia's face brightened. "I understand now."

~

"To Cecelia on a successful journey! May she continue to grow and flourish, the doors to her magic wide open," Aunt Susan toasted.

"I'll second that!" Maria chimed in.

"Mom would be so proud of you, as I am."

"Thank you, Dad, for everything. For being there and understanding." She hugged her father. "And everybody here." She looked at her boyfriend-turned-fiancé, Aunt Susan and Maria, and a few new members of the group.

Cecelia walked into her bedroom and placed the birthday card next to the wooden box. It began to glow. She walked out of her bedroom and closed the door, into the celebration.

Realistic Wizarding Ambitions

Lizbeth Myles

Ever since she was a little girl, Branwyn wanted what every wizard wanted: a tower of her own.

But wanting a tower was a great deal easier than having a tower. Her patron, Signeur Ricwin de Mermande, had a habit of summoning her away from her studies to perform parlor tricks at his banquets. It was irritating, but not as irritating as Signeur Ricwin's generous financial support of an attempted coup d'état against the Princess Regent, and his subsequent banishment.

Branwyn's debts piled up. But her creditors had an exaggerated view of what an unqualified wizard could do, and threats of violence regarding timely repayments were kept to a minimum. In due time, she finished her schooling, and completed her apprenticeship, and she earned the right to own property on mystical land.

All she needed was gold. An awful lot of gold.

For a year, she buried her pride and took on any mage-work she could find. She conjured water fountains and powerful currents to clean up after the nervous colts, proud chargers, and cautious mares that packed the horse market. She choked on soot as she cleaned chimneys with awkward sweeps of bristly magic, and went home covered in cuts and bruises after lifting petty curses from overvalued trinkets.

Every night she reminded herself that this was all good, honest labour. It let her practice her craft in all sorts of ways she'd never have imagined, and appreciate the value of imperfect solutions. Even so, she learned illusion magic just to disguise her face if ever she spotted another wizarding graduate while she worked.

And then there was the occasional fool who thought delving into the earth to find lost treasures was a sensible thing to do. Branwyn valued her personal safety, but she was also desperate, and while treasure was rare, the adventurous fools did pay exceptionally well.

It was a very, very long year, but by the end she'd scraped together enough gold, gems, and artifacts of arcane interest that an agent for the buying and selling of enchanted land and buildings was willing to see her. His name was Aimery, and he wielded a condescending smile with razor-sharp precision. After much hemming and hawing, Aimery offered her a tower on a small peninsula an eight-day ride from the nearest town.

"You'll love it," he said, smiling. "And it's the only one you can afford."

"Almost there," Aimery told her. He led the way along a dirt path overgrown with nettles, brambles and thorned vines, which he cut through with a freshly enchanted sickle. "Lucky we even had this one on the books. The tower market is booming at the moment."

"I know," said Branwyn, thinking of all the soaring wizard towers in the city, with their marble domes and stained-glass windows. She'd need to make several demonic bargains to ever have a chance of buying one. And she just wasn't that sort of wizard.

"But there's a real charm to this place." Aimery looked back and smiled at her. "I'm sure you'll like it."

"I hope so." It was hard not to sound bitter.

He sliced through another thick knot of vines. "Ah, here we are."

"At last," Branwyn muttered. She ducked under the maimed vines and entered a small clearing.

"She's a real fixer upper," said Aimery cheerfully.

Branwyn stared at the sight before her, momentarily speechless. This wasn't a tower; it was a ruin.

The upper levels had collapsed entirely. A fragment of the third-floor walls survived, but looked like they were about to crumble away like old cheese. The remaining walls were battered and full of holes, as though a colossal dog had used the tower as a chew toy.

"You must be joking."

"Not at all. There's a whole room on the ground floor that's intact. It's even got the remains of the original wooden door." Aimery stamped on the grass. "And you feel that? Real mystical ground."

On that, at least, she agreed. The healthy fizz of enrooted magic tickled at her boots.

"There are so many opportunities to customize. You can really make the place your own. An opportunity like this doesn't come up often. Certainly not at this price."

Branwyn winced.

The agent unfurled the title deed. He smiled broadly. "So, what do you say?"

Branwyn stared. Then she sighed. "I'll take a look around."

She made a show of examining fallen chunks of masonry, and the warped spiral stairs. She circled the tower and tapped cautiously at the stonework. All the while she hummed to herself as though she was thinking things over. She doubted Aimery was fooled for a moment, but she couldn't bring herself to just say yes. So she continued her wanderings for half an hour. And then she said yes.

Aimery lifted the repulsion curse that was seeded into the land, gave her a cheery wave, and left.

Branwyn shrugged off her pack and dropped all her remaining worldly goods on the broken steps. She stared up at the tower for a few moments, then sat down and buried her head in her hands.

What the hells had she just done?

The sole intact room of her new tower stank of mould and contained numerous small skeletal remains, so Branwyn spent the first night at her new home in a small tent pitched outside. She conjured a crackling fire, and a loaf of bread that looked freshly baked but tasted of nothing.

Breakfast was crafted eggs and beans, and if she stared really hard, she could almost trick herself into believing they had flavor.

In the fresh light of morning, the tower was no less of a ruin, but Branwyn was rested and filled with a restless optimism. She strode up the broken steps and surveyed the entrance hall. First things first, she had to get rid of all those tiny corpses.

She tugged at the magic that rested in the earth beneath her, teasing it out and using it to fuel her spells. The fresh magic tingled through her veins and down her spine in the most wonderful way. There was a new strength to her spells that almost made her giddy. As she swept away old bones and dry leaves, decomposed rotting furniture and cleansed the walls of black moulds, she suddenly envisioned how magnificent her tower could be.

She saw the sharp lines of crenelations at the summit that would offer her the most magnificent views. The vaulted entrance would have thick oak doors with shining brass hinges, flanked by enormous clay pots that would bloom flowers in deep blues and brilliant reds all year round. Enchanted tapestries would hang from every wall, keeping the tower warm in winter and cool in summer.

Before she began construction in earnest, she surveyed the rest of her land. There were plenty of trees and berry bushes, patches of mushrooms, and a pleasing assortment of wildflowers. With the help of a little levitation magic, she climbed her way to the top of a silver birch. The stillness there, as she sat between forest and sky, was beautiful. And then she spotted a clutch of thatched roofs tucked into a river bend only a few miles away.

A village. Aimery had not mentioned a village. Branwyn chewed at her bottom lip as she considered all the stories she'd read about villages and their local wizards. Many of them mentioned sharp implements and an excess of fire. Some talked about wisdom and healing. Others of reclusive wizards, too strange and distant to risk approaching.

Branwyn very much wanted to be a reclusive wizard.

But the temptation was still there. Magic meant that so long as she was on her land, she had everything she needed. It did not mean that she had everything she wanted. Memories of fresh bread and sweet, sticky jams taunted her.

But no, she had to be strong.

Winter arrived with undue haste, and with it came vicious storms and unrelenting snow.

It didn't take long before all Branwyn's work on her tower was undone. Great drifts of snow meant she didn't dare set foot outside, and it was all she could do to keep the freezing cold out of the few rooms she'd restored.

One morning, she woke to a terrible cracking that shook the air. It was as though the ground wanted to tear itself apart.

No, not the ground, the stone. Her tower was collapsing.

She fled outside, careless of the falling debris and the thick snowfall. She stumbled through the storm until she tripped into a thicket of half-buried thorny branches. For a while, she lay there, unwilling to get up. She didn't actually want to freeze to death, so she summoned a cheery little fire to sit next to her.

When she finally decided to move, her limbs were uncooperative and she couldn't feel her fingers. She held them up to her face. They were patched in blue and red. Frostbite. It would take her hours to heal them.

But first, she had to turn around. She had to look at the tower. For a few minutes, she was perfectly still, summoning up the courage. Then she drove her numb fingers into the palms of her hands and turned.

The storm had eased off, and through the delicate snowflakes her tower's brutal injuries revealed the ineptitude of all her repairs.

She had failed. Everything she'd worked for had collapsed in a single night.

Should she leave? But where would she go? What would she do?

A proper wizard wouldn't give up so easily.

She sat at her fire, her back to the tower, and tried to make some plan. It wasn't just that she had to rebuild; she had to work out what had gone wrong. Were her stones not strong enough? Had she built it too high? Perhaps her conjured mortar had too much lime?

Maybe this was how the tower had fallen into ruin in the first place. Maybe, despite the magic growing in the land, this was not meant to be the home of a wizard.

Maybe she wasn't destined to have a tower at all. She'd have to become one of those poor unfortunate wizards who found themselves living in a bungalow, or a wagon, or a cave–

A twig cracked behind her. Branwyn swept to her feet in a flurry of thick robes and mild panic. She turned to face the intruder, expecting a deer or fox. At worst, an irate boar.

It was a person, and a horse. A horse had snuck up on her. Embarrassing.

"Hello," the person said.

Branwyn glared at her, but this person didn't seem to mind. She narrowed her eyes at the path behind the new arrival. It had been a bad idea to clear out those brambles. People didn't ride horses through brambles.

"What do you want?" Branwyn brushed down her robes and straightened her spine as she tried to exude an aura of power and competence.

"I am Alys de Merville," the person said. "I am here to offer my services as an apprentice."

Branwyn stared at Alys as if she'd suddenly grown a second head. Which was the sort of magic that only the very foolish or very evil ever indulged in.

"What?" said Branwyn. "Why?"

"Well, you're a wizard, and I'm an apprentice wizard. I seek to avail myself of your knowledge and wisdom so I might progress in my education."

"I know *that* why. Why would you want to be *my* apprentice?" Branwyn could think of only two reasons: this woman was desperately poor, or she was a truly terrible student, and this was her last-ditch attempt to find a mentor.

"I've family in Odstone," said Alys.

"Odstone?"

"The village. It's about an hour's walk that way." She nodded east.

"Uh-huh," said Branwyn, unconvinced this was a sufficient reason.

"Look, I do have the necessary skills." There was a tiny note of irritation in Alys's voice. Branwyn felt a twinge of guilt; she really had been quite rude.

"I would be delighted to see a demonstration," she said, trying to sound sincere.

Alys proceeded to run through a standard series of spells, conjuring fire, water, and an elegant little gust of wind. Then she crouched down in the grass and coaxed a patch of vibrant red poppies out of the earth. She was showing off, but Branwyn couldn't help being impressed. And she was fond of poppies.

"I've got my apprentice fee too," Alys said, patting one of the saddle bags. She looked so very hopeful, and it was unlikely anyone else would ever ask to be Branwyn's apprentice.

"Fine. There's a room on the second floor that stays dry unless it's raining and there's a north wind. You can have that."

"Oh, thank you." Alys grinned, and Branwyn was afraid she'd start jumping up and down she looked so happy. "And this is Honoria." She patted the horse. "She says thank you too."

Branwyn stared at the horse. The horse stared back.

No, she was absolutely not going to start talking to horses.

Sometimes, Branwyn forgot she was no longer alone in her tower. There were days when she woke to the clatter of pans, or racing footfalls on the staircase, or, gods protect her, actual singing, and for a split second believed the place haunted. But interruptions in Branwyn's sleep aside, Alys was a conscientious apprentice.

Every morning, the tower stairs were swept from top to bottom. Every evening, the kitchen and potions room—more of a cupboard, really—were cleaned and tidied. She went to the village three times a week and brought back fresh fruit and vegetables. She even drew an elegantly illustrated botanical map of Branwyn's land.

When she completed the phoenix blaze display for the first time, Branwyn clapped. Then realised what she'd done and stopped. But it was too late. Alys was delighted by the approval of her spell-work. She practically glowed with pride.

"I'll pick up some eggs and flour at the market tomorrow. I've a wonderful idea for a new omelette, a celebration omelette," said Alys. She hesitated, then added: "You could come along, you know. See for yourself what they have."

"I had a look," said Branwyn.

"When?"

"Last autumn," Branwyn answered in a mumble. Unfortunately, it wasn't mumbly enough.

"Did you go to the market?" Alys's voice tingled with suspicion.

Branwyn sighed. "I saw some cottages as I balanced on the top of a birch tree."

"Right," said Alys. "Would you like a proper look? It's really quite nice."

It was hard to say no when Alys looked at her with those wide brown eyes, full of ludicrous amounts of hope.

"Fine," Branwyn said. "But I won't enjoy it."

Craftsmen from all the nearby hamlets and farms came to Odstone every week to tout their wares, and they all seemed to be in competition for who could shout the loudest.

Branwyn and Alys walked past the village smithy, and Branwyn flinched at every clang of the hammer. A barber snipping away at a wiry old man's hair gave Alys a quick nod, and she smiled back. There was a hatmaker, who didn't let the lavish prices of his creations dull his optimism about selling them to villagers who'd be lucky to own two pairs of shoes. Branwyn's eye lingered on a pink and purple steepled headdress. Alys nudged her gently.

"I'm sure we can barter," she whispered. "We are wizards, after all."

Branwyn quickly looked away. "I've no idea what you're talking about," she said, hurrying to the next stall where wicker baskets overflowed with ripe red apples.

"That's my sister over there," said Alys. "Would you like to meet her?"

No, thought Branwyn. Then she took a long, deep breath. "If you like," she said.

After introductions were made the sister, Ida, invited them to join her for a drink in the tavern.

"We'd love to," said Alys. "But perhaps another day. We'd best get back to the tower. After all, a wizard's work never ends."

Branwyn took another long, deep breath. "Actually, that sounds like a lovely idea," she said.

Alys looked at Branwyn and smiled.

When they headed back to the tower, they carried a dozen fresh eggs, a large bag of flour, and a basket of blackberries. Alys had insisted on the blackberries.

"Before I left Odstone, I was the best jam-maker in the village," she said. "You'll see."

"I like your sister," said Branwyn.

"She's a likable person."

Branwyn nodded, but didn't say anything else.

Work on the tower continued at a steady pace. Alys had a steady, secure way of forming spells, while Branwyn preferred energy and intricacy. It took a few months, but eventually something clicked between them. Days of careful stone working spells took moments. Levitating the stone up and into place became a joy instead of a chore.

Alys didn't ask Branwyn back to the village again, though she was not above heavily hinting that Branwyn might enjoy spending a little time there. But the furthest Branwyn would go was asking for the odd item on market day.

This didn't stop Alys from sharing stories about her sister. Or stories about the smithy. And tavern keeper. And potter. After a while, Branwyn was appalled to find that she rather liked sitting by the fire, sipping at lemon balm tea, and listening to Alys' tales.

And so, when Alys started to include snippets of news from travelling merchants about raiding parties and disgruntled nobles, Branwyn began to worry.

One afternoon, Alys arrived back at the tower with an odd look on her face. It took Branwyn a few moments to realise that this was what Alys looked like when she was sad.

"A farm just eight miles away was burned to the ground. No-one knows what happened to the family," she said in a rush. "People are scared. If those raiders come here, there's no-one to protect the village." Alys held her gaze in a way that made Branwyn feel deeply uncomfortable.

"You think we can protect them?"

"No, I think you can."

Branwyn stared at her for several very silent seconds, then said, "Alys, I can't even rebuild one modest tower. What exactly do you think I can do against a pack of angry pillagers?"

"You must have trained in combat magic."

Branwyn rolled her eyes. "Passing grade," she said. "Barely."

"It's also the right thing to do."

Branwyn thought of all the stories she'd read about wizards, and there were indeed some where the wizard, protective of the local people, had stood between them and danger.

That was not the sort of wizard Branwyn wanted to be, but she'd also wanted a beautiful tower, and an apprentice who didn't sing first thing in the morning.

The next morning, with a healthy dose of complaining from Branwyn, they began to build tower fortifications. They'd had a lot of practice sculpting stone, so they created a pair of stone guardians, twelve feet tall, with four arms, each one carrying a stone sword. Branwyn set repelling charms on each window, and grew ivy up and around the tower, each leaf imbued with an enchantment to absorb momentum.

Alys lifted magic from the earth, then sowed it back in traps of fire and oil. Branwyn was uncomfortable knowing they were hidden below her carefully planted rows of parsnips, but she couldn't deny that exploding vegetable patches would come as quite the surprise.

It was only a few days later when there was a frantic knocking on the tower doors. Branwyn opened it to find Ida, red-faced and out of breath.

"They rode into the village," she gasped. "Two dozen soldiers. They didn't hurt anyone, but they want our money and goods. They said they want it all packed up and they'd come back tomorrow. If they think we've given enough, they'll leave us alone."

Alys wrapped her sister in a hug. "It's going to be all right," she said calmly.

Ida trembled, and it turned Branwyn's stomach to see someone so scared. "They're not going to leave us alone, are they?"

"Stay here," said Branwyn. "Alys, get her some peppermint tea. I'm going to Odstone."

It was only when Branwyn stood in the centre of the marketplace ringing the village bell that she realised what she'd done. But it was too late now. The villagers were already hurrying out to see what the fuss was about. She was surrounded. Branwyn did her best look around, and met their eyes. And when most of the villagers were there, she cleared her throat.

"Sorry to bother you all. Ida told me about your unpleasant visitors. I want to help."

"Oh, bloody hells," muttered Branwyn. "It's *him*."

Alys poked her head above the windowsill. Below, two dozen armed and armoured horsemen approached. Their leader's armour gleamed with gold decorations, and precious gems that were sewn into his horse's saddle glinted in the sunlight.

"You know him?"

"My former patron. Signeur Ricwin de Mermande. Absolute arse. He's supposed to be banished."

"I don't suppose he remembers you fondly and you can talk him into going away?"

Branwyn gave her a look. Still, it felt wrong to not at least try and talk it out.

She held her head high as she descended the curved stairway. As she passed the villagers who'd taken up positions at the windows, she did her best to give them reassuring looks. Most of the villagers were hunkered down in the cellar. But those who had some skill with a bow had volunteered to help in the defence.

Branwyn shoved open the tower doors and swept outside. She marched forwards until she was just behind the parsnips, then addressed the riders.

"My name is Branwyn, wizard protector of Odstone, and it's time for you to leave." She was impressed at how confident she sounded.

Ricwin stared down at her. "Do I know you?"

"No," said Branwyn. "Of course not. I'm just a simple country wizard. And I'd like you all to leave. Now."

Ricwin rolled his eyes. "Archers!" he cried. The second line of horsemen drew their bows. "Loose!"

A dozen arrows flew towards Branwyn. She rolled her shoulders and flicked her wrist. The arrows fell harmlessly to one side.

Ricwin snorted. "I see the robes aren't just for show. Very well. Archers! The other arrows, if you please."

There was a bit of fumbling in their quivers as the archers struggled to find these other arrows. But in a few moments, they were ready to take another shot at her.

"Loose!" cried Ricwin.

Branwyn felt the shimmer of enchantment racing through the air towards her. When she knocked these arrows aside, they crackled with fire and then turned back towards her. She managed to slow them enough to let her dash through the tower doors.

"Alys! They don't want to talk!" She hurried up the stairs to the second floor window.

The riders had dismounted, and most had drawn their swords. At Ricwin's command they lifted their shields to cover their heads. There was a rustle of branches and Branwyn groaned at what was carried out of the forest: a freshly made battering ram.

"Forward!" shouted Ricwin. Branwyn nodded to the villager one window along, and he loosed an arrow. At that signal the rest of the tower's archers began to fire. Most of the arrows bounced off the attackers' shields. There were a few cries of pain where they got through, but not a single man fell.

The attackers marched on towards the doors, heedless of the vegetables they crushed beneath their boots. When the last man had stepped onto the parsnip patch a bouquet of gentle explosions erupted from the ground, and clouds of noxious smoke engulfed them. Branwyn tutted at the pastel colours. There was no need for blooms of pink and soft purple; Alys was showing off.

As their coughing fits worsened, Branwyn sent in a flock of conjured ravens, and directed them to focus on their prey's eyes. Eyes watering from the smoke, the attackers stumbled around trying to cut down the birds, and were met with outraged squawks and sharp beaks.

Meanwhile, Alys shot bolts of sparkling fire and lightning. They weren't strong enough to do any real damage, but the hits would sting. Finally, Branwyn released the great stone guardians of the tower. She was certain that this would be the coup de grâce required to drive them off.

At first it seemed to be working, but as the smoke cleared, it was clear the battle went poorly. Most of the ravens were dead, and the guardians were being chipped apart. Her magic was exhausted.

Alys yelped as an arrow flew through the window and sank into her arm. "It's nothing," she said.

Branwyn did not agree, but it was hardly the time to argue. She stared down at her failing guardians, her poor fallen ravens, her squashed parsnips, and failed to come up with a clever idea to turn the tide of battle.

She shot out sluggish trickles of lukewarm fire. There had to be something more she could do. This was her land, and her tower. Some obscure lesson from defense magic must be lurking in her mind, ready to jump out at just the right—

The tower doors suddenly slammed open, and the air was filled with screams. Not screams of fear, but screams of anger. Men and women armed with axes and knives rushed out to join the failing stone guardians in their fight. Under normal circumstances, they'd have been slaughtered, but they ran at a party of horsemen who were choking, bleeding, singed or extremely nauseous. Morale sapped, and faced with a band of roaring villagers and sharp steel, they ran.

"Did we win?" asked Alys.

"I think so," said Branwyn.

"Protector of Odstone, eh?" said Alys.

Branwyn flushed and looked down. "Sounded better than Branwyn, failed recluse."

Around them, villagers tended to the wounded, tied up prisoners, and carried their goods home. They smiled at Branwyn as they passed, and added to a little pile of gifts by the tower entrance.

"You're going to have to put up with quite a bit of gratitude from now on," said Alys.

"Right. Of course. I can do that. No problem." She fidgeted at her robes. "You do know they might come back?"

"Then we'll fight them again," said Alys.

As the last of the villagers made their way out of the clearing, Branwyn sat down in front of the tower doors. Alys slumped down beside her, the wound on her arm now bandaged, the healing magic beneath hard at work.

"The tower's still standing," she said.

"It's a good tower," said Branwyn.

Alys smiled. "It has a good wizard."

"I suppose the apprentice is acceptable too."

"A work-in-progress," said Alys.

Branwyn looked up at her tower. "Yes," she said. "I suppose we all are."

Acknowledgments

With the success of our first anthology, *Of Shadows, Stars, and Sabers*, we saw a great opportunity to continue with themed anthologies for the future. We thank everyone involved in helping bring *Of Enchantment, Enigma, and the Infinite* to life. You enchant us!

Many thanks to our fantastic editor Scarlett R. Algee, for formatting and final proofread edits. Thank you to Niall C. Grant for another gorgeous cover. And thank you to Mike Trobiano at Dash Creative Group for full cover layout and advice.

Thank you to the following donors to the crowdfunding campaign that made this book's production possible. You are magic! Thanks to: Ken Wheaton; Anna Tan; Michael Mulhern; Carrie Ancell; Dean Powell; Robert Tienken; Roger "Frying Tiger" Long; Michelle F. Evans; Ian Beaverstock; William T. Carmichael; Deborah A. Levinson; Ciaran Sundstrem; Cerise Cauthron; Leslie B. Lambert; Dana Gricken; David Perlmutter; Lee James; Dr Chet Morrison; Ken Zinn; Marianne Senechal; Rebecca Powell; Stephen Crawford; Dave M. Jones; Julian White; Deb Zuroski; Julie Kangas; Casey Lau; Gryftkin; Cliff Winnig; Ian Beaverstock; Arina; Roger Alix-Gaudreau; Bryan Ingram; Colette Reap; Ripley M; Edirin Oputu; Jeffrey A Hallett; Gloria Thomas; Steve Adkins; Allen V. Cheesman; Paraskevi Oppio; Kristin Pratt; Akira K; Harvey Hamer; Richard Czernik; Meghan Crockett; Michael H; Jeffery Heileson; Doug Mayo-Wells; Catherine Moffat; Ginger Stample; Gaffin Sheedeedy; Sean Dowd; Nic de Lisle; Philip Ness; Lucien Telford; Randall Reimers; Joseph Held; Thomas Dilligan; Robin Haglund; Katrina Brown; Steven Klotz; Geoffrey Knox; Scott Melton; Paula Turner; Bill Gray; Janice Thompson; Kyddryn Gaia; Tyler Martin; Pamela Twyman; Martyn Winters; Arianne Hartsell-Gundy; Roger Pearson; Andy Tinkham; Cat Treadwell; Glori Medina; Michael Harrold; Allen Born; Victoria Traube; Erik Cieslewicz; Steven Brief; Michael Stackpole; Stuart Yael Gordom;

Acknowledgments

Alan Nash; Jesse Reid; Laura Roberts; Judith Morton; Paul Moss; Mark O'Neill; and David Bradley.

And thank you, of course, to our wonderful writers, without whom this book would not exist:

Ai Jiang, Alice James, Angela Sylvaine, Anne Corlett, Chris Panatier, Cynthia Pelayo, D.K. Stone, Dana Gricken, David Quantick, Dennis K. Crosby, Eddie Robson, Eliane Boey, Eugen Bacon, Guido Eekhaut, Helen Glynn Jones, Ian Green, J.L. Worrad., James Bennett, Jenny Rae Rappaport, Jonathan Maberry, Kali Wallace, KC Grifant, Khan Wong, Lili Hayward, Lizbeth Myles, Mya Duong, P.A. Cornell, Ren Hutchings, Renan Bernardo, Sarah L. Miles, and Somto Ihezue.

About the Authors

Ai Jiang (江艾)

Ai Jiang (江艾) is a Chinese-Canadian author and winner of the Bram Stoker®, Nebula, and Ignyte Awards. She has also been nominated for the Hugo and Astounding Awards and is a Locus and BSFA Award finalist. An immigrant from Shanghu, Changle, Fujian, Ai currently lives in Toronto, Ontario. Her work can be found in many speculative fiction publications, including *F&SF*, *The Dark*, *Uncanny*, *The Masters Review*, and many more. Ai is a prolific writer of both short and long fiction. Her books *Linghun* and *I AM AI* continue to garner recognition. Her novella *A Palace Near the Wind* is now available via Titan Books. Learn more about Ai from her website: https://aijiang.ca/.

Alice James

Alice James—self-described as a science fiction and fantasy novelist, cat wrangler, and plant killer—is based in Oxford, England. Her paranormal romances, *The Lavington Windsor Mysteries*, star an amateur necromancer who helps solve murders by raising the dead to find out who killed them. She has had short stories published in *Andromeda Spaceways* and *Indie Bites*. Alice lives in an 18th century chapel with four cats and a lot of wine. Learn more about Alice on her website: https://www.alicejames.co.uk/.

Angela Sylvaine

Angela Sylvaine is a Bram Stoker Award nominated author and self-proclaimed cheerful goth who writes speculative fiction and poetry. Details about her sci-fi horror comedy novel, *Frost Bite*, her slasher novella, *Chopping Spree*, and her short story collection, *The Dead Spot: Stories of Lost Girls*, as well as her dozens of short fiction and poetry publications can be found at angelasylvaine.com.

Anne Corlett

After 16 years as a criminal defence lawyer, Anne Corlett decided to abandon the world of legal aid for a—worryingly—more stable and viable career as a writer. Since then, her short fiction has been published in various magazines and anthologies and has won or been shortlisted for several awards. Her debut novel, *The Space Between the Stars* was published by Pan Macmillan, with her second book, *The Theatre of Glass and Shadows* recently released by Bonnier. Set in an alternate version of London where a vast theatre district has grown up around an immersive show that's been running for centuries, it was inspired by the vast immersive creations of theatre company, Punchdrunk. Learn more about Anne on her website: http://annecorlett.co.uk/.

Chris Panatier

Chris is an artist and writer living in Dallas, Texas, with his wife, daughter and a fluctuating herd of dogs. He writes short stories and novels. *The Phlebotomist, Stringers,* and *The Redemption of Morgan Bright,* are published by Angry Robot Books. Learn more about Chris on his website: https://chrispanatier.com/.

Cynthia Pelayo

Cynthia Pelayo is a Bram Stoker Award winning and International Latino Book Award winning author and poet. Pelayo writes fairy tales that blend genre and explore concepts of grief, mourning, and cycles of violence. She is the author of *Loteria, Santa Muerte, The Missing, Poems of My Night, Into the Forest and All the Way Through, Children of Chicago, Crime Scene, The Shoemaker's Magician,* as well as dozens of standalone short stories and poems. Her latest novel, *Forgotten Sisters*,* is now available from Thomas and Mercer and is an adaptation of Hans Christian Andersen's "The Little Mermaid." Her latest novel, *Vanishing Daughters,* is now available. Learn more about Cynthia on her website: https://cinapelayo.com/.

D.K. Stone

D.K. Stone is a Canadian bestselling multi-genre author who has written both for adults and teens. *Switchback* (via Macmillan) (written as

Danika Stone) was selected as the "Best YA Books of 2019", and her thriller, *Edge of Wild* (Stonehouse, 2016) was selected as part of *Chapters* "Our Favourite Canadian Fiction." She was Writer in Residence for the Lethbridge Public Library, and has led numerous writing workshops. Learn more about D.K. from her website: https://danikastone.com/.

Dana Gricken

Dana Gricken is a multi-genre author from Ottawa, Canada. She's been published by Melange Books, Evernight Teen, Bella Books, and Oliver-Heber Books with more novels coming out soon. When not writing, she enjoys watching Star Trek, playing video games, cooking and baking, and hanging out with her family and adorable but mischievous cats. Connect with her at danagricken.com or @DanaGricken across all social media where she chats about her books and mental health awareness.

David Quantick

David Quantick was born in the North and raised in the South-West. His novels include *All My Colors*, *Night Trian,* and *Ricky's Hand*. David will also have two forthcoming solo author works publishing via Stars and Sabers: *Imagine a Friend* and *The Hyena*. David also has also written movies (*Book of Love*) and for TV shows, including *Veep* (for which he won an Emmy Award) and *Avenue 5*. You can see more of his film and television work on his IMDB page: https://www.imdb.com/name/nm0702880/

Dennis K. Crosby

Dennis K. Crosby is the multi award-winning author of the bestselling Kassidy Simmons Series (*Death's Legacy*; *Death's Debt*, *Death's Despair*). Since 2020, he has published three urban fantasy novels and numerous short stories. Learn more about Dennis on his website: http://www.denniskcrosby.com/.

Eddie Robson

Eddie Robson is the author of the SF novels *The Heist of Hollow London* (2025), *Drunk on All Your Strange New Words* (2022), *Hearts of Oak* (2020) and *Tomorrow Never Knows* (2015). He's also a scriptwriter and journalist: he created and wrote the BBC Radio sitcom *Welcome to Our*

Village, Please Invade Carefully (2012-14) and the Audible rom-com *Car Crash*, and has written for numerous animated TV shows as well as many different forms of *Doctor Who*. Learn more about Eddie on his website: https://eddierobson.wordpress.com/.

Eliane Boey

Eliane Boey is the author of technothriller *Club Contango*, and cyberpunk and space horror novella collection *Other Minds*, both published by Dark Matter INK. Eliane will also have a novella published by Stars and Sabers in 2027 titled *The Ah Huat Engineering Cookbook and Organizing Manual*. Her short fiction has appeared in *Clarkesworld*, the *Penn Review*, and *Galaxy*. Find her on Instagram @author.eliane, or Bluesky @elianeboey.bsky.social. Eliane writes science fiction and fantasy, and lives in Singapore. Learn more about Eliane on her website: https://www.elianeboey.com/.

Eugen Bacon

Eugen (*Yu-gin*) Bacon is an African Australian author. She's a Solstice Award recipient, British Fantasy and Foreword Indies Award winner, a twice World Fantasy Award finalist, and a finalist in other awards, including the Shirley Jackson, Philip K. Dick Award, as well as the Nommo Awards for speculative fiction by Africans. Eugen was announced in the honor list of the Otherwise Fellowships for "doing exciting work in gender and speculative fiction." *Danged Black Thing* made the Otherwise Award Honor List as a "sharp collection of Afro-Surrealist work." Stars and Sabers Publishing is also publishing her Sauútiverse novella, *The Nga'phandileh Whisperer*, in 2025. Read more about Eugen on her website: https://eugenbacon.com/.

Guido Eekhaut

Guido Eekhaut is the bestselling author of the Amsterdam crime books, the first of which, *Absinthe*, won the prestigious Hercule Poirot Award. He writes in a variety of genres, from speculative fiction to the Weird, but his best known for his often-unusual crime fiction. He lives in Belgium and Spain.

Helen Glynn Jones

Helen Glynn Jones writes fantasy and romantasy, as well as romance novels under the pen name Isadora Love. Helen is the author of *The Last Raven* (2025, HarperCollins) and its sequels. Learn more about Helen at her website: https://journeytoambeth.com/.

Ian Green

Ian Green is a writer from Northern Scotland with a PhD in epigenetics. His short fiction has been widely published. He won the BBC Radio 4 Opening Lines competition, the Futurebook Future Fiction Prize, and was shortlisted for Best Newcomer at the British Fantasy Awards. His debut fantasy trilogy *The Rotstorm* began with the Sunday Times bestseller *The Gauntlet and the Fist Beneath*. His biopunk eco-terrorism thriller *Extremophile* was one of *Financial Times'* BEST SCIENCE FICTION BOOKS of 2024. Find out more at www.ianthegreen.com.

J.L. Worrad

J.L. Worrad lives in Leicester, England, and has for almost all his life. He has a degree in classical studies from Lampeter University, Wales. He has found this invaluable to his growth as a science fiction and fantasy writer in that he soon discovered how varied and peculiar human cultures can be. He is the author of the fantasy novels *Pennyblade* and *The Keep Within*, published by Titan Books, and *Feral Space*, a space opera in two parts, published by Castrum Press. Find out more on J.L.'s website: https://jamesworrad.com/

James Bennett

James Bennett is a British Fantasy Award winning author. Raised in Sussex and South Africa, his short fiction has appeared internationally. His acclaimed debut *Chasing Embers* came out in 2016, the first of his Ben Garston novels. Other works include the well-received *The Book of Queer Saints* and his latest stories can be found in *The Dark*, *BFS Horizons*, and *Occult Detective*. A new collection, *Preaching to the Perverted*, came out from Lethe Press in September 2024. Feel free to follow him on Bluesky: @jamesbennett.bsky.social.

Jenny Rae Rappaport

Jenny Rae Rappaport has been published in *Nature, Lightspeed Magazine, Escape Pod,* and *Beneath Ceaseless Skies,* among other magazines. She is a graduate of the Odyssey Writing Workshop, and holds a BA in Creative Writing from Carnegie Mellon University. In the past, she has worked as a literary agent, a marine sciences field guide, and spent a semester observing monkeys as an intern with the Pittsburgh Zoo. Jenny lives in New Jersey with her family, where she divides her time between writing and genealogy. Read more about Jenny Rae Rappaport on https://jennyrae.com/, and follow her on social media on Bluesky.

Jonathan Maberry

Jonathan Maberry is a *New York Times* bestseller, five-time Bram Stoker Award-winner, four-time Scribe Award winner, Inkpot Award winner, and author of over fifty novels. He is also a comic book writer, poet, executive producer, and writing teacher. His vampire apocalypse book series, *V-Wars,* was a Netflix original series; his novel, *Rot & Ruin,* is in development for film with Alcon Entertainment; and his Joe Ledger thrillers are being developed for TV by Chad Stahelski—director of the *John Wick* movies. He writes horror, sci-fi, fantasy, adventure, thrillers, and more. Jonathan is also president of the International Association of Media Tie-in Writers, and the editor of *Weird Tales Magazine.* Read more about Jonathan Maberry on https://www.jonathanmaberry.com/, and follow him on social media on Facebook, Instagram, Threads, Bluesky, and Twitter/X.

Kali Wallace

Kali Wallace is a Philip K. Dick Award-winning science fiction, fantasy, and horror author and geophysicist. She writes novels for adults, teens, and children, as well as a number of short stories and essays. Her science fiction horror-thriller *Dead Space* won the 2022 Philip K. Dick Award. She is also the author of the sci fi horror *Salvation Day,* young adult novels *Shallow Graves* and *The Memory Trees* and the children's fantasy novels *The Secrets of Underhill* and *City of Islands.* Her short fiction has appeared in Clarkesworld, F&SF, Asimov's, Lightspeed, and Tor.com. She lives in the Pacific Northwest. Learn more about Kali on her website: https://www.kaliwallace.com/.

KC Grifant

KC Grifant is an award-winning writer based in Southern California who creates internationally published horror, fantasy, science fiction, and weird west stories. Many of her short stories have appeared in podcasts, magazines, games, and Stoker-nominated anthologies. Her weird western novel, *Melinda West: Monster Gunslinger* (Brigids Gate Press, 2023), described as a blend of *Bonnie & Clyde* meets *The Witcher* and *Supernatural*, is the first in a series. The second novel, *Melinda West and the Gremlin Queen*, is now available. She is also author of the short story collection *Shrouded Horror: Tales of the Uncanny* (Dragon's Roost Press, 2024) and co-creator of the *Monster Gunslingers* card game. Learn more about KC from her website: https://scifiwri.com/.

Khan Wong

Khan Wong is a Lambda Award finalist speculative fiction author. Khan's background includes nonprofit arts administration, arts funding, playing the cello, firedancing, hula hooping, and poetry. His debut novel, *The Circus Infinite* (Angry Robot Books, 2022) was longlisted for the BSFA Best Novel and was a finalist for a Lambda Award. His second novel, *Down in the Sea of Angels*, is now available. Khan will also have a novella publishing via Stars and Sabers in 2027 titled *Elegant Manifestations for the Beautiful and the Lost*. Learn more about Khan from his website: https://www.khanwong.com/.

Lili Hayward

Lili Hayward (also known as Laura Madeleine) is the bestselling author of *The Cat of Yule Cottage* and *A Midwinter's Tail*. After a childhood spent acting professionally, she changed her mind, and went to study English Literature at Newnham College, Cambridge. She lives in Bristol, but can often be found visiting family in Devon, including her sister, fantasy author Lucy Holland. Read more about Lili Hayward on https://lauramadeleine.com/lili-hayward/, and follow her on social media on Instagram and Twitter/X.

Lizbeth Myles

Lizbeth Myles is a Scottish writer and podcaster. She frequently writes audio drama for *Big Finish*, and has contributed to their *Doctor Who*,

Blake's 7, and *Survivor* ranges. Her story, "Peake Season," was a Scribe Award nominee. She's a three-time Hugo Award finalist, and has written for *SFX*, *Uncanny*, and *Doctor Who Magazine*. She can be heard on Hugo Award nominated *Verity!* podcast, *Hammer House of Podcast*, and the ENNIE Award winning *How We Roll* podcast. Learn more on Lizbeth's website: https://lmmyles.com/.

Mya Duong

Mya Duong is the fantasy author of the *Mindful Things* series, a poet, and a healthcare worker. Mya Duong (in English pronounced Mia Dwong; in Vietnamese, Duong pronounced yuung or zuung) grew up in Wisconsin, then moved to California. She has been working in healthcare for 25 years. She writes in her free time, and currently lives in the San Diego area with her husband and two dogs. Learn more about Mya on her website: https://www.myaduong.com/

P.A. Cornell

P.A. Cornell is an award-winning Chilean-Canadian speculative fiction author. In 2024, she became the first ever Chilean writer to be nominated for the Nebula Award for her story, "Once Upon a Time at the Oakmont," also a finalist for the Aurora and World Fantasy Awards. Additionally, Cornell has been long-listed for the 2023 and 2024 BSFA Awards, and in 2022, her story, "Splits," won Canada's 2022 Short Works Prize for Published Fiction. Despite her early interest in fiction, Cornell's first publications were in non-fiction as a journalist and copy editor. Since 2015, she's dedicated herself to writing science fiction, fantasy, and horror full time, and her stories have appeared in over fifty magazines and anthologies, including three "Best of" anthologies. P.A. Cornell has two forthcoming works publishing via Stars and Sabers: the novelette *Shoeshine Boy & Cigarette Girl* and her collection *The Astronaut Among the Flowers*. Learn more about P.A. Cornell on her website: https://www.pacornell.com/.

Ren Hutchings

Ren Hutchings is a speculative fiction writer, writing mentor, and lifelong SFF fan currently living in London, UK. Ren is the author of time travel space opera *Under Fortunate Stars* (Solaris, 2022) as well as the upcoming *An Unbreakable World* (Solaris, 2025) and *The Legend Liminal* (Stars and Sabers, 2025). Ren loves weird mysteries, pop science, elaborate book playlists, and pondering about alternate universes. Most of what she writes involves space, time, and/or uncanny liminal places. Read more about Ren on her website: https://www.renhutchings.com/

Renan Bernardo

Renan is a 2023 Nebula Finalist, an Ignyte Finalist, a 2022 Utopian Award nominee, and a Locus-recommended author. He's also a SFWA member. His work has been published in English, Portuguese, German, Japanese, and Italian. Renan's collection of Solarpunk/Climate Fiction stories, *Different Kinds of Defiance*, was published in 2024 by Android Press. His novella, *Disgraced Return of the Kap's Needle*, is now available via Dark Matter. Learn more about Renan from his website: www.renanbernardo.com.

Sarah L. Miles

Sarah L. Miles is a writer of prose and comics. She is also a comics journalist and book reviewer, and works in a comics and gaming shop. Sarah is also a competitive strongwoman, and enjoys tabletop gaming and Lego building, renovating furniture and painting things any color but white or cream. She lives on the south coast of England with her partner, and an ever-expanding collection of houseplants and books. Find Sarah L. Miles across social media as @iamgiantwoman and read more about her on her website: https://sarahlmiles.com/.

Somto Ihezue

Somto Ihezue (he/him) is an Igbo writer, filmmaker, and editor. He is an MFA student in Creative Writing at the University of Maryland. His works have appeared, and are forthcoming in *Clarkesworld*, *The Magazine of Fantasy & Science Fiction*, *Uncanny*, *Strange Horizons*, *NIGHTMARE*, *Beneath Ceaseless Skies*, *Podcastle*, *Escape Pod*, *PseudoPod*, *POETRY Magazine*, *Flash Fiction Online*, Flame Tree Press, and others. His work has been shortlisted and/or nominated for the British Fantasy Award (Sydney J. Bounds Awards), the Nommo Awards, the Afritondo Short Story Prize, the Utopia Awards, the Pushcart Prize and the British Science Fiction Award. He has received residencies, scholarships, and grants from Clarion West,

Tin House, Sundress Academy for the Arts, Voodoonauts, Horror Writers Association, Arts for All, and Milford SF. He is the assistant editor of the Publishing Taught Me anthology (SFWA & National Endowment for the Arts sponsored), and co-editor of *Will This Be A Problem? The Anthology*. He tweets at @somto_Ihezue, and find him on bluesky @somtoihezue.bsky.social. You can also visit his website at https://somtoihezue.com/